THE GYPSUM CREEK MASSACRE

ALSO BY KEN PRATT

The Royal Potter's Shop

When the Wolf Comes Knocking

Matt Bannister Series

Willow Falls

Sweethome

Bellas Dance Hall

The Wolves of Windsor Ridge

The Eckman Exception

Prairieville

Return to Willow Falls

Ballenger

Blood Vengeance

Dragon's Fire

Legacies of Spring

To Kill A Dragon

Slater's Gold

Leather Man's Journal

The Natoma Bride

Hollister

Everson Solstice

A Love to Die For

THE GYPSUM CREEK MASSACRE

THE JESSUP COUNTY CHRONICLES
BOOK 1

KEN PRATT

The Gypsum Creek Massacre

Paperback Edition
Copyright © 2024 by Ken Pratt

CKN Christian Publishing
An Imprint of Wolfpack Publishing
1707 E. Diana Street
Tampa, FL 33609

www.cknchristianpublishing.com

Paperback ISBN 978-1-63977-474-6
Ebook ISBN 978-1-63977-473-9
LCCN 2024947001

AUTHOR'S NOTE

The Jessup County Chronicles is a continuation of the Matt Bannister Series. Do you need to read the Matt Bannister Series to understand what's taking place in The Gypsum Creek Massacre? No. I will say if you did read the Matt Bannister Series, it would add to the depth of the story and those to follow because you'll understand the character's histories and relationships better. However, any essential details that are relevant to the story will be covered in this series.

It was 2004 when I first took a pencil in my hand and wrote the first words to what would become my first book. Seven years later, Willow Falls was written. A literary agent I had reached out to responded that *Willow Falls would never be published because it was too secular for the Christian market and too Christian for the secular market. It went straight down the middle and crossed the lines of both genres and there was no genre like that.*

I think she was wrong. I remember walking along the sidewalk in Sisters, Oregon, when I got a notification to open a link from my publisher. To my surprise, Willow Falls was the #1 Best Seller on Amazon, and it stayed there for a while. That book she thought would never resonate with people was just the beginning. The Matt Bannister Series went on to have eighteen books, and sixteen of them were the #1 Best Sellers on Amazon. The other two reached as high as #3 and #2 but didn't reach that #1 spot.

There is a wide following for the Matt Bannister Series, and I have met many great people and made many new friends who have supported me in more ways than they know. I recall many reviews that inspired me when I felt uninspired, direct messages with incredible encouragement when I was discouraged. In so many ways, my life has been touched by the people who have read my books and reached out to me in very positive ways. The fanbase for the Matt Bannister Series is made up of incredible people, and so, with that, I dedicate this first book of the new series to my friends, the wonderful fans of the Matt Bannister Series.

Thank you. Matt is Back!

THE GYPSUM CREEK MASSACRE

PROLOGUE

Branson, Oregon 1932

ALEXANDER WENTWORTH'S HANDS TREMBLED lightly with nervous anticipation as he drove his 1928 Chevrolet National up the steep dirt road filled with ruts and occasional exposed stones that climbed Bannister Hill, leading to the intimidating large home built with the strength of a military fort. The house had thick granite block walls for the first ten feet of height, with windows on all four sides and finished granite window seals inside to place plants, photos, or a pillow to sit on as one enjoyed the scenery outside.

Set on top of the heavy granite blocks were heavy logs built like a log cabin that rose another sixteen feet to allow for a second story and an attic space. The Bannister's home had a covered wrap-around porch with granite steps, walls, and support posts that circled the house. Each side had a comfortable bench swing, table, and chairs so that they could enjoy the view no matter which side they chose to sit on.

The second story had windows in each room, but the

west side of the house that looked out over Jessup Valley had a much larger window and extended deck in the master bedroom where they could sit outside and watch the sunset. Alex had seen the house on the hill for as long as he could remember, but he had never driven close enough to it to comprehend how large it truly was. He came to a stop in front of the house and turned his motor off. He could feel his heart racing and was intimidated as immediately two large German Shepherds were at his car's door, barking aggressively and snarling, daring him to open the door.

He remained inside, grabbed his leather briefcase, and waited for someone to come to his rescue from the two dogs. Looking around, he could see a black Ford Model T pickup parked under a lean-to built on the side of a single garage separated from the house. The garage's two doors were closed, not revealing what kind of car was parked inside. Alexander could see the barn not too far away with fenced pastures where a few cows and horses grazed in the afternoon sunshine. A lean-to with three walls and an open double doorway revealed an old 1880s black horse-drawn buggy protected from the elements.

A young man, no more than seventeen, came from behind the house carrying a garden hoe while the house door opened at the same time. A Black lady with long gray hair tied in a bun stepped onto the porch and clapped her hands loudly as she shouted, "Hey, you dogs, leave that man alone! Get! Go on, shoo. Shoo, I said." She waved the dogs away, but they ignored her and dared Alex to exit the vehicle.

The young man walked over and grabbed the more aggressive of the two dogs by the collar. "Sit!" he ordered with a jerk of the collar. The dog sat obediently. "Sir, you can get out of your car. She won't bite, he's the only one that might. I'll put them away while you're here."

The old lady shouted, displeased, "You were supposed to put them away already."

"I'm sorry, Miss Jackson. I forgot. I'll do it now." He led the male dog away while the female followed upon being called.

"You can get out of your rig. The dogs are gone. They won't bite unless you have bad intent," she said. "But if you ever do have bad intent coming here, you better stay inside that rig, or you may never get in it again."

"I assure you, my intentions are good," Alex said as he got out of his car, wary of his welcome. "My name is Alexander Wentworth. I'm a—"

"I know why you're here. Letting you in is against my better judgment, but come inside."

"You are Miss Rory Jackson. Am I right?" he asked with a widening grin. He admired the colored woman, even though he had never met her.

"I am."

"You knew all of them, didn't you? All of the Bannister family, I mean."

Rory's expression became indignant. "They are my family! Of course, I knew them all."

"Yes. Forgive me, Miss Jackson. I'm just excited to be here. I grew up—"

"Young man, I'm not the one you need to impress," Rory said, cutting him off quickly. She spoke frankly and to the point, "Matt does not like reporters. He never has. The only reason you're here is because of Christine's good graces. You better know that upfront. If you mess that up, you won't be welcomed back. And if you print lies about Matt or any of the Bannisters, Fasanas, or

3

Zieglers, I'll hunt you down myself. Am I making myself clear?"

"Yes. Perfectly. I understand," Alex said somberly. He had one chance to interview one of the most famous old-time lawmen that ever lived. Being granted permission to interview Matt Bannister was more than the chance of a lifetime, it was a dream come true. Alex was nervous and followed Miss Jackson into the large home.

"Christine is waiting in the sitting room." Rory led the way, stood beside a door, and held an arm out to invite him to enter. Alex entered a room furnished with two plush davenports and two leather back chairs. It was a beautiful room with cherry wood paneled walls decorated by many photographs and a few rifles mounted on the wall. A stone fireplace burned quietly while a window looked out over the beautiful Blue Mountains.

Alex's attention wasn't on the photographs, guns, or the large lighted hutch that contained multiple items, but on the silver-haired lady in her early seventies sitting in a wheelchair. She slowly stirred a cup of warm tea while she smiled pleasantly at him.

"Hello, I am Christine Bannister. You must be Alexander Wentworth."

"I am. What an honor to meet you," he said, extending his hand to shake hers. There was no denying the beauty that the woman must have been in her youth, as she had an undeniable beauty to her face despite her age. Her brown eyes glimmered with kindness, and she greeted Alexander with a warmness that made him feel at ease. "I am a journalist with the Jessup County Chronicles. I thank you for writing back to me and inviting me here."

Christine's lips rose, enjoying his nervous awkwardness. "Yes. Please, sit down and tell me about yourself."

He sat in a leatherback chair and set his leather bag down. "I just want you to know how excited I am to be here. Your husband is a living legend. I'm so thankful to have an opportunity to interview him, it truly is a once-in-a-lifetime opportunity. So, I thank you so much for talking him into seeing me."

Christine smiled with a slight nod. "Matt would not dare speak to a reporter if it was just him and I. Our grandson heard you wanted to interview Matt and asked him to share his stories so that someday, our great-grand-children will know what we stood for and why. That is why Matt agreed to meet with you."

"Then I'll have to thank your grandson. You'll have to forgive me, I'm just excited. It is my understanding that my grandfather worked for Matt."

"Oh? Who was your grandfather?" Christine asked with an ounce of skepticism. It was surprising how many people claimed their grandfather worked with Matt or told some wild tale of Branson's early days that was not true.

"His name was Jed Clark. He was my mother's father. He was killed on duty, or so my mother tells me, and I believe it because his tombstone has a US deputy marshal's badge engraved on it. My mother was very young when he died and doesn't remember him, and her mother didn't talk about my grandfather hardly at all. I don't know much about my grandfather or what happened to him. I tried to research the paper's archives, but as you know, the 1895 fire burned the Branson Gazette news-paper building to the ground. All those old articles and records are lost."

Christine's expression saddened. "Jed Clark. That is a name I've not thought of in years. Yes, he did work for Matt for a time. I personally did not know him very well.

I'll let Matt tell you about him, though. So, your mother
was one of his little ones?"

"Yes, ma'am. The youngest of the family."

Christine nodded quietly. Her eyes lit up as Matt
entered the doorway. "Well, here is the man you need to
talk to."

Alex stood immediately, his mouth dropping open as he
sputtered, "Marshal Bannister! Thank you for taking the
time to see me. I'm Alexander Wentworth. It is an absolute
honor to meet you and Mrs. Bannister, sir."

Matt smiled lightly as he entered the room. He wore
blue jeans with dirty knees and a tan button-up shirt with
the sleeves rolled up above his wrists. "I apologize for
being late. I was out back helping Walter plant trees.
Walter is a young man who lives down the hill and works
for us doing odd jobs and such. I have him planting trees
on the hillside. So you're a writer?" he asked, shaking
Alex's hand. Matt's skeptical expression studied Alex with
less friendliness than when he had entered the room. The
young man's handshake was too soft for Matt's liking.

"Yes. I'm a journalist with the Jessup County Chronicles." He was surprised by the strength of Matt's grip as
they shook.

"Have a seat." Matt waved toward where Alex had been
sitting. Matt stepped near Christine and leaned over her
wheelchair to kiss her before taking a seat on the davenport where he could hold Christine's hand. "So, Alexander,
what can I do for you?"

For a moment, Alexander stared at the man who had
made himself into a legend in law enforcement. Matt was
tall, lean, and unlike the stories Alex had read, Matt's hair
was no longer dark but had turned a grayish white, shy of
silver but still long and worn in a ponytail, exposing a high

forehead of thinning hair. His beard and mustache were grayish-white and well-trimmed. He wore silver-rimmed glasses, but his eyes were keenly aware. He watched Alex as if studying him.

"Please, call me Alex. I go by my full name at work, but I'm just Alex to everyone else. Mr. Bannister, I understand you have never liked journalists?"

Matt shrugged a shoulder while tilting his head. "I don't like writers in general, especially when they're trying to write about me. In fact, I have that original book over there framed, which you can look at later. That one was written by a local man way back in 1881 by the name of Marcus Swindoll. That's my bullet hole in it. I did that when I first came back to Willow Falls." He smiled in reflection. "Marcus never wrote another book about me or my family. So, I'll warn you now, if you do write something about me, it had better be true, or it will be your paper framed up there with a bullet hole through it, or if you lie enough, maybe your photograph will be hanging on my office wall."

Christine freed her hand from his and smacked his hand to scold him. "Matthew!" She explained, for Alex's benefit, "He keeps photographs in his study that I will not allow anywhere else in my home. They are the gruesome photographs of dead men, mostly."

Matt smiled as he took her hand in his again. "Alex, you've been warned. So, why are you here?"

"Matt, be nice. He is Jed Clark's grandson," Christine said.

"Are you?" Matt asked with interest.

"Yes, sir. My mother was a baby when he died."

Matt's eyes narrowed reflectively. "Your grandfather was a good man. I kept paying your grandmother his wages until she remarried about two years later. What happened to Jed has always been one of my biggest regrets. I couldn't save him. Before you leave, I'll take you to my office and show you a picture of Charlie Walker in his pine box outside my old marshal's office. That's the man that killed your grandfather."

Alex's mouth dropped open. He had just learned a lot that he did not know about his family history. "I'd like that. I was just telling Mrs. Bannister that the fire at the Branson Gazette back in 1895 destroyed all the information about everything up to that time. So, I hope to write stories no one remembers or knows about anymore. So much about you and this county was lost in that fire, and over time, people forget. Marshal Bannister, I'd like to bring those stories back."

"Ahh, just in time," Matt said as Rory entered the room carrying a tray containing three tall glasses of iced tea and a cup of warm tea. He took Christine's finished cup, set it on the tray, and handed her a new cup with a spoon before taking one of the tall glasses.

"Rory," Matt said, "Will you do me a favor and go into my office and bring me the photo of Charlie Walker." Once Rory left the room, Matt told the story of hiring Jed Clark and how he met his end at the Sperry residence in Natoma. Rory returned with the photograph, which was in a glass frame. "This is a photograph of Charlie." Matt handed it to Alex.

Alex stared at it for a long moment. "He's the man that killed my grandfather?"

"That's the man. I was there. I did not allow any photographs of your grandfather to be taken. He was a respectable and good man. I took care of your family for two years afterward. I held your mother when she was a baby. I'm assuming your grandmother is gone?"

"Yes." He nodded.

"She was a strong woman. So, how do you want to do this? What do you want to know about?"

Alex stared at the photograph of Charlie Walker a moment longer. He cleared his throat and answered, "I'm curious to know about something an old timer told me outside of the bank one day. He mentioned the Massacre of Gypsum Creek. Could you tell me what happened there?"

Matt's expression grew long with a saddened frown. He lingered in a long pause before speaking, "Well, that was a tragedy. I'm sure you can read about it in other newspapers. The press pretty well covered it across the state."

Alex read Matt's expression correctly and spoke softly. "Yes, but not *your* story. If I read correctly, you were on the train. You were there for all of it. That's the story I would like to write, Marshal Bannister."

Christine raised her brow and spoke frankly. "Alex, you're asking Matt to talk about something that he still has bad dreams about even after all these years. I don't want him to relive it and start having nightmares again."

Matt turned his head to gaze at his beautiful wife. "It's okay, my love. I'll tell him."

"Are you sure you want to?" she questioned.

Matt took a deep breath and nodded. "The Massacre of Gypsum Creek, as the newspapers called it, was"—he paused—"awful," he said after a moment as the memory played in his mind. His eyes welled up with moisture.

He nodded repeatedly and swallowed emotionally as he said, "It was soon after Christine and I married in September of 1884. A couple of my deputies, William

Fasana and Morton Sperry, my son Gabriel, and I had to go back to Portland to testify at the Felix Rathkey trial. That's the man that shanghied Gabriel and Evan Gray and sold them to the Captain of the Everson Solstice. Felix was sentenced to five years in prison but was released within six months. It pays to have some dirt on politicians, I suppose. Anyway, it was the last time we'd have to go back to Portland. We were all excited to be done with that chapter of our lives when we boarded the train. I was looking forward to coming back home to Christine when it happened. Let me tell you about it. The train was leaving Portland, and my cousin William was being loud and annoying as usual..."

CHAPTER ONE

September 1884

THE OREGON SHORT LINE STEAM ENGINE NUMBER 117 left Portland's concrete platform with an abrupt jerk that startled a gray-haired older woman in her midsixties. She was an obese woman with broad shoulders and a large belly traveling with her husband. They were sitting three rows forward and across from Matt Bannister, who sat with his son, Gabriel. Matt and Gabriel waved goodbye to Matt's father, Floyd Bannister, who stood with his stepdaughter, Maggie Farrell. Maggie was tearfully waving goodbye to William Fasana, who was sitting alone behind Matt and Gabriel. Across from Matt sat Morton Sperry, who kicked his feet up across the green cloth padded bench seat with a metal frame to face Matt and the others while they talked.

The passenger coach was shorter than the other two connected to the train and had ten rows of bench seating that faced forward. The other two passenger coaches were longer and may have had more comfortable seating, but the seats faced each other back to back throughout. Matt had no desire to look at people facing him while he tried to talk with his son on the journey home, so they settled for seats in the less comfortable third-class passenger coach, which offered less comfort, no food or drinks being offered, but more privacy at least.

They had just finished a weeklong trip for a summons to the Felix Rathkey trial. Felix was found guilty of several counts and sentenced to five years in state prison. Matt was disappointed in the judge's sentence and figured Felix would be paroled within two years or sooner if he had friends in high enough places, which Matt was sure he did. With the trial finally over, Matt and the others were grateful to be on the train back home and putting Portland behind them.

"I don't like this, Amos!" the obese old woman said with a loud and uneasy deep voice. "I don't like this at all. We should have taken a sternwheeler like we always do or paid for better accommodations, at least."

"Lucille, the train is much faster. We'll be there in four or five hours, depending on the rail speed. It's a little jerky to start, but once we're moving, it's not bad. Trust me, you'll have more time with Penelope when we arrive hours earlier than we would have on a sternwheeler. There is nothing to worry about."

"I don't like these seats," Lucille complained irritably while shifting her weight on the uncomfortable seat. She lowered her voice so she wouldn't be overheard. "If I get hemorrhoids from this, it will be your fault."

"Sweetheart, you didn't want to travel with strangers facing you the whole way, so here we are. It's only four or five hours, six at most, and we'll be there. We can take a sternwheeler back home if you like."

She rolled her eyes. "My bottom is going to be bruised and sore for a week sitting on these seats even if I don't get hemorrhoids. I should have brought a pillow to sit on."

William hid his face behind Matt's head and quipped loudly, "For crying out loud, woman, shut your mouth and go to sleep! You're worse than a whining kid." He quickly smacked the back of Matt's head condemningly. "That's rude, sir! You should apologize to the lady."

Matt smiled slightly as the woman twisted in her seat to glare at him. Matt pointed backward with his thumb. "It wasn't me, Miss. It was my cousin back there horsing around. I'm sure he didn't mean anything by it, did you, William?"

William laughed. "I apologize, Miss. I was hoping to embarrass my cousin. He needs to be humbled here and there. You're riding in the train with the US Marshal Matt Bannister and his equally gifted deputies, myself, the one and only William Fasana. Oh, he's easy to forget, but over there is our most recent acquisition, Morton Sperry. We picked him up at a freak show. Matt has a foolish notion of proving that even freaks can be lawmen, so we're taking him back home to try him out. We might as well talk since we're all on this train for a while. Right? So, who might you be, Miss?"

Morton gazed at William with a half-humored expression but only shook his head slowly.

The older woman's husband stood while holding the seat to keep his balance as the train picked up some speed. He gazed sternly at William through a pair of silver-rimmed glasses. "Thank you for apologizing, young man. I thought I would have to punch you in the mouth. I may be old, but I can still punch any man who disrespects my lady. Now, I may not win the fight, but at least I'd get one solid shot in." He was a small man wearing a clean, pressed black suit with a bleached white shirt and red bowtie. He had a narrow face with aging blue eyes, a well-manicured white goatee, and a handlebar mustache. His gold-plated pocket watch and chain connected to his suit vest and silver lion-head cane topper left no doubt of his being a man of some influence and wealth.

William had long, wavy blond hair that fell across the shoulders of his blue vest over a gray and white checkered shirt. He kept a blonde goatee about three inches long and had a rough and weathered face that made him look slightly older than his early forties. William's blue eyes twinkled with a spirited humor. He raised his hands in surrender and said in his deep voice, "It was a bad joke on my part, and if you were to punch me in the mouth, I know my boss would sit right there and say I deserved it. And certainly, I would. My sincere apologies to your lovely bride."

His bride, Lucille, held a wide-brimmed white hat with an attractive floral arrangement on the side and a lace veil. She was wearing a bright red and gold-colored dress with gold rings on her fingers and a pearl necklace and earrings to match. She nodded, accepting the apology, and said, "Thank you for apologizing." She turned back around.

Amos turned sideways in the aisle seat to look back at Matt quizzically. "So, you're Matt Bannister? The Wyoming deputy marshal?"

Matt was in his mid to late thirties and had long dark hair that he kept in a ponytail. He had a square-shaped face and a well-trimmed beard and mustache. His brown eyes were alert but friendly. He was a tall, broad-shouldered man with a muscular build. "I am. But I'm a US marshal now. I have an office in Branson."

A stranger sitting a few seats ahead of Amos and Lucille

said, "Thank goodness, I'm surrounded by lawmen. If the train's robbed, I guess the robbers won't get my last dollar-fifty."

"Was that a joke?" William questioned with a straight face.

"No," the man answered uneasily. "I was just saying I'm glad you're on the train. I lost all my money in Portland. All I got left in the world is my dollar-fifty."

"What makes you think I'd risk my life to stop a robber from taking your dollar-fifty?" William questioned, primarily out of boredom. "Your dollar-fifty is out of my jurisdiction. I only protect pretty women. You can protect yourself and any children on board. I'm not fond of smelly children either," William said with a friendly wink to a small Indian girl sitting two seats behind at the back of the passenger coach with her parents. She was about six years old and dressed in a blue dress with white ruffles around the collar. She smiled shyly.

Amos asked Matt, "Do you ever think about writing a biography of your adventures?"

Matt shook his head slightly. "No. I don't even like to think about some of my memories. I sure don't want to sit down and write about them."

"How many men have you killed, if I may ask?"

"I don't take any pride in counting," Matt answered, annoyed by the question. He asked to change the subject, "What do you do, sir?" More than a dozen people were sitting nearby, which was more than enough people for Matt not to want to be the topic of conversation.

"I am retired mostly, but still president of my company for now," Amos said with a proud smile. "My sons and son-in-law are taking the business over nowadays. We're going to The Dalles City to visit our daughter and grandchildren.

What else do we have to do at our age other than enjoy the life we have? Those grandchildren bring life, I'm telling you. They keep me young." He grabbed his hat and spoke to his wife as they moved seats to the one in front of Matt. He sat next to the window but turned to look back at Matt comfortably. He reached his hand over the seat's back to shake. "Amos Stafford. This is my wife of forty-eight blessed years, Lucille. Is he your son?" He motioned to the handsome young man with dark brown hair and brown eyes with a hint of a mustache beginning to grow on his upper lip, sitting beside Matt.

"Yes. His name is Gabriel." Matt and Gabriel shook the man's hand. Matt nodded to Lucille, who barely showed interest enough to glance back. Matt was slightly annoyed that the man wanted to socialize. He hoped for a quiet ride where he could talk to Gabriel.

"Gabriel, you're a handsome young man. Are you interested in being a lawman, too?" Amos asked.

"Actually," William Fasana said while hurrying across the aisle to sit in a vacant seat in front of Morton and across from the elderly couple. He sat on the edge of the bench seat facing Lucille. "Gabriel mentioned something to me about opening a bordello with midgets called Half Price. Isn't that what you said you wanted to name it, Gabriel?"

Gabriel's face reddened. "He's lying. No, sir, I have no intention of being a lawman. I don't know what I'm going to do yet."

Amos ignored William's attempt at humor as he advised, "Can I give you some advice? Time waits for no one, young man. Before you know it, your youth will be gone, and whatever you invest your youth in will be where your career is. If you waste it away, labor is all you'll do.

Educate yourself about a trade, and you'll do okay. The world's a cold place if you haven't got a trade. I'm sure your pa will agree to that."

"I certainly will."

"Twenty years ago, I opened a little tack and feed store in Portland and it prospered. Believe it or not, our little feed store grew into one of the largest milling companies on the West Coast. A large percentage of the wheat and other cash crops grown in the Pacific Northwest and beyond are milled and exported through one of our facilities. You'll see one of our milling facilities when we enter The Dalles City. The train will go right by it so you can't miss it. It's close to the river and has five tall storage silos. We've got a pretty big operation just like that at three locations. I'm not trying to brag. My point is that we started as a small feed store but grew into a corporation that buys, processes, sells, and ships agricultural goods, from flour to cornmeal worldwide. Young man, that was never a vision I had, but the Lord blessed us, kept blessing us, and took our little Ma and Pa shop in a whole new direction. So, my advice is to find the trade the Lord has for you and stay faithful. Who knows what the Good Lord will do for you, too? I can tell you're a Christian. Am I right?" Amos asked with a kind smile.

"I am. My grandfather was a reverend," Gabriel answered.

Amos nodded. "Are you interested in the ministry?"

"Maybe. It would fit my personality more than being a lawman."

"There's a direction you might be called in. There's a definite need for good ministers. I'm not talking about handsome, well-dressed men or even good speakers who can speak a crowd up into a wave of emotion or laughter.

I'm talking about men who can teach the truths of God's Word in such a way that it sticks in the hearts and minds of the listeners. We need honest Bible teachers who teach what the Bible says and not happy-go-lucky gibberish to please the ears, especially in Portland."

"Yeah, you do!" William interjected. "We came to Portland because Gabriel and his friend were shanghaied." He told the tale of what had happened in Portland. Amos and Lucille listened with interest.

William finished, "My old buddy Felix Rathkey is spending the next five years in prison, and we're on our way home from the final trial. Thank goodness we don't have to go back to Portland. Speaking of prisons, felons, and hell holes, this ugly man next to me is Morton Sperry. He's not really a freak, per se, but he is the former leader of the notorious Sperry-Helms Gang that terrorized the state's eastern half for a long time. A murdering thief he was." William leaned slightly forward to speak to Lucille, "We like to think he's been rehabilitated into a lawful, upstanding state, but looking at your gold and diamond rings there and pearl necklace and earrings, old habits might become more tempting than he can withstand. I moved to this seat to stop him if the temptation becomes too much."

"Is that a true story?" Amos asked Morton.

Morton nodded slowly, not appreciative of William's eagerness to speak of Morton's past. If anyone ever looked as infamous as their reputation alluded, it was Morton Sperry. His green eyes held a cold gaze without a hint of emotion in his blank expression. His hair had been recently cut short, but the thick brown goatee added to his rough and savage-like exterior. "It is," he answered without the slightest bit of shame. He tilted his head to the side, interested in seeing Lucille's earrings and necklace a little bit better. "Are those real pearls? Just how much are they worth, do you think?"

William almost laughed but controlled his stoic expression. "We watch Morton like a wolf around a small lamb. He is likely to attack without warning when something shiny is within reach. The glitter and shine nag at him like a bitter woman."

Lucille raised her hand to touch her earring subconsciously. "Luckily, the marshal is behind us."

"No, ma'am," William said while shaking his head. "Matt's no help at all. Trust me. He stood back and watched a Portland police officer, who happened to be a former fisticuffs champion, beat me black and blue, and he didn't do a thing to help. He said it was out of his jurisdiction. And I'm his cousin!" he exclaimed.

Matt replied, "Miss, you should ask William why that officer hit him."

She turned her head back toward Matt. "Do I really want to know?"

William's lips turned upward. "You can be a proud Portlander, Miss. I was trying to bribe one of your good men in blue. You'll be glad to know he refused the bribe and took great offense or his marital troubles out on me, one of the two. Either way, Matt was no help at all."

"You are a very uncouth man," Lucille said, unimpressed with William.

"I'm also unkept and free. So, if you have any nieces or daughters you don't like, you could introduce them to me, and I'll become a disappointment to them, too."

"How long will this train ride take?" Lucille asked her husband.

"Roughly four or five hours, maybe six."

Lucille took a deep breath and exhaled. "Mr. Fasana, I only need to listen to you for five hours or so. I have a feeling you won't be quiet, will you?"

William remained sitting on the edge of the seat with his legs in the aisle inches from her. "Why would I, ma'am? This is where we can all become friends if we just talk and get to know each other."

While William continued talking to Lucille, Amos turned toward Matt and lowered his voice so he wouldn't be overheard, "I'm glad you're on this train. I no longer trust wiring large sums of money to and from banks. A bank's mistake nearly cost me a fortune, and it took about three weeks to get their mistake figured out. I now deliver the harvest payroll in person. This is the second time by rail. I have about two hundred thousand dollars in a safe riding in the mail car with four armed guards, but having you here is extra security, and I like that."

CHAPTER TWO

THE TRAIN ROLLED ALONG THE TRACKS BUILT beside the Columbia River through the thick forests of the Cascade Mountains of the Columbia Gorge at a steady speed of twenty-five miles per hour. Five hours had passed, and the green forests had been replaced by sparse bunch-grass, sagebrush, and rock cliffs as they came out on the eastern side of the Cascades onto the arid Columbia Plateau. They were still fifteen miles outside The Dalles City and the passenger coach swayed slightly as it was pulled along the tracks. The swaying motion had made the little Indian girl sitting in the back with her parents sick to her stomach, causing her to vomit on her dress and the floor.

Matt and Gabriel moved to the back row to sit across from the Indian family. Matt handed his canteen to her mother, who sat on the aisle end of the bench seat. "Here, I have an apple she can have as well. It will put something back in her stomach and stop her from dehydrating."

Her father was a thin Indian man dressed in loose

clothing with suspenders holding his britches on. His black hair was cut short, and he appeared to be a beaten man in spirit to the point of surrendered timidness. His wife was broader in the shoulders and heavier with a round face. She smiled at Matt appreciatively and took the canteen. "Thank you." She told her daughter, "Alice, you must sit up and drink water. This kind gentleman has an apple for you, too."

The little girl sat up with a sickly pale frown and glanced at Matt before taking a drink. Her mother explained, "It's only her second time riding the train. It makes her sick to her stomach."

"My stomach gets a little queasy, too. How far are you folks going?"

"Dalles City," her mother answered. "You?"

"Walla Walla. Tomorrow, the fellas and I will take a stage over the Blues back home to Branson. We have a long trip ahead still. Another three or four days before we'll be home."

She pointed at his badge. "You're a marshal?"

Matt held out his hand to shake. "Yes. I'm Matt Bannister."

"Oh," she said with recognition. She shook his hand. "My name is Ona, my daughter Alice, and my husband, Gilbert Redbird."

Gilbert shook Matt's hand limply but with a friendly nod.

"You're Indian, too?" she asked.

Matt nodded. "My grandmother was Nez Percé."

"We heard about you and Chusi Yellowbear. We never met him, but he traded with our friend, who knew him well. He said you were Chusi's friend. He read us the newspaper about what happened to him."

Matt was surprised to hear her say Chusi's name. He nodded sadly. "Yes. He was a friend of mine. Chusi gave his wife's wedding dress to my fiancé at the time to wear when we married. It's a beautiful dress."

"Did she wear it at your wedding?" Ona asked curiously.

"Yes, she did," Matt answered with a reflective smile.

"Chusi gave her a great honor to wear that dress. Your wife must have been very special for him to give a White woman his bride's wedding dress. I'm assuming your wife is white, yes?"

Matt nodded. "They became good friends."

"Did he enjoy seeing her wear it at your wedding?"

Matt frowned. "He'd already been killed. But if he were there, he would have cried his heart out because I'm guessing my wife would have reminded him of his own bride on their wedding day. She was beautiful."

Ona smiled sadly. "Our friend was very sad to hear that Chusi was dead. Many of our elders are dying, though. The way the White men have forced us to give up the old ways and live as they do has killed the spirit of our elders long before they die. My husband works in the wheat fields for a White man. We live there. On the bright side, they are starting an Indian school for our children. We went to pick up Alice from the Indian school in Salem. She will be home with us and the other children from now on. We are thankful for that."

Matt noticed a small golden cross necklace on the breasts of Ona's dress. "Are you a Christian?"

Ona nodded. She was thankful to have someone to talk to on the trip as her daughter was feeling sick and her husband wasn't a talkative man. "I became a Christian when I was around twelve. A missionary told me about

Jesus. My husband isn't so willing to believe. He doesn't know how anyone claiming to know Jesus can be so mean."

"No," Gilbert spoke for the first time. There was a bitter tone to his voice, "I don't know how a God that claims to love everyone could be so mean. Good people struggle to survive and die, while the worst of people get rich and thrive. There is no justice in the world. I was a Christian, but not anymore."

Matt spoke thoughtfully, "You could look at it like this: the Bible says this is the closest the wicked will get to Heaven. So why wouldn't they thrive? This is their heaven. And truth be told, their heaven isn't that good, nor does it last that long. But on the other hand, this is the closest a Christian will get to hell, and it isn't that bad. People are merely people, they make mistakes and are fallible. We are certainly not like Jesus. I serve Jesus, not people."

Ona spoke, "You must be a Christian, too?"

"I am."

"When our missionary left, Gilbert's boss burned down our church, and we still haven't been able to build a new one. Every Sunday, we have to meet in a field or the barn if it's raining to listen to the boss man read from the Bible and hear the sermon. We cannot read, so we don't know if he is telling us the truth. The boss man does not believe in it, but it is his job to read it. Sometimes, I don't trust his words. We must work and do so happily despite the hardships. At least we have a home off the reservation, and now all of our children are at home while going to school."

"Where do you live?" Matt asked with interest.

"We live on the Livengood Plantation."

"Plantation?" Matt questioned. "Is that like a slavery plantation?"

"I wouldn't know. We live and work there. Gilbert

24

works in the fields, and I work in the garden and vegetable fields."

"So, your boss burned the church down, and yet, has church?" Matt questioned, not quite understanding the reasoning.

Ona nodded. "Yes. Well, it was the old man that burned it down. He died. He didn't believe we needed church, so he burned it down. He always said if God loved or wanted us, we'd be white. I don't believe that, do you?" she questioned. Her expression appeared more concerned than confused.

Matt grinned with disgust. "No. Nowhere in the Bible does it say that. If I heard someone say something like that, I'd probably hit them in the mouth. That is not true."

She smiled with apparent relief. "I didn't think so. He was a horrible man and mistreated everyone, even his son. But he died, and now his son owns the plantation. He is a good man and built the school so all our children could be at home. But his son, oh boy, that young man is a lot like his grandfather. I hope we save enough money to live elsewhere when that boy takes over the plantation."

Gilbert spoke quietly, "Ona, just leave it be."

"I was just saying Rickson is like his grandfather."

"He doesn't need to know that!" Gilbert snapped. "The last thing we need is to bring trouble to the house."

Matt asked, "What kind of trouble are you talking about? We're just talking."

"He means you," Ona said plainly. "It's too bad you weren't staying in Dalles City. Gilbert's boss and his men do whatever they want. The local lawmen do nothing to stop them from hurting our people. We are treated no better than cattle."

"Cattle are worth more," Gilbert said bitterly while staring out the window toward the river.

Matt listened carefully and questioned, "If you are mistreated, why not leave? There are jobs elsewhere."

"To where?" Ona questioned. "No one leaves the Livengood Village on their own. There is nowhere else to go except to the reservation. We make money from our work and have a house, and now that they have built a schoolhouse for our children, we will not leave. Can you imagine your child being taken away from you and being sent to a government school far away and only seeing them twice a year while the government raises your babies?"

"No, I can't imagine what that would be like."

"Your mother loved you, and you know the love you have for your son. We love our children like any white mother or father loves theirs. We don't have the right to raise our children like you do until now. Now that the school is open to younger children, we can bring Alice home. For that, it is worth staying where we are."

Matt wrinkled his nose at Alice. "It must be nice to know you'll always be home with your mommy and daddy."

Alice smiled slightly, unsure what to think of the big man talking to her. She feared men with badges, and she clung to her mother's arm tightly.

"Well," Matt continued, "If I can assist you in any way, let me know. I'm going home, but I can always return if needed. So, where do you work? You said it was some plantation?"

Ona nodded. "Yes. The Livengood Plantation. It was not a good place like the name says, but it is getting better with the schoolhouse. Isabel is the teacher and said a church is to be built next. She is the owner's daughter, so I believe her."

"Who is the owner?"

Ona answered, "Mr. Emrick. He is nice to us. But his son, the boss man, and his pals are the mean ones."

"Who is the boss man?"

Gilbert's patience had run out. He ordered firmly, "Not a word, Ona! That's enough talking! He can only cause us trouble and has no cause to come there. So hush and don't give him one!"

───────

WILLIAM FASANA DISCOVERED that Mr. and Mrs. Stafford were not interested in speaking with him after Matt and Gabriel had moved back to sit by the Indian family. He turned his attention to two fellows wearing laborer's clothing and sweat-stained hats. William invited them to play poker to help pass the time. They were quickly joined by the stranger with a dollar-fifty William had spoken to earlier. His name turned out to be Gus Walden. Gus was going to northern Idaho to find work in a mine.

The other two men, Joel Jones and Emory Fisher, were going back home to a small town in eastern Washington after spending a few days of pleasure in Portland. The two friends worked on a wheat farm and knew who Amos Stafford was. They were pleased to meet the man and found the conversation ended after telling Amos what an honor it was to meet him and who they worked for. Amos replied that his son-in-law might know their employer, but he had never heard of him.

William, Gus, Joel, and Emory sat in four aisle seats

facing each other while playing poker. An overturned hat belonging to Joel centered in the aisle functioned as the pot for the betting. There were no high dollar amounts but mere change being bet. The game wasn't meant for anything other than entertainment. A young teenage boy watched quietly while his mother read a book, uninterested in conversing with anyone.

William turned to the boy who was leaning over his shoulder watching. As irritating as it was to William, he wasn't too concerned about it. "Hey, boy, why don't you jump seats over there and stare at Gus's cards? Maybe you could even signal me if he has a good hand. We'll share the profits."

Gus was not humored. He cast a disapproving glance at the boy. "I wouldn't do that." Gus had a limited amount of money and the game wasn't going his way.

The boy's mother lowered her book. "Michael, come sit down."

William leaned back to get a good look at the woman. She wasn't too pretty, but cute just the same. She was in her midthirties, with light brown hair held in a bun under a wide-brimmed decorative hat with spectacles on the bridge of her nose. Her face was long and narrow, with a thin nose and small lips that refused to smile. Her blue eyes met William's and she went back to her book without a nod or indication of noticing him.

William said, "Miss, he's fine. He's not bothering me and we're minding our language as best we can."

Her book lowered. "My son doesn't need to learn how to play cards. Come sit down, Michael," she said plainly.

"Oh, Ma," the boy complained as he obediently moved back to sit by her. The train may have been exciting initially, but Michael had become bored sitting there.

"I'm William," he said to the lady.

Her eyes shifted up to him without interest. "I know. You've been telling everyone."

"Well, yeah, that's how you meet people, miss. Do you have a name, or do you want me to call you Gerty?"

Gus giggled. He had tried to talk to the lady earlier and was met with the same lack of interest. "Two pennies." He bet two pennies and tossed them into the hat.

She lowered her book with a glower. "Gerty? My name is Molly, if you must know. Molly James. No, I'm not related to Jessie, so don't ask. My husband's name is Cletus. Have you heard of him?"

"Who?" William asked.

"My husband. Cletus James."

William chuckled. "No, I can't say I have Cletus James. But it does sound like quite the venereal disease. Does it itch?"

Her cheeks reddened while the men laughed. "You are a despicable man."

William's grin was broad. "Thank you. So, Miss James? Are you related to Jesse?"

Molly's eyes widened with anger. "I just told you I wasn't! Leave me be."

William laughed and turned back to his poker game. "Two cents, huh, Gus? You must have a winning hand. Well, heck, I've won twenty-eight cents so far, so why not meet your two and raise you, boys, one more? Three cents to stay in, Joel."

Amos Stafford had overheard the conversation between Molly and William and couldn't help the slight smile that lifted his lips. He knew his wife was not amused at all. "Miss James, I'm curious. You asked William if he had heard of your husband. Is there a reason why? What does your husband do for a living?"

Molly's head lifted noticeably. "He is the county sheriff. We also own the Fourth Street Market, the Amber Light Hotel, and the Golden Star Restaurant in The Dalles City. And I know Clete would probably love to humble Mr. Fasana if he would dare to step off the train."

William spoke through a soft chuckle, "The train is stopping there for lunch if you and the sheriff would like to join us."

Lucille Stafford said with interest, "Mrs. James, that sounds like a lot of work for one family. You must be busy."

Molly wrinkled her nose. "We have a large family and good employees. The James family is very prominent in the The Dalles City area," she said proudly.

As he dealt the cards, William quipped, "They were prominent in Missouri a few years ago, too."

Molly took a deep breath. "I hope Clete meets us at the train station. Maybe he'll teach you some respect."

Gus looked at Molly and shook his head. "He'd best not try it. William is a Deputy US Marshal, so is that man there, and way back there is Matt Bannister."

"I don't care. I won't be disrespected by anyone."

"Miss," William said, "I was trying to be respectful. You should have known—"

A loud boom was heard, followed by a rough jarring that forced Matt forward off his seat and into the back of the seat in front of him with a brutal, jarring hit. Several startled screams from the passengers in the coach joined the choir of cracking wood and thundering booms that vibrated a man's chest. All too quickly, the passenger coach's wheels were pulled free from the rails as the front end shifted slightly toward the river.

The steel wheels bounced over the wood railroad ties, jarring the riders with every bounce the wheels hit every two feet, making it hard to stay seated. The rough ride created a nonstop rattling that severely shook the passenger coach up and down so rapidly that the screams of the frightened people vibrated with uneven volume and consistency. A loud thundering roar like an approaching tornado filled everyone's ears with distant screams, cracking wood, the squeals of twisting steel, and slamming bangs that were so loud and powerful that they penetrated a man's body to his very soul.

Terror went through the passengers with every jerk, bang, squeal, and crack of shattering wood. A second ground-shaking explosion erupted, sending a shock wave through the coach and elevating the panic while the thundering, heavy slamming and pounding grew ever closer. Suddenly, the iron coupler that connected the third-class coach to the rest of the train broke free and slammed into the higher-class passenger car ahead of them, ripping into its wooden frame like a spear through flesh with an explosion creating a hailstorm of sharp shards of splintered wood and glass as the two cars collided slowing the coach to a near sudden stop as it tilted heavily toward the bank of the river.

Behind them, the momentum of the caboose and the twisting angle of the coach snapped the iron coupler, allowing the caboose to slam into the backside of the coach with spine-numbing force. The hit from behind propelled the coach off the rails and pushed it over the edge of the steep bank. The passenger coach began to roll as if in a nightmare a hundred feet down the embankment toward the Columbia River.

Matt was thrown viciously out of his seat and slammed

against the roof, which buckled under the weight. Then, he rolled over the windows and slammed against the seats. The back of Lucille Stafford's neck landed against the metal edge of the seat's back before she was sent reeling like a rag doll out of control against the broken windows, roof, and bench seats before being tumbled around the coach again as the passenger car continued to roll down the bank. Like everyone else, Matt was tossed helplessly back and forth as the railcar rolled down the steep hill, finally coming to rest on its side in the Columbia River.

CHAPTER THREE

THE TRESTLE OVER THE GYPSUM CREEK CANYON
was the perfect place to stop the train. It was inaccessible
except by rail or the Columbia River. The nearest wagon
road was five miles south, and the closest home was seven
miles east. The Oregon Short Line Railroad track followed
a narrow strip of land between the Columbia River and the
basalt cliffs of the Columbia Gorge that averaged four
hundred feet high. The narrow area between the river and
cliffs where Gypsum Creek entered the river would ensure
the passengers had nowhere to flee, making their job
easier.

Everything was in place, and now they waited. Six
heavily armed men wearing flour bags over their faces
waited for the black smoke of the train to appear around a
bend. Taking note of the drawings in a book about knights
during the Middle Ages, their horses were draped in dark-
gray sheets from head to tail under the saddle blankets to
limit any trace of identification from a witness. Burlap bags
were tied around the horses' lower legs and hooves.

The men covered their faces with flour bags, but to conceal their identities even more, they wore spectacle frames with or without lenses under the flour bags, so any witnesses would say the man or men they saw wore glasses. They dressed identically, having soaked their pants, shirts, long coats, and sheets for the horses in a vat of dark-gray dye. Their boots were covered by burlap bags tied to their legs, and their hands were covered by cotton gloves dyed gray that were tight enough to give them finger dexterity. The six men had cut a square hole in their long coats, providing access to their gun belts. The six men were well prepared, and each man knew exactly what his job was, which was to make the robbery go as quickly and effi-ciently as possible without the use of bloodshed, preferably.

A shipment of a two-hundred-thousand-dollar payroll was being transferred to the Stafford Milling Company to cover the farmer's harvest payments. The money was in a safe inside the mail car, protected by four paid guards, none of whom knew the safe's combination. However, the robbers knew the owner, Amos Stafford, was on the train with his wife. The robbers did not doubt that Amos would rather open the safe than see his bride of forty-eight years suffer. It was a good plan that should go without any need-less bloodshed or permanent harm to Mrs. Stafford. At most, a squeeze to one of her arthritic hands would cause her enough pain for the love of her husband to open the safe willingly.

Most importantly, Gypsum Creek was isolated enough to give Randy Paulson and his pals time to locate Amos Stafford and convince him to open the safe. The mail car had no access from the outside to open the door, but the men inside would open the door if Amos loved his wife as much as they heard. The plan was simple and efficient, and no one would get hurt if everything went according to plan.

To stop the train at the mouth of Gypsum Creek, their plan was simple: blow up the trestle, and the train would have to stop, allowing them to board and take it over. To escape, they'd ride up the creek into the narrow canyon, come out five miles up the creek, and split up, peeling off at different access points to meet up later. With the streambed's running water over the rock base and loose gravel, the burlap bags tied around the horse's hooves should leave no viable trail to follow.

As to being recognized or someone being able to describe the men or horses, every aspect of identification was covered except voice recognition. They all knew and agreed that if any of them knew someone on the train, a tap to the gut meant that man could not speak and the next man would. It was to protect them all as one man being recognized put them all at risk. Once they left the train and were deep in the canyon, they would change their clothes and, later that night, have a bonfire to burn any evidence while celebrating their sudden pay raise.

Randy and his pals waited on a steep slope of scree-rock along the base of the cliffs above the tracks for a good view of the coming train. In the creek bed, a hundred feet below the trestle, Isaac Chandler waited for the signal to light the fuse that would ignite the blasting cap, blowing the dynamite and destroying the trestle. The locomotive engineer would have no choice but to stop the train. It was a solid plan, and by tonight, the six men would be wealthier, earning just over thirty-three thousand dollars apiece for a day's work. It would be higher for Randy and his partner Stan Meldrum, who planned the heist, and lower for those whose only function was to do as they were told.

Randy Paulson smiled slowly as the black smoke of the train rounded the bend about a mile from the trestle, providing plenty of space for the train to slow to a stop. He held his revolver in his hand with the hammer pulled back but hesitated to pull the trigger.

"What are you waiting for? Pull the trigger," Stan said, watching the train's black smoke and steam plume pushing the engine forward at a reasonable speed. A single shot in the air was the signal for Isaac to light the fuse.

Randy shook his head. "I want to confine them in this narrow section right down here, not find ourselves contained in a long narrow strip as we ride away. The train's stopping right down there." He pointed directly in front of them, close to the trestle. "I don't want to leave any time for them to shoot us in the back as we're leaving."

"Good point," Stan agreed.

David Ruddick disagreed. "It takes trains a while to stop. He's chugging along pretty good. You better pull the trigger."

"I will as soon as he reaches that boulder."

"Which boulder?"

Randy hesitated another fifteen seconds and pulled the trigger, firing a loud shot into the air. "Get ready, boys. We're about to become much richer men."

GYPSUM CREEK WAS a small river that began in the high Cascade Mountains and snaked its way down onto the western edge of Oregon's central high desert plateau. Squib Creek was another small river that started in the high country of the Blue Mountains and flowed west, where it crossed the plateau and eventually joined with Gypsum

Creek just before plunging over the edge of a natural bowl in the ground that started the Gypsum Creek Canyon which grew more profound over the next five miles until it the met the Columbia River.

The mouth of the canyon was about a hundred feet deep and one hundred and fifty feet wide. During spring's snow melt, Gypsum Creek became a torrent of rushing water, but after the dry summer months and now being late September, the river was shallow, not more than a foot deep in the center. Though the Gypsum Creek Canyon walls were sheer and high, they ended at the Columbia Gorge, where the river's banks were steep but navigable on horseback.

Isaac Chandler had spent his younger years working in a silver mine in Nevada and knew black powder explosives intimately from his experience as a powder-man. His job was to plant the twelve sticks of dynamite on the trestle, set the blasting caps, string the fuse line down the trestle to the creek bed, wait and listen for the signal, and last, light the fuse. It wasn't necessarily a hard job, but he wasn't as young, agile, and vibrant as he was twenty years before. Now he was in his midforties, well over two hundred pounds, and climbing around on the steep bank and trestle wasn't as easy as it might've been when he was a thin twenty-five-year-old that weighed a hundred and fifty pounds.

Isaac stood in the creek bed gazing up at the bottom side of the trestle far above him. He had already chased a ground squirrel away from the black fuse laid out thirty feet along the rocky edge of the creek. Every aspect of the robbery was planned to protect the six men from being identified, including the dynamite and fuse being used. The dynamite was already at hand, but they couldn't risk using a safety fuse that burned slower, nor could they afford to risk buying a fuse cord from the hardware store. An answer to their problem was found when Isaac said he could make a reliable fast-burning fuse using a roll of yarn dipped in natural honey covered heavily with finely ground black powder.

Isaac carefully unwound his cord as he clumsily climbed down the cross braces of the trestle's legs to the ground and along the creek bed. He laid it out and was ready to light it when a young ground squirrel he'd been watching became curious about the black line stretching across the gray rocks and got his feet tangled on the cord. Isaac would have shot it, but he didn't want to alarm his partners. In truth, he had enjoyed watching the critter run around and play. He straightened the line and tossed rocks at the squirrel to chase it away. His job was simple: light the fuse when he heard a gunshot and run to safety. His horse was with his partners a safe distance away. It couldn't get any simpler.

Upon hearing Randy fire his revolver, Isaac struck a match and lit the end of the fuse. He watched the flame quickly crawl along the ground, and then suddenly, it stopped. He could hear the rumble of the train approaching and hurried over the rough river rock, and to his horror, he found the cord soaking in the edge of the creek. It must have been moved by the squirrel running around because he had placed it two feet over along the edge of the bank. He couldn't see it due to larger rocks blocking his view.

Isaac quickly lit another match, but it went out in his rush to light the cord. He lit another match and tried to light the fuse, but it had soaked up water and was too wet to burn. He stepped forward a few feet and lit another match, but once again, in his rush to light the fuse, it was blown out before he could ignite the cord. In his growing panic, he dropped his box of matches and quickly picked them up.

Randy fired his gun again. The roar of the train was getting louder as it drew closer. Isaac's hands shook as he finally got the fuse to light. The cord burned quickly, but it still had thirty feet to travel before the trestle and then up a hundred feet to the dynamite. He watched the flame snake across the ground. Verifying there wasn't another issue, he turned and ran. He could hear the train approaching fast and the ground began to vibrate. He glanced back at the burning cord and tripped over a rock, falling face-first onto the creek's bank.

A few seconds passed, and then two consecutive loud explosions hurt his ears. Knowing he was too close, he covered his head with his hands as splinters of wood rained down on the creek bed. A moment later, the ground shook so violently that it nearly sent his body into the air. Like a nightmare, the pounding, rumbling, and loudness of the crashing railcars seemed to continue for hours, and then suddenly, a large explosion, louder and more potent than the dynamite, echoed in his ears. Pieces of iron and scalding hot water showered down from the air as the boiler exploded, tearing the locomotive apart.

Isaac screamed as the boiling water rained down, burning his back. Screams, more terrified than his, roared like a crashing wave along with the loud booms, snapping and cracking of wood, and the squeals of bending iron. Isaac scampered into the cold water to relieve his burning skin. It was beyond the limits of his imagination as he watched in utter horror as the canyon filled up with crashing rail cars. The terrified screams coming from a passenger coach standing upright on one end with its back end straight up in the air forced all the passengers toward the bottom, and then it slowly fell, slamming into the cars under it and rolling to its crumbling roof on the river rock. Smoke began to rise from the engine's hot box and the mail car as the lanterns inside it had broken.

"Oh, my Lord, no," Isaac gasped with the horrifying realization that he was responsible for a catastrophe.

––––––––

ON THE RIDGE, Randy Paulson watched with growing horror as the locomotive was less than twenty feet from the trestle when it blew and had no time to stop. The engine dropped and plowed through the remaining support timbers, shattering them like toothpicks as the trestle fell. The steam engine hit the ground nose first, busting the coupler to the tender, which was filled with split oak. The tender then plowed into the steam engine, causing the boiler to explode with great ferocity. The mail car, a wooden box car with no external way of opening the door, hit the falling trestle, shearing part of the roof and sidewall off. While turning horizontally, it hit the base of a splintered timber about twenty feet tall that ripped through the mail car walls like a knife through butter coming to rest halfway through.

The following baggage car, a wooden boxcar, was quickly torn apart by the trestle's twisted rails and jagged remains, scattering pieces of the roof, walls, and baggage across the wreckage. What was left of the baggage car crushed the backside of the mail car. A steel-framed flat car hauling a beautiful new black carriage and a large piece of mining equipment nose-dived and tipped over, crushing the shiny, new horse-drawn carriage under its heavy steel frame. However, the mining equipment supported the flat-car's weight as it rested angled toward the river upside down.

The first-class passenger car flew over most of the overturned flat car, but the bottom of the front end collided with the uprighted steel wheels of the flatcar. In an explosion of splintered wood, the steel wheels plowed through the wooden passenger car's floorboards and wall like a branding iron through rice paper before the first-class coach rolled off the pile of debris and slammed down on its flattened side in the creek bed beside the mail car.

The second-class passenger coach's steel wheels slipped off the tracks and hit the edge of the railroad ties and gravel, slowing its momentum with jolting significance. In a terrible collision, the heavier third-class passenger coach and caboose rammed the second-class coach, cutting through the back left corner in an explosion of splintered wood. The crash shifted the angle of the second-class coach so that it slipped over the edge of the deep ravine horizontally. The front of the passenger coach hit what was left of a heavy support post, which spun the back half around as it fell so that the back end of the passenger coach hit the creek bed vertically, bowing the roof and sidewalls out before it slowly fell back and landed upside down collapsing the roof on the creek bed's stones.

In the same way, the third-class passenger coach slid off the rails and was rammed by the caboose, which sent both rolling several times down the steep bank and coming to a stop twenty yards or more in the Columbia River. The caboose landed upright and rolled deeper until all that was left was the smokestack from the woodstove sticking a foot above the water. The third-class coach landed on its side and slid along the gravel bottom, coming to rest in four to five feet of water.

For a moment, the shock of it all left a haunting silence. Then the screaming began. Like the roar of an audience, the screams grew loud and panicked. Cries of pain, fear, and desperation rose up the cliffside. Then, the first flumes of smoke began to appear from the mail car at the bottom of the twisted wood and steel pile.

"They're going to be burned alive," Mark Duffy said, utterly shocked by what he'd witnessed.

Randy was equally in a shocked daze. His words were barely more than a whisper, "We can't stay here. We have to go."

"They need help. We need to help them," Mark said, forgetting about the flour sack over his head.

Stan Meldrum pulled the bag off his face and rubbed his eyes. He was in his early fifties, and his short brown hair was growing heavier with gray and balding on top. He was clean-shaven and had a rectangular face with a long nose and thin lips. His blueish-gray eyes stared in horror as he hoped in vain that what he had witnessed wasn't real. He waved a pointed a finger at Mark. "Randy's right. We have to go. If we stay, we'll hang for this. We can't do anything for them. Let's go." He kicked his horse and turned toward the Gypsum Creek's deep ravine that would lead them into the canyon.

"What about the money?" Dave Ruddick questioned.

Randy pointed at the rising black fume. "Do you see that smoke? Soon, all of that down there will be a raging fire. We can't do anything about it. Most of those people are probably dead, and if not, they will be. All of those rail cars are made of wood. All that wood is varnished and will burn like pitch-coated kindling with this breeze. No one is putting that fire out tonight." He swallowed and nearly choked as his throat went dry. "We'll come back if we can, but let's get out of sight."

They could hear screaming and crying as they rode into the shadowed crevice of Gypsum Creek's narrow canyon as it cut through the cliffs. They found Isaac standing in the shadows, breathing heavily. He was shaken up.

Randy was furious. "You were supposed to light the fuse when I fired my gun! That train could have stopped!" Randy yelled. He had never considered there might be a wreck.

Isaac had pulled the hood off his head, revealing his medium-length blond hair and round face. His blue eyes were moist. He had a thinly grown blond beard and mustache about three inches long that made his round face look fatter rather than longer. Isaac was forty-five years old. He was slightly shorter than average height at about five feet and seven inches tall but over two hundred and fifty pounds. Isaac gasped and fought to keep his emotions under control. His voice was tight, and it was just over a whisper: "A squirrel got the fuse tangled in its feet, I think. It was in the water."

Randy shouted angrily, "People are going to die because of your screw-up! Isaac, I want you to stay here and watch what your stupidity caused. You stay here and watch them folks burn! Don't follow us, or I'll shoot you myself. You watch your mistake burn, and don't ever screw up again, or I swear I'll put a bullet in your head!"

CHAPTER FOUR

MATT WAS JOLTED, JARRED, TOSSED, AND THROWN around like a rag doll as the passenger coach rolled down the embankment and came to a sudden stop, slamming him against a shattered window. Disoriented, he was quickly startled by the cold water that flooded over his head as he lay against the window's broken glass. He got to his hands and knees, stood on wobbly legs, and grabbed hold of the top of a bench seat, which was the outside edge of an aisle seat, to steady him as the water continued to rise to his hips and then near his chest. The coach rested on its left side, so the center aisle and two rows of seats were now the right-hand wall as he stood on a window. Chaos was all around him as he tried to get his wits together while warm blood drained over his face and into his eyes. Matt was in shock like everyone else around him, and it took a moment to get some orientation of his surroundings.

Cries and screams for help were coming from both ends of the passenger coach as everyone aboard was stunned, hurt, and panicking that they would drown. They had no idea how deep the water would rise or how far from the bank they had rolled. The seat Matt had been sitting on was now beside his head, connected to the wall, which placed all of their weight on the outside edge of the coach. He could see the blue sky through the windows overhead and knew the coach wasn't submerged, but it was sitting at a downhill angle that threatened to slide deeper into the river. It took a moment to comprehend what had happened, but his immediate reaction was to holler over the screaming, "Gabriel! Gabriel!"

"Dad," Gabriel said, barely peeking over a seat's back. He had backed away from the incoming water as far as he could, pressing himself against the bench seat. His eyes were wide and mouth open while he took a breath unsteadily. His body quivered as he stared blankly at Matt. "W...W...what happened?"

Matt quickly pushed through the chest-deep water, stepping on broken glass and gravel under his feet to reach his son. "Are you hurt?"

Gabriel was in shock. "I...I...think so. My arm hurts."

Matt could see at first glance that Gabriel's forearm was broken. "Let's get you out of here."

The chaos was overwhelming. Everyone needed help and everyone was in pain. Morton pulled himself up from his knees, gripping the top edge of a seat, groaning in agony while holding his back. Amos Stafford was trying to keep his wife's head above water while sobbing. His wife, Lucille, floated half submerged but remained calm, too stunned to cry. She was alive but unmoving while staring straight up at the windows above her while her husband cradled her head and shoulders to his chest. Molly James held her injured son's head in her arms as well to keep his head above the water. She was screaming for someone to help her get her son's leg free from under the seat. William was quickly at Molly's side to help free Michael's leg from the twisted steel frame of the bench seat. Gus Walden stood with a pain-filled grimace while leaning against a bench seat, holding his back. Emory Fisher screamed for someone to help him free Joel's arm, which was pinned underneath the coach, securing Joel in a watery grave.

In the immediate confusion and growing panic, Matt glanced back at his Indian friends and saw that Gilbert, despite cuts and bruises on his body, had his wife and daughter in his calm arms, reassuring young Alice that they would be okay. They were cut, bruised, and tattered by the tumbling of the coach, but their injuries appeared minor compared to many others. What struck Matt immediately was Gilbert's ability to remain calm in the chaos. It was as noticeable as a red coat in a snow-covered field.

"Dad, your head," Gabriel said with frightened concern.

Matt touched his scalp and noticed a deep slice near the top of his head. He didn't remember hitting his head, but the amount of blood pouring down his face and off his ears suggested that it was a severe laceration.

Gabriel trembled as he stared at Matt numbly. "I can see your skull." He began to weep.

"Let's help everyone get out," Matt said.

William pulled one of his silver-plated revolvers from his holster and stuck the barrel under the seat to use it as a pry bar to leverage it up enough to pull Michael's leg free. William's shoulder was dripping blood from a cut from broken glass.

"Matt," Amos Stafford wept, "Lucille's hurt." A gash across Amos's forehead painted his face red as the blood dripped like rainwater. His spectacles had been lost in the tumbling, but a cut on his nose showed where his glasses were driven into his flesh. Matt went to Lucille's side.

"Oh, no!" Gus Walden hollered in desperation. He took notice of a deep gash in his leg that bled so profusely in the water that he feared his artery was cut. "I'm bleeding to death."

William glanced at the wound, annoyed. It was on the outside of the leg, far from his artery. He yelled, "No, you're not! Get your head on straight and help me! Matt! I need your muscles!"

Lucille grabbed Matt's wrist. "My back is broken. I can't move my legs. Let me say goodbye to my husband. You go help them."

"Don't say that," Amos groaned from a depth deep within where the very foundation of his love for his wife was found. "We'll get you out of here. Won't we, Matt?"

"Matt, the boy's going to drown!" William screamed urgently.

Gilbert Redbird lifted his daughter out of the coach through a broken window, followed by his wife. Ona was much larger than Alice, and the tight squeeze of her going through the window cut her body with the tiny shards of glass stuck in the frame. Once she was able to sit on the exterior wall and see the carnage of the wreck, she gasped and hugged her daughter tightly to hide her eyes and ears from the screams. Ona wept.

Gilbert Redbird remained inside and pushed his way through the water to Matt. "The windows are our only way out." He pointed toward the front of the coach. The front end was crushed, with the front iron deck crumpled like tissue paper inside the coach, blocking any exit. A gash in the side wall of splintered wood opened up to the blue sky, but it wasn't big enough to get anyone out. "The windows are the only way to get people out," Gilbert repeated.

Matt nodded with understanding, but his concern went to Morton, who appeared to be in severe pain. He rested a hand on Morton's shoulder. "You have to get out of here. How bad are you hurt?"

Morton spoke through a pain-filled grimace, "My back and ribs. My ribs are broken, I swear. But I'll be fine." The side of his face was bruised and beginning to swell, his nose and a cut on his hand bled.

Matt sloshed through the water, adding more weight to the front of the coach, but stopped when an unnerving chill ran down his spine as the coach slid a few inches deeper into the river. He had no idea what kind of terrain the coach rested on or if it was tittering on the edge of a deep hole.

"Matt! Damn it, hurry up!" William shouted anxiously. Molly James struggled with all her might to keep her son Michael's head above water as the water level rose another inch. The boy was bawling with heavy sobs, scared to death and anguishing in pain the more his mother strained to lift and tug his upper body. Gilbert Redbird stepped beside Molly and took hold of Michael to hold his head above the water line. Molly stepped back and leaned heavily against the side of the rail car to be out of the way. The sudden weight pressed against the side caused the coach to slide downhill another foot on the loose gravel underneath, which brought a loud chorus of terrified screams. Molly stepped away from the wall and broke down into heartwrenching sobs as her son's face was covered by water.

Gilbert readjusted his feet and pressed upward with his legs to force Micheal's nose and mouth out of the water.

The young man screamed, blowing bubbles in the water until a muffled snap was heard, and then Michael's high-pitched screams broke free from the rising water as the bone in his trapped leg snapped.

Matt dipped under the water to grab the revolver from William and lifted as hard as he could to pry the twisted steel frame up enough for William to pull the boy's ankle free. A silent prayer for Jesus to help free the boy's ankle slipped out of Matt's closed lips as he strained with all his might to bend the seat's metal frame just enough to loosen its grip on Michael. The revolver was the only tool they had to use as a pry bar, and it didn't have enough leverage to do the job. Matt's head lifted from the water. "Get me a rifle! I need a rifle!"

Gus Walden shouted, "Cut the boy's foot off, and let's get out of here before we drown!"

Michael screamed in terror. "Mommy, don't let them cut my foot off!"

Molly James sobbed bitterly. She knew if the men could not free her boy's foot, then they would have to cut it off to save his life. She leaned against Gilbert Redbird and tried to comfort her son but could not get any words out of her mouth between her desperate sobbing and wailing, knowing her son was just moments from drowning.

"I'm not cutting his foot off!" Matt shouted angrily. "Get me a rifle!" He knew that he and his deputies carried rifles onto the train, as did one of the other men.

Morton Sperry knelt with a pain-filled grimace and felt around the floor for one of the rifles. After a few moments and three fresh cuts from broken glass, Morton lifted his rifle from the water. "Matt, here!" He tossed it to Matt and then bent over as the action aggravated his ribs. Matt dunked back into the dark water and wedged the barrel between the folded metal and the floor. With a longer tool to use as leverage, he prayed it would be enough to lift the seat. He used his legs to push upward and pulled on the rifle with all his might. William also went underwater and reached across Matt's body to yank the boy's foot loose. Morton stepped through the water and grabbed the seat to help lift. He made eye contact with Emory Fisher and shouted, "Come help us!"

Emory Fisher was standing idle next to the submerged body of his friend Joel Jones. He couldn't believe his life-long friend had drowned despite his best efforts to save him. Emory looked at Morton in shock and said, "Joel's dead."

Enraged, Morton yelled, "So will this kid be if you don't get over here and help! Your friend's gone, but we can save this boy. Now help us!"

Emory slushed through the water and slipped his fingers under the seat just as Matt and William came up for a breath of air. Matt looked at Morton as he caught his breath. "If it doesn't loosen this time, I'll need your knife." The moving around and sloshing of water had caused the coach to slide a bit further downhill, raising the water level more. Gilbert had lifted Michael as far as he could, and now his mouth and nose were barely out of the water. Matt knew if the coach slid any further downhill, the boy would drown if they did not cut off his foot.

"No, no, no," Molly bellowed, knowing it may be the only option of saving her son's life. Michael was too terri-fied to say a word as the water was at the edge of his lips.

Matt went back underwater and strained to pry the seat up just enough to free the boy's foot. The five men crowded together to unbuckle the crumpled frame. Matt lifted as strenuously as if it was his son trapped to a certain death if he couldn't bend the steel. With great effort, he could feel the bench seat beginning to give. A moment later, William finally pulled Michael's foot free.

Gilbert said, "We'll have to carry him through a window."

William glanced at the splintered wood of the gash in what was now the ceiling and knew the passenger car walls were not designed to support much weight. The front exit door was no longer operational. "What about the back door?"

Gilbert shook his head. "It's jammed like the front. The back deck is compressed against the door. It won't budge," Gilbert said.

From outside, the smell of smoke was beginning to seep into the coach while the sound of screaming and wailing people could be heard crying out for help.

Molly James held her son close to her heart, weeping and thanking God that her son was still alive. She looked at Matt and asked, "Are we trapped in here?"

Gilbert answered, "I got my family out the window. We'll get you and your boy out that way too."

Matt used the rifle's barrel to break the glass shards around the windows above them, careful not to let the falling shards hit him as they fell. When he finished, he told Gabriel, "Climb up there and help the ladies out. Morton, you too."

Gabriel lifted his broken arm. "I don't think I can." His teeth were chattering from the pain of his arm and cold water.

Matt helped lift Morton out of a window, Gus Walden was on the outside assisting Molly and then Michael James out of the coach and to the shore to keep a minimal amount of weight on the weak framed walls. Emory Fisher,

Gabriel, and Gilbert climbed out next, leaving Matt and William alone inside the coach with Amos and Lucille Stafford.

Lucille had begun coughing up mouthfuls of blood and did not want to be touched. Tears flooded her eyes as she gazed into Amos's while he lovingly held her head and shoulders out of the water. She spoke through short breaths, "I'm not afraid to die, Amos. I just never thought it would be like this." Her bloody lips trembled emotionally.

"You're not dying here," Amos said emotionally. "These men can lift you out the window. You have to get through this so you can see our grandchildren again. Okay? We can overcome this, Sweetheart."

She began to whimper. "I'm dying, Amos. I can't move my legs and I'm bleeding inside. I won't fit through the window anyway. There's no reason to go through the pain of trying. I won't leave this train alive. I already know it." She coughed a fine mist of blood into the air. Her eyes welled heavily mixing the tears with the water on her face as she gazed lovingly at her husband. "You gave me a good life, Amos. I love you so much."

He closed his eyes emotionally and rested his head on hers, suddenly feeling faint. His voice strained to fight the anguish that fought to burst out in screaming wails, "I can't leave you here. I won't! We have to try." The desperate expression on his face pleaded with her not to give up on him.

"Amos, no. All I want is for you to stay with me until I am gone or let the marshal drown me, but do not try to lift me out, please. I can't take any more pain."

A sudden burst of emotion escaped his mouth as he wept.

Lucille touched his cheek gently. "Show me your smile, Amos. I want to see you smile." She forced an emotional smile as the tears left her eyes. "Thank you for the forty-eight greatest years of marriage a woman could ask for. We almost made it to fifty."

Amos burst out in a loud sob that he couldn't control. "Don't say that, Lucille," he said in a high-pitched voice. He looked at Matt and pleaded, "Please, help me get her out of here. She'll die if we don't get her to a doctor."

Matt already knew she wouldn't fit through a window. He gently put a hand on Amos's shoulder and frowned empathetically. "She's right, Amos. She is bleeding inside and doesn't have long. I am sorry, but there is nothing we can do."

Lucille looked at the laceration on Matt's head, which revealed the white of his skull. "Leave us and go get some help for yourself. You look like you'll bleed to death before I do."

Matt took hold of Lucille's hand and nodded sadly. "I'll see you in Heaven."

Once Matt had crawled out of a window and left Lucille and Amos alone, she lifted an arm around her husband empathetically as he gave in to his tears and wept violently with his head resting upon her. "Amos," she said with a voice just above a whisper, "Shhh, my love." She coughed up more blood. She forced a slight smile as her eyes grew heavy. "Thank you...for loving me. Thank you for a lifetime with..." she coughed, "my best friend...and giving me our children. You made me happy. Fat and happy." Her voice had grown slower and softer to a mere strained whisper. "I'll always love you."

He squeezed her closer to him in a firm hug, refusing to

let her go. His words were choked with emotion. "I love you, Lucille."

"I know…" She coughed up more blood. For a second, fear showed in her eyes as she struggled to get a breath. Her breathing was growing shallower. "I…love…you. I'll… see…you in…Heaven." She looked at the blue sky through the window above her. "Can…you…hear it? It's beautiful." Her eyes seemed to focus on something and widened.

"The yelling?" Amos questioned. All he could hear was the distant cries for help, screams of pain, and wailing from the rest of the train.

A smile formed on Lucille's lips as her eyes grew brighter with life, but there was nothing that Amos could see except the blue sky. "I see Jesus. He's beautiful…" As suddenly as Lucille said the words, she was gone.

Amos, left alone inside the twisted railcar, held his wife's body close to him and wailed loudly.

CHAPTER FIVE

MATT HONORED LUCILLE'S WISH TO BE LEFT alone with her husband. He was just barely able to squeeze through a broken window to make it out of the coach, receiving several minor cuts and scratches on the undersides of his arms and sides from bits of glass in the seal that were too small to knock out. Once on top, the nightmare inside the passenger coach he had experienced became minimal compared to the reality Matt's eyes struggled to comprehend. Standing on the third-class coach's edge, he stared in disbelief at the collapsed trestle now snapped and splintered timbers, scattered ties, and warped rails entangled in an indescribable mass of wood and steel that were functioning railcars moments before. Visible flames were rising from a split-in-half boxcar at the bottom of the pile, and they were quickly spreading to other rail cars, including a collapsed passenger coach lying on its side near the flames. Matt could see half of a man's body lying underneath that passenger coach. The body of another man was impaled on a broken board that was pointing upward at a forty-five-degree angle about twelve feet above the coach. But more horrifying was a man pinned under a heavy timber from the fallen trestle who was still alive and screaming mercilessly as the flames roasted his legs.

There were many frantic screams, weeping, wailing, injured moans and pleading for help, prayers, and cursing that could be heard in the hellish choir. The red caboose was nowhere in sight except a short chimney pipe sticking six inches out of the water further out in the river. A dead body floated near the bank, which Matt supposed was a railroad employee. Although the scene was utterly horrific and overwhelming, for the few of them who were able, there were people trapped inside the two passenger coaches who needed help.

"Oh, Lord, give me and the others the strength to help them," he said quietly before jumping down into the river in a hurry to help where he could. Gilbert Redbird followed him with a splash in the water. Gus jumped down but groaned loudly as his injured back was jarred. He froze in excruciating pain before he slowly stumbled forward to collapse on the bank.

"My back's no good," he said with a grimace.

Matt joined William, Morton, and Emory Fisher at the bottom of the Gypsum Creek bed and looked up where the trestle used to be. The heavy timbers that supported the trestle were snapped like matchsticks, and the hardened steel rails were bent and twisted, intertwined with the decimated rail cars. Amazingly, there were a few stunned people scattered around who had crawled out through broken windows or a torn gash in the sidewalls.

One man sat on the creek's bank, wailing uncontrollably for the loss of a loved one. Another man lay prone on the rocks with his head in his wife's lap, both bleeding and traumatized. She silently ran her hand through his hair comfortingly. Another woman covered in blood from a severe gash across her forehead that peeled her scalp back until it hung like a flap of hair stumbled over the riverbed, mumbling randomly in shock as if she was lost in her own private world. Yet another, a young man, pleaded with William and the others, desperately seeking help to save his young wife, who was pinned inside the crushed rail car. His wife lay on her stomach inside the second-class passenger coach with a jagged wooden shard from the roof penetrating through her leg, pinning her in place. There was barely enough room for a man to crawl inside to offer any assistance.

William got down in the shallow creek to peer inside and then looked at Matt with a sullen expression. "That splinter of wood is probably saving her life. That's about where the artery is, isn't it?"

Matt got down on his belly in the cold stream to look inside through the blood stinging his eyes. The coach's roof was not designed to support its weight and had collapsed, turning the roof into a splintered pin cushion on the creek's rocks for the passengers to fall onto. There were several dead inside, and others impaled like the young lady. He shook his head with a growing, helpless feeling. The shard of wood penetrating the back of her leg was about two inches thick and rose above her to pierce the red velvet cushioned seat dangling overhead. If they had a handsaw, they could cut it and free her leg and hope the artery wasn't damaged, but there was no handsaw available, leaving no other way to break the splintered wood without hitting or kicking it, which would cause more damage to her leg.

Another concern that couldn't be overlooked was that the weight of the heavy frame, steel axle, and wheels pushing down on the coach would become too much for what little remained of the wooden walls and crush anyone who crawled inside. The fire was growing and had spread to the first passenger coach, where the survivors trapped inside screamed in terror and prayed for a miracle, but the fire continued to expand into a furnace of consuming flames. Matt could feel the heat from the fire growing hotter as he peered at the frantic woman trapped inside the second-class coach. She was a young lady in her early twenties or late teens and quite attractive. Her eyes pleaded with Matt as she begged, "Help me, please!"

Matt looked at the outside of the shattered structure and, despite his better judgment of self-preservation, said, "Give me your gun, William."

"Are you going to shoot her?" William asked, horrified, as he drew his one remaining revolver and handed it to Matt. Matt's gun belt was now underwater in the flooded passenger coach.

"No. I'll crawl in there." He took hold of the gun and scooted on his belly through a twisted, narrow window. William grabbed him. "Let me go, I'm smaller."

Matt forced William's hand away and continued manipulating his broad shoulders through the window to crawl inside under the double cushioned seats that were back to back and facing the opposite row of seats so that everyone who rode in the second-class passenger coach was facing someone that they could talk to. The red fabric seats were all empty now, but there was no shortage of dead and injured bodies all around him. The young woman grabbed

Matt's hand desperately and pleaded with him to save her life. She appeared uninjured in any other way except for her leg. Matt could feel the heat from the fire quickly consuming the other rail cars while the screaming continued, but little by little, it became fewer cries and prayers from the first-class coach as the sound of crackling flames grew louder.

"Help me! Please help me. I don't want to burn. Help me!" the young lady wailed.

A sharp pain in Matt's knee nearly made him curse as a splintered board jabbed into his knee. "Miss, I'll do my best." The uncanny sound of the crackling fire raging nearby and the heat coming from it all reasoned that it would not be long before the entire passenger car would be engulfed in flames, too.

"Sir," a soft voice spoke from six feet away. "Take my baby. He's already gone, but at least...his father can bury him. My son, please take him."

Matt was horrified to see the woman was alive with a shard of splintered wood six inches wide that had impaled the lady's back and stuck out of her abdomen. Not far from her, a man lay with a broken neck twisted unnaturally. Another man was beheaded, and another man was nearly severed in half at the chest as their blood mixed with all the other blood from torn-up bodies that discolored the creek's water. Matt nodded to the woman to acknowledge her while taking notice of all the horror that surrounded him and the few survivors who were trapped inside, most unconscious but breathing. The woman strained with a pain-filled grimace as she lifted her baby, wrapped in a blue baby blanket, from her chest, holding her child out for Matt. "Take him, please."

Matt gasped. The child appeared uninjured but was life-less in her outstretched hands.

The young lady with the impaled leg pleaded urgently, "My feet are going to burn! Please help me!" she begged.

The sound of a loud crack in the sidewall sent a wave of alarm through Matt and got his attention back on what he was doing. He crawled a few feet through the bloody water to the young woman with a shard of wood through her leg. "What is your name?" he asked to calm her down.

"Deanna."

"That's a beautiful name, Deanna. This will hurt, but I'll get you out of here." He put the gun against the wood splinter and fired. The vibration of the bullet passing through the wood caused the woman to scream in pain. He fired again to put another hole through the wood and broke the board just above her thigh. Matt pulled on the board impaled in the seat cushion above them and tossed it aside.

Deanna screamed in agony as Matt lifted her leg, forcing it upward and, with effort, pulled it free from the jagged splinter. He hollered to William and the others, "Pull her out!"

Gilbert Redbird was already inside, helping whoever he could to escape the fragile and endangered coach. He crawled across the dangerous roof and helped guide Deanna out of the coach to the safety of the creek bed. William stuck his head in the window and yelled, "Matt, get out of there! It's shifting! I don't know how long it will hold."

Matt crawled further into the coach to reach the baby, who appeared to be sleeping peacefully without a mark on his body. Matt took hold of the baby, who was still warm, freshly killed by a broken neck. A strange, deep emotion overcame him and he lifted his eyes to look at the baby's mother. The agony in her expression was evident, but she was calm despite being trapped in a hopeless situation. Matt shook his head helplessly. His voice quivered with emotion, "There's nothing I can do to help you. I'm sorry. I can't remove that." He motioned toward the splintered wood extending out of her abdomen. She was already dying.

The torment the woman was experiencing between her physical pain, losing her child, and knowing her situation was helpless was unimaginable. Every breath she took or word she uttered expanded her abdomen, pierced by the piece of wood. Her agony was unmistakable with every wince her expression made as she said, "My name...is Margaret Pihl. Please...deliver my baby to my husband... Joe, in Walla Walla. Please." She swallowed and choked on the blood that came out of her mouth.

Matt could feel the warmth of his tears penetrating his eyes. "You have my word, Miss. I promise you."

Smoke rolled into the rail car, filling it with the rancid smell of burning bodies. Terror filled her eyes as she pleaded with Matt with a twisted expression of torment, "I don't want to burn to death. Please...shoot me."

A cold chill, icier than any he had ever felt before, ran down his spine. "I..." he gasped. He had put down many hurt animals to spare their suffering, and he had killed too many men in his lifetime, but this was different. He was horrified by the thought of shooting an innocent woman.

"Matt!" William shouted. "Hurry up and get out of there! It's starting to burn!" The crushed sidewall of the railcar was now burning and spreading fast.

"Sir, don't let me burn to death. Please!" she pleaded. Her eyes clouded with tears that shined in the firelight as she spoke softly. "Free me so I can go home to the Lord.

Tell Joe I love him. Tell Joe...tell him...I'm sorry I couldn't protect little Jacob. I'll burn if I must," she tried to swallow but choked on the blood. "But get Jacob back to Joe before you get trapped in here, too. Please, sir."

Matt held the child in his left arm and nodded. "I promise you I will. I'm sorry, Miss." He took a deep breath and pointed the revolver in his right hand at her head for a guaranteed killing shot.

"Thank you," Margaret said and closed her eyes. "Jesus, I'm coming home."

"Jesus," Matt said with a heavy heart, "forgive me." He closed his eyes with the revolver only a short distance from her head and pulled the trigger. He opened his eyes to see a blurry world through his tears and smoke. Margaret Phil was dead. He tossed the gun out a window while shouting angrily, "Take that!" He held the baby close, crawled to a window, handed baby Jacob to William, and forced himself out the window across the heavy river rocks and cold water.

"Are you alright?" William asked, knowing what Matt had done.

Matt stood still and stared downward at the red tint of the water passing over his feet as he stood in the creek. His breathing was quickened and his hands shook uncontrollably. He gazed at William, but no response came.

"Matt, are you okay?" William questioned.

Matt shook his head slightly with a far-off look in his eyes. "No," he said softly. He blinked repeatedly to force the moisture in his eyes away. Matt bent down, peered at where Margaret Pihl lay, and noticed yellow flames had already spread to her feet. He knew he had done what was right, but knowing it was right didn't make it any easier to digest.

"No! No! No! Deanna, no! Please don't leave me! No!" the young man bellowed, overcome by emotion, as he held his beloved Deanna in his arms. Morton Sperry kneeled at her legs, trying frantically to stop the bleeding. All of his efforts were in vain as the young and pretty lady named Deanna succumbed to her torn artery.

Morton had helped the young man as best he could, but now that Deanna was gone, he slowly rose and approached Matt and William, keeping his elbow tight against his ribs. He spoke quietly. "They were just married yesterday. They were on their honeymoon."

William watched the young man wailing and shook his head sadly. There were no words he could think of to say. There was just tragedy and brokenness everywhere he looked.

Matt was upset by the experience of what he had seen and having to shoot an innocent woman to spare her the suffering of burning to death. His body was cut up and blood covered his face from the open head wound, but hearing Morton's words and the young man's deep emotional wailing hit him like a fist punching his chest. It was not hard for Matt to empathize with the young man's sorrow when he thought of his newlywed wife, Christine. However, he knew he could not imagine the depth of what the young man was feeling. For a moment, he could feel himself losing his self-control. He was overwhelmed with emotion and squeezed his lips together, blinking rapidly to clear the smoke and tears from his eyes. He rubbed his beard around his mouth, taking notice of the smeared blood on his hand.

"Are you alright?" Morton asked Matt with concern.

Matt held out a hand with his index finger lifted. He needed a moment to pull himself together. "No. No, I'm not. Let's get that man and his wife's body up on the tracks away from this smoke. Anyone else, too. How many more are trapped inside there?" Matt asked, nodding to the coach he had just come out of. He stepped toward the coach.

William grabbed Matt's arm and spoke firmly. "None! Matt, if there was, they're dead now. The coach is on fire. There is nothing more we can do." William's eyes filled with very rare thick tears. "I won't let you go in there. This is already hell without you getting trapped inside there, too."

Gilbert Redbird put a hand on Matt's arm. "We've done all we can do. Come, Ona can fix your scalp. Your skull is showing and that is not good."

Of the seventy-four passengers and railroad employees on the train, fifty-nine were dead, and the rest were injured with varying injuries from severe internal injuries and broken bones to mere lacerations. Only one man, Emory Fisher, walked away without a single scratch. However, helplessly watching his lifelong best friend drown was an injury that perhaps cut deeper and would leave a more prominent scar than many others.

MATT SAT on the Columbia River's bank, feeling exhausted and weak. At the same time, Ona Redbird washed his wounded scalp and then twisted a few strands of hair into thin braids on both sides of the laceration and tied them together tightly to close the wound. The wound was four inches long, and it took her some time to tie the braided knots and seal the cut tightly. Her daughter Alice watched intently to learn how to do it.

Gabriel sat by his father, grateful to know that Matt's wound was not as severe as it appeared. The amount of blood that had covered Matt's face and shirt was startling. Gabriel feared his father might bleed to death.

There were fifteen survivors, and all were in the last two passenger coaches. Those who could helped the more seriously injured and tended to their needs as best they could with their limited means.

The fire raged, sending a large plume of black smoke into the air. The survivors moved down the bank to escape the smoke and nauseous odor of the many bodies being cremated at once. The smoke was sure to be seen and help would come, but there was nothing more they could do except wait.

William was soaking wet as he and Morton walked down the tracks to where Matt sat. William tossed Matt's wet gun belt down with a heavy thud as he said, "You're going to need that. The trestle didn't fail and this was no accident. Morton and I walked to the other side of the trestle. It was blown up. That first explosion we heard was dynamite. We found part of the fuse and paper scraps from the dynamite used. All this"—he waved at the injured people waiting on the bank and smoke rising above them—"was done on purpose. The only access is up that canyon, and Morton found horse tracks going that way."

Matt's expression hardened as a wave of rage filled him. "Gilbert said we weren't too far from town, so help should be here soon. I'm not going home and letting someone get away with this."

"Me neither." William's eyes went to Molly James as she sat on the bank with her son. Molly's long, light brown hair was loose and windblown, her dress was bloodstained and filthy. "It shouldn't take long for someone to see that smoke cloud and come looking."

Matt pointed up the river where the smoke from a double-paddle wheel tugboat came as fast as it could, and four men were standing on the bow. "It looks like help is on the way now."

CHAPTER SIX

OFFICIALLY NAMED THE DALLES CITY, BUT commonly called Dalles City. It was invaluable as the epicenter of central Washington and Oregon's heartland, where most of the wheat and other cash crops were grown and shipped down the Columbia River to Portland. Dalles City was one of the most inland harbors on the West Coast, eighty miles east of Portland, and was located in the beautiful Columbia River Gorge.

Amos Stafford had changed the name of his small company store to what would become known as the most prominent name in Oregon's agriculture market, called simply enough, The Stafford Milling Company. The Stafford Milling Company owned a few extensive milling facilities, including one in Albany, Portland, and The Dalles City, Oregon. Sea-faring ships lined the company's Portland waterfront pier to carry wheat, flour, barley, and other crops across the Pacific and Atlantic Oceans. The foreign trade market was a significant part of the Stafford Company's business, but the Stafford Milling Company was becoming a familiar sight for flour bags, cornmeal, and oats across the United States.

Getting the crops, whether milled or not, to Portland from the lower Willamette Valley in Albany could be done by rail or the Willamette River. Shipping by rail was quicker but more expensive. To cut costs, the Stafford Milling Company used barges pulled by shallow-hulled steam-powered tug boats to pull the barges seventy miles or so up the Willamette River to Oregon City. The product had to be transferred to rail cars to get around the Willamette Falls, and it was cheaper to use the train for the remainder of the journey to the Stafford Milling Company in Portland from there.

Unfortunately, The Dalles City was a different story—a more significant amount of product needed to be shipped at a quicker rate than in Albany. Transferring the product west was a labor force of its own. Barges were used to haul the harvested crops from the Upper Columbia to the outside of Dalles City, where the mighty Columbia River Falls created an obstacle. The cargo was offloaded and put aboard a portage train around the falls and rapids to Dalles City for processing. A barge was used to transport the finished product from Dalles City forty miles down the Middle Columbia River to just above the mighty Cascade Rapids and again offloaded onto a portage train to travel seven miles around the rapids and transferred back onto a barge to be towed sixty miles on the Lower Columbia River to Portland for final shipping.

To see tugboats pulling barges down the Columbia River to Portland and returning with everything from food to farm equipment was a common sight. The Columbia River was Central Washington and Oregon's highway to feeding the world, as most of the wheat from both states was grown in the eastern and central arid country between the Cascade and the Blue Mountains, which were approximately two hundred miles apart.

A tugboat was pulling a barge west when it witnessed a sudden thick and quickly rising black smoke cloud ahead on the riverbank. It was uncommon, and when the sound of an explosion and continuous thunderous banging reached the boat, the captain knew it had to be a train wreck. It was the only reasonable possibility of black smoke at that location. He sped the motor to get around a slight bend, and seeing the seriousness of the tragedy, he decided to return to The Dalles City to bring more men to help any survivors.

News of the train wreck spread quickly. The Dalles City Constable, Perry Whitmore, immediately notified the county sheriff, Cletus James, who was Perry's brother-in-law. Knowing the train wrecked at the Gypsum Creek trestle fifteen miles or so west of town, where it was only accessible by horse, rail, or the river, Perry secured the use of an empty barge and tugboat to take as many men, tools, and medical supplies as possible to the wreck to assist any survivors. However, Perry and Cletus had an urgent and more personal need to get there as fast as possible. Cletus's wife, Molly, and their son, Michael, were coming home on the train today. They got aboard another tugboat that wasn't pulling a barge to hurry to Gypsum Creek.

Cletus James could barely breathe as he stood on the bow of the tugboat as it hurried to the rising smoke of a train wreck. His heart pounded with the horror of the unknown as the bow of the boat cut through the water, not nearly fast enough to get there to satisfy Cletus's anxiety. His beloved wife and oldest son were on the train, and he feared finding them among the casualties. The boat's captain had told him to expect the worst because the trestle had failed and the wreck looked fatal. To Cletus's most unimaginable horror, he had never experienced such an overwhelming sensation of doom that filled him when he got his first look at the flames devouring the pile of wreckage. "Oh no!" he gasped with a frightened quiver in his voice, unable to say another word through his tightening throat.

The trestle that once stood a hundred feet above the mouth of the Gypsum Creek Gorge had fallen, intertwining with the locomotive and the rail cars that crashed into the creek bed—a large pile of twisted steel and wood burned in a raging fire. The roaring flames made it a nightmare to imagine anyone survived. The sight before his eyes shook Cletus to the core. He wasn't a praying man usually, but he prayed his family wasn't somewhere within the flames.

There were about a dozen or more people spread out along the bank of the river, some lying prone, but all appeared to be injured and covered with blood. Strangely, the people who walked on their feet walked like the living dead along the railroad track. As the tugboat slowly approached the riverbank, the captain noticed the caboose underwater and changed course to move around it, increasing Cletus's anxiety all the more as he searched the bank for his family. His heart missed a beat when he spotted his wife and son. Cletus leaped from the bow into the water and ran ashore as quickly as possible. A man begging for help tried to stop him, but Cletus ran up the hill shouting, "Molly! Molly!"

Molly James had been lying prone beside her son, trying to comfort Michael in his anguish of having a broken lower leg. Hearing Cletus's voice, Molly stood and held her arms out, beginning to weep, relieved to see him.

Cletus ran to her and wrapped his arms around her in a tight hug. "I was so scared I lost you!" Molly held onto him tightly and sobbed uncontrollably. "Are you okay?" He broke the embrace to look at her. "Is Michael okay?" He was quickly at Michael's side. "Are you hurt?"

Molly wiped her tears as she explained, "His leg is broken. We must get him to the doctor before anyone else arrives."

Cletus shouted for his deputy to help and they carried Michael down the bank to the tugboat and placed him on the short deck. Michael was screaming in pain.

"Cletus!" Perry Whitmore shouted and waved him over. "This is Matt Bannister, the US marshal from Branson, and his deputies, William Fasana and Morton Sperry. They're telling me the trestle was blown up. They don't think this was an accident."

Cletus shook his head, unconcerned. "We haven't got time for that right now. I have to get my son to the doctor while I can. His leg is broken. Help's coming, but we have all these people to get to town. They all need help." He gazed at the dry blood that covered Matt's face and shirt and the blood that covered both Morton and William's wounds and clothing. "Let's get you three to town, too."

Matt said, "Take the most seriously injured. My son, Gabriel, and Morton, if there is room left. They need to be looked at before I do. William and I will stay here and help where we can."

"Another tug is bringing a barge that will carry everyone. Where is everyone?" Cletus asked, looking around.

"Dead," Matt answered plainly.

"This all that survived?" Cletus asked, dumbfounded.

Molly James walked up the hill and took hold of Cletus's arm. "Matt, I'll make sure you and your men have rooms at our hotel. They saved Michael's life," she explained to Cletus.

Cletus gasped emotionally. "Thank you. Thank you." He shook their hands. "They've loaded a few of the worst injured on the tug. We'll make room for your son and your deputy." He spoke to Morton. "Let's get you looked at."

Matt watched the tugboat leave, knowing Morton would watch over Gabriel until he got to town himself. He took a deep breath and felt the warm tears fill his eyes. He sat on the ground overlooking the blue river. If he was alone, he might have sobbed, but he held it within.

He sniffled as he said, "Jesus, my Lord, I can smell the bodies burning." He sniffled and fought the tears. "Shooting Mrs. Pihl did me in, Lord. It just doesn't seem right to be put in that situation. None of this is right. Help me to remain strong enough to get through this day. Help Gabriel's arm and young Michael's leg heal. Lord, there's so much death today. I don't know how or why we survived and the others didn't, but thank you. I pray you'll be with the families of those who perished and those who went through this with us. Thank you for sparing Gabriel, William, Morton, and the rest of us who did survive. I'm hurting, Jesus. I have never seen so much death before. If the trestle was blown up, I ask you to help me find the people responsible to bring some justice or explanation for all of this."

"Matt," William called as he approached. "The other tug is coming."

Matt lifted his eyes to see a tugboat pushing a barge full of men with pry bars and other tools and supplies coming to help any victims still trapped, but seeing the flames roaring, they all knew it was hopeless. When the men aboard stepped off the barge, Matt directed the men carrying tools to the third-class passenger coach in the water to assist in freeing Lucille Stafford's body. Amos was refusing to let her body go. Amos and Lucille's son-in-law had heard of the wreck and came to check on his beloved in-laws. He slid down into the passenger car with Amos and mourned with him until Amos could find the strength to let his bride of forty-eight years go.

The horror of the wreck and heavy loss of life was too much to bear. Tragedy had struck, and if it had been an accident, it could have been understood. It could be reasoned through and accepted, but this wasn't an accident. There was a person or persons responsible for the deaths, the life-altering injuries and scars left on everyone who survived and the loved ones of those who perished. There was someone to blame, and whoever it was intentionally created a tragedy that was too horrific to understand.

CHAPTER SEVEN

MATT SOAKED IN A HOT BATH, FEELING THE exhaustion and soreness of his body from being tossed around the rail car. The hot water felt good on his sore muscles, bruises, scratches, and cuts. He was beat up and had no desire to get out of the bathtub. The shock of the wreck and all that had happened had not sunk in until now that he had time to relax and think about it. He had seen death in many forms over the years, but he had never been surrounded by tragedy and death like he was today.

He thought of Lucille Stafford, who knew her time was at hand, and the young bride Matt had freed from the splintered board that impaled her leg. But the most haunting thing above and beyond the rest was the woman named Margaret Pihl, who would have been burned alive if he had not shot her. It may have been the right and merciful thing to do, but it weighed heavy on Matt's heart. It didn't feel right. A man should never have to be put into a situation like that.

Matt had carried Margaret Pihl's baby onto the barge

and held it until he arrived in The Dalles City. If there was one thing he could do that might make some sense out of the tragedy, it was to deliver little Jacob Pihl's body to his father in Walla Walla. Matt told the local mortician what the baby's name was and to embalm the child as he would be taking the baby with him when he left town.

William Fasana carried a bottle of whiskey into the hotel's bathhouse. He had bathed and had changed into clothes that the townspeople had donated to the survivors since none of their personal belongings in the baggage car had survived the fire. William pulled a chair beside Matt's bath, sat down, opened the bottle, and took a long drink. He sat silently for a moment and then took another long drink. "I heard they cut a hole in the side to get Mrs. Stafford out. They just cut Joel's arm off to pull him out." He handed the bottle to Matt.

Matt shook his head, refusing a drink.

"I know why they blew up the trestle. The sheriff got word from the railroad that there were two hundred thousand dollars in the safe that belonged to Mr. Stafford. Mr. Stafford's son-in-law says the safe is fireproof, so the sheriff hired men to stand guard until the fire is out. The railroad is sending another train filled with investigators tomorrow to determine what happened. I already told them what happened. All that death for money. I hope you're ready to go hunting, Matt, because I'd sure like to shoot the people responsible like we did ground squirrels back in our youth."

"Did you wire my dad and Maggie to let them know we're all okay?" Matt asked.

William nodded. "I did. I also wired Tom and Elizabeth, as you asked. Truet, too. He'll tell Christine and Audrey. I acquired some horses for you and me tomorrow. I want to find those men, whoever they are. I'll never forget today, not ever. I want the men responsible," William said with watery eyes. He took another drink.

Matt said quietly, "I have a feeling we'll be pretty sore and beat up by morning. We may need a few days before we feel like moving much at all."

"Well, you're no fun," William said without his usual flare. "I'll go oil our weapons. I'll see you in the morning. Matt, you know we were blessed today, don't you? All those prayers Aunt Mary says, Christine and I'm sure Audrey says, I think the Lord heard them. How could he not with all those women babbling on like that? But..." he paused to take a deep breath. "Seriously. We were this close," William said with a shaken voice, barely holding his thumb and index finger apart. "I guess it just makes me want to say I love you. That's all."

"I love you, too, William," Matt said. "Hey," he called, stopping his cousin from leaving. "Think about the lives you saved today, not those we couldn't. What happened today was a tragedy, the worst I've ever seen, but we survived it. Because of you, others did too."

William shook his head sadly. "But that young lady didn't survive. That pretty young bride. It was their honey-moon, Matt. Sometimes, life makes no sense to me. How do you comfort someone when something like that happens? I overheard some man say the wreck was God's will, but I can't believe that."

Matt shook his head slowly. His neck was beginning to stiffen up. "It wasn't God's will. It was the will of whoever put the dynamite on the trestle and blew it up. That is an act of evil, and that comes from man, not God. What happened today was a decision that a person made, and the consequences of it led to the deaths of that young lady and

76

everyone else, even children. Not one child survived. The trestle being blown up had nothing to do with God. Evil comes through the minds and hearts of men and the actions they decide to act upon. This was a man-made tragedy."

"Murder," William corrected. "What they did was murder. Tomorrow, they'll pull all the bodies out they can, and it will become a massacre."

Matt nodded sadly. "William, we'll find the men responsible. Until then, don't drink all of that bottle, or you won't be any good tomorrow at all."

"I'll be fine. I'll see you in the morning."

———

FOUR YOUNG MEN in their late teens and early twenties settled around a freshly made campfire away from Gypsum Creek to avoid the smoke from the fading flames. The sun was low over the western horizon, promising to show a sunset's brilliant orange and yellow glow. The men from town that came on the barges could do little except pull the bodies of Lucille Stafford and Joel Jones from the third-class coach, one from the caboose and another from the river. The fire was too intense to put out, and all they could do was take the injured and dead that were retrievable back to town. There wasn't much threat of a wildfire despite the heat from the flames, and there was little to do until the fire burned itself out.

As evening fell, the men returned home on the last barge, leaving the four young fellows who volunteered to stay the night at the wreckage with the promise to be paid twenty-five dollars each by the Stafford Milling Company. Their job was to ensure no one sifted through the wreckage to find the safe or scrounge for any valuables among the dead, which was most unlikely as the fire would burn all night.

Coal was the most preferred fuel for locomotives around the nation, but coal wasn't found in Oregon, timber was. Timber was Oregon's most plentiful natural resource. The railway from Portland to Walla Walla was mainly an easy grade as it followed the Columbia River through the Columbia Gorge rather than going over the Cascade Mountains, making the journey most practical for a wood-burning locomotive. No one knew right away how many cords of wood fueled the flames, but one thing was for sure: no one would be walking around in the burning coals overnight.

Randy Paulson, Dave Ruddick, and Stan Meldrum rode their horses along the railroad tracks to the edge of the Gypsum Creek to get their first glance at the wreckage now that the flames had burned down and only a few young men sat around a campfire. Randy's eyes scanned the remains for any sign of a safe, and he smiled when he spotted the large square safe lying on its back, covered in burning coals.

They rode down to the river's bank and crossed over the creek and up the other side to where the four young men sat around the campfire talking. One of the young men asked, "Randy, what are you fellas doing out here?"

"We heard about the accident and thought we'd come take a look. What about you all?" Randy questioned. Randy was in his midforties. He was tall, had a muscular build, and had thick black hair that covered his ears. Though his hair was thick with no threat of thinning, Randy could not grow a beard or mustache that grew thick enough to look good, so his square-shaped face remained clean-shaven. It was to his eternal frustration because he was the only one of his siblings who could not grow a beard, but he was the only one who wanted to have one.

The young man grinned. "We're being paid twenty-five dollars each just to stay here. That's more than I made in two weeks. So yeah, I'll do it! It's easy money."

"Do you know if anyone is coming back? Are the sheriff and tugs done for the day?" Randy asked.

The young man answered, "They'll be back tomorrow morning. I heard there are still people in those rail cars and they'll pull the bones out tomorrow. It's a gruesome thought to think about them burning over there."

"So, you boys are doing what? Why are they paying you so much to stay here doing nothing?" Randy questioned.

The young man shrugged. "Maybe it just feels like the right thing for them to do, I don't know. Everything's burned except in that rail car. The owner of the Stafford Milling Company's wife died in that one. They cut a big hole in the side to pull her out, she was pretty fat. Mr. Stafford was an emotional wreck. Some other man died in there, but his arm's still underneath. We were here when they did that. It was pretty gross."

Another young man spoke excitedly. "Matt Bannister was on the train, too! He was covered in blood but survived. We got to see him."

"The marshal, Matt Bannister?" Dave Ruddick questioned. Dave was a thirty-eight-year-old divorced man with a rough disposition. He kept his brown hair cut short and a thick beard that hid most of his face about an inch long, leaving a pair of hardened brown eyes for the world to see. He was average height but stocky and muscular.

"Yes. Matt Bannister. Two of his deputies, too. Everyone was talking about it."

"Huh," Randy acknowledged. "Anything else?"

"Other than the easiest twenty-five dollars we ever made? No."

"How bad was the marshal hurt?" Dave Ruddick asked.

"Which one? Perry Whitmore wasn't hurt at all…"

Dave had no patience for stupidity. He growled, "What do you mean which one? The United States Marshal, Matt Bannister, you idiot!"

"Well, we have Constable Whitmore too," the young man explained to defend himself.

His friend answered, "He was walking, but he was hurt. You don't bleed like that and not be hurt."

"Huh," Randy said, looking around. There was not another light anywhere in the darkness. "So, it's just you four fellas? No one else is coming out here or with you?"

"Not until tomorrow morning."

"But you all don't know what you're protecting?"

The young man shrugged. "The wreck."

"No," Randy corrected. "You're protecting two hundred thousand dollars in that safe over there."

"Whoa! They didn't tell us that!" one of the boys said.

"Yeah, that's what you boys are here to protect. But they didn't tell you that or give you any weapons, so we'll just have to take it."

One of the young men laughed. "I'd like to see that. The fire's still burning."

"Well, that's true," Randy said, adjusting himself in the saddle. "But the safe is in a creek and there's the Columbia River, so we should have plenty of water to cool it down. Unfortunately, we can't have any witnesses. I can't tell you how sorry I am." He pulled his revolver and shot the nearest young man. The other men with Randy pulled their weapons, and within seconds and eight shots later, all four of the young men around the campfire were dead.

———

WITHIN FIFTEEN MINUTES of hearing the shots, Leon Goodrich and Isaac Chandler rode out of the darkness and down the steep incline to the creek with four metal buckets, a shovel, and some gelignite explosive putty for the safe.

"Alright, let's get some water on and around that safe. Get a lasso and pull it out of the coals so we can blast that thing open. The sooner we get it done, the sooner we'll get paid," Stan Meldrum ordered.

Dave Ruddick said, "Stan, you and Randy didn't say anything about the safe being protected by Matt Bannister and his deputies. He'll trail us."

Stan was a supervisor at the Stafford Milling Company and had confidential knowledge about when and how the harvest payroll was coming. "I had no idea about that, but we came too far to turn back now, Dave. We can't do anything stupid, though. So we'll hide the money for now and wait for him to leave town before dividing it. I'm afraid killing those four kids was stupid enough, but we had no choice. In fact, I'm going to put another bullet in their heads to verify that they are dead. You fellas get to work carrying water."

Dave Ruddick said, "If it were just Constable Whitmore and Cletus, I wouldn't be so worried, but Matt Bannister is protecting this shipment, and stealing from him sounds foolish. He'll come looking for us and looking to kill."

Isaac Chandler's hands shook since witnessing the train falling into the gorge and burning. He turned his head, closed his eyes, and even covered his ears, but the screaming penetrated past his large hands no matter how hard he pressed against his ears. He wept, prayed for forgiveness, and even sobbed, but the guilt wouldn't leave him. Being back at night and knowing so many died because of him was a weight that ate at him. "Matt Bannister will kill us all. We drew his blood."

"He's just a man," Randy Paulson snapped. "Isaac, Leon, Dave, start hauling water and let's get this done."

"Boys," Randy said. "Tonight, our lives are changing for the better."

Half an hour later, they had the safe pulled out of the coals and cooled off. Dave held a lantern while Isaac pressed the gelignite onto the lock. Gelignite was a more powerful explosive made with nitroglycerine instead of black powder. It was made into a perfectly stable and safe waterproof putty until ignited. Isaac applied a blasting cap, laid out twenty feet of his homemade fuse, and lit it before he and others ran further away. The gelignite blew with a large boom that blew the door open as they hoped it would.

"Yeah!" Randy yelled, seeing the door fly open. "Isaac, you just redeemed yourself! Wow! You know your dynamite, that's for sure."

The others patted Isaac on the back and praised him for opening the safe. Randy hurried to the safe, reached inside, and pulled out a bundle of mostly burned bills. His excitement faded to a devastated gasp. He tossed it aside and reached in again to pull another burned bundle of bills. "They're all burned. Give me the lantern."

"Let me look," Stan said as he bent into the safe to find that the money had burned in the fire. Not a single bill was salvageable. He threw a handful of burned bills down and cursed loudly before kicking the safe.

Randy was angry. "I thought you said the safe was fireproof!"

"It is!"

"Well, it sure doesn't look like it, Stan!"

Stan cursed. He pointed at Isaac. "This is your fault! If you had just done your job, we'd have the money and all these folks would be alive!"

Isaac held out his hands helplessly. "The squirrel—"

Stan cursed and quickly charged Isaac to tackle him to the ground and start beating him.

Randy stepped between the two men and stopped Stan. He shouted, "Hey! It's bad luck. That's all. Okay. We had a good plan, but it just didn't work out. We still have to cover our tracks and act like nothing is wrong. All our lives are in danger, and more so now because all these folks died for nothing. Not even a single dollar." He bit his bottom lip, overwhelmed by the cost of what they did. "Look, we are all in this together. We all know if one man goes down, we all will follow. We have to stick together, all of us. Like it or not, we have to be like brothers because if we start fighting between us, we'll all go down, and no matter what, we will be hung for this. So, Stan, you may not like Isaac, but he's our friend and you have to get along with him."

Stan shook his head irritably. "All the planning, preparation, and work we did to open this safe is for nothing!" He cursed. "I had plans."

"We all did," Dave Ruddick said, downtrodden. "Let's go home. There's nothing left for us here."

Randy sighed. "No, there's not. Let's go."

CHAPTER EIGHT

MATT BANNISTER WOKE UP LATER THAN USUAL and could barely move from the sore muscles and bruises that ached all over his body from being thrown around the rail car. His back and neck were stiff, limiting his usual limber movement. He bent over to stretch his back and tilted his neck as far as the stiffness allowed. He would've liked to stay in bed and rest his weary body, but he could not. He dressed slowly and went to the room next door to ensure William was awake before going downstairs to eat a warm breakfast. He sat across the table from Morton Sperry. "How is your back?"

Morton was finishing his breakfast. He slept most of the night after the town doctor had given him some morphine to ease the pain. "Sore. I'm no good today, Matt. My body feels like it's been kicked by a horse from head to toe."

Matt felt very much the same way. "Get some rest. William and I will try to track the men responsible for blowing the trestle. I'll be honest, though, I wish I could stay here. My body has never hurt so much."

Morton warned, "You won't be any good out there. You don't know this country, and if you get into trouble, you won't be as quick and limber as you usually are. You and William should take a day to let your bodies heal up a touch. I don't think we will be good for a week or two. Maybe not even that for me. I'm just glad my back didn't break like Mrs. Stafford's."

Matt rubbed his face. He couldn't turn his head entirely in either direction without a sharp pain shooting down his neck. "Maybe you're right. I can't turn my head."

"That wreck was something right out of a nightmare," Morton said reflectively.

William slowly came down the stairs with tightened lips. His back was stiff. "I don't know if I can ride, and no, it wasn't the whiskey I drank." He winced as he slowly sat at the table. "I knew I was going to be sore, but I wasn't expecting to hurt like I am."

"Change of plans, William. I can't twist my neck much at all, and I'm hurting too. I think we'll rest today, and I hope we feel better tomorrow. I'm sure the railroad will send Pinkertons to investigate and find those responsible," Matt said.

"I'm glad to hear that. My back feels like it's been worked over with an iron bar."

"In essence, it was," Morton reasoned.

The Dalles City Constable, Perry Whitmore, entered the hotel dining room with an exasperated expression. "I'm glad to see you all up and around. Marshal Bannister, somebody shot the four boys we left out there and blew up the safe. We have four dead bodies, and not one of them was armed. They were just sitting by their campfire, where we found them. All of them were shot at least twice in the chest and once in the center of the forehead. They were just teenagers for the most part. Someone killed them in cold blood."

Matt said, "Mr. Stafford told me about the safe on the train. How much was in it again?"

"I don't know for sure, but whoever did it got nothing because the money was all burned. It was part of the harvest payments for all the farmers around here. What I do know is the railroad communicated last night that they'd send a crane and men from the railroad this morning. I imagine they are already getting close. We went out there this morning and found the boys. No one imagined they'd be in any danger." He was clearly troubled by the young men's deaths. "They weren't even armed."

Matt rubbed his neck with a grimace. "Whoever blew up the trestle wanted what was in that safe. Was there just money or was there something else like gold? Silver?"

"I don't know. I didn't talk to Larry Harmon, Clete did. Larry's the Stafford's son-in-law who manages the Stafford company here."

"Where is your county sheriff?"

"Clete and I came back on the tug to notify the four young men's families. He's finishing that horrible job, and I was sent here to talk to you. Marshal Bannister, I know you and your two deputies are probably hurting badly today, but the fact is, we could use your help to find these murderers. Those kids meant a lot to us."

Matt frowned, followed by a reluctant sigh. "It looks like I'll be going to the train wreck today after all. I don't know what kind of foot traffic you have out there, but maybe I can find the murderer's trail. The railroad will send their people to investigate the wreckage. Pinkertons will most likely come here to track the killers down. But I can tell you right now that the railroad will care a lot more about the damage done to their trestle and trying not to be sued by the families than about your local boys or the money. Neither were theirs."

William rolled his shoulders uncomfortably. "I don't know if I can ride, Matt. My back and shoulders are messed up. Where is Gabriel?"

"Sleeping. He had a hard night," Matt replied downtrodden. They shared a hotel room, just as Morton and William did.

Perry Whitmore said, "Marshal, if you feel like it, you can ride with Clete and me. We're getting a posse together to try to track them, but with all the rock, it's hard to say which way they went. It appears they stayed either on the tracks or in the creek bed. We know the territory and the people around here, so we hope someone saw something to help us identify the murderers. You're welcome to come with us if you want."

"Do you have any suspects?" Matt asked.

Perry shook his head. "Not at the moment."

Matt grimaced. "I suppose William already reserved horses for us today, so I might as well go and see if I can find a good track and trail."

William offered, "The horse tracks I saw yesterday went toward the creek bed heading up the canyon."

Perry said to Matt, "One tug already took our mortician and group of volunteers out there to collect the bodies and sift for personal belongings to help identify them. He says it will be a two-day job because there are so many dead. There will be a tug waiting for us with a barge in tow because a bunch of men want to help get the wreckage cleaned up. Clete is a little headstrong, but I know I'd like you to lead our posse." He added humbly, "Neither of us have your experience. So, we could use your help."

Matt hesitated. "Perry, you have to understand we are all hurting, so my help might be limited. I'll get a horse and meet you on the dock, but I can't guarantee anything. I'm just not up to my usual self."

William spoke sincerely. "You're in no condition to go looking for a gunfight, Matt. Hell, it hurts to move. You can't even turn your head."

"I don't plan on looking for a gunfight. The sheriff and Perry can gather their posse and team up with the train full of Pinkertons, which I'm sure are coming. I'm only going out to look and see if I can get them started in the right direction." Matt turned his upper body slightly to look at Perry. "You might ask any stores in town if someone has bought any dynamite recently that normally doesn't. That's a good place to start."

———

As the double-paddle wheel tugboat pulled a barge with thirty-some men volunteering to help do what they could with the train wreckage, Matt stood at the edge of the barge holding the reins of a rented horse while watching the railroad track that followed the river and the terrain beyond it.

The Cascade Mountains extended from Canada to California, separating Oregon's lush and fertile Willamette Valley on the west side and the arid high desert of Central Oregon on the east side. The Dalles City was on the eastern edge of the Cascade Range, where rock outcroppings, sagebrush, Ponderosa Pine, and blue spruce trees replaced the lush green Douglas Fir, Oak, and Cedar Trees that carpeted the western half of the state.

The foliage around Gypsum Creek was sporadic bunch

grass, bare ground, and rock with few outcroppings of sagebrush and few bushes along the creek bed that entered a canyon that cut a narrow gash between the basalt cliffs that rose hundreds of feet above them. Matt had been studying the railroad tracks along the cliffs, looking for the most likely escape routes if he were to commit the crime himself. The most reasonable escape along the river would be by boat, but on horseback, the canyon leading deeper into the interior was the most concealed route. He had no idea how far the canyon went or what was between its beginning and end.

Matt's curiosity about the layout of the interior landscape and the community itself was quickly satisfied as there was no shortage of information to be found from the collection of men aboard the barge.

"Gypsum Creek Canyon goes back about five or six miles to Casper Falls. That's where Gypsum Creek and Squib Creek meet and make a nice little waterfall. That's where the canyon starts, I guess. That's on Peter Lang's land. He's a farmer. He's a good man, but he won't let me sluice for gold at the bottom of the falls. You see, Gypsum Creek comes down from the Cascades. There's gold there, you'll understand. Now, Squib Creek comes from the east across the high desert. If there's any gold in that creek, it's a hundred miles that way. Here, there are just a few trout, carp, and catfish that taste like the mud at the bottom. The Emricks built a dam and made themselves a ten-acre lake. I've never been through the canyon, so I have no idea what's between here and the falls, but there is no gold at the mouth of the creek on the Columbia that I found. It's all under the falls, I tell you," an old man named Jock Livingston said. He was an employee of the Stafford Milling Company.

An old timer with a rough exterior and a severe burn scar covering half his face named Clint Rogers spoke, "Jock, there ain't no gold down this far in the creek. I know that. The only gold to be found in Gypsum Creek is west, up higher in the Cascades. Now, Marshal, what he said about Squib Creek is true. It ain't got nothing except mud in the bottom of it. I own about an acre along it."

"Outlaws?" a man questioned when Matt asked about local outlaws. "You got the Darnell family, the Hatch brothers, Roy Clegg and his pals are troublemakers. We got all kinds. But the only person stupid enough to blow up a train to steal the payroll for the local farmers and then burn it is probably Chase Swanson," one man volunteered.

"No, you're wrong," another man interjected. "Chase would blow himself up carrying the dynamite out here. If there was ever a stupid criminal around here, it is him, though."

Another man confidently said, "Marshal, I'll bet my last dollar that the half-breeds did it. You know, the Crowe Brothers. They are the only ones cruel enough to do this and then come back to murder our young'uns overnight. It was those damn half-breeds, I'll bet you."

Matt let the men talk and asked questions occasionally to get a feel for the locals. He took in the names and opinions and what information he could. If there was anything he did find interesting, it was that the Crowe Brothers came to The Dalles City more often than they came to Branson, and their reputation was well known among the locals.

As the tugboat pulled the barge around the bend, they got their first glimpse of the wreckage still smoldering from the day before as a small group of men poured water on the smoldering coals to get closer to the heart of the wreckage.

It was strange for Matt to be back at the train wreck and see the twisted steel rails draped like limp noodles over the locomotive, overturned tender, steel axels, wheels, brake irons, and frames on a heap of smoldering coals, and a few heavy timbers of the trestle that hadn't burned all the way through. In the mix of debris and ashes were many charred, smoldering bodies lying in plain sight.

"Oh, my Lord," one man said, shocked by what he saw. He was the only voice that spoke as a sudden silence crept over the talkative barge. All the men were stunned by what they were witnessing.

"Are those bodies?" a young man asked as the barge slowed to a near drift past a collection of charred skeletal remains that were partly covered by sheets. What little could be seen of the blackened bodies that were lined up where the barge was docking against the shore was enough to upset a man's stomach, but it was the sickening odor that caused one man to rush to the edge of the barge to vomit.

An overwhelming sense of dread filled Matt's chest as he knew that one of the unrecognizable bodies had a bullet hole going through the skull, and he would have to look at each one of the bodies to identify that charred body as a young lady named Margaret Pihl.

"You were in this wreck?" Matt heard a man ask him.

Matt nodded slowly as he watched the volunteers search for more bodies in the steaming wreckage.

"You're a lucky man to come out alive. I've never seen anything like this before."

"None of us have," Jock Livingston commented.

Matt looked at the man for the first time. "I was in that coach in the river. Unfortunately, many people weren't so lucky. If I had been in either of those two"—he pointed to where the steel wheels of what were passenger cars— "I wouldn't have survived. Most of the people in those coaches died."

"Any idea how it happened?" the man asked. "I mean, I heard the trestle was blown, but do you know if that is true? Is it true that Stafford's payroll was stolen?"

Matt shook his head slightly. "I don't know."

"Well, it looks like the cavalry arrived," the Dalles City Constable, Perry Whitmore, commented.

A train from Portland had already arrived with a steam-powered crane mounted to a flat car lined up where the caboose and passenger coach were in the river. The train pulled three empty flat cars, followed by two box cars and two passenger coaches.

Matt stepped off the barge with Perry Whitmore and Cletus James, who walked straight to his deputy, who had remained there to keep some order while he and Perry returned to town to notify the four young men's families. His deputy stood off to the side, watching two men wading in the river, trying to connect steel cables from the crane to the passenger coach.

The deputy approached the three men, shaking his head. "Clete, I'm glad to see you. I guess the Pinkertons and railroad police are taking over. I was told to get out of the way until I could go home. They're not very friendly, and we're not wanted here."

"Really?" Clete asked. "Did you tell them this is our county and you have authority?"

"No, sir."

"Who's in charge?" Matt asked.

The deputy pointed. "Do you see that short man in the black suit directing the photographer what to take pictures of? That's the king dog, and he acts like it, too.

His name's Marty Rook. He works for the railroad. I don't like him."

Matt left Perry and Cletus and walked up the bank onto the tracks, where the trestle was blown, to introduce himself to Mr. Rook. "Hello, I'm the United States Marshal Matt Bannister. I hear you're the man in charge of the investigation?"

The man's eyes scanned Matt with annoyance. "Marshal Bannister. Yes, I am. Marty Rook is my name. I heard you were on this train. I'm glad to see you survived." He shook Matt's hand.

"Thank you. It was a bloody nightmare."

"Yes, I can imagine so," Marty said, gazing back at the debris.

"I heard the safe was opened, but the money was burned. Is that right?" Matt asked.

"With all due respect, Marshal Bannister, that is confidential railroad business and of no concern to you or the county sheriff. I'm the man in charge here. My team will conduct the investigation and the search for the criminals responsible. If you don't mind me saying so, you're free to leave. I have a lot of work to do."

Matt spoke frankly. "Well, with all due respect, I was on this train and helped rescue people from those rail cars before they burned. I think I have the right to know exactly what happened. I'll ask again: did they get any money or not? Because they murdered a lot of people to get it."

"This is railroad business, you have no authority here to—"

"As a federal marshal, I think I have all the right in the world to know why the train I was riding was sabotaged," Matt sneered.

Marty spoke heatedly. "You were a paying passenger, no

different than anyone else. Keep it that way. Unless you saw the vandals, we have nothing more to say."

A tall man wearing a suit and derby hat listening to their conversation interrupted, "Marty, Matt Bannister is a United States Marshal and was on this train. If the robbers knew he was on the passenger list, they could have blown the trestle with the intent to take his life so that he couldn't intervene. You said as much earlier today. I advise you to take full advantage of his skills to help you solve this crime. He can only help us, and that's reason enough to let him assist."

Marty glared at Matt and walked away with a wave of his hand.

"He seems to have an issue with me," Matt said, watching Marty walk away.

The man grinned. "He's more concerned about you taking over and finding the criminals before he does. My name is Corbin Hazelton. I'm a former Pinkerton Detective now working for the railroad. Marty is the man in charge but doesn't have much practical experience with criminals."

"Or lawmen either. I was about to throw him down the hill into the river to cool him off. You're doing the investigation and he'll take the glory, then?" Matt asked, already knowing the type of man Marty was.

Corbin nodded while raising his brow. "Pretty much. I am stuck working with those four men loitering in the shade. They are your basic tough railroad bulls with some gun experience, not always on the side of the law, by the way. Listen, I'm the one leading the hunt for the criminals responsible for this and wanted to say we'd be honored if you and your deputies wanted to join us."

Matt narrowed his eyes questionably. "Is Marty a railroad man just here to save the railroad's reputation, or does he have a real purpose for being here?" Matt asked with an aggravated glance toward Marty.

"His job is to hide what he can and smooth over the public to limit any bad press. That safe was marketed as fireproof, but if the public finds out the payroll for a private citizen kept in our safe was burned, it could be an embarrassment to the company. That's why he didn't answer you. It is a fireproof safe, but I don't think any safe can endure that kind of heat for so long and keep its integrity. The money was burned. Whoever caused this got nothing in return except future death sentences."

Matt asked, "There wasn't anything else in the safe besides Stafford's money?"

Corbin waved toward what was left of the train. "No. What other reason do men need to do heinous crimes like this than for money? Two hundred thousand dollars is a fortune to most people. The question is, who knew about it? *This* payroll transfer was a confidential secret within the Stafford Milling Company, which alone tells me it was an inside job. It was being transferred with complete secrecy, or so they thought. Blowing up the trestle wasn't an accident."

"When do you plan on tracking them?" Matt asked.

"In the morning. We found several horse tracks up the hill, and we know they escaped up the canyon. We followed about a mile up and found some tracks in the sand but no identifiable marks."

Matt nodded with a slight grimace from his stiff neck. "You didn't go any further?"

"No. We might follow their tracks all the way back to town or kingdom come and find nothing except a wasted day. I want the rats to relax and think we couldn't follow them. As I said, I suspect it was an inside job. I figure someone in the Stafford Milling Company will start talking if we give a little leeway before we push it hard enough to make them nervous. I'll look for the nervous rat. If you want to find a rat, you lay out some grain where you know they are and wait, you don't go tearing up the barn looking for them. If you'd like to track them, be my guest, but me? No. I have other plans to catch them. I imagine you folks are staying in town. If you're open to it, you could meet me for dinner this evening."

Matt pointed at the four toughs standing in the shade. "Who are your deputies?"

"They're hardly deputies. They are railroad bulls, regular toughs hired to protect the trains. I handpicked them because they are experienced with military training and weapons. I don't associate with them because they are crude in nature, but they are dependable and tough men. As you probably know, this is a bad bunch we're after, and I don't expect to take them alive."

"That doesn't hurt my feelings any," Matt replied. "Well, I have a body I need to identify before they haul them away."

Corbin wrinkled his nose with distaste. "They all look about the same, and there isn't much left to identify."

Matt took a deep breath and exhaled before speaking softly, "Unfortunately, she'll be easy to identify. I shot her in the head to spare her the torture of burning to death."

"I'm sorry," Corbin said empathetically. "I can see the carnage, but I doubt I could imagine the nightmare you went through."

"I'll have some nightmares about it, I'm sure. It was the worst thing I've ever seen. It's nice to meet you, Corbin."

"My pleasure. By the way, what I said earlier is true. If

the rats saw your name on the passenger list, this might have been done to kill you. That makes it personal, so you're welcome to do whatever you need to do to find these rats. We won't get in your way. All I ask is that you leave the Stafford Milling Company to me and my men so we're not stepping on each other's toes. Rats scurry, and I don't want them fleeing until I have a noose around their necks."

Matt's lips curled up just a bit. "Thank you. I wasn't leaving town until I caught them anyway."

Corbin chuckled. "From what I know about you, I didn't think you would."

CHAPTER NINE

RANDY PAULSON, DAVE RUDDICK, LEON Goodrich, Stan Meldrum, Mark Duffy, and Isaac Chandler sat at a table in the back of Gable's Steel Cable Saloon, having drinks while playing a quiet game of poker among themselves. The saloon was full of customers, and the overbearing conversations were about the train wreck, the murder of the four youths, and the fools who burned the money inside the safe.

A man sitting one table over from them said to his friend, "Hey Jack, let's blow up the train trestle, cremate everyone inside, and hope the money doesn't burn. What a bunch of fools," he scoffed with disgust. "Fifty-nine human beings burned to a crisp for nothing."

Rumors flew faster than a hummingbird's wings, with speculation from the payroll being burned in the fire to gold bars that were taken. If there was anything that most people agreed on, it was the criminals deserved to be hung on the spot wherever they were caught.

"You know it had to be the Crowe Brothers, right?"

Randy Paulson thundered. He was leaning back in his chair, holding his drink. "Who else could be so cold-blooded and heartless enough to blow up a trestle with a train full of women and children crossing it? The Crowe Brothers, those soulless savages, are pure evil," he spat out.

Randy expected Pinkertons and investigators by the dozens, even if all had gone according to plan and no one got hurt. Unfortunately, their simple plan turned into a massacre of fifty-nine innocent lives of men, women, and children, along with the murder of four local young men. Every element of law enforcement was investigating their act of savagery and would be milling around town asking questions. Randy knew his best defense was to go on the offensive and accuse someone else of their crimes. The most believable villains to accuse were the Crowe Brothers. As long as he did his part to get the public to blame them, Randy and his pals were free of suspicion. Not that Randy and his pals were outlaws. They had regular jobs and were known as decent men. The truth is, they saw an opportunity and took it.

Randy's eyes lifted when he noticed a group of men walk in through the bat doors of the saloon. One of the men stepped over to the piano player and interrupted the music.

"Excuse me!" he shouted over the conversations that filled the saloon. "My name is Corbin Hazelton. I'm a former Pinkerton Detective investigating the train disaster. These are my deputies, and we're being joined by US Marshal Matt Bannister and his deputies. If you have any information about the wreck, please talk to us. We know it wasn't an accident. Matt, do you have anything to say?"

Matt Bannister stepped in front of the others and slowly scanned the many faces in the saloon. He spoke loud and sharply. "This is a small county despite its size, and most everyone knows everyone else. Am I right? Someone in this town, maybe in here, knows something, or they will learn something over the next few days about who committed these crimes. We will find the people responsible. I kid you not. If any of you were involved and want to take your chances with a gun, I'm all for it. But I guarantee you those men involved will be left standing upright in a pine box for the whole town to see before I leave here. I will have no mercy on those responsible at all! You have my word on that. Turn yourselves in, and it will go a lot easier for you. I'm staying at the Amber Light Hotel and will stay here until the men responsible are caught, dead or alive is up to them. I'll be there in about an hour if you have anything to tell me. Make it easy on yourselves." He nodded once and walked out the door with the others to go to the next saloon.

"I'll be right behind you," William Fasana told the departing group.

"I know him," Mark Duffy said. Mark was a tall and thin man, forty years old. He had wavy brown hair that fell just below his ears and a long and narrow face with a bushy six-inch long beard that was turning slightly gray.

"Who? Matt Bannister?" Leon questioned.

Mark shook his head slightly. "Him." He nodded toward William Fasana, who approached their table. Mark stood with a grin. "William, what the heck are you doing with a badge?" He laughed.

"Well, someone has to watch Matt's back for him. It might as well be me. I'm his cousin, after all. So, you're still here, huh? I thought you'd move further along the gambling trail. San Francisco or somewhere more prosperous than here by now."

Mark shook his head, happy to see William. "No. I found out the hard way that I'm not a good enough gambler to afford to leave here. So, here I am. How are you, my old friend?"

"Stiff as a stick. I was on that train, and I'm feeling a bit beat up. I would accuse you of doing it, Mark, but I know you're not smart enough to pull that off." He paused and lowered his brow with a questionable gaze. "Wait...the dumbasses *did* burn their money. Were you involved in that, Mark?" he teased.

Mark's smile faded as he said, "No! I don't think I'd have the guts to anyway."

"That's true," William said. "Seriously, what are you still doing around here, Mark? The last I heard, you were planning to go south."

"Do you remember that woman called Peaches?"

"The whore that handed out peaches with two dollars etched into the skin?" William questioned. "Yeah, I remember her. Why? Is she hocking herself with rotten apples for two bits now? She wasn't much of a looker back then."

Randy and the others at the table laughed. Mark spoke slowly. "No. Her name is Clair. I married her."

William's deep voice rose to a higher pitch as he laughed loudly and slapped a hand on Mark's shoulder. "Well, curse me red. I guess I spoke a bit too much, huh? Well, good for you. I'm sure she's prettier in a housedress."

Mark nodded uncomfortably. "Yeah. Anyway, we're doing good. She's a good wife."

William bit his bottom lip and shook his head with a slight grin. "I bet so. I bet you still call her a pretty peach when you're drunk, am I right? I see you're having a few stiff drinks before going home, huh? She's always been a looker...after enough liquor," he said with his brow raising.

Mark frowned. "Come on, she's my wife."

"That explains why you're out here gambling instead of at home with her. She always got on my nerves, too. But, good for you, Mark. A man should settle down and plant his roots." He grimaced as he said, "I just didn't expect you to do it here with her."

Mark answered defensively, "Well, she won my heart. I have good friends, a good home, and a job, so I have all I need. I left all that wildness of youth behind me, and I'm happy with it."

"Then it sounds like you're happy enough. You can't ask for more than that, and you shouldn't. Good to see you, Mark, but I need to catch up with my cousin before he causes too much trouble."

"What is your name?" Randy Paulson questioned. He stood from the table to introduce himself to William since Mark wasn't doing so.

"William Fasana. I know Mark from his wandering gambling days before he settled down and became happy."

"I'm Randy Paulson. Mark is a good friend of mine. We all work together, so we're out having a drink." Randy introduced the rest of the table to William. "So you were in that wreck, huh? I heard it was a bad one."

"It was bad enough to kill fifty-nine people and injure plenty more. It wasn't good odds for survival. Luckily, our passenger coach rolled into the river instead of the fire. It was an easier grade down into the river. We survived, but I can't say we're not hurting."

"I'm glad you folks survived. And good luck finding those responsible. I hear it was the Crowe Brothers."

William shook his head. "No, it wasn't. Morton is their

cousin, and he spoke to one of the Crowe relatives today, who said the boys were nowhere near here. We can trash that idea right now. The men we're looking for are still out there, and like Matt said, we'll find them."

"Morton, who?"

"Morton Sperry. He's one of our deputies."

"Morton Sperry of the Sperry-Helms Gang?" Randy asked skeptically.

"Yeah. Do you know him?"

Randy shook his head. "No. I've never met the man, but I know his name and reputation. He's a lawman now?"

William answered, "Yeah, Matt has a unique effect on outlaws. Join him or be killed by him. Nice to meet you all. Mark, we'll meet again before I leave town. Tell Peaches hello, for me. Oh! Tell her I'll finally pay that two dollars she put on credit for me." He laughed as he walked away.

Mark spoke quietly as he watched William walking away. "He hasn't changed a bit. I'm surprised he hasn't been shot yet."

CHAPTER TEN

CLIFF EMRICK WAS BORN AND RAISED ON THE Emrick family plantation, deep in the heart of Louisiana. It was one of the largest plantations in Louisiana at the time and grew two crops: tobacco and cotton. Cliff's father, Basil Emrick, was a proud Southerner and owned a large number of slaves who worked the fields and harvested the crops.

As Cliff grew older, he married his sweetheart, Marie, the daughter of a neighboring plantation owner. Cliff and Marie's future looked bright, but changing times were coming in the late 1850s. Cliff's father, Basil, warned of unsettling times that he could see coming in the near future. The talk of politics and a growing division between the southern and northern states were like two tides that would clash, and the threat was frightening for those caught in the middle. Fearing the rumors and growing support for the southern states to secede from the Union would undoubtedly lead to a war that would be futile in Basil's view. The South's present wealth and way of life were destined to be destroyed.

Basil was a former Union officer, a graduate of West Point, and he knew if the South seceded from the Union, it would bring a war that would devastate families and kill thousands upon thousands of men from both sides. It would invariably enforce a draft and eventually destroy the southern economy and quite possibly the very lives of his grown and teenage children.

Basil could see the writing on the wall of what was ahead and made the difficult decision to sell the Emrick Plantation while the times were still reasonably good and take his sons and daughters to the far west where a war between the states would not touch them. He had read about the potential for growing wheat on the Columbia Plateau and the potential for shipping it overseas on the Columbia River. Basil had read about the local Indians along the Columbia River being moved to reservations, and an idea formed in his mind. He took his wealth and used his children's names to buy parcels of adjoining land on the Columbia Plateau, a wheat-growing paradise, and founded the Livengood Plantation.

Oregon forbade slavery, but it did not prohibit hiring Indians to work the land for a wage. Basil Emrick approached the state government for permission to create an alternative to a government-run reservation called the Livengood Plantation. Basil built a small village with cabins and furnishings and approached the reservation to recruit farm laborers, promising the Livengood Plantation wasn't just a name, it was a better way of life. It was a place where Indians could leave the reservation and come live in an Indian community, work, and earn the money to enjoy a better life. Over the next twenty-three years, the plantation grew and prospered. The Emrick Plantation became the largest wheat grower in Oregon if not the West.

Basil Emrick rebuilt the Emrick mansion from the original plans and enjoyed a long life in the kingdom he had created before passing away one year before. Now, the plantation belonged to Basil's oldest son, Cliff Emrick.

The Livengood Plantation was a few miles outside of The Dalles City. Wheat was their primary crop. Winter and spring wheat kept the farm busy year-round. The plantation consisted of the Emrick mansion, a large colonial home with a wide porch with four tall columns facing west to watch the sunset over the golden wheat fields along the rolling hills as far as the eye could see.

A large carriage house was the only building near the mansion, where their buggy and private coach were stored. The Emrick's cook and his family and the gardener's family lived upstairs in the carriage house in private residences. They were responsible for tending to the family's collection of horses, milking the cows daily for fresh milk, tending to the henhouse, and performing other daily chores.

Out of sight of the big house, a mile away was the bunkhouse and cookhouse where the plantation field manager, Randy Paulson, and his field supervisors lived. Further away was what was known as the Livengood Village, a cluster of thirty-six small homes, a general store, and several large barns where the animals and field equipment were all kept. Among the large barns and sheds were tall grain silos.

The Indian men and teenage boys worked in the fields while the women cooked their meals and cared for their children, but also grew a community garden to help feed themselves. It was a community of laborers that never needed to go to town as the Livengood Village's general store supplied everything needed at elevated prices.

Unlike his father, who would spend his days carrying a

bullwhip into the fields, rant and rave, and intimidate or punish the workers, ensuring his manager and supervisors ran the plantation like the one back in Louisiana, Cliff preferred to stay clean and work from his office in the mansion. Cliff disagreed with the brutal tactics that his father believed in and fired his father's heartless farm manager, Stan Meldrum, and Stan's top foreman, Leon Goodrich, the day after Basil died.

Cliff hired Randy Paulson to manage the farm under the condition that he treated the laborers and their families fairly and ran the farm with upright integrity. Cliff had more important things to work on in his office, such as the payroll and other financial matters that kept the farm prosperous. He ordered what to plant and where depending upon the market and demand. Cliff and his wife, Marie's twenty-seven-year-old son, Rickson, oversaw the daily work details to ensure Randy and his field bosses were doing their due diligence.

Cliff and Marie sat on the front porch enjoying the morning sunshine while drinking coffee and reading the morning's paper about the train wreck. He looked at the picture of the burning train cars piled up under where the trestle once stood in disbelief. It sickened Cliff's stomach to learn the trestle was intentionally destroyed. Still, the story only got worse when he read about the four local youths being murdered and the Stafford payroll being burned. Having read a little further, he read the list of known survivors. No name was more surprising than his employees Gilbert and Ona Redbird and their daughter Alice. Cliff turned the paper around to show the picture to his wife.

"Marie, did you know about this train wreck? It's horrible."

Marie Emrick nodded. "Yes. I heard about it last night at my meeting. The whole town is talking about it. I thought you already knew."

"No. Did you know the Redbirds were on that train? They survived, thank the Lord, but they were on it."

"I don't know who you're talking about. Do they work for us?" Marie asked with an uncaring shrug.

"Yes. Gilbert is one of our top hands. I'm glad he's okay, but it doesn't say if he's hurt. I think I'll go by the bunkhouse and grab Randy to check on them."

———

"MR. EMRICK?" Gilbert questioned with concern when he opened the door to see Cliff standing there with Randy. Cliff seldom came to a man's house in the Livengood Village. "Did I do something wrong?"

Ona stood behind Gilbert, holding young Alice close at her side. Their other two children were outside playing near Squib Creek. "Mr. Emrick, Sir," Ona greeted him meekly.

Cliff smiled to ease their discomfort. "Gilbert and Ona, may I come inside and sit for a bit? Randy can stand by the door if that's alright with you?"

"Of course. This is your house," Gilbert said, waving toward an empty small room with unfinished wood flooring. A plain table with five chairs beckoned them. Blankets on the floor revealed where the children slept.

Cliff's brow narrowed as he looked at their living conditions. "I wasn't aware that your home was so empty. We need to get you some furniture."

"That would be nice. Thank you, Sir."

"Please, let's have a seat." Cliff sat at the table on a

wobbly chair. "And new chairs, too. I want to take care of my employees, but this won't do. This is *your* home, Gilbert, not mine. You pay your rent and it is where you live. And I'll respect it as *your* home."

"Thank you, sir," Gilbert said warily. "Did I do something wrong, sir?" He cast a nervous glance at Randy, who stood just inside the door like a stone pillar with his hands clasped in front of him.

Cliff lowered his brow and shook his head slightly. "No. I read in today's paper that you two and little Alice were in that train that wrecked. I just wanted to come by and see how you three were doing and ask if you needed any medical care. Because if you do, let me know."

"No. We were lucky. Cuts and bruises only. I'll be at work tomorrow," Gilbert said.

Cliff held up a palm to stop Gilbert from talking. "You must be very sore, Gilbert. I want you to take tomorrow off and relax. So, tell me, what happened? Did you see anyone who might've caused it?"

"No. There were a lot of loud booms, and then we were thrown out of our seats as the train rolled down into the river," Gilbert said. "How we came out with just bruises and small cuts, I'll never know. Others died. Even in our rail car, people died."

Ona volunteered, "We were fortunate. God was watching out for us. Gilbert burned his arm badly helping others."

"You did? Let me see." Cliff watched as Gilbert rolled up a loose sleeve to expose a wrapped-up wound. Ona untied a soft fabric to reveal a large blister across Gilbert's forearm covered in a homemade salve. "Ouch," Cliff said with a grimace. "You got that from helping others?"

Ona spoke, "He helped others get out of burning railcars."

"White folks?" Randy Paulson asked from the door.

Gilbert nodded. "Yes." His eyes revealed he was not fond of Randy.

Cliff watched Gilbert respectfully. "You're a hero then. But you didn't see anything that could help the law try to find the men that caused the wreck?"

Gilbert shook his head with a sorrowful expression. "There was nothing to see. Everything went crazy, and we were in the river. There was only screaming, fire, and terror to see."

Cliff nodded understandably. "Well, I admire your heroics." He clicked his tongue. "Gilbert, I know how hard you work, and I want you and Ona to be happy here. So, I will get you folks some furniture to sit on after working all day. I'll have the fellas get you new chairs and mattresses for the boys, too. Do you and Ona need a new bed?"

Gilbert shook his head slightly.

Ona spoke softly. "We don't have a bed."

Cliff groaned unhappily. "Then let's get you one. Everyone deserves a bed. Let me ask, do you two like living here?"

Gilbert nodded. "Very much. We like living here."

Cliff motioned to Randy. "Are the fellas treating you and the other folks okay?"

"Yes," Gilbert answered, afraid to answer any differently.

"Good. If not, you let me know. We like having your family here. But like I said, I will work on improving your living conditions. Gilbert and Ona, you both came here years ago and have never complained about a single thing. Not even about my father when he was alive. I know he wasn't nice to any of you. He wasn't nice to me most of the time, either. It's my farm now, and things are changing for the better for all of you. We have the school now so that young lady can come home," he said with a smile while motioning to Alice. "And, in the spring, we'll build a nice church building where we can all worship together. We'll hire a real reverend, too. You can hold me to that promise. You're a hero for helping those folks, Gilbert. Take tomorrow off and relax. You deserve it."

"Sir," Gilbert said carefully, "I must work or lose money."

Cliff offered an appreciative smile. "You'll be paid for tomorrow. We'll call it hero's pay. Take tomorrow off and the next day if you need to." He stood from the table and waved a hand around the house as he spoke to Randy frankly. "Take a look around, Randy. This is *not* up to the standards that the Livengood Plantation set when you were hired as the manager. The village is your responsibility, and *this* is squaller! Get these folks some beds and new chairs. I can *not* believe they don't have a single mattress or a davenport for the family to sit on! Who else does not?"

Randy's face reddened. "I don't know."

Cliff sighed irritably. "You have a budget for this stuff. Where does it go if you're not purchasing what's needed here?"

Randy stumbled for words. "Stan was the manager..."

"I fired him a year ago! What about this year's budget?" Cliff questioned Randy severely.

"It went to firewood for heat and cookstoves. Restocking the store and so on," Randy stated with a shrug of his shoulders.

"Get these people taken care of, Randy. And anyone else who needs something. These folks work hard for a living and should at least have a bed to sleep on! If I find out you're using the money for something else, you'll be demoted or fired, Randy. I'm dropping you off at the bunkhouse and I want you to get to work getting these folks some furniture. Now let's go."

Once they climbed into the buggy to leave the village, Randy said, "I'll replace the Redbird's furniture and get them new beds right away, Mr. Emrick."

Cliff shook his head with frustration. "Good. I'm not asking for the best quality, just a bed. I don't understand where you spend the money allotted to the village. Every month, the budget is spent, but the Redbirds have nothing! So where does it go?"

"Like I said, wood for the cookstoves, and the store uses most of it," he said, knowing it was a lie.

"The store earns money, not loses it. If I find out you've been pocketing it or gambling with my money, you won't have a job. I am disappointed. It is called the Livengood Plantation. My father may have intended it to deceive the Indians into a form of slavery or as close to it as he could. But I don't believe that way. I want to enrich their lives! They've had enough taken from them. The least we could do is give them a way to live well and have nice homes. They make us wealthy, and they deserve a lot more than what I just saw. If I can't trust you to do your job fairly, I'll find someone I can trust."

"You can trust me, sir. You have my word on it."

"Can I?" Cliff asked sharply. "I want you to prove that to me within the month. You're Rickson's friend, Randy, not mine. I owe you nothing except your wages, but if you fail to earn them, then someone else will. Your job is to manage the village and the labor force. My job is to worry about the plantation. I should never have to go into the village or worry that they are not being taken care of, ever! Do you understand me?"

"Yes, sir."

"Good. Enjoy your day off, but tomorrow, you better be working on getting them some furniture."

RANDY STEPPED into his bunkhouse room and peeked out the window to watch Cliff Emrick drive his buggy toward home. He cursed Cliff's name heatedly once he was out of sight.

"What's wrong with you?" his roommate Dave Ruddick questioned. Dave was hungover and lying on a plush davenport with a wet rag on his forehead.

"Cliff is questioning where the village money went. He's upset that the Redbirds are sleeping on the floor."

Dave grinned despite his headache. "I guess we shouldn't have had a bonfire that night, huh?" Two months before, on a hot Saturday night, Randy and his pals invited some women back to the Livengood Village for a party. They started a bonfire in the center of the village, but alcohol and a mean streak led the men to burst into some of the houses and carry out mattresses and other furniture to burn.

"Yeah," Randy agreed. "At least the Redbirds didn't tell him where their beds and davenport went."

"If they ever do, you can tell Cliff that Rickson was there, and it was his idea. Blame him," Dave said.

"If the train had gone right and we had the money, I would tell Cliff he could go to hell." Randy was good friends with Stan Meldrum and Leon Goodrich and missed them being at the plantation. They all liked Basil Emrick far more than they liked Cliff. "I wish Basil was still alive. That old man would have been partying with us that night."

"Yeah," Dave agreed. "But times change. Hey, I was thinking, Mark's friend William said they knew it wasn't the Crowe Brothers, so that means Matt Bannister isn't going anywhere soon if he was speaking true. We need to make sure no one gets weak knees or gets drunk and spouts off. The marshal seemed quite serious last night."

Randy sat down in a wooden chair and looked at his friend. "Isaac is the one that caused this mess and ruined our chance of getting out of here now that Cliff is the boss. I should have put a bullet in Isaac's head and buried him in one of the fields somewhere for fertilizer. If anyone is going to talk, it's him."

"He can't disappear too soon or it might look suspicious."

"Oh, heck, Isaac is a good man. I'm not going to do anything to him. It could have happened to any of us." Randy sighed with discouragement. "We'll be fine if we keep our mouths shut and do our jobs like nothing happened. But I'd like to get Cliff off my back. He gave me one month to prove I can take care of these savages and give them a comfortable home or I'll lose my job. He humiliated me in front of the Redbirds. I don't take kindly to that. How about we pay them a visit and ask what color of davenport they want? Cliff's babying them now that he thinks Gilbert is a hero, so maybe I should, too."

Dave sat upright slowly and placed his bare feet on the floor. "Give me ten minutes, and I'll ride with you."

———

RANDY STEPPED off his horse and tied the reins to a hitching rail near the Redbirds' home. He did not bother to knock but burst into the house uninvited. He stood just inside the door with a harsh scowl.

Startled, Gilbert sat at the dining table with wide eyes, staring at the two men. "Hello," he said, not knowing why they were there. Growing more uneasy and frightened, he began to breathe harder.

Randy stepped closer to the dining table with a menacing scowl on his lips. "I'm telling both of you only once that if you say a word to anyone about Cliff Emrick berating me before leaving here, I'll hang you up in the barn and whip you both until you can't work for a week. Am I understood?"

Gilbert nodded. "Yes, sir."

Ona swallowed nervously. "We wouldn't tell anyone."

"As Cliff promised, I'll replace your beds and furniture, but what happens in the village or out in the fields stays quiet. If anyone ever says a word to Cliff or his daughter now that she's teaching at the school that puts me or one of my friends in a bad light, there will be hell to pay! Am I understood?"

"Yes, sir."

"Let me see that blister on your arm." He turned to Dave. "Ona and Gilbert were on the train the other day. Gilbert burned himself trying to help people get out of the fire. White people, at that. He's quite a hero to Mr. Emrick."

"Really?" Dave questioned. "Did you see anything? Like, who did it?"

"No," Gilbert said as he rolled up his sleeve to show his wrapped-up forearm. "Ona, would you unwrap this?" he asked his wife.

Ona unpinned the cloth and unwrapped his arm, exposing a six-inch long blister about three inches wide on the inside of his forearm.

Randy gently grabbed his wrist to look at the burn. "That's a heck of a blister. You know the best thing you can do is pop it. Dave, do you have your knife?"

"Yeah." He reached into his pocket and pulled out a small knife. He unfolded the blade and handed it to Randy.

Ona shook her head. "No! That is not a good idea. I have medicine on it."

"Your witchcraft crap? Herbs and such?" Randy questioned.

"Medicine."

Randy felt Gilbert gradually pulling his arm back. Randy jerked Gilbert's arm forward, and instead of carefully puncturing the blister at the base to drain it, he sliced it open across the top carelessly with one swift swing of the knife, releasing the fluid inside.

Gilbert shouted and pulled his arm out of Randy's grip reactively. The water and blood flowed. He glared at Randy angrily but kept his mouth shut.

Randy folded the knife and spoke pointedly. "Now, you have no excuse not to work tomorrow. You had better tell Mr. Emrick you took the day off if he asks, but you had better be at work. Remember, Mr. Emrick's the owner, but I'm the boss. You folks deal with me and my friends, not him. If I'm fired, my friends will make you suffer for it. You know the rule: what happens in the village or fields stays here. Right?"

Gilbert held the cloth to his bleeding burn that was cut too deep and seethed, "Yes, sir."

"Ona?" Randy questioned.

"Of course, sir."

CHAPTER ELEVEN

THE FOLLOWING DAY, MATT ATE BREAKFAST WITH Morton and learned that William had left the hotel a few hours earlier to play poker at the only saloon open twenty-four hours a day. Matt walked several blocks to the Witching House Saloon to find William sitting at a poker table with a drink first thing in the morning. William offered a guilty smile when he noticed Matt. "Sorry, boss, but I couldn't sleep and felt my hands burning with luck."

"You must be feeling better, William," Matt said. "That's good because we have a busy day ahead of us. Morton is joining us today, so wind this game up."

The day before had been a waste of a day as the county sheriff, Cletus James, invited Matt and his deputies to ride up Gypsum Creek Canyon to track the men responsible for the train disaster. Matt had spent the day riding through a long and narrow canyon that ended thirteen miles out of town, having learned little to nothing. They could track the horse's faint tracks covered by burlap to the busiest road south of town, where the burlap was removed, but their tracks entering the road were swept clean, not giving them a single good track to study. The busyness of the road and two days' worth of heavy wagon and horse traffic coming and going covered any trace on the hardened ground with a light layer of shifting dust in the breeze. William and Morton had stayed in the hotel and rested. William had fallen asleep early and woke up much earlier than usual.

William's deep voice spoke loudly. "I should let you know that these gents let me enter their game, but I probably should have stayed in bed listening to Morton snore. Hot hands don't always mean luck, come to find out. I think it might've been the blankets and a bit of delirium. They're beating me so bad, Matt, that it's making my back ache again. I don't know if I can ride with you today."

"Good. An aching back and will keep you alert," Matt replied. He had a pretty good idea that William was letting the men win. "I'll meet you at the livery stable. We're going to talk to the Redbirds today. So hurry up."

"Well, fellas, one more hand before I go."

MATT PULLED the reins of his rented horse to a stop in front of a headgate that stretched across the driveway. It read:

THE LIVENGOOD PLANTATION. FOUNDED 1861.

Matt looked around, and all there was to see was the golden color of harvested wheat fields, as far as the eye could see, on gently rolling hills in every direction. They rode forward for half a mile and then turned toward a large white colonial home with four tall columns on the oversized front porch. There was a wide veranda on the second story with the exact dimensions of the lower porch under the high roof and multiple large windows on the front.

Matt had never been to the southern states where slavery and plantations were, but the large home in front of him, with its smooth circler driveway, manicured green grass, and well-trimmed thick hedges around the porch, was about as close to a southern plantation as he'd ever be. It was a beautiful home set in a lovely oasis of green with decorative bushes and a few fruit trees to give some shade.

As they approached the large home, an old Black man with gray hair attending to the few weeds under the hedge noticed them and went inside the house. Matt and the others dismounted their horses and tied the reins to a wrought iron hitching post as the front door opened. A man in his late twenties stepped out onto the porch. He had a twisted smile as he approached William with an extended hand.

"I can only assume you're the marshal, Matt Bannister? I heard you were in town. I'm Rickson Emrick. Welcome to the Livengood Plantation," he said as he shook William's hand. "It's an honor to have you here at our home." Rickson was handsome with a clean-shaven face and dark blue eyes. His light-brown hair was short on the sides and longer on top, combed straight back and held in place by a dab or two of pomade. He was a well-dressed man wearing black suit pants with white pinstripes and a white shirt that wasn't buttoned fully, exposing a small patch of sparse chest hair.

William's brow lifted as he licked his lips with a

growing grin. He put his left-hand fingers on his chin and spoke in a feminine, high-pitched voice to impersonate a female,."Thank you, Mr. Emrick, you're quite handsome and have a very strong grip. Wowzie! You can call me Matthew anytime." He fluttered his eyebrows with a seductive smile while his blue eyes floated up and down Rickson's body seductively. "Mmm!" he grunted with a slight jerk of his body.

Rickson's welcoming smile faded as his mouth dropped open, and his brow deepened while he stepped back from William. His upper lip lifted into a slight snarl of disgust. Simultaneously, he wiped the palm of his right hand against his pants. His words failed him as he tried to comprehend that the deadly lawman that so many feared was a homosexual.

Not wasting a moment, William rolled his head dramatically toward the large white carriage house. "Do you want to show me the hay loft, handsome? We could…talk." He finished with a wink.

"Hell no! I'm not going anywhere with you!" Rickson snapped angrily. "Get the hell off my property! Go!" he shouted with a pointed finger up the driveway.

"William, knock it off," Matt said with a slight chuckle. He reached out to shake Rickson's hand. "I'm Matt. Forgive my cousin. He's just fooling around."

William said in his usual deep voice, "I'm William Fasana. Nice to meet you."

Rickson's expression grew more hostile instead of relief. "Were you making fun of me?" he asked William, shaking Matt's hand reactively.

William chuckled uneasily. "Not intentionally, anyway. Was it a good imitation of your pals or something?"

"What?" Rickson stammered, more offended. "Do I

come across as a homosexual to you?" He took a step forward with inflamed eyes burning into William. "Do you want me to punch you in the face?"

"No, not really," William answered. "If you want to know the truth, I was poking fun at my cousin because you thought I was him." William smiled. "Bad joke, I take it?"

Matt spoke to ease the tension. "Rickson, never mind William. It was a bad joke directed at me, not you. I apologize for any offense. I suppose you're wondering why we're here, right?" He wanted Rickson's attention on him and not glaring at William.

Rickson glared at William for a moment longer before moving over to Matt. "So, you're Matt?"

"I am."

Rickson gazed at the man dressed more like one of his Indian laborers than a United States Marshal. Matt and his deputies were wearing clothes that were given to them by the town's citizens. He wore dark pants with a stained green button-up shirt that was partly unbuttoned with the sleeves rolled up while holding a brown Stetson in his left hand. Rickson narrowed his eyes as he took notice of Matt's long dark hair held in a ponytail, full-faced beard, brown eyes, and tanned skin that gave him a bronzed color. "Have you got Indian blood in you?"

"I do. You?" Matt asked, taken off guard by the question.

"No! I'm perfectly white. So, you're Matt Bannister? The marshal who killed all those people?"

Matt nodded with a slight chuckle. "Just as much as you're perfectly white, I'm me, yes."

"Are you a homosexual?"

"No. I'm married." He lifted his ring finger to show his new silver wedding ring.

"Then what's so funny? Why was he making fun of me?" Rickson questioned with an irritated wave at William.

"William, will you apologize to him?" Matt asked, not masking his frustration.

"I'm sorry. I just thought it would be funny. It had nothing to do with you, I swear. I was trying to embarrass him." He pointed at Matt. "My sincere apologies."

Rickson nodded, satisfied with the apology. He looked at Matt. "So, how can I help you?" The friendliness they were met with was gone.

Matt's brow lifted upward slightly. "Correct me if I'm wrong, but by how you came out here and greeted us before William pulled his stupid stunt, it seemed you might have been expecting me?"

"We heard you were in town and investigating the train wreck. A couple of our employees were on board. We figured someone might come here to question them. I saw his badge." He cast a cold glance at William.

William took a deeply offended dramatic breath and gave a light scoff. He spoke with the feminine voice. "It's a broach, sweetheart."

Rickson jabbed a finger in William's direction. "Don't ever call me that again! You're already on my bad side, you son of a—"

"William!" Matt shouted angrily, cutting Rickson off. "That's enough! I mean it." He looked at Rickson. "I'm sorry. Yes. I would like to know if the Redbirds saw anyone or anything that will help identify the men that blew the trestle."

"Sure." Rickson grimaced slightly as he put his attention back on Matt. "I wasn't aware that Indians could be federal marshals."

Matt's brow lowered. "I'm lucky enough to be three-quarters perfectly white," he said with a touch of sarcasm. "Can you point me in the Redbirds' direction and maybe we can talk afterward?"

"Sure. Follow that road for about a mile and a half and you'll come to the Livengood Village. The Redbirds live in house number nine. You'll find them. If you want to return when you're done, my parents should be available."

William reached his hand out to shake. "Listen, I apologize. I had a few drinks this morning and was just having fun. I don't want to leave here on bad terms. But you ought to know before we become best friends that I'm what they call a bleached Indian."

"A what?" Rickson questioned. He refused to shake William's hand.

"Well, my mama married an Indian, but she didn't know that. You see, she was blind in one eye and color blind in the other. So when I popped out, she decided to bleach me white to make sure I was perfectly white. Some people care about that, you know."

Rickson had no response. "You'll find the Redbirds that way."

Morton Sperry climbed into his saddle and laughed lightly. "William, you're nuts."

Matt looked at William as they rode away from the house. "Why in the world would you do that? You obviously aggravated him."

"Because he thought I was you." William laughed to himself. "I wish you weren't with us, Matt. Can you imagine what he'd tell everyone in town if I had all day pretending to be you like that?"

Matt chuckled lightly. "William, I'd be so tempted to shoot you. On a serious note, no more whiskey in the mornings, okay? It brings out a bit of, well, a side of you we don't need when we're trying to be serious."

———————

ONA REDBIRD'S lower back and right hip were inflamed and hurt worse today than the days since the train accident. Grunting, she stood from an unstable dining chair and hobbled slowly to the door of her home. She hoped it was Mr. Emrick's men knocking to deliver new dining chairs as Mr. Emrick had promised the day before. Her brow lowered when she opened the door to see Matt Bannister and his two deputies. "Yes?" she questioned with concern, noticing the badges on their shirts.

Matt's smile was friendly. "Mrs. Redbird, it's good to see you again."

"Yes?" she repeated without the friendliness she had on the train or the familiarity of a slight friendship that Matt had expected her to have when seeing him again.

Matt's brow wrinkled slightly, disappointed that she didn't appear to recognize him. "I'm Matt Bannister. I spoke to you on the train. You fixed my head up," he said, pointing at his scalp she had tied back together.

"Yes. What do you want?"

Matt grinned uncomfortably. "I was hoping to speak with you, your husband, and your daughter about the train wreck?"

"Gilbert is not here. He is at work."

"Oh," Matt said slowly while observing her. He wondered why her countenance had switched from being who she was on the train to wanting to close the door in his face. "Well, may we come inside and talk to you?"

Reluctantly, she stepped back with a pain-filled grimace and pulled the door open.

Matt stepped inside the dark two-room cabin with a nook of a kitchen. Blankets were laid on the floor with three filthy pillows. The dining table and five unmatching chairs were the only furnishings. "Are you feeling okay?" Matt asked as William and Morton followed him inside.

"My hip hurts today. Sit," she waved toward the table. She hobbled slowly with a gimp to the table and sat carefully. "How is your head?" she asked.

Matt ran a finger over the many tiny knots of hair that lined his scalp wound. "The doctor said he couldn't have done a better job suturing it himself. Thank you. Have you seen a doctor about your hip?"

She shook her head. "No need."

"Okay," Matt said, putting the subject to rest. "So, how long have you lived and worked here?"

"Nine years."

"Nine years?" Matt questioned with a raised brow. "Well, Ona, it was nice to meet you and your family, but I can see you're hurting, so I won't beat around the bush. We are investigating who might've caused the wreck and murdered four young men from town who were protecting the wreck overnight. We know someone used explosives to blow the trestle so the train would crash into the ravine. I was wondering if you, Gilbert, or Alice saw anyone outside of the train?"

She shook her head slightly with a pain-filled grimace. "No. Mr. Emrick asked us the same thing yesterday. None of us saw anyone that wasn't hurt or dying."

"Rickson Emrick asked you about that?" Matt asked with interest.

"Not Rickson. Mr. Emrick, Rickson's father, Cliff, came here."

"If I may ask, what did he say?"

"He asked if we were okay and if we saw anything that would help the sheriff. We told him no. He told Gilbert not to work today."

Matt nodded understandably. "I know we're all sore and hurting. I certainly wouldn't want to work while feeling like this either."

"No," she agreed.

A sudden crack was heard, and Morton's rickety chair collapsed sideways, sending him to the floor. He lay there for a moment as it jarred his ribs and back.

"Are you alright?" Matt asked, standing suddenly.

"I'm fine." He stood slowly and spoke to Ona, hiding his discomfort. "I'm sorry I broke your chair." He slowly bent over to pick it up, the chair leg split down the middle. "I'll replace it."

William shook his head. "I didn't want to say so, Morton, but you have been getting fat since marrying Audrey."

Morton ignored William's comment. "Again, I'm sorry. I'll buy you a new chair before we leave town."

"No," Ona said. "Mr. Emrick sat on that chair yesterday and said he'd get us new chairs and beds. He even told Gilbert he'd get paid for not working today."

Matt questioned. "Gilbert must be a hardworking man to want to work anyway, huh?"

"No," Ona said plainly with a bitter twitch to her lip. "The boss man came in here and made Gilbert work. He cut open the burn on Gilbert's arm. I told him not to."

"Who is the boss man?" Matt questioned.

"Randy is his name, but we must call him boss or sir, or we get in trouble."

"So, Mr. Emrick told Gilbert to take today off, but this Randy forced Gilbert to work?" Matt asked to clarify his understanding.

"Yes. He came later after Mr. Emrick shouted at him for us not having beds."

"Why don't you have beds?"

"The boss man and his friends took them out to burn in their big fire. They were drunk and celebrating with women from town around the fire. They were very mean to everyone. Rosemary ran and hid in the field, or she would have been...you understand?"

Matt nodded quietly. "I think so. Who is Rosemary?"

"She and her husband Donnie live four houses down in number five. She is young and pretty. Donnie was beaten up that night. Rickson likes Rosemary too much."

"Rickson was here that night when they burned your beds?"

Ona nodded. "Yes. We don't want any trouble. The school is open, and all our children are taught here now. We don't want our children to go away. Isabel is good with the children and not like her brother at all. Please, don't cause us any trouble."

Matt remained quiet for a moment. "I just came by to ask if you had seen anyone outside the train. Causing you any trouble is not my intention."

"We did not see anyone. So, you can go."

"Yes, we can," Matt said, standing. "Gentlemen, let's go back to the big house. Ona, I hope your hip feels better. You should be looked at by a doctor if you're not feeling better soon."

"I will be fine," she said with a touch of anxiety.

"I hope so," Matt said. "Ona, you mentioned that the boss man cut Gilbert's burn open. If I remember right, it was a significant burn. Was that Gilbert's idea so he could work?"

"No. Gilbert's arm was held down, and he cut it open."

"You folks take care. It was nice meeting you," Matt said. "Oh, one last thing. Has Mr. Emrick ever come to your house before?"

"No," Ona replied.

CHAPTER TWELVE

Matt paused beside his horse and gazed at the white schoolhouse built near the community store. The schoolhouse was decent-sized and had a bell tower and brass bell to call the children to school.

"Gentlemen, go into the store, look at the prices, and ask around a bit. I'm going to the school."

Matt ascended the four steps to the schoolhouse and opened the door. It was a one-room schoolhouse with multiple rows of desks and chairs filled with Indian children. Most older ones had short hair, but the younger children had long hair. His entrance caused the students to turn around to see who was late.

"Can I help you?" a young lady in her midtwenties asked. It was clear from her tone that she did not appreciate the interruption. She held a book she was reading in her hands. Behind her, the blackboard had four categories of mathematical problems for the four age groups she was teaching.

Matt smiled and waved at little Alice in the front row.

"Yes. I am Matt Bannister, a US marshal. I was wondering if I could speak with you for a moment?"

The young lady, clearly annoyed, looked at the clock on the wall and closed the book. "Children, let's take an early fifteen-minute recess."

Matt watched the twenty or so children leave the schoolhouse to play excitedly. "They like recess," he commented once they left.

"Of course, they're children. So how can I help you, Marshal?" she asked.

"Honestly, I don't think you can, but I am curious about your school. Little Alice might have mentioned she was on the train with her parents when it crashed. I'm looking for the people responsible for that. I came here to talk to her parents. May I ask you an odd question? Why are *you* here?"

"I live here. My name is Isabel Emrick. This is my home. Does that answer your question? Maybe, being a federal marshal, you think only the government should teach these children and strip them of their heritage. That's what the state schools do. You can quote me on that if you want to, but I'll deny saying it. We have regulations to meet, and we do. Does that answer your question?"

Slowly, the corners of Matt's lips lifted as he gazed at the young lady. She had straight, shoulder-length, light brown hair that appeared to shine in the sunlight that came in through the window. She was a very attractive lady with dark blue eyes that held on to him firmly and an aggravated sternness that dared him to challenge her further.

"I think you misunderstood. I'm not questioning the validity of the school or its intent. I'm curious why you want to teach these children and not teach elsewhere?"

"I already answered that question. This is my home,

and these children need to be home with their families. The answer is not any more mysterious than that."

"Do you feel safe here?"

Isabel grimaced at the stupidity of the question. "Do I really need to answer that? This whole plantation is my home. Of course, I feel safe here."

"Do your father's employees? Meaning your students and their parents, do they feel safe?"

Her brow narrowed. "What are you getting at? Of course, they feel safe. This is their home, too."

"So, the night Rosemary hid out in the fields while the boss man, his friends, and your brother beat up her husband and pulled the beds out of the Redbird's home to throw on the fire, they all felt safe?"

"I don't know what you're talking about. Rosemary is a friend of mine and so are the other mothers and women in the village. If anyone is afraid, they haven't told me about it."

"How close of friends are you?"

"What are you getting at, Marshal Bannister?"

"Do you spend much time together like friends will occasionally do, or is it more cordial acquaintances? I ask because I just found out a young lady named Rosemary hid in the fields in fear while your brother and employees beat up her husband. Other folks had their beds burned by a drunken bossman and his friends. I was just there, and the Redbird kids are sleeping on the floor. These folks seem to like you, but it seems odd how none have spoken to you about it. That indicates fear of someone or something to me. Maybe the bossman or your brother?"

"My father is very kind to these people. My grandfather, who founded this plantation, was not, I'll admit that. My grandfather was mean to everyone, but my father is nothing like him. And I'm not either."

"Your brother?" Matt asked gently.

She widened her eyes. "Rickson is...Rickson. He was close to my grandfather. They were like two peas in a pod."

Matt hesitated. "I respect what you are doing here. If I can suggest it, you might want to start sitting down with the ladies here and have some deeper conversations to earn their trust. Maybe then they'll tell you more about what's really going on. Who is the bossman named Randy? What can you tell me about him?"

"His name is Randy Lee Paulson. He goes by Randy. He is the plantation manager in charge of the field bosses and the Livengood Village. Other than that, I don't know what to tell you. He's always been nice to me. But I was also away at college."

"I see. Well, it was very nice to meet you, Miss Isabel. Have a good day."

WILLIAM AND MORTON entered the Livengood Village store to see what was for sale and compare prices to other places in town. Small rural stores were known for marking up their prices with the laws of supply and demand, and this store wasn't a whole lot different. It was smaller than most and provided the basics for food, clothing, and other needs for a family's survival. Blankets and fabric were along one wall with all the needles and primary threads needed for sewing. Canned foods and bags of basic kitchen staples were on a center rack, and kitchen wares and other items were lined up neatly around the store. Behind the counter were candies, coffee, tea, beads, and feathers in different colors for those with a more creative side.

The back door opened, and a short, plump woman with dark brown hair and a round face walked behind the counter. Her face brightened when she saw William. "Well, the tomcat has finally come home! William Fasana, of all the places, I never expected to see you. What are you doing here? Don't tell me you're working for us now?" Her grin was wide, and excitement glimmered in her eyes as she approached him.

"Peaches?" William questioned, mouth gaped open as he stared at her. She had aged ten years, if not more, and gained plenty of weight. "You work here?"

"Well, yeah!" She gave him a quick hug. "I married Mark Duffy. You remember him?"

"Mark told me that."

"You saw Mark? He didn't tell me you were in town."

William laughed. "Well, he wouldn't, now would he? He's probably afraid I'd steal you away. I was your best customer, after all."

She laughed with a light tap on his chest. "Oh, stop it. I'm a married woman now, and all that is behind me. What's with the badge on your lapel? Don't tell me you're a Deputy US Marshal."

"Part-time when I'm needed. So you and Mark live here?"

"Yes. We have a nice apartment in the bunkhouse. Mark's a field boss, and I work here. We're saving up to buy a business, whether a saloon or a hotel, we haven't decided. I hate to cook, and that's another great thing about living here: we have a cookhouse. There is always good food to eat. In case you can't tell." She laughed as she patted her belly.

"You may have gained a pound or two over the years, but you're still worth stealing away from that dull blade of a husband you have."

"William, you haven't changed a bit." She laughed with a good-natured slap to his shoulder. "I'm afraid you couldn't steal me from Mark back then and surely can't now. I do love my husband."

"Well, that's most unfortunate for me. I always seem to find the right one, just a bit too late. I came all the way back here just to look for you, and darn it, you're married. I should have run Mark out of town years ago and swept you up like a dirt pile." He looked at Morton and rolled his eyes, causing Morton to smile.

"Oh, hush. What are you doing here, anyway?"

"Business. We were on that train, and now we're investigating it."

"Oh. So, why are you here? You don't think anyone here had anything to do with it?" The concern on her face was evident.

"No. We had a few questions for the Redbirds. They were on the train, too. We hoped they had seen someone, but they didn't. Our boss sent us in here to see how badly you are robbing the natives."

"Robbing?" she questioned.

"Yes, Peaches. Your prices are so much higher than average that it would take a team of mountaineers to climb them."

She laughed with a headshake. "Hardly. By the way, Willliam, my name is Clair. I'd appreciate it if you called me by my name and not peaches. That's from long ago, and that isn't me anymore."

"Clair," he said slowly, "how much do you make here? I know you pocket at least half of the money."

"I do not!" she exclaimed with a good-natured laugh. "Rickson and Randy hold me accountable for every penny I take in."

"Right," William said skeptically. "I met Rickson and Randy and don't see them as all that straight and narrow as bookkeepers, you either. But that's none of my business. We just came in to see the prices, and you." He smiled fondly. "It's good to see you again, Peaches."

She shook her head. "Get out of here, William. And Willy-Boy, it's good to see you again."

He laughed and waved a pointed finger at her warningly. The only people that could call him Willy and get away with it were his relatives. Willy-Boy was her nickname for him years before. "Take care, old friend."

———

MATT, William, and Morton were met by the gardener, an old Black man who had not introduced himself but, expecting the men, escorted them around the large and elegant home to the backyard. Well-groomed hedges and rose plants lined a stone pathway through lush green grass to a large white gazebo with a round table covered with white linen. There was a vase of fresh flowers in the center and plates and glasses set for them with a pitcher of lemonade and an assortment of cut melons in a large glass bowl.

Cliff Emrick stood to welcome his guests. "Hello, gentlemen. I am Cliff Emrick. My wife is unable to join us, but my son will be joining us before too long." He shook each man's hand as they introduced themselves. "Please, sit and make yourselves welcome to all the fruit you can eat."

"Thank you," Matt said as he sat across the table, feeling at ease in Cliff's presence. Cliff Emrick was a portly man with a well-fed stomach and a welcoming smile that appeared genuine. His clean-shaven face and balding head, except for the short brown hair on the sides, gave him a friendly and non-threatening appearance. His blue eyes shined with mutual respect and kindness.

Cliff scoffed at the food with a nonchalant wave. "Oh, certainly, fill your bowls and have at it. Rickson told me you went to question the Redbirds. Were they able to offer any information about the crime?"

Matt shook his head. "No."

Morton reached for the large spoon to get some fruit. "I won't be shy. That cantaloupe and watermelon look too good to pass up."

"I agree," William said, waiting for Morton to hand him the large spoon.

Cliff furrowed his brow as he watched Morton. "Morton, the Sperry name sounds familiar. Do you have family around here?"

"No," Morton answered.

Cliff turned his attention to Matt. "Marshal Bannister, where does the investigation stand as of now? A good percentage of that money was to pay for part of my harvest. We are not in desperate need like some of our neighbors for what is owed them, but we all like to be paid what we're owed for our labor."

"Of course. Well, I can't really say too much about it. We're doing our part, and a former Pinkerton Detective is also investigating it. So are your local lawmen. The railroad is taking it very seriously, and I wouldn't want to be one of the men involved. That's about all I'll say. It's only been a few days, and I am not leaving until we find the men responsible."

Cliff shook his head. "I read about it in the paper. It's an absolute tragedy how many people died, including Lucille Stafford. She was an exquisite lady. We are heartbroken. She and Amos are very good friends of ours. We've had them here a few times over the years, and we've been to their place in Portland many times. Let me know if there is anything I can do to assist you in any way. I was hoping the Redbirds had some information to give you."

"Nope. It's interesting. Ona was very friendly and talkative on the train. But today, she was acting like we never met. She sewed my head shut." He leaned over to show the line of hair tied tightly.

"It looks like she did a magnificent job. I read that you were on the train. I spoke with Gilbert and Ona yesterday to see if they were okay. I had no idea they were on that train until I read their names on the list of survivors in the paper. I hope they are feeling better today. Gilbert's burn looked pretty bad. I understand he was helping with the rescue?"

Matt nodded. "Absolutely. He didn't say much on the train but took an active role in the rescue. He did a lot, and most impressively, he stayed calm and collected despite the chaos. It truly was a nightmare."

"He's like a hero then?" Cliff asked.

"If there were a hero, then yes, it would be him. He jumped right in to help save as many as he could."

Cliff smiled proudly. "He's a very good man. I hope he's resting well today."

"No. He is working."

"Why would he be working? I told him I'd pay him."

"Ona said the bossman, Randy, came over, cut his burn open, and made him work."

"What?" Cliff shouted. His dark blue eyes hardened with aggravation. "I'll take care of that today."

"Tell me, Mr. Emrick, you have a large farm. I understand it's the largest wheat farm in the county, if not the state. How many employees do you have to work it?"

Cliff spoke plainly. "We have about forty Indian men working for us. Not including their wives and children if they have a family. Several are single men."

Matt questioned, "Why was the church burned down? Ona told me about that on the train."

Cliff looked downward with tightened lips. "My father burned it down after a missionary left. In truth, my father ran him off the property and told the congregation he went on his own. My father burned it down to stop any more missionaries or pastors from coming here. There was no church service until I started them up again. None of the natives can read, or very few can, so I write the sermons, and my son will read them in a church service we provide. Occasionally, Randy will read them. He's the plantation manager.

"Marshal Bannister," Cliff added quickly, "you have to understand that my father was not a nice man. He sold our slaves and plantation in Louisiana before coming here and named this place the Livengood Plantation to deceive the natives to live and work here. It was all part of his plan to have the closest to slave labor that he could. Not surprisingly, he hired very cruel men to oversee and manage the fields and village where our employees live. Our help was terrified of my father and the men he hired to run this place, and that's why none of the Indian folks left. They were too afraid to. I know that because my father told me so. He was proud of it.

"I'm not." Cliff continued, "My father died last year, and I took over the plantation. The first thing I did was fire the plantation manager and two other men. I cannot say that I respected my father. I despised him. I believe in helping the natives. It's sad to see them on reservations and I can't stand to see the families here having to send their children away to be taught to read and write. We can do that here, so we built a school which my daughter teaches. We had to get permission, but we did that. Honestly, money did that, but it was worth every dollar. I plan to build a church next."

"I respect that," Matt said, setting his glass of lemonade on the table. "I agree children should be at home with their families. Mr. Emrick, I've heard nothing but good things about you from the Redbirds on the train and again today. I don't know you, but you seem like an upstanding man. I promised Ona I wouldn't cause her or Gilbert any trouble, but I think you need to know, if you don't, that it was Randy who pulled the Redbirds' beds out of their house to burn them during a party. Ona told me a young lady named Rosemary hid in the field that night while Randy and his friends beat up her husband. Ona made it sound like Rosemary was fearful of being molested by the drunk men. In particular, she mentioned your son."

Cliff took a deep breath. "Marshal, you're telling me a lot of things I don't know anything about."

"Ona said your son may like Rosemary a little too much."

"If that's true, there will be a stop to that. And Randy is on very thin ice as it is. Speaking of which, here comes

Rickson now." He stood to greet his son. "Rickson, you met the marshal and his deputies earlier."

William said, "He didn't meet Morton earlier. This ugly fellow is Morton Sperry." Morton stood to shake Rickson's hand.

"Nice to meet you," Morton said.

Rickson paused. "Sperry? I know that name."

"Doesn't it sound familiar? I couldn't place it either," Cliff said.

Rickson put his attention on Matt. "Did you learn anything from the redskins?"

"Rickson," Cliff said irritably. "I told you not to call them that."

"Yeah, and like I said, I'm twenty-seven years old, not thirteen." He sat in an empty chair and lit a cigar. "So, gentlemen, since there's nothing to learn out here, why are you still here?"

Cliff answered sharply, "They're my guests, Rickson. That's all the reason you need to know."

"That's fine. I just asked, is all."

Morton chimed in during a moment of silence, "By the way, I broke one of the Redbirds' chairs I sat in. I told her I'd replace it before we leave town."

Cliff waved it off with his hand. "Don't worry about it. I told Randy to replace those and their beds. And he will immediately, or he'll walk away without a job. As I was saying earlier, Marshall, I want these children who grow up in the Livengood Village to be educated and become functioning adults. I hope that when they grow up, they can go to college and make a life for themselves, and maybe one or two will want to come back here and help run this plantation."

"Not while I'm running it," Rickson said.

Cliff tightened his lips with frustration. "Rickson, why don't you go bring Randy in from wherever he is? I want to talk to him and you both. Tell him I want to talk immediately."

Rickson chuckled arrogantly and stood. "I'll let him know. Marshal Bannister, it was nice to meet you."

Matt stood. "You too. Well, I think we're about done here ourselves. Nice to meet you both. Thank you for lunch."

"You didn't eat anything," Cliff pointed out.

"No, but the lemonade was fantastic. Thank you."

Through a slight smirk, Rickson said, "Marshal Bannister, if you ever decide to give up being a lawman, you can always work for us. Half breeds are welcome too."

Cliff stood quickly and shouted, "Get out of here, Rickson! Go get Randy and get your butts back here! Now!" His face was reddened with anger.

Rickson snickered as he walked away.

"Marshal Bannister, I am so sorry. I am humiliated and shocked at my son's disrespect. Please forgive me for my son's..." he sighed heavily. "I don't know what to do with him. I see more of my father in him every day."

"I won't hold anything against you," Matt said. "I would appreciate you ensuring that no trouble comes to the Redbirds, such as retaliation for confiding in me. That's what they fear will happen."

Cliff was adamant. "It won't. I can assure you of that. I do appreciate you telling me what you shared today. And I will take care of it right now."

William poured a glass of lemonade and gulped it down. A wry smirk lifted his lips. "Cliff, will you do me a favor and tell your son that deep down, I think he's a real sweetheart."

Cliff rolled his eyes. "Right. He reminds me more of my father every day."

CHAPTER THIRTEEN

"OKAY, PA, WHAT DID YOU WANT TO TALK TO US about? Are you giving us a raise for doing such a great job?" Rickson asked as he led Randy into his father's office.

"Close the door," Cliff said. He was standing next to the desk, holding a glass of lemonade.

Randy closed the door and sat in a leatherback chair beside Rickson. "Is it time for a raise, Cliff."

Cliff stared at Randy with a hardened, stone-faced expression. "Why did Gilbert work today when I told him to take today off? And you know that because you were right there."

"He wanted to," Randy answered. "Who am I to stop the man from working? So, I popped the blister for him, and he worked."

"And I heard you burned the Redbirds' beds at a party?"

Rickson answered, "That was my doing, Pa. We were drunk and running out of firewood." He chuckled.

"Is that funny?" Cliff asked without any humor.

"It was, yeah."

143

Cliff leaned against the front of his desk and leaned forward toward his son to be heard clearly. "Rickson, I don't have to will this plantation to you. I can will it to Isabel and know it will be run right. But it won't be you running it nor you, Randy. I am this close"—he held his thumb and finger close together—"from firing you as it is. If I ever hear of you harassing Gilbert, Ona, Donnie, Rosemary, or any of them again, you can kiss your job goodbye. I will meet with all our natives and tell them they don't need to be afraid of you or anyone who works here except me. I'm the one who owns this place, and I will make the rules! They will have every opportunity to come here and talk to me personally anytime they want to tell me if any of you mistreat them again. And I will fire you. That includes you, too, Rickson! I am sick and tired of your disrespect for me and everyone else around here. You either change how you treat people or move out and find a different way to make a living. I'm done putting up with you! You've been warned. Randy, I want beds, a davenport, and chairs in the Redbird house by the end of the day today, even if you have to take them from your place. Now, both of you get out of my sight!"

"Pa, you can't be serious. Isabel doesn't know a thing about growing crops."

"Rickson, I love you, but I'm getting to the point where I can't stand being around you. I meant what I said. I will sell this place before I let you own it."

Rickson laughed. "No, you won't."

"No?" Cliff challenged. "I'll change my will tomorrow. That's how serious I am. I'll go to town and talk to Amos Stafford about a price and put that in my will, and the money will go to Isabel. Once I go to Heaven, what do I care about what happens to this place? It's the people I care about and how they are treated. I don't trust you, Rickson. I think your grandfather's influence is way too strong, and I fear that it will lead to more cruelty. That won't happen if I have anything to do with it. I fired Stan Meldrum and Leon Goodrich for a reason. How you can be friends with them, I don't know, but no son of mine should be."

Rickson snapped angrily, "This is my birthright! Grandfather built this place for me. So I can pass it on to my children. It is my birthright!"

"Well, son, your choices have become your Jacob then, haven't they? You've stripped this place from yourself. Now, go outside and cry about it, don't be crying about it in here. Do what the Bible says and repent, maybe you can earn it back. That's all I have to say."

Rickson glared at his father with a scowl. "Let's go, Randy. Let's go to town and get the Redbirds' crap."

"What does your choices have become your Jacob, mean?" Randy questioned, confused by the statement.

Cliff answered pointedly, "Esau traded his birthright, his fortune, and his blessing to his younger brother Jacob for a bowl of soup. It's the same thing Rickson is doing with his stupid choices, immaturity, and disrespect. You have a great future in your hands, Rickson, but you're going to lose it if you can't treat people right. It's not hard to be nice. You just treat people with the same kindness and respect that you'd like to be treated with in all circumstances."

"We have to go get some furniture," Rickson said, leaving his father's office with Randy right behind him.

STAN MELDRUM TOOK a seat in a chair facing a table where three men sat looking at him. He had been called into the conference room to be questioned by the train incident investigators. Stan had spoken to other employees who had been interviewed and knew what to expect.

"Stan Meldrum, my name is Corbin Hazelton, this gentleman is Marty Rook, and that gentleman is John Reed. We are investigating the deliberate destruction of a railroad trestle and the intentional derailing of the train in an attempt to rob the Stafford Milling Company's payroll. Not excluding the murder of four young men and fifty-nine passengers."

"You're looking at the wrong man here," Stan replied.

"Yes. It seems maybe so. Your work record states you were the manager of the Livengood Plantation for about twelve years. But you lost that position a year ago and was hired here as the production foreman. That proves you're a leader of men with a lot of experience. That's not a bad living."

"Not bad."

"Do you have a family?"

"No."

"I see here that your old cohort from the plantation, Leon Goodrich, was let go at the same time you were and he now works for you. Are you two good friends?"

"Yes," Stan admitted. "Best friends."

"I see. Being a supervisor, you have an elevated level of authority that puts you in the inner circle of all things management, including certain knowledge that others aren't privileged to. You would agree to that, right?"

Stan nodded. "Obviously."

"So, you knew when to expect the payroll and how it would arrive?"

"I did."

"Did you happen to mention it to anyone? Your friend, perhaps? A coworker? A customer impatient to get their money? Anyone at all?"

Stan shook his head. "As you mentioned, I've been the boss for a long time. If there is anything I honor, it is the confidentiality of my employers. No, I didn't mention it to anyone. I reassured our customers that the payroll for their crops was coming and would be here soon. That is all."

"You have a good work record. You are reliable and have good marks. Are you a church-going man?"

"No."

"Do you own a horse?"

"I worked on the plantation for fourteen years in total. Of course, I own a horse. You can't do that job and not own one."

"I understand. Do you board it?"

"No. It's kept on my property just outside of town."

"But you walk to work?"

"I do."

"How far away is your place?"

"I don't know what that has to do with anything, but about a mile from here."

"It doesn't. I'm just asking. How long does it take you to walk that?"

"Twenty minutes or so."

"Have you ever bought dynamite from any of the hardware stores around here?"

Stan nodded. "When I was the foreman of the plantation. We had rocks to move in the fields and dynamite worked well for that."

"Have you bought it since?"

"No. No need. Look, I'm not the man you're looking

for, nor do I know of anyone involved. We're all devastated by the loss of all those people, especially Mrs. Stafford. She was good to us. I met her numerous times out at the plantation, and she was wonderful. Even to a low-scale man like me. I would be the first to tell you if I knew anything."

Corbin grunted. "Yeah, that seems to be the case with everyone here. Mr. Meldrum, on the day of the attempted robbery, it says you and your best friend, Leon Goodrich, had left the morning of the tragedy to meet with Cliff Emrick to discuss a new contract with your old employer, the Livengood Plantation. But no contract was turned in. Can you explain that?"

Stan nodded. "I didn't meet with Cliff. I met with his son, Rickson Emrick. He is taking over the plantation nowadays. We went field by field, made a plan for next year's crops, and then sat down and debated numbers. It was preapproved through management here. Rickson asked Leon and me to meet with him because we have vast knowledge of the plantation and what can be grown. Like you said, I ran that place for twelve years as the manager. Rickson and Randy, my replacement out there, are just getting their feet wet. It's a big place with a lot going on. That's why I was asked to go there. They needed help.

"Unfortunately, the next morning, I was carrying the contract to work to turn it in when my attention was drawn to the pier. All those men were boarding a barge to help with the train wreckage. I wandered down and set the papers on the pier to ask what was going on, and the damn wind picked up the papers and blew them into the river. I was so pissed. I came in here and told our manager what happened. All that work for nothing. I'll have to meet up with Rickson and redo it on my time instead of company time now. That is why the contract was not turned in."

"You didn't help with the train wreckage?"

Stan shook his head slowly. "I was tempted but missed work the day before and needed to stay here and get caught up on my work."

"Rickson Emrick can confirm your alibi?"

"I'm sure he can. I was with him all day."

"LEON WAS a little worked up about being interviewed, but he got through it just fine. They know nothing," Stan said, pouring a drink for himself.

"Thank goodness for that. They aren't going to find out anything. We're safe," Randy said with confidence. He and Rickson had brought a wagon to town to buy furnishings for the Redbirds but were at Stan's home when he got home from work.

"No," Stan said, "my concern is that fat slob of a row boss you fellas brought into it, the explosive expert, you all said. I know he is your friend, but he could bring us all to the gallows. Fifty-nine dead, plus four more. None of us would escape the noose. He is the weak link in our chain. You fellows had better watch him closely—Leon's fine. I'm fine. You both are fine, but him? I don't trust him. He's soft."

"Isaac has been a bit melancholy since the accident," Randy admitted, "but he didn't mean to blow the trestle up right before the train crossed it. The fault isn't on him but a ground squirrel, of all things. Isaac will be fine. He knows it wasn't his fault."

Rickson had not participated in the robbery but had covered for the others who left the plantation. He had approached Amos Stafford's son-in-law, who ran the

Stafford Milling Company, to request permission for Stan Meldrum to come out to the plantation for a meeting to renegotiate a contract for next year's crops. Since Stan and Leon Goodrich were quite familiar with the plantation, it only made sense for them to negotiate with the Emricks.

When it came to the largest producer of crops, the management of Stafford Milling jumped high or low for the Livengood Plantation, and the meeting was scheduled. The paperwork had already been done and would be accidentally ruined somehow before it was set on an official desk. It was a ploy to cover for Stan and Leon to miss a day of work and still be accounted for when an investigation began. Everyone had an alibi, and all alibis depended on Rickson's word.

Rickson was angry at his father and in no mood to listen to Stan complain about his friend. "Isaac will be fine, Stan. Right now, I'm far more concerned about my father. If he changes his will, I'll be robbed of my birthright. I can't let that happen, fellas. My grandfather primed me to inherit the plantation since I was a child. He always said my father was too weak to run it. And he is. I'll kill him before I let him sell the plantation to the Staffords or give it to my sister. It's my birthright! It was built for me."

Stan had already heard an earful about what had happened earlier in the day with Cliff. "Rickson, you know there is no love lost between your father and me. But right now, you need to be kind to the savages, treat everyone, especially your father and sister, with the utmost respect, and become a good religious boy until this investigation is over. Once all these do-gooder investigators go back home with their tails tucked between their legs, then we can plan something along those lines. But for now, behave yourself and keep your mouth shut."

Rickson snarled as he lifted his drink. "It's *my* plantation," he grumbled.

"One thing at a time, Rickson. Promise your father you're going to do better and put on an act. I don't like the man, either, so we'll take care of him soon enough if you really want to, but you better think that over carefully before we do anything," Stan said.

Randy solemnly said, "We better take the wagon and buy some mattresses and chairs before the furniture store closes. I must have those delivered today or I'll be fired."

"Fine," Rickson said. "Let's go get that done so I can tell my beloved pa I helped pick them out."

CHAPTER FOURTEEN

WHEN MATT RETURNED TO HIS HOTEL, HE WAS given a telegram from Gabriel's mother, Elizabeth Smith. He went upstairs to his room and found Gabriel sitting on his bed against the wall, reading a book missing its hardback covering. His arm was in a plaster cast, resting comfortably on a rolled-up blanket and pillow. "What are you reading, Gabe?"

Gabriel laid the book down. "I'm not sure. The title page is ripped out, and it doesn't have a cover, so I don't know. I think it is a love story, though. I found it downstairs in a bookcase."

"Well, love is an important part of life," Matt said, sitting tiredly on his bed across from Gabriel's. "We've never talked about it too much, but do you have any love interests? Are you courting anyone? I ask because you're reading a romance book and getting to that age where love is a part of life."

Gabriel smiled as his cheeks reddened just a bit. "Kind of."

"May I ask who she is?"

Gabriel bit his lip, hesitant to say. "I don't think you really want to know."

"Why wouldn't I? Gabriel, I may not have raised you and been the father I wish I had been, but you know all that. It doesn't mean I don't love you. I do. You're the only son I may ever have, and I missed so much of your life. I'll take whatever I can get to be a part of your life now. So tell me, who is the lucky lady that has your attention?"

Gabriel was still hesitant to say, "Tiffany."

"Tiffany Foster? The Tiffany I brought back from Prairieville?"

"Yeah..."

"Really? Isn't she your cousin now?" Matt teased.

"No! She is not related. She just lives with Aunt Annie."

"Are you courting her?"

"Not technically."

"Do you love her?"

Gabriel's face reddened. "I don't know."

"You're seventeen. I fell in love with your mother long before that. I remember when I first realized I truly loved her. It was down on Pearl Creek one summer's day. I watched her run through the shallow water because a crawdad touched her toe. She was screaming and scared to death. It was so cute. And I thought, Lord, I sure love that girl. And I did. I really did. I was about fourteen or so at the time."

"Do you still love my mom, even though you're married to Christine?"

Matt nodded slowly. "It's a different kind of love. Your mother and I loved each other as teenagers, but we're much older now and very different than we were. There is no longer a romantic love but a strong love for her as a person. When you fall in love with someone, you give a part of yourself to them, and whether it lasts to marriage or not, they always own that small piece of your heart. The love I have for your mom makes her very dear to me."

"I like Tiffany a lot," Gabriel offered.

"I bet you're excited to get back home and see her. Huh?"

"Yeah. Are you excited to get back home to Christine?"

"Far more than you know." He pulled the telegram out of his pocket and held it up. "Your parents want to know when we will return to Willow Falls. I can't give them an answer." He paused. "I don't know how long I'll be here, Gabriel. Yes, I want to go home, but I could be here for a day or two or a week or two. I can't leave until the men who caused that train wreck are caught. It's just something I can't do. But I can put you on the portage rail around the falls and board a sternwheeler to Wallula, where you can take a stagecoach home. I think that's something we ought to do. Your parents are terribly worried about you and want you home. And you'd get to see Tiffany in a few days. That's something to look forward to. Right?"

Gabriel shook his head anxiously. "I don't know if I want to take another train."

Matt's brow raised questionably. "There's not much of a choice. The portage rail is the only way around the falls, and then you get on a sternwheeler. It's not that far, just twelve miles or so. Listen, what happened on the train isn't going to happen again. The portage train goes back and forth all day, every day. It's safe. The train would have been safe, too." He paused. "In less than an hour, you board the sternwheeler, and you get off in Wallula. I'll give you money for the stagecoach. You've taken it before, so you know how that works. I think we need to get you home, Gabriel."

Gabriel's lips tightened as he rolled them inwardly. The anxiety he felt could be seen in his expression. "I don't know if I'd like traveling alone."

"Gabriel," Matt said gently. "Your mother is worried about you and wants you to come home."

Gabriel's breathing grew more profound as his eyes glazed over with a thin coat of moisture. Tiny beads of sweat formed on his brow, and his voice rose higher in pitch as he said, "I...will never be able to forget what I've seen and all the screaming I heard as people burned alive." A tear silently rolled down his cheek. "How do I know if I take a portage train, it won't wreck? If it does, and if I'm stuck inside, who will get me out, Dad? I don't want to burn to death." His bottom lip quivered noticeably.

Matt spoke gently, "Gabriel, what happened on the train wasn't the train's fault. That was an act of evil committed by a human being. It was horrible, unimaginable, and tragic in so many ways. We were lucky enough to live through it, and we'll always carry the memory of those who didn't. That can be a very heavy load to carry as time moves on if you can't find a way to reconcile and come to terms with what you have experienced. I'm not saying it's easy to forget, it *will* bother you. That train wreck is one of the worst things I've ever experienced, so I know it has to be shocking to you. I am telling you that you *cannot* live your life fearing what will come next or worrying that it will be bad.

"Our mind can paralyze us with fear by thinking about all the *what ifs*...that is one question you could contemplate all day, every day. What if you walk outside and a stray bullet falls from the sky? What if you use the privy and sit down and get your jewels bit by a black widow? You can come up with a thousand frightening thoughts, but more than likely, not one of them will happen. We can scare ourselves into insanity if we don't get a hold of ourselves and shake the cobwebs off. It takes courage to live this life, son. Do you know how many times the Bible says to *be strong and courageous?*"

Gabriel shook his head.

"Thirteen times, in various forms. Three hundred and sixty-five times, the Bible says to *fear not.* Now, I'm not great at mathematics, but if you add all that up, I think we who know the Lord and have faith in him should be brave and courageous more often than afraid. Don't be afraid of more bad things happening, Gabriel. Fear is a poison that can control everything you do if you don't take control of it now. I didn't raise you, son, but I know for a fact that neither Tom nor your mother want you to grow up to be afraid of living. I won't allow it either. You're going home tomorrow, and you're going to stand tall, step onto that train, and do it like a man. Are we clear?"

"Yes, sir," Gabriel replied softly.

"Wait," Matt said with a slight grimace. "This is bad timing, but it will have to be in a couple of days because the railroad is using the sternwheelers to bring the families of the deceased to town to identify and collect them. Tomorrow is going to be a rough and busy day. Look, I'll let your mother know we'll get you heading home with or without me in a few days. Now that that's settled, how about you and I go to a nice restaurant downtown and have dinner?"

———

MATT AND GABRIEL went to Milgard's Restaurant on the corner of Third and Main Street. It was a nice restaurant with a dozen tables covered with white tablecloths, a vase of flowers, and a water pitcher. They were almost done eating dinner when the county sheriff, Cletus James, walked into the restaurant with his wife, Molly, and another couple.

"Marshal Bannister," Cletus said as he removed his hat. "Are you here for the oysters? It is oyster night."

Matt shook his head with a wrinkled nose. "No, I'm not. Mrs. James, how are you feeling?"

She smiled slightly. "Tonight is my first time out of bed if that answers your question."

"It does. How is Michael?"

"In bed with a broken leg. The doctor says it will heal, and Michael will walk normally again, hopefully. I see your son is on the mend."

Gabriel smiled half-heartedly. "Yes. I'm still very sore, though."

"I think we all are," Molly said. "Thank you again for helping get my son's leg from under that seat. I've thanked the Lord at least a thousand times for Michael and me surviving that terrible tragedy. I'm also praying you and the others will find the criminals that caused it."

"I'm confident we will," Matt replied. "Cletus, could I have a word with you?"

"Yes. Molly, I'll join you and the Ragcliffs in a few moments. You know what I want? Oysters and a lot of them." He sat down at the table. "What can I do for you, Matt?"

"I'm curious. What do you know about Cliff Emrick?"

"He's a pillar in our community. He's a great man. Why? No. Don't tell me that you suspect him?"

Matt wrinkled his nose. "No, I don't. I was just wondering if he was as nice and caring of a man as he seems?"

"When it comes to Cliff, what you see is what you get. He is a genuine good man."

"What about Rickson?"

Cletus grinned quietly before choosing his words carefully. "Rickson is Rickson."

"That's precisely what his sister said. I take it that's not good?"

"He is very obnoxious and arrogant. He's not so well-liked around here." He held up his hand to explain. "Rickson is a spoiled kid who grew up to be one of the most arrogant men you will ever meet. Everything revolves around him, and hell has no fury like an unhappy Rickson if something doesn't go his way. It wasn't Cliff who spoiled him, though. It was Cliff's wife and his father, Basil, in particular. Basil was a horrible man, which rubbed off on his little Livengood Plantation prince. That should tell you about everything you need to know."

"Does he have many friends?" Matt asked as Cletus stood to join his wife and friends.

"The field bosses out there are his friends and about everyone he buys drinks for when he comes to town. Besides that, no. Enjoy your dinner. You should try the oysters and the special sauce."

Matt smiled. "No, thanks."

CHAPTER FIFTEEN

Enzio Corrales had entered the Amber Light Hotel and asked the desk clerk to see Morton Sperry. Morton was notified that Enzio wanted to speak with him and stepped outside, where Enzio was waiting. Enzio led Morton around to a side alley to talk quietly. "Morton, you need to come home with me. Your cousins Adrian and Tyee are here and they want to talk to you."

Morton felt a chill run down his spine. "Why are they here?"

"They came to see you. I sent Uncle Roman a wire to let them know the boys were being blamed for the train, according to you. Adrian and Tyee left three days ago and just arrived. They're waiting."

Morton took a deep breath and exhaled nervously. "Enzio, I didn't want to see them. I was asking if they were in town," Morton complained.

Enzio was a cousin of the Crowe brothers on their father's side. He wasn't related to Morton, but Enzio was a part of the Crowe Brothers outlaw gang in years past and knew Morton from past experiences. After his first child was born, Enzio quit the gang and found work with the Oregon Steam and Navigation Company, transferring cargo from the train to the sternwheelers to support his family. He shrugged his shoulders innocently. "I know. I didn't invite them here, but they are here now."

"They should have stayed where they were," Morton said. He knew if the two Crowe brothers were seen in town, they would be arrested, if not shot on sight, for the widespread belief that they were responsible for the trestle and murder of the four young men. Morton also knew that his cousins possibly endangered his life since he was now a US deputy marshal. Morton was uneasy and nervous and wanted to take Matt with him, but Matt and Gabriel had not returned from dinner, and William was at the saloon. He had no choice but to go alone to face his cousins. He walked with Enzio to the east side of town, where a line of poor shacks was built a little way outside the city limits.

The home was small and cluttered with the belongings and bedding of Enzio and his wife, their three children, and his wife's older parents. Adrian and Tyee Crowe were sitting around the table eating when Morton entered. Their dark eyes displayed no semblance of emotion except cold-blooded fury that glared at Morton.

"Adrian, Tyee," Morton greeted cautiously. He had removed the leather thong from his revolver's trigger before entering the home in case he needed to use his gun. The two men were his cousins, but blood only ran so deep when betrayal and the law separated the blood ties.

Adrain Crowe, the eldest of the brothers and leader of the gang, nodded toward an empty wooden chair set against the table. "Secure your gun's hammer and sit down. Keep your hands on the table."

Morton slowly pulled the leather thong back onto the hammer and sat, refusing to take his eyes off Adrian.

"You accused us of robbing a train?" Adrian's eyes narrowed as they burned into Morton.

"No. The town is accusing you. I asked Enzio if you were in town. He said no. And that's what I told Matt."

Adrian's head rose. "Matt is in town, too? What are you doing here, Morton?"

"We were on the train." He explained what had happened. "Now we're looking for who did it."

Tyee spoke for the first time. "It wasn't us, Mort. We were in Prairieville."

"I know it wasn't you. Enzio told me that. I never accused you. We've been telling people it could *not* have been you."

Adrian spoke evenly. "That's good because you are no longer a part of our family, Morton. We came here to kill you if you were accusing us. I should kill you now, but this isn't the right time. I imagine we'll cross paths again since you're a lawman now. Stay out of our territory or we'll kill you on sight."

Tyee added, "You chose the wrong side, Mort. You will be dead before long. Cousin Jesse has it in for you."

Morton took a deep breath and sighed. The Crowe and Sperry families shared Jesse Helms as their cousin. "What Jesse did to that girl in Hollister was horrific. I should have let Matt kill Jesse—next time, I will. And as far as my family goes, they'd best not try to harm me or Audrey. That would be the worst mistake they could make."

Adrian's lips rose chillingly. "Does that go for us too?"

Morton nodded slowly. "It does."

Adrian laughed lightly. "Morton, I'll give you one chance to make amends. Bring the marshal here so we can ambush him, and you'll earn back our good graces in our family, anyway."

Morton slowly stood. "It's good to see you both. I suggest you get out of town tonight and don't come back until we make an arrest. We don't know who blew up the trestle and killed all those people, but you're being blamed for it. Don't let anyone see you leave, but get out of town."

Adrian's hand had slowly maneuvered down to his holster casually. "We'll worry about that later. Next time we meet, if we do, I may do your mother a favor and take her your scalp for her wall. I'll make it into a dream catcher."

Morton gazed at his cousin, knowing very well that the words were not a warning to take lightly. "You can try, Adrian. I hope it never comes to that, but until then, take care."

———

WILLIAM SAT at a poker table in the Witching House Saloon with his old friend, Mark Duffy, and Mark's friends, Randy Paulson and Dave Ruddick. Two other gentlemen, KC Green and Kevin Wiegel, played with them. The poker game had evenly spread among winners and losers over several drinks.

Randy laughed at something William had said as he set his drink on the table. "William, I wish you lived around here. You're a sight more entertaining than these other fellows. Too bad you're a lawman, though. We could have you working on the Livengood with us, and trust me when I say the living is good."

"Oh yeah?" William questioned. "Well, I'm liking The

Dalles City area better than I used to. Do you think your boss would pay me better than Matt does?"

"Guaranteed."

William rolled his eyes. "The works probably a bit safer, too. Matt's almost gotten me killed a few times now. Check this out." William stood and pulled his shirt up to show a red scar that was reasonably new across his right side. "I was slit open with a knife back in July. I killed the kid, but not before he cut me. And just a few days ago, I was almost killed in a train rolling down the side of a bank into the river." He laughed with a shake of his head. "Matt's my cousin and I love him, but his sense of excitement is far too dangerous for this gambler. This is my love, right here," he said, sitting down and patting the poker table. He leaned toward Mark and said, "The only thing that would make this game better is if your wife was here with one of her free peaches. Oh! Sorry, they were only free for me!" He laughed. He was quickly joined by everyone at the table except Mark.

"Her name is Clair, and I don't appreciate that, William. I know you're just making fun, but she's my wife now."

"Oh, come on, Mark, have you lost your sense of humor since saying, *I do*? Heck, if I decide to stay here, we might be working together. What do you guys do, anyway? You got an entire town of Indians out there, what's left to do?"

"Supervise," Randy answered. "We have to keep them savages working and keep them in line. It's easy work for us and we get paid to do it."

"How many men does it take to do that?" William asked.

"It's a huge plantation with a lot of different fields. Indians are lazy, we need to keep them motivated and working."

"Like slaves?" William asked.

"No. They're employees, like us, just lower." Randy smiled. "If you want a job, I can get you one. It comes with room, board, cookhouse, and anything you want."

William grunted. "Let me think about it. I'm here for a few days anyway. Matt and I are determined to find the men responsible for that train."

KC Green offered, "We pulled so many charred bodies out of that...well, it became a furnace." He shook his head, troubled. "I'd like to kill every one of those men, no matter who they are."

William spoke, "We'll find them."

"And what makes you so sure about that?" Randy asked.

"Because it's what we do," William answered.

Randy's attention went to the sound of a crowd on the street yelling with excitement that flowed into the saloon. A man pushed the bat doors open and shouted, "We caught them! Two of the Crowe Brothers and one of their gang members! Come on, we're going to string them up!"

"What?" William asked as the news reverberated through the men.

Randy Paulson stared at Dave Ruddick for a second and then reacted with a wide grin. "Let's string them up!" he yelled, quickly gathering his money from the table and following the crowd outside.

"I got a rope!"

"We need three ropes," a man shouted over the crowd.

"The blacksmith shop has beams to hang them from!"

"Wharton's barn! Take them to Wharton's barn."

"Just slit their throats and be done with them!"

"We're innocent!" Tyee Crowe shouted. His hands were bound behind his back and he was being pulled by his arms along the street by the crowd of hostile men. Tyee was beaten up and bleeding from his mouth, nose, and a gash above his eye.

A man planted a hard fist into Tyee's face with a murderous shout, "Go to hell, you murdering half-breed!"

Adrian Crowe fared no better than his younger brother. His swollen face was beaten black and blue and bleeding as well. The two brothers had been spotted entering Enzio's house by Enzio's neighbor, Wade McKay. Wade notified Perry Whitmore, The Dalles City Constable, who collected his deputies and a few others and waited outside Enzio's house for the Crowe brothers to come outside. When the two brothers decided to leave town, they were circled by a group of armed men and forced to surrender. Enzio was taken as well and was now being marched downtown toward Ish Carnes's livery stable to hang.

Enzio, like his cousins, was beaten up by several men and bleeding, but not with the fury that Tyee and Adrian had suffered. Enzio was terrified and weeping uncontrollably as he was being led to a cruel death. "I have a family," he sobbed with desperation. "Stop! Stop. I'm innocent. I was at work! I was at work! Perry, you know me. I have a family!"

His plea was met with a fierce strike of a fist by his neighbor, Wade McKay. Wade did not like Enzio to begin with. Knowing his neighbor was not just related, but helping the men who murdered his nephew was more than enough reason to want to hit the man. "Everyone on the train had a family! So did the boys you all killed. Stevie was my nephew, you son of a..." Wade's heavy fist, filled with rage, slammed into Enzio's face.

William followed the crowd, surprised that Constable Whitmore wasn't taking the men to jail to be tried in a court of law. The fact was the world would be a safer place if the Crowe brothers were hung, but William knew the Crowes were innocent of the crimes they were about to be hanged for. He approached a young boy of about fourteen who was following the crowd of angry citizens and offered the boy five dollars to run to the Amber Light Hotel to let Matt know what was happening. The amount of money and the chance to meet the marshal were not enough to persuade the young man to leave the crowd and miss the opportunity to watch the outlaws being strung up like the vermin they were. Being rejected, William looked around and saw three prostitutes standing outside on a saloon's porch, watching with interest. William quickly approached them and made the same offer. One of the ladies who appeared the most concerned agreed and hurried down the street.

"William, there's no time for whoring!" Mark Duffy yelled at his friend with a laugh. "Come on, we're stringing them up!"

A man following in the crowd looked at William and shouted to the others, "Hey, does having Constable Whitmore, a county deputy sheriff, and a US deputy marshal with us make this a legal lynching?" he questioned with a laugh.

The city constable, Perry Whitmore, answered without looking back, "It does in my law book."

"We'd string them up with or without you, Perry!" one man responded. It was met with collective agreement from the others.

"We didn't do it," Adrian Crowe repeated as he was pushed along the street.

Perry held out his hand to stop the crowd in the middle of the street. He turned around to face Adrian and the other two. "I said hold up! Shut up, all of you!" As the crowd quieted, Perry stared at the three bleeding men. "You heathens are about to meet your maker and face your judgment. And there is nothing that you can say to stop it. So, pretend like you're *brave* heathens and die like men, not weeping women!" he shouted and slapped the side of Enzio's face.

"Constable Whitmore," Enzio sobbed through his bloody mouth. "You know me! You know this isn't right. You know I'm not a killer!"

"I don't know anything of the sort, Enzio! I know that you're related to these monsters and you were hiding them. That makes you as guilty as them in my eyes. Ish, lead the way. Let's hang these savages."

"Yeah!" a shout led to a roar from the crowd of forty-some men and growing.

Adrian Crowe was shoved forward and fell to the ground. He was pulled back to his feet by his long hair while another man kneed him in the face. Recovering from the knee, Adrian snarled and shouted through his wrath, "My father will avenge us! Your town is going to burn!"

"Send Roman and we'll hang him too," Perry said, unconcerned. He walked beside Ish toward the livery stable.

A man hit Tyee Crowe in the back of the head mercilessly. "You're going to die, and we'll be dancing on your graves!"

"Dancing? Pissing is more like it!" Wade McKay said bitterly.

"Piss on their father's grave too!" an old man named Oscar Harrison screamed, enraged. His chest heaved up and down through his enraged breaths and his bulging eyes.

When they arrived at Ish's livery stable, Ish pulled the

doors open to enter. He called for his hired man, who worked nights. "Fred, push that buggy outside! I need a horse saddled, too. We have some lynching to do!"

"Are we going to do them all simultaneously?" a man asked.

"No. We're going to make this night last and hang these criminals one at a time. We're going to save the best for last," Perry answered.

The wagon repair shop was in the back of the livery stable, where a solid beam had a single pulley chained to its center. Ish grabbed a ladder and set it against the beam to remove the chain connected to the pulley. He waited for Fred to bring him a rope, which he fed through the pulley. It wasn't a thick four-strand braided rope with a noose tied correctly, but a lighter weight two-strand braided rope with a quickly tied slip knot brought to Ish to slip through the pulley. Once a horse was saddled to pull the rope, Perry yanked Enzio from the group and pulled the narrow slipknot over his head, pulling the slack to tighten it around his neck while three other men roughly held him. Enzio wept, begged for mercy, prayed, and sobbed.

Seeing an opportunity to help the innocent men, William Fasana stepped forward and jerked the horse's reins out of a man's hands. "I'll lead the horse," William said sharply. "It should be a lawman's job, not a citizen's."

"You're not even from here," the man argued, wanting the privilege to say he hung the outlaws.

William answered with a harsh, raised voice, "I'm a US deputy marshal. It's my duty to pull the reins to lift these boys off the ground. Not yours!"

The man protested with a few curse words but backed away.

Enzio, sweating like a swollen creek, begged, "Please,

don't. I'm innocent! Please...you all know I'm innocent." His knees grew weak, and he would have fallen if not for the two men holding his arms.

"Someone shut that murderer up!" Dave Ruddick exclaimed. A solid fist to the side of Enzio's face stunned him.

Adrian Crowe spoke through a gash in his lip. "Listen to me, Enzio is innocent. You can hang me, but Enzio is innocent! He didn't do anything to deserve this. Let him go and hang me."

Perry grabbed Adrian's jaw and glared into his cold brown eyes. "Are you saying you're responsible for the train?"

Adrian shook his jaw from Perry's grip with a sharp jerk. "I'm guilty of many things, but I'm not guilty of that! We got to town tonight!" he sneered with an enraged snarl. "If you want to hang me and my brother like this, then do it! But Enzio is innocent. Let him go!"

Perry shook his head. "No. Innocent or not, it's one less savage. You're going last so that you can watch your cousin and your brother die. It is our pleasure to watch you all suffocate to death."

Adrian's eyes glared dangerously at the constable. "Enjoy it! My father will kill you slowly." He spat in Perry's face.

Perry wiped his face with his hand. "Like I said, we'll hang him too."

"You know I'm innocent," Enzio wept. "You all know it. Perry, James, Henry, Eric, you all know me. Wade, we're neighbors. You know I'm innocent. My wife and children need me," he sobbed. "I didn't know they were coming. I didn't do anything wrong!"

Wade shouted at his neighbor, "I watched you invite them into your house! You were helping them."

Tyee Crowe headbutted the man holding his right arm and tried to break free but was quickly constrained and earned a severe beating by several of the men. Tyee lay on the ground, trying to get his breath. His hands were tied behind his back like the others and any attempt to escape was futile.

"Stand him up so he can watch," Perry said heartlessly. When Tyee was on his feet, Perry quieted the group of men and announced loudly, "Adrian and Tyee Crowe, and Enzio Corrales, I sentence you three to hang by the neck until you are dead for your crimes. I'll give you one chance to admit your guilt. Tell me you're guilty and I'll make your death quick. If not, I'll close the livery stable doors and make your hangings last all night."

"We didn't take any money," Adrian said heatedly. "I told you we didn't do it!"

Randy Paulson hit Adrian in the side of the face. "Of course, you didn't take the money. It was burned! Hang them! Let's get this over with!"

"Yeah!" someone yelled, and a loud agreement followed.

Perry glanced at Enzio and then waved a hand toward William. "Pull the horse!"

"Enzio..." Tyee called his cousin's name. He couldn't finish what he wanted to say and just shook his head slightly, helpless to save his cousin from a death he did not deserve. The sorrow and guilt showed in the moisture that clouded his eyes. "I'm sorry."

Adrian's lips tightened as fury filled him. "Damn you, Perry, I told you Enzio is innocent!"

Perry ignored him. "Deputy Marshal, Fasana, pull that

horse!" Perry repeated as the crowd of men cheered William on.

William remained still and switched the reins to his left hand to free his gun hand. "I'm not ready yet. I think we should wait for Matt."

Perry refused to be disobeyed. He yelled, "I said to lead the horse forward, now!"

With his left hand, William held the reins close to the bit to control the head better. His right hand drew his silver-plated revolver and pointed it at Perry. "I said we're waiting for Matt! He should be here soon."

"William, what are you doing?" Mark Duffy screamed, outraged. An outraged crowd quickly followed him. One man reached for his revolver to draw it from the holster.

"Don't!" William shouted as his gun turned to the man. "You're not that fast, Pal. The next person who tries that will be dead. We're waiting for Matt, like it or not!"

"Lead the horse!" A man hollered. He was a stoutly built middle-aged man with a balding head and unshaven face. His desperation to see the three men hang showed in his reddened cheeks and bulging eyes.

William shouted above the angry crowd, "I am not hanging these men until Matt agrees. If you want to draw your weapons and take your chances, go for it. But six of you will be dead before me. I promise you that! Then the rest of you might be dead, too, when Matt and Morton arrive. This isn't a gunfight you want."

Perry stepped closer to William and pointed a finger in his face. "I'm the city constable, and I'm telling you to get out of my way. We're hanging these killers right now!"

William pressed the barrel against Perry's stomach. "And I'm telling you, we're waiting."

No one in town knew William better than Mark Duffy.

He pushed his way through the crowd of angry men. "Get out of the way! I'll do it," Mark snapped. He was stopped by William's arm raising to aim the revolver at him at point-blank range. Mark stopped in his tracks. "You wouldn't."

William pulled the hammer back until it clicked and offered a slight shrug. "Do you want to find out?" His cold blue eyes left no doubt of his sincerity to pull the trigger.

"You don't live here!" a man shouted. It began a series of incomprehensible shouts and curses as they all shouted over each other.

Randy Paulson knew if the three men were hung, then the mystery of who caused the train wreck would be solved. He peeked in the livery stable's tack room and found a bullwhip tied to a saddle. He loosened and kept it coiled in his hand as he maneuvered through the hostile crowd to the front right side, where he had a direct angle to the horse's hind end.

"Oh, hell with it!" the angry red-faced man with bulging eyes shouted. He pulled his knife and stepped forward to stab Enzio. William's attention was drawn to the man with the knife, and he swung the gun toward the man. He was about to shout a warning when Mark reached across the saddle and grabbed William's wrist, forcing it upward. At the same time, Perry attacked William. William's gun fired, shooting into the hay loft floor, which spooked the horse, but he held tight to the reins as he fought to remain upright while Perry tried to wrestle him to the ground. The horse neighed and stepped to the side just as a loud crack of a bullwhip sounded across the horse's hindquarters.

The sting of the whip and loud crack startled the horse, and it lurched forward at a full run, ripping the reins out of William's hand, pulling him off balance, and causing him to fall to the ground with Perry on top of him. William accidentally fired his revolver into the base of the wall, traumatically scaring the horse more so.

Enzio was yanked off his feet by the panicking horse and slammed the back of his head against the beam while the rope tightened around his throat, crushing it until the narrow rope cut through his flesh like a knife through soft butter. The coarse rope cut through his neck, decapitating his head from his body as the slipknot was pulled through the pulley and fell to the ground on the other side of the beam. The horse ran out of the building into the city street, dragging a bloody rope behind it.

Enzio's body dropped to the ground with a heavy thud, pouring out blood onto the dirt floor like an overturned fountain. His head rolled to a stop a short distance away.

There was a stunned silence before the sound of a man vomiting and the loud cry of Tyee bellowing out Enzio's name. "I'll kill you all! I will kill all of you!" Tyee screamed and then dropped to his knees in sobs.

The sound of a few men gagging or puking grew louder while William sat on the ground, staring in horror at Enzio's head. He glanced up to see Randy rolling up the whip. "You…" William said, too stunned by the sudden unexpectedness and horror of what was before him to complete his sentence.

Randy ignored him. "Mark, go catch the horse or saddle a different one. We have two more to hang. I'll lead the horse this time."

Hearing Randy, Perry repeated to the crowd, "We have two more to hang. Catch that horse and bring it back. That one didn't go quite right, but Enzio's dead! We have two more murderers to hang."

William stood and holstered his revolver. "You decapitated him."

Perry spun around and yelled, "That's your fault! I told you to lead the horse forward and you refused. This mess never would have happened if you'd done what you were told. I'm the law here. This is my responsibility, not yours! Now get out of here! We have work to do. Go!"

"Get another rope. Let's hang a Crowe!" someone shouted.

"Randy, saddle a horse. Let's get this going."

"Hey, let's stick Enzio's head on a fence post," someone in the crowd laughed.

"Get out of my way!" Morton yelled as he forced his way through the men. He stopped and stared in horror at Enzio's decapitated body and head lying in a large puddle of blood in front of his cousins, who were being held.

Matt Bannister fired a shot in the air and shouted, "Get back! The first man that interferes, I will kill! All of you go home! No one is hanging anyone. Now Go!" He got his first look at the horror of the body lying there a few feet from the head. For a moment, he couldn't look away. "What in the hell happened?"

Clearly, a hanging had gone wrong, but beyond that, he had no idea what the circumstances were except it being an illegal lynching. Adrian and Tyee Crowe were horrified by what had happened to their cousin. Both brothers were covered with blood from being beaten with their hands secured behind their backs. Tyee had fallen to the ground, taking deep breaths to grasp what he had witnessed. Adrian stared at the body without any emotion except wrath.

Morton knelt to check on his two cousins and used his knife to cut their bound hands loose. Both brothers collapsed on the ground, physically and emotionally drained. Enraged by the treatment of his cousins, Morton glared at the men in the crowd that lingered. His wild and hardened green eyes penetrated the men dangerously as he shouted, "These men are my cousins. My family! Get out of here! All of you leave now before I do the same to you!" He turned his head toward William. "You should have stopped them, William!"

"I did!" He didn't like being yelled at.

"Yeah, it looks like it," Morton said spitefully. "I'm taking my cousins back to Enzio's. And him..." He pointed at Enzio's body. "He was innocent! He's got a family. Now I have to tell his wife and children what happened."

William raised his hands innocently and explained to Matt, "I tried to stop them, but I was attacked, and someone whipped the horse. It happened so quickly I couldn't stop it."

"Did you see who it was?"

"Yeah. It was that man named Randy. I was playing poker with him earlier. He's my buddy Mark's friend."

Morton watched the men leaving the livery stable. "Matt, I'm taking them back to Enzio's. I don't know what else to do other than start shooting people."

Matt had never seen Morton as upset. He nodded understandably. "We'll have Enzio's body taken to the funeral parlor. And Morton let his family know the constable's office is going to pay for his funeral. I'll see to it." Once Morton walked his cousins out of the livery stable, Matt asked, "Where did Perry disappear to?"

William looked around the livery stable that had cleared out substantially. "I don't know."

Ish Carnes answered, "They went to get a drink. I

suppose he didn't want to tangle with you and your deputy, Marshal."

"Well, tangle with me, he will. Does he expect you to dispose of the body and clean this up?"

Ish frowned. "I was wondering the same thing. Everyone ran out when you arrived."

———

THE DALLES CITY CONSTABLE, Perry Whitmore, was in Gable's Steel Cable Saloon with a large group of others complaining about their lynching being interrupted by lawmen who didn't belong to their community.

"You should have shot that blond-haired deputy marshal!" one man exclaimed of William. His frustration was evident in his voice. "We had them! We had the Crowe's!" he shouted.

"We could have had all three of them hung by the time the marshal and his deputy arrived."

"Did you know his deputy Morton Sperry was part of the Crowe family? No wonder they haven't found the robbers. He's probably in on it," Randy Paulson proposed. "I'll bet Marshal Bannister had it all planned out and hired that outlaw Sperry so they could partner up with the Crowe Brothers. Didn't Morton Sperry lead the Sperry-Helms Gang? I'm sure of it. Now we know why they protected the Crowe Brothers! Right? Think about it: Marshal Bannister and his deputies were in the last railcar, which was the safest. We should gun them all down and make our community safe again!"

Mark Duffy was perplexed. "I never expected William to save the murdering Crowes. I wouldn't expect that even if he wasn't a lawman."

Randy Paulson slammed his fist down on the table furiously. "They killed those people on the train and murdered the four boys for our money! We know they did it. Don't we, Perry?"

Perry Whitmore carried a mug of beer to the table and sat down. "I wish they'd all go back to wherever they came from. I'm really beginning to dislike Matt Bannister and his deputies."

"Speak of the devil," Mark said, looking toward the bat doors.

Matt Bannister stepped into the saloon with anger burning in his hardened eyes. He scanned the room from left to right like a predator seeking its prey. "Perry!" Matt yelled and walked quickly to the table Perry was sitting at.

Perry stood. "Matt, what do you—"

Matt swung a hard right fist that connected with Perry's jaw. The hard jolt of Matt's fist sent Perry downward into the edge of the table before he bounced off the table onto the floor. The other men stood surprised by the sudden attack. Matt kicked Perry in the ribs and then bent over to grab him and pull him back to his feet before slamming him down on the table, only to hit him in the face again and let Perry's weakened knees collapse underneath him as he slithered to the floor. Matt kicked him in the face one last time and then paused to look around the saloon with a wild look in his eyes.

Matt shouted angrily, "You don't accuse a man without evidence! And you sure as hell don't lynch a man without evidence of a crime! It wasn't the Crowe Brothers that blew up the trestle or killed your young men. You fools murdered an innocent man. And I will file a complaint with your local prosecutor and the governor about what happened tonight."

William held his revolver, watching for anyone who drew a weapon. He wished he had his other gun to fill his left hand, but the barrel was bent on the train when it was used as a pry bar to free Michael James.

An older balding man with a stout frame shouted angrily at Matt, "The Crowes aren't innocent of anything! They deserve to die. All you did was guarantee more folks are going to die. Those heathens will go on the warpath now! Roman Crowe murdered my family during the Snake War, and justice has never come. You ruined my chance to get even. I'll never forgive you for that!"

Matt stared at the man with fury in his eyes. "I don't need you to forgive me. I couldn't care less about that. Roman's sons did not kill your family, and the man you all murdered tonight wasn't a Crowe! If you want vengeance, take your cowardly ass and go get it! But you get the man who is responsible, not his family! You're a coward! If they had anything to do with the train or murders of those young men, I'd say hang him where they stand, but they didn't. They weren't around here. They were in Prairieville!"

"I beg to differ," Randy Paulson said. "I saw them riding by the Livengood Plantation, and Enzio was with them. They're murderers, and I say we go collect them and finish what we started right now. And, Marshal, there's more of us than there are of you. I'd go back to your hotel until sunrise and then leave town if I were you!"

"You're a liar. You didn't see them ride by the plantation."

"Are you calling me a liar?" Randy questioned.

Matt nodded. "I just did. They were in Prairieville, and there is proof of that. All I have to do is send a wire to the postmaster there, and he can verify that Tyee signed for and picked up the wire from Enzio a couple of days ago. So, if you want to make false allegations, that's fine, but it makes me wonder why."

Randy cursed Matt in his humiliation.

"Anyone else have any evidence they'd like to share that proves Enzio and the Crowe Brothers are guilty?" Matt shouted. When no response came, he said, "I thought not. You murdered an innocent man tonight." He kneeled and looked into Perry's dazed and swelling eyes. "And you are to blame. I'll do all I can to ensure that badge is taken away from you and you're prosecuted. From this day on, stay out of my way and far away from me."

"Bannister," Randy said to get Matt's attention. "We know who did it. And you let them escape. Or maybe you teamed up with them and are doing us all wrong."

Matt narrowed his eyes as he looked at Randy sitting at a table with his friends. "Why don't you investigate that possibility? Better yet, try to prove it."

William spoke, "Matt, that's Randy. The man who whipped the horse."

Matt's gaze stayed on Randy as a slight, cold smirk lifted his lips. Matt waved a pointed finger at him as he said, "You're Randy? I've heard a lot about you."

"What...what have you heard about me?" Randy didn't like the expression on Matt's face.

"Nothing good." Matt waved his finger but said nothing more. "Let's go, William."

CHAPTER SIXTEEN

"MORNING, MORTON," MATT SAID AS HE JOINED Morton at a table for breakfast. Morton appeared to be exhausted and wore an irritable expression. "How are you doing this morning?" It was Matt's first time seeing him since he left with Adrian and Tyee the night before.

Morton cast a glance at his friend and nodded silently. "Nothing will happen to any of them for Enzio's death, will it?"

Matt hesitated to answer carefully. "I hope so. And by them, you mean The Dalles City Constable Perry Whitmore, of course. He was the one in charge. If anyone can be held accountable, it would be him, and I'll file charges against Perry with the district attorney today and file a report with the governor's office. There's not much more that I can do than that."

"Shoot him," Morton suggested.

"Shoot Constable Whitmore?" Matt questioned. "That wouldn't make us much better than him, would it? But if it makes you feel any better, I did leave him bleeding on the saloon floor."

Morton looked at his friend and offered a slight hint of a smile. "I'm glad to hear that."

"Morton, all I can do is file complaints to the proper authorities, and coming from a US marshal, the complaint should be more persuasive than a regular citizen. But quite frankly, this is a tight-knit community where a few families run everything, and Perry Whitmore is part of that family. So, there is a pretty good chance that nothing will come from it. I'm sorry to say."

Morton shook his head slowly while he moved an egg around on his plate with a fork. "Who are we kidding? Enzio was an Indian and they don't matter. Nothing is going to come from it unless Uncle Roman and his boys make it right. Uncle Roman might even come to take care of Perry and Enzio's neighbor himself. I don't think they'll let this go."

"Do you really think this might get Roman Crowe on the warpath again? He's getting old."

Morton exhaled. "You don't know my uncle. Enzio was special to him because he is the only living son of Uncle Roman's deceased sister. My brothers and I are just nephews on Aunt Linda's side of the family. Enzio is Crowe blood. Uncle Roman may be getting older, but he's still dangerous. And if he does come here, Perry and Enzio's neighbor will disappear."

"Well, if they disappear, we'll know where to look for them, I guess. How did it go last night?" Matt asked.

Morton shook his head somberly. "Enzio's wife and children were devastated last night, Matt. I don't ever want to tell a woman that her husband is dead again. It broke my heart. Now they'll all have to go to the reservation because no one can provide for them. I don't know why I let you convince me to stay your deputy until the trial for Felix is over. It's over now, Matt. We're done. When we get back to Branson, I am turning my badge in for good."

Matt looked at the wedding ring on Morton's finger. Morton and Audrey had married just two days before going to Portland in a lovely wedding similar to Matt's and Christine's at the church. The reception was a small affair at Joel Fasana's house. For a wedding gift, Joel sold them his house for a very affordable price. Having a larger home was a blessing as they were raising three of Morton's nephews and a niece. In Morton's absence, the oldest nephew, Travis, was helping his aunt, Audrey, with the younger three. "Audrey will be glad to hear that, but I'm not," Matt said.

Morton offered a sad smile. "I know. I appreciate your friendship, Matt. I really do, but my family needs me at home, and I can't afford to make these weeklong trips. I just got married and spent two nights with my wife. I've spent my weeklong honeymoon with you and William. And what really irritates me is we have no idea how long we'll be here trying to find the men responsible. We haven't got a clue who did it," he said, heavily burdened. "You know, it's easier to be an outlaw than it is to be a lawman. When I ran the Sperry-Helms Gang, we were the aggressors. The only blood we saw was what we had caused.

"I swear, ever since I joined you and put this badge on my chest, my world has become nothing except tragedy, horror, and things I never want to see or experience again. All I see is evil, death, and torn-up bodies, which I didn't cause. Seeing it now is different. Trust me, I've seen more grotesque and wicked things since joining you than I ever saw when I was leading an outlaw gang of cold-blooded killers. Maybe I'm being punished by God, I don't know. What I do know is I am tired of the gore, evil, and the worst that humanity has to offer. Injustice rules and justice is never found. I can't take it anymore, Matt. And you know what else? I want to see my wife at night, not William."

Matt smiled, lightly humored. "I can understand that." The cook brought him a cup of coffee and a plate of eggs, hash browns, toast, and sausage. It was the hotel's breakfast plate. "Thank you," Matt said to the cook as he left their table.

Morton shrugged his shoulders, waiting. "You're not going to try to talk me into staying?"

Matt shook his head. "No. You have a family now. They need you at home. That's perfectly understandable. Just don't go back to leading an outlaw gang because I'd sure hate to track you down."

Morton smiled for the first time. "I don't think that's an option for me anymore. My wife would drop me like a rock."

"Glad to hear it. Morton, if that's what you need to do, then I do understand. No hard feelings. But I will tell you that I happen to know Tim Wright is not running for reelection as the Branson Sheriff next year, and if you want, I'll help you win it."

Morton thought for a moment. "That's a year away, but I'll talk to Audrey about it."

"It's only a year away. Maybe I can talk you into staying with us until then?"

Morton chuckled. "No. I'm turning my badge in as soon as we get home. And there is nothing you can say to change my mind. Last night was the final straw. I'm done. I never want to go through that again."

———

MATT RECEIVED an urgent request to join Marty Rook and the other railroad investigators for a meeting at the Crystal Sage Hotel. The Crystal Sage was on Second Street and reminded Matt of the Monarch Hotel his brother Lee owned in Branson, except the Crystal Sage was much brighter with white walls and cedar flooring. The chandeliers were large sparkling crystals that gave a diamond rainbow effect to the walls and floor around them. Matt was directed to a conference room where the investigators were joined by The Dalles City Constable Perry Whitmore and his brother-in-law, County Sheriff Cletus James. After a general greeting and invitation to get a cup of coffee and a pastry, Matt sat at a long table.

Marty Rook, the Railroad Incident Investigator in charge of the accident investigation, stood beside a blackboard mounted to the wall. "Thank you for coming, Marshal Bannister. Since day one, the good folks of this community knew who the guilty party was, and nothing was done about it. Do I need to remind you all that the Oregon Short Line is under tremendous pressure to arrest these criminals and ensure the public that there is no reason to fear this event happening again? Not excluding the damage to the trestle and the threat of lawsuits from the lives lost and injured.

"We need to make an arrest to show the state, the nation, and, for that matter, our investors that we are competent to do what we were hired to do. The public cares far more about arresting the guilty party and justice being paid for the tragedy they caused. This accident was a massacre, pure and simple. A devious intent to kill and harm as many innocent victims as possible. If you doubt that, go over to the wharf and stroll through all the bodies laid out for identification. This incident has already earned us some terrible press and promises a loss of stocks. In the public's view, we are not doing enough, and I agree with them!

"On day one, before the sun set on that day, everyone in this community knew without a shadow of a doubt who was responsible, and yet, we haven't made an arrest." He paused to take a drink of water. "Last night, Constable Whitmore arrested three members of the Crowe Brothers Gang for the tragedy at Gypsum Creek Canyon. But a passenger on the train who has invited himself into our investigation overrode the town constable and our most wanted criminals rode away as free men. May I ask why, Marshal Bannister, you thought it was in your authority to interfere with guns drawn to release the murderers responsible?" He stopped pacing and glared at Matt.

Matt quickly realized he was only invited to the meeting to be blamed and perhaps publicly shamed. He knew very well that Marty Rook did not like him and might try to use Matt's involvement as an excuse for their lack of satisfactory results.

Matt cleared his throat. He spoke evenly. "The Crowes didn't do it. They could not have because they were a three-day ride away from here back at home in Prairieville. Their cousin, Enzio Corrales, sent a wire the day of the accident, telling them my deputy, Morton Sperry, questioned him about that crime. It took Adrian and Tyee Crowe three long and hard days of riding to come here with the intent to confront Morton because they misunderstood and thought Morton was framing them for the train disaster.

"They may be cousins, but there has been bad blood between them since Morton started working with me. Adrian and Tyee Crowe had no interest in the train. They just didn't want to be blamed for a heinous crime that they didn't commit. Unfortunately, they were spotted, and Perry Whitmore was summoned, but he did not arrest them. Constable Whitmore decided a lynch mob would be better suited and made a show of it. Enzio Corrales was wrongfully taken and ended up decapitated before I arrived."

"According to Perry, Enzio was harboring the notorious killers who were wanted by the railroad," Marty replied.

"Have you not heard a word I said?" Matt questioned. "The Crowe Brothers are a dangerous gang, there is no doubt about that, but they are innocent of this crime. I'll speak slower so you understand. They...didn't...do...it."

Marty glared at Matt for a moment without saying a word. "Have you discovered who may...be...responsible?" he asked with the same sarcastic tone.

"No."

"You haven't? Well, neither have some of the best minds in the railroad's employment and local law sitting around this table. An amateur should not be able to outwit the experience and knowledge in this room, including yours and the local law officers. Unless you can name who else may be involved, we have no choice but to trust the locals who know more about the people in this area than we do. In fact, I'd say they know a lot more than we do, and they suspect the Crowe Brothers Gang. The general public wants us to take them dead or alive. We need to wrap this investigation up and make arrests or bring about their deaths, which is fine, too. We need to solve this crime and move on for the good of the railroad. Take it or leave it, that is up to you. I want the Crowe Brothers Gang arrested or dead. Either way will suffice for public approval."

Matt scoffed with disgust. "You better hope they're dead then because if the Crowe brothers go to trial, you'll be humiliated," Matt said pointedly. "I'll send Morton to talk to them today and take them to Portland to turn themselves in. You'll get immediate praise from the public, but then you'll look like the fool you are when your case is dismissed because they were a hundred miles away on that day. And I'll tell the papers that you cared more about public opinion than justice. Might I suggest you let your men and I work and you stay out of it?"

Marty's brow lifted. "Really, Matt? Well, I did not want to mention this. But there was an accusation that perhaps you are involved."

Matt laughed. "Really? May I ask by whom?"

"That doesn't matter. I swore to protect the individual's identity because he feared for his life—"

"I bet," Matt interrupted.

Marty Rook continued, "What matters are the coincidences that may add to the speculation about you, which might be worth investigating, too. You can consider yourself a suspect, Marshal."

Matt chuckled.

"That's ridiculous," Corbin Hazelton said plainly.

Matt cocked his head to the side and spoke with a grin. "Maybe you could stop speaking in riddles and tell me what you are talking about. If it concerns me, then I have a right to know. If I am being accused of having any part in this crime, then I also deserve to know who is accusing me."

"Yes, he does deserve to know," Corbin agreed.

Marty sighed, frustrated. "I do not know the man that accused you, nor will I say who told me of it. But you were in Portland for a week before the accident, and on the same train car as Amos Stafford, the very last rail car, which would suffer the least damage, and interestingly, your deputy is cousins with the Crowe Brothers Gang. That gives you access to them, but more concerningly, your deputy walked away with them after you let them go free. That doesn't look good. I'll remind you the public view will be the judge of this tragedy, *not* a court of law."

Matt shook his head. "I know who made the accusation because he said it last night. I think you're a fool if you put any faith into that. But go try to find the Crowe brothers if you want to. They are Roman Crowe's sons and know every crack and crevice of that country to hide in. You won't find them without Morton or me, and we won't help you. I'm telling you now, if you send these good men after them, few, if any, will come back alive. It would be stupid to do because the Crowe brothers are not the men responsible. I guarantee it. And it's the worst-case scenario for you because they can prove it.

"You're reaching for whatever you can to grab to make you look good, but some of us care about real justice, and between all of us here, we'll find the men who did this. And then you can shine as bright as the sun as far as I'm concerned. I don't need the credit; but truth and protecting the innocent from being strung up like rabid dogs, now *that* is something I do believe in. And that is precisely what happened last night.

"If you want the Crowe brothers so bad, send Constable Whitmore and his merry men from last night to bring them back. I assure you Adrian and Tyee would love to see him again. But in the end, it will come back on you because they were not around here when the trestle was blown." Matt stood. "If that's all you got and all you can say, then good luck. But as for me, I'm not a part of your investigation nor under your authority. Do what you have to do, but I'm intent on finding the guilty party. The public you worry about so much can wait, as far as I'm concerned. And one last thing, stay out of my way. Good day."

CHAPTER SEVENTEEN

ISAAC CHANDLER AND MARK DUFFY HAD FILLED two heavy freight wagons with extended eight-foot sideboards from one of the silos containing barley on the plantation. They drove the two wagons into town to deliver the product to the Stafford Milling Company.

After weighing the two wagons loaded to the brim with barley, Isaac and Mark stood back and watched as a pair of young men employed by the mill began shoveling the wheat into a hopper which led to another silo. Isaac noticed the barge usually tied to the Stafford Milling Company's private shipping pier had been moved and anchored several hundred feet downriver, and the largest passenger sternwheeler that ran the forty-mile section of the Middle Columbia River was moored to the pier. The large red and white sternwheeler was a work of beautiful craftsmanship but was usually seen coming and going from the riverboat terminal a mile upriver. The oddity of it made Isaac wonder why it was there.

Curious, Isaac asked one of the young men shoveling

the wheat. "Say, what's happening with the docks? Is the riverboat terminal having problems with theirs?"

The young man paused to wipe the dusty sweat from his brow. "No. Today is the day the boats brought all the families here to identify their dead family members from the train crash. You could hear a bunch of wailing and crying earlier. They're over there in the railroad's warehouse. Their little dock isn't big enough for the boats, so Mr. Stafford had them dock here. It's a shorter walk than if they docked at the terminal. Right over there is where they have the bodies," he said, pointing at a warehouse built on the shore next to the railroad's small pier.

A few hundred yards away was the portage railroad's station, maintenance shops, and turntable. By appearance, it was a maze of tracks, stationary rail cars, and buildings varying in size. A short pier reached a hundred feet from the bank for river deliveries. A medium-sized warehouse the railroad used for storage was built next to the dock. The warehouse had been emptied and cleaned for the day's purposes. Isaac could see a crowd outside the warehouse, loitering on the pier and milling in and out of the warehouse door. By their body language, Isaac could tell the people were mourning the loss of their loved ones as several held each other and wept.

Mark Duffy wrinkled his brow. "Weren't most burned? The fire was crazy."

The young man shrugged his shoulders. "I don't know how they are doing it. I just know they are. Go over and take a look if you want."

Mark tilted his head, curious. "I think I will. Come on, Isaac."

"I...I don't think I want to," Isaac said with a burdensome weight filling his chest.

"Oh, it's not like you know any of them. Come with me," Mark pressed.

"You might," the young man offered. "Amos Stafford's wife died in that wreck, and other people from here. She's not over there, though. That's where the unclaimed bodies are."

Mark and Isaac walked along the waterfront to the warehouse and quietly strolled through the mourning families. The warehouse had been emptied and swept clean before being filled with over fifty closed pine caskets ranging in size from toddler to adult. A small stand stood at the head of each casket with burned jewelry, buttons, pocketknives, watches, or whatever else could be used to identify the body. When the personal belongings were identified, the person's name and hometown were written on the casket to be shipped by river, rail, or wagon.

It took a few days to collect the bodies and carefully search around each one for anything that might help identify the person. The railroad organized travel arrangements to The Dalles City from the west with a sternwheeler reserved for families of the accident victims. That sternwheeler left Portland and came up the Lower Columbia River to the Cascade Rapids, a long series of thundering rapids that the sternwheelers could not cross. The passengers and baggage were transferred to a portage rail for the six-mile journey around the rapids and then loaded onto the largest sternwheeler the Middle Columbia had to offer for the remainder of the trip to The Dalles City.

Families from the east of The Dalles City came on a sternwheeler down the Upper Columbia River to just above the magnificent Cielo Falls, where they were transferred onto a portage rail for the twelve-mile journey to The Dalles City.

Organizing the families of the passengers to identify the deceased and meet with the injured who were still in The Dalles was a challenge that took a couple of days to organize. There was an urgency to return the injured and deceased to their families. The burned bodies were not complete enough to embalm, and adding to the deterioration process was the eighty-degree weather. The smell of decomposing bodies was strong, even though the bodies were doused with lime to keep the odor limited.

There were railroad officials, attorneys, priests, and reverends to help meet with families from different locations and of various financial statuses, from wealthy to poor. The local mortician asked for help from other morticians in Portland and other towns to help prepare, comfort, and organize funeral or travel arrangements for the families. The warehouse was full of people there to identify their loved ones, but there were also people from town whose curiosity got the better of them and came to watch. There was no active effort to separate the two.

Isaac had heard how many deaths had occurred, but seeing the caskets lined up in rows one after the other and seeing the weeping families and the sound of their brokenness brought the reality of it to life. No longer was Isaac drinking his guilty conscience away with friends far from the dead and the safety of the Livengood Plantation. He never had to face the horrors of digging through the ashes for a wedding ring on a charred bone or sifting the ashes for a button or shoe buckle found under a child's unrecognizable body. But now Isaac could see fifty-eight coffins, minus Mrs. Stafford's, in front of him. He could see the personal remains of jewelry, buttons, shoe buckles, hair pins, broaches, and even a partly burned child's doll that had once belonged to living human beings just days before.

They all died because of a squirrel getting the fuse caught on its feet. It was a good excuse, but the fact remained: Isaac wasn't fast enough to light the fuse in time for the train to stop. The weight of it being his fault hit him deep enough that he couldn't breathe from the tightness in his chest.

"Twinkle, twinkle...little star...how I wonder...what...you...are..." A man tried to sing but began a guttural sobbing while he rocked back and forth in a chair, holding a deceased baby in his arms. The child had been embalmed and looked as though it was sleeping peacefully. An opened casket was beside him that already had Jacob Pihl's name written on it. Beside the infant coffin was an adult coffin with Margaret Pihl's name on it. The man's broken cries, mixed with an attempt to sing to his baby son, touched Isaac's heart. He gazed at the collection of pine coffins and tables of personal belongings and the painful tears in the sorrowful faces of the people around him. His chest tightened more, compressing his lungs as he found it harder to breathe. Isaac walked quickly out of the warehouse and turned the corner to brace himself against the building with one hand while he bent over slightly to focus on his breathing. He took a deep breath and followed it with another.

A middle-aged father walked by him with his arms around his ten-year-old daughter, who clenched tightly onto a silver necklace as she cried bitterly at the loss of seeing her mother's belongings. The father carried a small box filled with the other personal effects.

Isaac's lip trembled as his eyes warmed with burning tears that clouded his vision. He wiped his eyes, refusing to break down in tears. He leaned back against the building, looking skyward, repeatedly blinking to force the tears away as a wave of deep emotion hit him like a landslide, burying him in guilt and shame. He took another deep breath and looked toward the pier to see, to his surprise, Matt Bannister watching him. Matt's expression wasn't one of compassion or empathy but of a predator studying him.

Isaac quickly walked back toward Stafford's Milling Company.

———

MATT HAD BEEN WAITING and watching through the families' heartbreaking pain since the boats and train arrived. He wasn't sure what he was waiting for, but he watched each person come and go. He watched Isaac and Mark enter the warehouse and noticed Isaac's hesitation and how upset he was when he exited. He studied Isaac's body language and watched Isaac walk away, glancing back at Matt like a frightened dog, making sure it wasn't being followed. Matt's attention shifted back to the warehouse door to see Mark Duffy gazing at him, then at Issac and then back to Matt. Matt gave a short nod to let Mark know he had noticed.

Matt watched Mark leave the warehouse, casting a quick, nervous glance back toward him, but it differed from what Isaac gave. Isaac's expression was filled with panic, but Mark was concerned.

Matt walked into the warehouse and noticed the man holding the child immediately. He knew exactly who the man was and approached him slowly, offering a compassionate small smile to anyone who made eye contact with him.

"Mr. Joe Pihl?" Matt asked the inconsolable man. He kneeled. "I'm Matt Bannister."

Joe Pihl wiped his face with his forearm and reached a handout to shake Matt's. His eyes were reddened and watery. "Thank you for your wire. Thank you."

Matt had sent a wire to Joe notifying him that Matt had identified Margaret's body and had little Jacob embalmed. "You're welcome. My deepest condolences to you."

Joe nodded with a sniffle. "You were with them on the train?"

Matt spoke gently. "They were in a different train car, but I met your wife. She couldn't be saved, unfortunately. I'm sorry. Margaret asked me to tell you that she was sorry that she couldn't save your son and that she loved you."

Joe nodded with understanding as his face crumpled into quiet but deeply felt sobbing. "I loved her so much," he gasped. "Oh, Lord. I loved her so much."

Matt remained quiet and put an empathetic hand on the man's shoulder.

After a moment, Joe got himself under control and asked through a sniffle, "How much do I owe you?"

Matt shook his head slowly and answered, "You don't owe me anything."

Joe held baby Jacob close to his chest and sobbed.

Matt patted his shoulder. "If you ever get to Branson, look me up. Again, I am sorry. Take care, Mr. Pihl."

———

"OH, HELL WITH THAT!" Mark said sharply. He and Isaac had stopped short of the granary mill along the river's bank to talk privately. "Isaac, that could have happened to anyone, well, almost anyone. You should have shot the squirrel and been done with it. What's done is done. You can't let seeing those dead folks bother you so much."

Isaac rolled his eyes. "Mark, you were on the hill. It was my job to blow up the trestle, and I screwed up. I killed all those people. Men, women, and children. Even that baby." He clenched his jaw and ran his top lip over his teeth as he inhaled heavily through his nose. "I killed those children."

"For crying out loud, Isaac, a critter messed it up, not you. That's not your fault. You can't blame yourself. It worked out, okay? We didn't get what we wanted, but we're getting away with it. Consider that our lucky share and sparing our lives is more profitable than any amount of money. How it happened doesn't matter anymore. What's done is done. You need to put it behind you and go on living."

"That's easier said than done. I only agreed to do that so I could quit the plantation and buy a farm somewhere. No one was supposed to get hurt!"

Mark was losing patience. "What are you going to do, Isaac? Stay here and mope about the graveyard weeping? What's done is done. Get over it!"

"I just wanted to buy a farm of my own, Mark. I will never do anything like this again. Next time, you all can count me out."

"Hush! Here comes the marshal, Matt Bannister. I knew he was watching you. Damn it, Isaac!" Mark quietly exclaimed. He watched Matt approach and said, "Marshal Bannister, what a horrific thing over there. I've never seen anything so sad."

Matt nodded as his eyes searched the two men. "It is indeed. The men responsible for all those deaths probably won't sleep very well for the rest of their lives. I pray not, anyway. A man's conscience has a way of getting to him no matter how hardened he is over time. It's a sorry way to live a life if you ask me. All those women and children. I'm glad it's not me that has to carry that weight."

"Marshal, it almost sounds like you think we might have something to do with it," Mark said with annoyance.

"No. No. I just noticed we all came out of there feeling the same way, or it seemed to me. I had a meeting this morning with the head investigator of the train wreck. It seems we're narrowing in on those responsible. I suspect we'll start making arrests soon enough."

Isaac's eyes widened momentarily. His breathing grew a bit heavier and his hands began to sweat. He wiped them on his pants, but he didn't say anything.

Mark plugged one nostril and blew out a line of snot onto the ground. He blew the other nostril and then sniffed. "Constable Whitmore had them caught last night until you let them go. At least one is dead. It seems a bit redundant to arrest them again."

Matt wrinkled his nose. "They didn't do it. It would be impossible for them to have. No. The people we are looking for are locals. They know the territory and a bit about hiding tracks. If you two know of any group of friends of six or so that we should be looking at, let me know."

"I'll do that," Mark said. He swallowed forcefully.

"Oh, one more thing," Matt said. "Why is your friend Randy so insistent to blame anyone for that crime? He claimed to have witnessed the Crowe Brothers ride past the Livengood Plantation that day, but it is effortless to prove that they were a hundred miles away and that Enzio was at work. So, what Randy said sounds a lot like a lie to me. He even accused me of being involved. Do you gentlemen have any idea why Randy would do that?"

"No," Mark said while taking a deep breath. "He was drunk."

Matt raised his brow to consider that answer. "That always sounds like a pretty good excuse, but it's not. I think there is more to it than that. Let Randy know I'm not as gullible as Constable Whitmore. It sounds to me like Randy's trying to cover his trail by hanging someone else. That's what I see. And truth be known, that could implicate you two as his friends. My advice is if that's so, and you were involved, you'd be better off letting me know and turning yourself in before anyone else does. That old saying, the early bird gets the worm, is especially true here. It could save your life. If you're not involved, you have nothing to worry about. But if so, well, you better hope no one talks to me before you do. I can be found at the Amber Light Hotel if or when you're ready to talk."

CHAPTER EIGHTEEN

MARK DUFFY FOUND STAN MELDRUM INSIDE THE mill and told him about Matt Bannister following him and Isaac from the warehouse and what was said. Stan was aggravated and told Mark to go back to the plantation and bring everyone involved in the robbery to his home at two o'clock for an impromptu meeting of great urgency. He would find a reason to leave work, but Leon Goodrich would have to stay and finish his shift.

Rickson Emrick, Randy Paulson, Dave Ruddick, Isaac Chandler, and Mark Duffy arrived at Stan's small home just outside of the city limits. It was just after two in the afternoon.

Rickson was irritated and the first to speak as he entered. "What's this all about? I just told you yesterday that my father was considering changing his will if I don't change my ways. We agreed I'd be the perfect son until this investigation is over. How do you think it will appear if he finds out I brought all the fellas into town during the middle of the workday? He's going to assume it's to get drunk. That's not a good start, Stan!"

Stan took a deep breath and held up a hand, patiently allowing Rickson to vent. "I know, Rickson. Okay? I know. But it cannot be helped and I'll tell you why later. But right now, we have an issue with him!" He pointed at Randy Paulson.

"Me?" Randy questioned, stunned.

"Yes, you!" Stan's voice turned harsh. "What in the world were you thinking about? Do you think we are higher than the law, Randy?"

Randy was quickly on the defensive. "No! But before you start raising your voice at me, you had better tell me what you are talking about?"

"Why on God's green earth would you dare to open your mouth and say a single word?" Stan cursed angrily. "Are you stupid, Randy? I told you fellas to keep your mouths shut! Not a word. Did you really say to Matt Bannister that you witnessed the Crowe Brothers riding by the plantation the day of the accident? They were nowhere around here!" he screamed, throwing his glass against the wall. The glass shattered and spread across the floor. "But that wasn't enough. You accused the marshal of the crime? He was a passenger on the train! You are the stupidest man I know! For crying out loud, Randy! How dumb are you?"

Mark offered softly, "He's not the dumbest. Apparently, Perry believed him."

"Shut up, Mark!" Stan snapped. "I want all of you to listen to me so closely that I never have to repeat it. Keep your mouths shut! You don't accuse anyone. You don't hint to anyone. You don't support that it is anyone. You do your jobs and keep your mouths shut. Are we clear? Because if one of us talks too much or messes up, we all hang! That's how serious this is."

Randy had been a bit intoxicated and let his tongue get the better of him. He lowered his head, knowing he had messed up. "I know. I can fix it, though. I can talk to Matt and tell him I lied and apologize for accusing him. It was just stupid talk. I'll do that tonight and smooth it over."

"Good. You do that," Stan said. He looked at Isaac Chandler. "None of us wanted anyone to get hurt in this robbery. What happened is tragic, but it happened. We have two choices on how we can handle that. We can let it haunt us until we break down and go crazy, which will only lead us all to the gallows eventually. Or we can choose to realize it was a rodent's fault and not anyone one of ours. We have to put this tragedy behind us and keep focusing on what's important: our jobs, family if you got it, and the future. We can't change the past because it's in the *past*. Sitting around and crying about it won't do us any good. It doesn't have to control your future, but it will if you keep looking back. Isn't that right, Isaac?" His annoyance was heard in his voice.

Isaac lowered his head and mumbled, "Yes."

Stan leaned forward and shouted, "Then lift your head and look me in the eyes! No more mumbling or feeling sorry for yourself. It wasn't your fault! It could have happened to any of us. So put it behind you, Isaac. If you can do that, we will be in good shape, and we'll all live happily ever after. Can you put it behind you?"

Isaac nodded. "Yeah."

"Good." He patted the big man's shoulder. "You're a good man, Isaac. You did nothing wrong, it was just bad luck. And if you want to know the truth, we should have fired that light the fuse shot sooner. It's not all your fault, big man."

Isaac's head raised with the admission of their error. "You mean it's not all my fault?"

Stan shook his head as he got a new glass and poured himself a drink. "We all share some of the guilt. Listen, everyone. Now that we are on the same page. Let's forget about what happened and just live our lives as normally as possible. Our concern needs to be keeping the law from suspecting any of us. Our answer should always be we know nothing about it. We have no answers because we know nothing about it, period. Randy, it would be best if you spoke with the marshal and told him you have a grievance against the Crowes. Say they stole your woman or kicked your horse or something. But don't say something stupid like they married your ex because the marshal's deputy is their cousin. It won't be hard for him to figure out another lie. Keep it simple, reasonable, and believable."

Randy asked, "And what about me accusing Matt? He'll wonder why I did that."

"Well, why did you?" Stan asked irritably.

"I was hoping he'd be arrested."

Stan chuckled to himself. "Randy, don't think anymore. Just tell him you were angry about him saving the Crowes. Okay, gentlemen, get back to work. Randy, you stay. I'm not through with you, we're going to talk. Rickson, you can stay too. You other fellas, we'll be a while, so get back to the plantation and cover for Randy and Rickson."

"Rickson and Stan, I apologize for saying what I did," Randy said after the others left the house.

"Hush. We can handle that." Stan lifted the curtain to peek outside to see if the others had left the property or were loitering outside the house. When he watched them all ride away, he turned to his friends. "Mark said Isaac is breaking. The weight of seeing those dead folks shook Isaac up. The marshal noticed it, followed them to the mill, and dangled bait out there for them to talk first to save their life. Isaac will squeal like a kicked pig soon if we don't all do our part to keep him on the straight and narrow. So watch him and keep him on the plantation until this all blows over."

———

THE COLUMBIA RIVER was nearly a mile wide in some places as it flowed west toward the Columbia Gorge. The river narrowed at a horseshoe bend to a mere hundred and forty feet before plunging over a twenty-foot waterfall that echoed down the gorge for miles in a torrent of whitewater before shooting through a maze of narrow chutes of deep water contained by black basalt walls that refused to erode after thousands of years of the swirling and raging current.

The Columbia River dropped eighty feet in half a mile, creating dangerous rapids of white water that sped wildly between small islands of basalt that could carry a man away and pull him underwater quicker than any hope of help could provide. Where the raging chutes of water collided together, large whirlpools threatened to suck anyone unlucky enough to fall in to a watery grave. The swells of the river's rapids could be larger than a man and had sunk many pioneers' rafts while trying to float their wagons downriver to The Dalles City.

The horseshoe bend and falls began a twelve-mile series of sporadic rapids and falls known as the *upper cascades* that made the area the perfect place to catch spawning salmon in the narrow passages of raging water. The ferocity and swirling of the chaotic water made it hard for the salmon to see the spears, hooks, and dip nets the natives along the Columbia River had used for thousands of years to harvest the salmon.

In 1805, Lewis and Clark canoed down the Columbia River Gorge, surrounded by high basalt walls on both sides covered with thin soil and brown grass dotted with sagebrush, protruding boulders, and sheer rock faces. As they flowed down the river, they came to a horseshoe bend that narrowed the river and plunged over the waterfall into thundering channels of wild whitewater that was the first of a series of rapids over the next twelve miles that cut chutes through basalt islands called collectively as the narrows.

Three miles below the falls were the short narrows, a mile-long series of thundering rapids. A few miles further were the long narrows, where the river dropped fifty feet over two miles, creating rapids so fierce and powerful that it was a magnificent display of nature's wonder.

Twelve miles downriver, Lewis and Clark came upon the only large basin they had encountered in the gorge. It was a large area of flat ground several miles in length and width on the river's bank surrounded by high basalt hills. To their amazement, they discovered an estimated ten thousand natives from the local Wasco and Wishram tribes and many other tribes from all around the Pacific Northwest and beyond who had assembled to trade, play games, and gamble.

The spawning salmon coming up the Columbia River were plentiful. Salmon made up a vital part of the trade for beads, furs, horses and other goods for generations. The tribes along the Columbia River had mastered the art of catching salmon all along the twelve-mile section of narrows by spear, hook, and dip net. It was the abundance of salmon and other foods that brought the thousands of natives from hundreds of miles away to the Columbia River to trade for as long as there have been human beings on the American Continent.

That basin of fine land with such historical significance along the Columbia River, where Indians came from all over the Pacific Northwest and beyond to trade, had been settled by the White man and became a prominent stop along the Oregon Trail—named after the French word for a series of narrow channels and chutes of rapids, *dalles*, the name stuck and The Dalles City or also known as Dalles City was founded.

In 1855, a treaty was signed where the local Indians throughout the area were moved to a reservation to the south, away from the Columbia River. However, the local natives were reserved the right to remain and fish on their ancient fishing grounds along the falls, chutes, and narrows.

In recent years, white settlers saw the potential for profit, and salmon canneries were built up and down the Columbia River. Two canneries near The Dalles City had prospered significantly by using water-powered fish wheels in the narrow channels of the river with buckets that would scoop through the rushing water, plucking the fish out of the depths and dropping them into a chute that led to a box, which was quickly replaced when full and taken to the cannery to be processed.

Chinese and White laborers did much of the work, leaving the natives to their traditional ways of fishing, using spears, hooks, and dip nets from the banks or wooden platforms built over the dangerous waters. The animosity between the Indians fishing traditional waters the traditional way and the invasion of white settlers with their canneries, fish wheels, gill, and seine nets pulled in by horses for more significant numbers of salmon to process in the canneries was reminiscent of the bison being massacred for the price of their hides.

The cannery owners claimed areas as their own and forbade the Indian population from fishing there, and any Indian caught fishing in the area claimed by the canneries were likely to be run off, if not shot and killed for stealing fish. Twenty-five fish wheels were turning along the narrow channels along the chutes of water from The Dalles City narrows and downriver along the Cascade Rapids.

The natives knew they would be prosecuted to the fullest strength of the law if they killed a White man for fishing in their area, but once in a while, a White man would be found floating in the calmer waters near The Dalles City. There was no decerning if he had fallen in accidentally and was slammed against the rock walls or had been beaten to death and thrown in for fishing in the Indian's fishing grounds.

Emory Blalock founded the Blalock Cannery, the largest of the two in The Dalles City. He gave an ongoing invitation to his friends to use the Blalock fishing grounds whenever they wanted to, providing they did not harm the fish wheels or take from the bins of caught fish. The Blalocks kept dip nets, long gaff hooks, or a throw net under their office porch for those friends to use at their leisure if they stayed upriver from the fish wheels.

The cannery was just east of the city, set back away from the river a reasonable distance to keep it safe from the spring floods. The wheelmen set the fish wheels and watched the catch boxes or bins while the skinners drove wagons back and forth to transfer the bins to and from the cannery. Both started work earlier than the production crew and got off work earlier while the cannery's production crew finished canning the day's catch. It was after four o'clock, and like the grist mill's water wheel, the fish wheels could be lifted out of the water and stopped for the night when the wheelmen and skinners went home.

Rickson Emrick didn't have the patience to sit by a slow-moving creek with a pole and wait for a fish to nibble at his bait like his father enjoyed doing for trout. Rickson liked the excitement, wildness, and daring of catching salmon with a dip net. It was challenging and almost immediate during the summer salmon runs as the heavy fish migrated up the Columbia to spawn. A man could catch six or seven salmon an hour if he wanted to, as long their arms and back held out trying to lift the fifty-to-seventy-pound beasts out of the river with a twelve-foot-long pole.

The salmon weighed anywhere from thirty to over a hundred pounds. Keeping one's balance on the rough, uneven basalt rock while lifting a wiggling and struggling wild salmon out of the water and onto the shore was more challenging than a man watching might think. It was one thing, perhaps the only thing Rickson respected the Indians for. They made it look easy and flawless.

Randy Paulson walked past the last fishwheel and beyond where they usually dipped for fish.

"We're not stopping here?" Isaac asked, waving toward the frothing white water as it sped through a nine-foot-wide channel six feet below them. Stretching across the river were islands of bare black basalt rock, rough and uneven, with various chutes of raging water spitting out a consistent spray of fine mist that reflected rainbows in the sun. The roar of the river was loud and intimidating, but even miles away, the roar of the waterfall echoing down the gorge could be heard.

Randy responded, "No. I thought we'd go upriver a ways. We've never fished upstream. Phil, the cannery supervisor, told me it's better fishing."

The four men, Randy, Dave, Rickson, and Isaac, had tied their horses at the cannery office, collected two dip nets, and walked to the river. They followed the frothing water for nearly half a mile before it joined a more considerable rapid in a collision of forces that created a series of whirlpools before breaking up in a series of chutes racing through the basalt islands.

The men separated into two teams, each team with a dip net: a long twelve-foot pole with a three-foot-wide metal circle with a three-foot-deep net attached. Randy handed a net to Rickson while Dave and Isaac took another net up the river.

Rickson placed the net into the swirling pool of deep water and let the current push it downstream in an arc as he pulled the net out of the water. He could tell by the weight that he hadn't caught anything. He did it again and again before he strained to pull the net out of the water with a large sixty-pound Chinook salmon wiggling to break free inside the net. Rickson heaved the net toward the bank, where Randy caught it and assisted Rickson in moving the net over the rock. Randy used a wooden club stored with the nets to hit the salmon's head and kill it while still inside the net so as not to risk it flopping back into the river.

Upriver, Dave pulled a salmon of about the same size out of the water after several empty tries. Isaac caught the net and clubbed the fish with a hard whack. They continued to sweep the nets through the water, and within an hour, they caught five salmon, which was plenty for their salmon feed that night. Randy took hold of the net as he and Rickson decided to call it a day.

Randy and Rickson left their catch on the rock bank and approached the other two men who were still fishing. Dave was using the net while Isaac waited to catch it.

Rickson pointed across the river and asked excitedly, "Look at the size of that bear! Is that a grizzly?"

"Where?" Isaac questioned as he raised his hand over his brow to block the sun's light from interfering with his eyes.

"Over there by that bush. I swear that's a grizzly." Rickson pointed his finger with urgency. "Right there! If I had my rifle, I'd have a new rug!"

"I see it!" Dave exclaimed, pulling the empty net out of the water.

While Isaac's attention was across the river, Dave lifted his net and dropped it over Isaac's head and shoulders. Rickson immediately pulled the rim down over Isaac's arms, confining his broad shoulders and arms inside the net.

"Hey!" Isaac laughed. "You caught a fat one," he joked.

Dave pushed him forward with the pole toward the edge of the bank, quickly being helped by Rickson and Randy. Isaac could not swim and was afraid of falling into the frothing water. Isaac put up a hard-fought fight, but with three men pushing him, he drew closer to the edge and cried out in terror as he fell eight feet into the swirling water with a splash. Dave pushed the pole downward, joined by Rickson and Randy to try to hold the caught man down at the bottom. They struggled to hold Isaac there while the force of the water pushed against his body.

Suddenly, the weight of the net lightened significantly as Isaac broke free of the net. He surfaced and gasped for a breath while reaching an arm skyward for help. His body swirled in a circle of a large whirlpool. He cried out again with only his face above the water, and then he was gone, sucked down into the river in the center where the forces of the two chutes collided together. Two minutes later, Isaac's body surfaced facedown fifty yards downstream in the center rapids. His body hit a rock and twisted around it while floating downriver, riding the swells like a lifeless bobber bouncing up and down with the water's wild flow.

"It looks like he learned to swim," Rickson said. He put his hands to his mouth and hollered, "Hey, you're supposed to spawn upriver!" He laughed.

Randy glanced up and down the riverbank and didn't see anyone else who would witness their treachery. Randy liked Isaac, but friendship only goes so deep before the risk of losing his freedom to a hangman's noose becomes more important. Randy could feel a mean streak, colder than an iron bar in December, fill him as he watched Isaac's body bounce against another rock before continuing downriver.

Dave turned around and lowered the net while shaking his head, not finding Rickson's humor funny. A glance at the brushline along the rocky bank sent a chill down his spine when he saw a man wearing an orange shirt forty yards away watching them. It was an Indian man in his thirties or forties holding a long dip net in one hand and a wadded-up net in his other. Dave's eyes widened with alarm. He immediately tried to pull his revolver, but he had neglected to unsnap the leather flap that held it in the holster. He unsnapped the cover and jerked his revolver out of the holster. He pointed the gun without aiming and fired his double-action Smith and Wesson .38 caliber too quickly to hit his target. The Indian man had dropped his nets and ran along the brush that lined the river's bed.

"Indian!" Dave exclaimed and pulled the trigger as fast as he could toward the fleeing man, who was as nimble as a deer across an open area before disappearing behind the green leaves of the vegetation that lined the edge of the river. There wasn't a lot of brush, but just enough to create a green line along the riverbank before the high hills of dry bunch grass, sagebrush with sporadic rocks that rose high above the gorge.

Randy grabbed Dave's wrist and forced the revolver downward. "Stop shooting! Don't draw more attention than we need. Let's go!" He began running across the uneven rock toward the opening the man had crossed. Dave and Rickson followed him. They found the trail, which was nothing more than a thicker layer of soil on top of the basalt that had fallen from the hills above and pushed aside by the water current to create soil deep enough to support the foliage that grew. As they ran along the trail, getting glimpses of the man's orange shirt while following the flat impression of moccasin tracks in the dust, Randy wished he could get a clear shot at the man running much quicker than them.

As suddenly as the vegetation could appear thick and green, it could vanish into an open area of barely an inch of soil where the brown grass and sagebrush grew sporadically, with the rock breaking through the soil in between. They had run a good distance when they entered a stretch of open ground where the mountain turned to stone, leaving bare rock to cross. The stretch of barren, uneven, and sharp rock without a clump of grass was perhaps a hundred yards long before the first sign of brown vegetation could be seen in the distance.

As they ran into the barren bank of the river, Randy heard Dave fall behind him and curse bitterly. Randy slowed to glance back to see Dave on his knees while holding his palm upward. His palm had been torn open by landing on basalt, leaving a painful cut that bled heavily. Randy turned, looking for the Indian's orange shirt, but he had disappeared in a matter of seconds.

Dave got back to his feet. "Where'd he go?" Dave asked, determined to find the witness of their crime. He was sweating heavily and wiped his brow while breathing hard.

Out of breath and with a cramp forming in his side, Rickson slowed to a stop and bent over to catch his breath as he caught up with his friends.

Randy tried to catch his breath as his gaze scanned the barren rock. Sweat poured down Randy's face from the distance they had run. "He has to be around here hiding," Randy said through his heavy breaths. "He wasn't that far ahead of us. Shoot him if you see him."

The three men separated to search the barren landscape in the hope of finding the Indian man hiding behind a rock or in a shallow crack of the jagged river's bank. Rickson walked along the river's edge and noticed a narrow slit of an opening along the river's bank about four feet wide and twenty feet long that stretched back from the river's fury. Rickson knew instinctively that it was the only place in the immediate area that the man could have climbed down into to hide. Rickson didn't have a weapon on him and wasn't sure if the man they were looking for did or not.

Rickson smiled, knowing he had found what they were looking for. He whistled above the sound of the river's churning water and waved the two men over. "Over here," he shouted. He pointed repeatedly downward to point out the aperture in the ground.

Randy and Dave hurried over and had their revolvers ready when they peered down into the eight-foot-deep crevice with about a foot of water inside. There was no trace of the man.

"Where did he go?" Randy questioned.

Dave searched the surrounding area carefully. There was nothing to see. "He wasn't that fast, was he? Could he have made it to that brush line without us seeing him?"

Randy shook his head. "No way. He must be around here. Let's keep looking."

"Did he jump into the river?" Rickson questioned with a gaze at the torrent of the rapids that no one in their right mind would dare to enter.

"He would if he had no choice, and he didn't," Randy said, stepping to the bank's edge to peer down eight feet below at the churning white water that sped by dangerously. "If he did, he's as good as dead."

"Dave, would you recognize him if you saw him again?" Rickson asked.

Dave nodded slowly. "I think so. He was just an Indian with an orange shirt and a red patch on his knee. I saw that."

"He had long hair. I know that much," Randy added.

Rickson scanned the river's raging water and banks. "Chances are he'll mind his business if he does survive the river. He must have jumped in. Well, let's get our fish and go home. Maybe someone will find that jackrabbit floating beside Isaac. Isaac will find him for us."

"Speaking of," Dave was not humored, "do we have an answer for why Isaac drowned?"

Randy shrugged his shoulders. "He went fishing."

"I know that, but maybe we should think ahead and tell folks so they can look for him."

"Of course. Just say we went fishing and he fell in. He couldn't swim, we all know that. Remember to act upset and cry if you can," Rickson suggested. "One thing is for sure, he won't say a word to anyone now. Well, it was a fair trade, a fat man and an Indian for five salmon. The river gods should be happy. Let's get our fish and go home."

CHAPTER NINETEEN

"THEY'RE FARMERS, NOT KILLERS OR ROBBERS," Cletus James said with a hint of agitation. "The only reason they carry sidearms is for rattlesnakes, badgers, and other critters. I don't believe for a moment that the fellas from the Livengood Plantation can be involved in the train robbery. I know you are a seasoned marshal, and there is no doubt you've earned the right to speak your opinion, but I think you're wrong, Marshal Bannister. Just because Issac left the warehouse used for the dead upset doesn't mean he was involved. That was upsetting for everybody, including me. I hope no one in our community left there feeling good about it."

"I'd hope not too. I know they are your friends, but that's who I suspect at this point. I just wanted to stop by and get your opinion. I have lost all respect for Constable Whitmore, and I won't be working with him again," Matt said. He had stopped by the county sheriff's home to speak with him privately about his suspicions. They were talking on the front porch, with the smell of turkey and homemade noodles boiling on the stove, which made Matt's stomach growl.

Cletus frowned. "Perry is my brother-in-law, so I have to stand by him."

"Well, I can't understand why when he's in the wrong," Matt said. "I can't tolerate his urgency to accuse and condemn on a whim. That's not how the law works, and he clearly wants to hang folks and be the hero, no matter how absurd the accusations may be. You might want to try to restrain him before he murders more innocent men."

"I'll do my best. As you know, my authority only goes so far."

"You're his family. He might listen to you."

Cletus's wife, Molly, asked, "Have you spoken with the Pinkertons about Isaac and the others?"

Matt shook his head. "Corbin was a Pinkerton Detective, but now he works for the railroad. The others with him are just street toughs who got a better job. They are doing their own investigation, and the last I heard this morning, they hadn't discovered anything substantial. Well, I'm sorry to disrupt your dinner, it smells delicious," he told Molly. "I think I'll stroll through the saloons and listen to what is being said."

"If Isaac and the boys show up there, don't accuse them without some evidence."

Matt smiled. "I won't accuse them until I have proof that they did it. Right now, I don't have anything except a gut suspicion."

"I personally have suspicions about the Darnell family or Hatch brothers. Maybe they even teamed up, I don't know. They deny it, of course."

"Cletus, let me ask you. If it was you last night, would

you have done the same as Perry or arrested those three men pending a trial? Be honest, please."

"I would have arrested them if I could. That's what Perry should have done. We all know Enzio is related to the Crowes, but that doesn't make him a criminal. I think Perry is just angry about what happened and gave in to the crowd. I agree that what happened to Enzio should never have happened."

"I'm glad to hear that. I don't have any evidence to back up my suspicions. I have been doing this job for a long time and if you had seen the expression on Isaac's face, you might suspect them too."

Cletus shook his head. "Not one of those fellas have a criminal history, to my knowledge, and the Livengood Plantation is a successful enough farm that they don't need the money. Those men are paid very well. I just don't see it, Matt. We are a fairly small community, and Isaac and all of those fellas knew my wife and son were coming home on that train. Heck, their employees were, too, the Redbirds. I refuse to believe that they would risk killing my family or the Redbirds. I can't picture them wanting to murder everyone on the train just to open up a safe. There are other folks around here who have more sordid pasts. That's who I am looking at."

"I won't argue. I may very well be wrong," Matt admitted. "Seeing Isaac and Mark today just got my attention, is all."

"Matt, I would suspect the people I mentioned to you. Personally, I'm letting the ex-Pinkerton man figure it out. That's what he was hired to do. I'm just a simple county sheriff with a county that is so rural, large, and spread out that most folks leave one another alone outside of town. Most of our trouble is right here in town with drunks in the saloons. And if you want to know the truth, I'm just thankful to the Lord Almighty for having my wife and son still here with me."

Matt nodded understandably. "Amen to that. I just wanted to come by and see what you thought about that group of men. We are looking for a group of men about that size."

"I won't say it can't be them, but I don't see it being them," Cletus clarified for the final time. "I know you're taking this personally, but maybe you should let the ex-Pinkerton handle it, too. Too many hands in the paint bucket makes a mess out of a simple job."

"Maybe. But I'm not leaving until I find the men responsible. It is personal."

Perry Whitmore approached the porch on horseback. "Cletus, I didn't realize you had company. Hello, Marshal Bannister."

Matt gave a halfhearted nod, taking notice of Perry's black eye.

"Where are you off to?" Cletus asked his brother-in-law.

"I'm actually here to help you. The boys from the plantation stopped by to let me know that they were fishing up past the cannery and Isaac fell in. They can't find him. I'm guessing his body is either trapped on a rock or floating at the bottom of the chutes. We're going out to look for him."

"Do they know he's dead?" Cletus asked.

"Yeah. He was washed out and drowned. Isaac couldn't swim."

"That's too bad. I'll get ready and grab my deputies and join you."

"Isaac drowned?" Matt asked. "Is that a normal kind of accident?"

"It happens. Apparently, Isaac was dip netting and caught a large one, lost his balance and fell in," Perry explained.

"Marshal, do you want to join us?" Cletus invited.

"What friends were with him?" Matt asked.

"Rickson, Randy, and Dave. They were upset and returned to the plantation to let Mr. Emrick know."

"Did he lose the dip net?" Matt questioned.

Perry grimaced. "I don't know." Isaac was his friend, and it showed in Perry's downtrodden countenance. "You can come help if you want."

"No. I think I'll ride out to the plantation and give my condolences," Matt answered.

Cletus scoffed. "You just won't leave it alone, will you?"

"I'm just offering my condolences for their friend."

"Yeah, right." Cletus chuckled lightly. "You do that, we'll go look for Isaac."

Perry questioned, "What are you two talking about?"

"The marshal can tell you if he wants to," Cletus said and entered the house.

Molly spoke, "He thinks Isaac and the others robbed the train."

Perry shook his head. "Yeah, you better let that idea go. There are a whole bunch of Indians out there that can verify that all of them were at work that day."

Matt's head lifted with interest. "Have you questioned them?" He had only spoken to the Redbirds who were on the train. He had not talked to any of the other Indian families that lived on the plantation.

"No need. I know my friends. I'm going to look for one of them right now. Tell Cletus I'll meet him at the docks."

MATT DIDN'T WASTE any time renting three horses and insisted that Morton and William ride to the Livengood Plantation with him. It was dusk when they arrived at the Emrick's large home. They hitched their horses and pulled a rope that rang a bell inside. The maid answered the door and left them on the porch while she went to notify Cliff Emrick that he had visitors. After a short moment, the maid, a much older Indian lady with a permanent frown, led the three men through the house to the gazebo in the backyard.

Cliff and his family sat at the table eating salmon steaks with all the trimmings. Cliff told the maid, "Anna, get these men some chairs. Marshal Bannister and, I'm sorry, I forgot your two deputy's names." After William and Morton introduced themselves again, Cliff said, "Yes, that's right. Thank you for reminding me. Are you men hungry? Anna can fix all of your plates right away if you'd like. We have plenty."

Matt answered for the three of them. "No, thank you. We just wanted to stop by real quick and wish you and your family our condolences for the loss of your friend, Isaac. I heard he drowned today."

Cliff wiped his mouth with a cloth napkin raised from his lap. "Yes. It was tragic news that has all of us quite saddened. I cannot say I knew him very well myself, but he was friends with Rickson."

"Hmm, mm," Rickson said with an annoyed expression.

Cliff's brow lowered at his son's apparent dislike for the three men. In the sudden silence that was becoming uncomfortable, he said, "Well, thank you for riding out here to offer your condolences. They are appreciated."

Matt looked at the dark-haired, fair-skinned bride of Cliff's. She was in her early fifties, solemn, quiet, and had a far-off gaze in her eyes. "This must be your lovely bride? I have yet to meet you, miss. I am Matt Bannister, and these are my deputies, William and Morton." He held out his hand to shake.

Marie Emrick glanced at Matt and his deputies for the first time. She was about as unfriendly as a poked badger protecting its home. "My hands are clean, thank you," she said, refusing to shake Matt's hand. "Thank you for your condolences, but you're interrupting our supper."

"Mother!" Isabel scolded. "There is no reason to be rude. Hello again, Marshal Bannister. Thank you for the condolences."

Cliff said, "Marie, Isabel is right. The marshal was nice enough to come out here to offer his condolences. The least we could do is be polite." He asked Matt, "Are you sure you would not like some dinner? We have plenty."

Marie's sideways glance at her husband revealed she was not pleased with his gentle scolding.

"No, thank you." Matt looked at Rickson, who had not said a word. "I don't want to bring up a terrible subject, but Rickson, I heard you were there. If I may ask, what happened?"

Rickson raised his eyebrows while he chewed his salmon. He grimaced irritably and cursed as he pulled a fine, nearly translucent salmon bone out of his mouth. "Anna!" he hollered irately. "Excuse me for a moment," he said to Matt. Anna came out of the house immediately. "Yes, sir?"

"Take this bone to Oscar and tell him if another bone jabs me, I will shove that salmon bone down his throat!"

"Yes, sir," Anna said nervously, taking the bone and disappearing into the house while giving Matt a nervous glance as she passed by.

Isabel shook her head, embarrassed by her brother.

Rickson added to his parents, "Oscar's getting lazy with the meals if you don't mind me saying so. You should fire him." He turned to Matt with an annoyance. "I'll tell you what happened. Isaac tried to pull a salmon out of the water without waiting for Dave to help him. He lost his footing on the wet rock and fell in. We couldn't get to him in time and the current dragged him under. It was hard enough to watch without talking about it. Are we good?" he asked with a bit of hostility.

Matt nodded slightly. "Yeah, we are good. Are dip nets expensive to replace?"

"I don't know," Rickson said with a slight grimace. "I don't own one."

"You don't? Did Isaac?"

Cliff smiled, catching onto what Matt was getting at. "Marshal, we don't own any of those. We're friends with Henry Blalock, who owns the Blalock Cannery. He keeps nets and stuff under the office porch that we can use. The fellas were using those nets."

"I see. Well, I won't keep you any longer. Where would I find Randy and Dave? I should offer them my condolences, too. I spoke with Mark and Isaac earlier today, and I know they are close friends."

Rickson answered, "They aren't here. They are helping with the search for Isaac."

"Oh. Constable Whitmore said they weren't helping and came out here."

"We brought the fish home. They went back to help."

Matt's brow lowered questionably. "If my friend drowned, I wouldn't worry about bringing the fish home."

Rickson took a deep, frustrated breath before speaking sarcastically, "Well, that's the difference between you and me, isn't it? The fact is Isaac was an employee. We can replace him. We went there for dinner, and we caught it. Whether we are heartbroken or not, we still have to eat."

"Rickson, please," Cliff said calmly and added to Matt, "Clearly, Rickson is upset by what he witnessed, so please forgive his rudeness and give him a little grace. This is not typical of him."

Matt answered respectfully, "I understand. Well, you folks have a good night. Oh! And Isabel, it is good to see you again, too," he said with a friendly smile. "Let's leave this fine family to their supper, gentlemen."

As they were leaving the gazebo, Marie spoke as she raised her cloth napkin toward her face. "Thank goodness. The stench of half-breeds was tickling my nose." She sneezed into the napkin.

"Mother!" Isabel exclaimed quietly.

"What?" Marie questioned with a stern voice. "It's true."

Hearing Marie's words, Matt paused and turned around with a chuckle. "Mrs. Emrick, I'm glad you had a napkin handy to blow that stench out of your nose." He paused, biting his bottom lip, fighting the temptation to say more.

Cliff laid his fork down and spoke apologetically. "Forgive my missus, marshal. She's had too much wine today and is suffering from a bitter stomach. She is not up to her usual pleasant self, I'm afraid. I am humiliated by how my wife and son have treated you tonight. I do apologize."

Matt gave a dismissive wave of his hand, but his eyes remained on Marie. Usually, he could shake off such nasty comments like a wet dog, but her tone and arrogance struck him like a slap across the face, and he found it hard to hold his tongue. "I think it's only fair since your lovely missus spoke her mind that I should, too. You have a beautiful home, Mrs. Emrick. You have a nice family and the world at your fingertips. And I must admit, there is no doubt that your daughter gets her beauty from you."

Marie put her fingers together over her dinner plate while her expression slowly warmed into an appreciative smile. "Thank you."

"You're welcome. All that is true. I do mean it. Unfortunately," Matt said, shaking a pointed finger hesitantly. "You remind me of a pumpkin that's sat out in the field too long. It looks great, but it's rotting from the inside out. The Bible says what's in the heart comes out of the mouth. Your bitterness, arrogance, and self-righteousness make you a repulsive woman. Rotten to the very core."

Marie's eyes grew enraged. She stood suddenly, grabbed her dinner fork, and threw it at him. "How dare you! Get out of my house and don't you ever come back!" she shouted, her facial expression was filled with hate.

Matt turned his shoulders to let the fork fly by him. William watched the fork buzz past and land in the yard. Matt had warned him not to say a word, but he said, "Throwing a hissy fit won't make you any more becoming."

Rickson stood and pointed a finger at Matt while raising his voice. "You don't talk to my mother like that! Who do you think you are? Get the hell out of here before I bust your jaw!"

William could not help himself and spoke in a feminine voice. "Ohh, sweetcheeks. You have no idea how that manly talk arouses me, but—"

Rickson tossed his chair out of his way and stepped toward William with clenched fists.

Cliff had been squeezing his lips tightly, trying to restrain himself, but it was going too far. He stood quickly and stepped in between his son and William, pushing Rickson back. He shouted, "Rickson, sit down!"

"No! That son of..."

William's mocking laughter fueled Rickson's fire.

"Sit down and shut up!" Cliff yelled. "There will be no fighting at the dinner table. I'll take care of this. Marie, sit down! Rickson, sit!" When Rickson and Marie had taken their seats, Cliff took a deep breath to collect his composer. "Marshal Bannister," Cliff said calmly, trying to remain a gentleman. "I am appalled by what you said. It was not appreciated, and there was no reason for you to insult my wife at our dinner table. Now, if you would be gentleman enough to apologize to Marie, I would appreciate it."

Matt's lips rose just enough to notice as he watched Marie glare at him. "I meant what I said. And I have a feeling, Mrs. Emrick, that you will hate me a lot more very soon."

Cliff grunted a dumbfounded chuckle. "What do you mean by that?"

Matt regretted saying it as soon as he had. She had angered him, and he had made the mistake of saying too much. "I shouldn't have said that. I apologize."

Cliff was clearly upset. "Then I think you had better leave."

"Have a good night," Matt said as he walked away without looking back. He walked through the house and approached the maid, Anna. He asked her to follow him out the front door, where they could talk in private. In response, she shook her head vigorously, afraid of being caught. He asked quietly, "Were Randy and those men here the day the train wrecked?"

"I don't know," she said with a frightened voice. "I work in this house. They are never here. Please, go. I can't be seen talking with you." The anxiety of being caught talking to him was evident.

Matt nodded and left the house to join the others at the horses.

William shook his head at Matt. "That salmon sure smelled good. I wish you would have been more pleasant until after we'd eaten our fill. I'm hungry."

Morton agreed. "We could have handled insults long enough to eat. Can you go inside and ask if it's too late to join them for dinner?"

Matt laughed lightly. "Do you think Cliff would invite us to join them again?"

William grinned. "No. But I'll give you a dollar if you go back in and ask anyway."

Matt laughed. "Let's go back to town."

CHAPTER TWENTY

CELILO FALLS ON THE COLUMBIA RIVER WAS HOME to the native people for thousands of years. Tribes would cross hundreds of miles to meet with thousands of others from tribes around the Pacific Northwest and beyond to trade where The Dalles City now stood. Life for the Indians on the mighty Columbia was one of wealth and plenty down through the centuries as the salmon, herring, lamprey and sturgeon fed the people and supplied a rich bounty for trade. The river provided a never-ending supply of riches that the men labored to catch and the women worked to preserve, along with wild berries and venison. The land gave them all they needed to thrive.

In 1853, a smallpox epidemic broke out among the tribes along the river, inducing a heavy death toll. The news of the outbreak spread among other native tribes, and self-preservation brought a sudden end to the trade market. Now, thirty-one years later, the rich fishing was being dominated by the salmon canneries along the Columbia River from Astoria to The Dalles City. The natives were being pushed out of their generational fishing grounds and competing with a dip net and spear against the modern industrial seine and gill nets, fish wheels, and men that would just as well shoot an Indian trespassing on the cannery's claimed territory. The White men were taking over while the Indians were being pushed aside to small corners of the earth where their lives were forever changed.

Celilo village was on the south side of the river near the great Celilo Falls. It had been the permanent home to countless generations long before the first White man ever stepped foot on the American Continent until 1858 when the natives were forced onto a reservation. With the right to fish during the spring, summer, and fall salmon runs, Celilo Village was home to a mixture of teepees, small dome-shaped wigwams covered by skins, and other temporary shelters. In the fall, they would return to the reservation, where they could sell or trade the dried salmon loaves and cured meat of their seasonal catch to help sustain their families through a cold and harsh winter.

Randy and his friends rode into Celilo Village as the sun neared the western horizon, casting an orange glow over the river. Several men stood on the banks, trying to catch another salmon or two. Randy had never been to the village and made a distasteful scowl as he looked at the variety of poorly built huts and other temporary lodgings around a plank-built long house. Randy rode his horse in front of an old gray-haired elderly woman slowly walking toward her wigwam to block her way.

"Hey, old woman, I'm looking for a man with an orange shirt and a red patch on his jeans. Have you seen him?" he questioned.

The old woman spoke mildly in her native tongue,

sounding like gibberish to Randy. She changed course to walk around the horse's head, ignoring him.

"Hey!" he shouted as he softly kicked the horse, moving forward to block her way, refusing to be ignored. "I'm talking to you!"

The old woman gently placed her hand on the horse's soft muzzle and quietly walked around it without looking at Randy.

Randy watched her walk away, dumbfounded by her lack of respect or fear.

Mark Ruddick chuckled. "I don't think your charming personality took her in. She didn't look at you once."

"I don't think she knows English or is deaf and dumb," Randy reasoned. His attention moved to a young girl about nine or ten holding a cloth doll in a beaded blue dress. "Hey, girl, do you speak English?" Her hair was cut above the shoulders, which indicated that she had gone to school.

She nodded quietly, frightened to see a group of armed White men in their village.

"Good. Have you seen a man in brown pants with a red patch on the knee and an orange shirt come through here? We're looking for him because he's a bad man," Randy explained.

She shook her head silently. Her large brown eyes watched him nervously.

"Where is your momma? You got a daddy somewhere?" She nodded.

"Well? Can you get them for me?" Randy asked impatiently. "Where the hell is everyone?" he said hastily, looking around.

She turned to point toward the river while nervously biting a fingernail on her other hand.

Randy glanced down to the falls, where about a dozen

men were spread out along the turbulent waters, holding long dip nets or spears to catch the spawning fish. The strong scent of salmon filled the village air. There were racks with filleted sides of salmon drying in the sun near many of the homes. A line of tubs, pans, and containers of ground-up salmon were lying in the sun to create salmon loaves.

An old man came out of a shabby-looking hut that the old woman had entered. He spoke, "Can I help you?"

Randy got right to the point. "We're looking for a man who may have come here today wearing brown pants with a red patch on his knee and an orange shirt. Have you seen him? The law wants him for attacking a young girl, and you don't want that kind of man around your people either," he lied.

The old man's brow raised as he looked at the men. He had spent a good amount of his adult life dealing with White men and didn't like the type of men that were in front of him. The best way to answer a White man was to keep it short, simple, and direct. "If I see him, we will bring him to you."

The old man was quickly joined by a younger man in his thirties, unlike the old man, who had long gray hair that hung freely over his shoulders and was dressed in baggy clothes covered in small tears and patches of various colors. The younger man had a short and respectable haircut and wore newer clothing. The younger man spoke his native language to the little girl, who quickly went to her mother, who had stepped out from behind their wigwam. Her mother put her arm around her daughter anxiously.

The younger man listened as the old man spoke in their native tongue. The younger man then spoke to Randy in English. "I overheard you say you're looking for a man with a red patch and an orange shirt who attacked a girl. You're right, we don't want men like that here. But you should know that the women here make shirts and patches from what material they have. Most of the time, it is what is cheapest or given to them by the government. It is always a color no one else wants, like orange. Many men have orange shirts and brown pants. Some even wear orange pants and a brown shirt. The women use what they can to make clothes for their family."

Randy answered sharply, "This man had brown pants with a large red patch on his right knee. Not everyone has that, do they? Have you seen him?"

"No. I haven't seen him. I'll ask around, but I want you to know that many men have red patches, and the knee is the most common for a patch. Do you have more that we can identify him with? What did this man look like?"

"He looked like an Indian!" Randy exclaimed impatiently.

The young man tilted his head questionably. "Surely, the girl he attacked can say what he looked like. We don't all look the same, just as you men don't. Did he have long hair, short hair, a round face or narrow? Small eyes or big? Was he tall or short? Old or young?"

"Are you playing with me?" Randy questioned dangerously. "He had an orange shirt and brown pants with a red patch on his right knee! Have you seen him?"

The younger Indian with short hair questioned skeptically, "The girl couldn't say what he looked like? If he changes his clothes, we would never know him from anyone else."

"She didn't say!" Randy snapped coldly with his eyes burning into the man. "What is your name?"

"Paul. You probably couldn't pronounce my given name. It's—"

"I don't care what your heathen friends call you!" Randy snapped impatiently. "I know the man we're looking for is here because we followed his trail."

"From?" Paul questioned.

"The river!"

"You followed his trail across rock? He must be a big man to leave tracks in rock."

Randy glared at Paul with hostility for a moment, knowing he had fallen into a trap. His lips lifted slightly. "Fine. We'll search the village ourselves. Fellas, let's search the place." He dismounted and tried to hand the reins to the old man to take. The old man refused to hold Randy's reins. Instead, he said a few words in his native tongue and turned his back to walk away from Randy.

"Don't walk away from me!" Randy shouted angrily and kicked the old man in the butt, which pushed him forward, causing the old man to stumble and begin to fall, but he was caught and pulled upright by his son. Paul forced himself to restrain his anger. He explained, "He will not hold your horse's reins, nor will anyone else. This is our home, and you are not welcome here."

"Do you think we care?" Randy asked, dismissing Paul's words. He added to his friends, "Search everything. If you find the man, shoot him and the folks hiding him, too."

Paul was alarmed. "If the color of a man's clothes is all you know of him, you may find the wrong man."

Randy jabbed a pointed finger near Paul's face. "He was young enough to run like a scared coyote. I know he's here. And I think you know exactly who I am talking about. If you're hiding him, I swear I'll burn your whole village down and leave all of your bodies for the vultures!"

Paul's eyes narrowed, loathing the man who spoke to him. He gave a slow wave around the village. "Go look. But do not harm anyone."

The men split up and began storming into the living structures. Mark Duffy shoved a middle-aged woman out of his way to go inside a flimsy-looking hut, not caring that she scuffed the side of her face when she landed on the ground.

Leon Goodrich grabbed a child by the hair and flung the boy aside to enter an old plank-built shack with his revolver drawn. It was one of the only wooden structures with a stovepipe sticking out of the rooftop. He came out manhandling a screaming Indian girl about thirteen years old. Her mother yanked her out of Leon's grip and put herself between the stranger and her child. She glared at Leon, wild and fearless.

Stan Meldrum came out of a hut eating a piece of dried salmon.

Dave Ruddick carried a weaved basket with sensational beadwork filled with ground-up dried salmon out of a residence and dumped it onto the ground before taking the basket to his horse and tying it to his saddle with the rear saddle strings. A woman in her late forties ran toward him to retrieve the basket, refusing to allow him to take it. She scratched at Dave's face and was met with Dave's hardened fist driven into her abdomen so hard that it lifted her feet off the ground. She fell to her knees before collapsing in a fetal position, unable to catch a breath.

"Hey!" Paul shouted as he approached to check on the woman and help her to stand. "That basket is very old. It was given to her by her grandmother. You cannot take it."

Dave Ruddick put his hand on the butt of his revolver warningly. "Who is going to stop me? We'll do whatever we want, and you all better sit down and keep your mouths shut, or this could turn ugly."

Paul looked at one of the women and spoke in his native tongue, which was Chinookan. It sounded like gibberish to Dave.

"What did you say?" Dave questioned with a stern voice. "Were you talking about me?"

"No. I told her to let you search the village."

"Good. You savages aren't as dumb as I thought."

"I know who you are," Paul said, carefully looking at Dave's thick beard that covered most of his face.

"Oh? Who am I?" Dave questioned.

"You work at the plantation. I remember you coming to the reservation looking for men and women to work. I'm a teacher there."

Dave snickered at the notion. "A heathen teaching little savages how to be American? You should've hired on with us and saved yourself the trouble."

Paul shook his head. "I'm teaching our children how to keep our traditions and still have a future in a changing world."

"You'd be better off digging irrigation ditches for us. That's the only future you and all those children have."

Paul shook his head. "The children are learning to read and write. They are learning all that your children learn in school. But our children will still know our traditions and our language will still be spoken."

"Has anyone found him yet?" Randy asked loudly as he came out of the largest structure in the village. It was an old, weather-beaten, plank-built long house about fifteen feet tall, twenty feet wide, and a hundred feet long. It was where several families lived, a storage room, and a meeting place where they could all gather in one spot around a fire.

"No," came several responses.

A boy in his young teens with his hair cut short from going to a government school ran up from the river. His skin and clothing were damp from the mist of the waterfall. "My sister said you were looking for a man with a red patch and orange shirt. I saw him outside the village. He said he was going south to the reservation."

"What is his name?" Randy questioned with interest.

The thirteen-year-old boy shrugged questionably with a glance toward Paul. "I didn't ask him. He was in a hurry. He's a good hour or two ahead of you on foot. If you go now, you should catch him."

Paul spoke, "Little John, you saw the man leave the river? Did you know him?"

"No. I don't know who he was. He wasn't from here."

Paul spoke to Randy, "Not every Indian that fishes the river lives here. The man you are looking for isn't from our tribe."

Randy could see the boy swallow nervously and his fingers fidgeting. The boy was lying, but Indians, by nature, were liars just as sure and true as the sun is hot. Randy stepped toward the boy slowly. "What did he look like so I'll recognize him?" He turned his head toward Paul. "I don't want to accuse the wrong man."

"We'd appreciate that," Paul answered.

Looking around the village, Leon noticed that the men fishing at the river were carrying their catches back to the village. A crowd had grown around the five men since Dave took the basket and hit the woman. "Stan..." Leon said uneasily, "They're coming out of the woodwork like roaches. I don't like this." He had no idea where the crowd had come from, but they did not appear very friendly.

A man in his forties with a broad and thick muscular

build led the others up from the river. Undoubtedly, he was a tough and powerful man with a round, pockmarked face. His dark eyes burned with fury after hearing what was happening in his village. He spoke roughly, "Why are you here spilling our food and stealing Nunna's basket? Little John, come away from him," the man ordered in English.

Little John stepped away obediently, but Randy grabbed the boy by the hair on top of his head, where it was the longest, jerked him back toward him, and forced the boy to his knees. Randy pulled a knife from his belt and held the eight-inch blade to the boy's throat. "You're lying to me, boy! You all better bring the man with the patch to me right now, or this little lying brave is a dead one. I'm not bluffing! Bring him here now!" he shouted.

Little John's mother began weeping as several of the women gasped. The men grumbled, and others slipped away quietly from the crowd. Paul spoke urgently, worriedly, "He's not lying! We aren't hiding anyone. Have you found him? You searched everywhere, right? Where else could he hide? Look around you. There is no place to hide. Listen to me, okay? Listen. I have to take Little John back to school with me in two days. Okay? He's a good kid, so how about you let him go? He was trying to help you."

The stern man with a pockmarked face warned with a cold sneer, "Let my son go!" His eyes burned with murderous anger.

Randy warned, "One step closer and I'll cut his throat! Where is the man with the orange shirt and red patch on his knee? Bring him to me! We'll trade the boy for the man."

Paul's voice rose. "We don't know who or where he is! How can we?"

"I'll cut his throat!" Randy exclaimed. "And then we'll

kill someone else until you dense dogs give me the man I want! That's the only deal I'm making!" Randy applied more pressure to the knife. "Where is the man with the orange shirt and red patch?" he shouted. "I know he's here!"

"We don't know!" Paul exclaimed, trying to keep control of the situation before it turned into a tragedy. "Can't you hear? We don't know!"

Suddenly the sound of multiple weapons being cocked took the steam out of Randy's threat as ten native men came to the front of the crowd holding rifles and revolvers aimed at him and his friends. Two native men had their bows at the ready with arrows aimed.

"Let him go or die!" Little John's father said, stepping around Paul. "Now!" he shouted with a fierce glare.

Randy took a deep breath as he weighed the odds of him and his friends being killed and buried in the desert. Their horses would be eaten and the skins added to the collection that covered some huts or made into blankets. For all practical purposes, they may have been a rock's throw from the railroad tracks, but they were in a foreign land with no help to hear their cries if he didn't release the boy. Angry, Randy released the boy's hair and sheathed his knife. "Let's go home."

Little John's father warned sternly, "If you come back, you will be killed on sight! Do not come back here. Ever!"

Randy stepped into the saddle as four Indian men surrounded Dave's horse and untied the basket to return it to Nunna.

Paul spoke, "You heard his words. If you come back, you will not leave."

Randy glared at Paul. "Then the same can be said to

you, any of you. There will be no peace between us. Let's go, fellas."

When the five men rode out of sight, a man named George Tessay crawled across the roof of the tall longhouse and dropped to the ground. He wore brown pants with a red knee patch and an orange shirt. He had been aware that the men he witnessed murder another White man might come looking for him at the village. He had warned the others of the possibility. He put a hand on Little John's shoulder. "Are you alright?"

"Yes."

George smiled slightly at his cousin's son. "Thank you. Thank you all."

"We're family," the old man said in Chinookan.

Paul watched the men ride in the distance and said, "We all heard Constable Whitmore murdered Enzio last night. These men wanted to murder George for witnessing them kill a White man. I heard the federal marshal Matt Bannister is in town and that he has Nez Percé blood within him. He must be a good man because he beat the constable for what he did to Enzio. I should go see him."

"No," Paul's elderly father said. "They killed a White man, which is of no concern to us. We should mind our business and let the White man's law take care of its own. The less White men that come here, the better."

"Father," Paul said, "If we don't do something, those men will always be a threat to George or the first man they see with a red patch. Or if their words are true, any of us who go to town. But if those men are hung for killing one of their own, George Tessay will be free of them forever. So will we." Paul added. "I will ask the federal marshal to come here to speak with George."

CHAPTER TWENTY-ONE

Gabriel Smith was bored waiting in the hotel room and decided to take a walk around town. He walked to the cemetery and strolled along the rows of graves until he came upon a cedar plank with the words carved by a knife that said: *Teddy Gray—Died 1882*.

There was no other information about the man or his life for the world to know. Gabriel realized all too suddenly that a man's life had been summed up with his name and the year of his death. The cedar would decay over the years and when his marker was gone, there would be no trace of the man's life to be remembered.

What Gabriel did know was that Teddy Gray was a family man who loved his wife and children. He had a dream and brought his family from New York to start a new life in Oregon's lush Willamette Valley. He had the passion to follow his dreams and the courage to move thousands of miles to make a better future for his family. Life has been called many things by philosophers and poets, but it's never been called fair. Gabriel knew it wasn't for Teddy Gray.

The journey west proved to be full of troubles and tragedy. Teddy lost his beloved wife and two younger children to disease and had to bury them one at a time along the trail. Teddy continued west with his two older boys and stopped in The Dalles City, just short of the lush Willamette Valley on the west side of the Cascade Mountains. Teddy Gray had lost the fire that fueled his passion and surrendered his dream in trade for a job at the local feedlot to support the only solace he found for his sorrow, whiskey. He had become a broken man and was quickly recognized as a town drunk. Late one night, Teddy Gray left one of the saloons and was found the following day in an alley, beaten to death. His murderers were never identified.

A senseless murder ended Teddy Gray's life, but there was no mention of his untimely cause of death or the family he lost nor the two teenage boys he had left alone carved into the cedar plank. There was just his name and the year he was found in the alley.

His two boys would eventually fall in with a pair of outlaws. Rodney Gray would die in the Blue Mountains near Willow Falls by a bullet from Charlie Ziegler's rifle. Evan Gray would be adopted into Gabriel's family.

It was nearly two months before when Gabriel and Evan were shanghaied in Portland. Evan was currently on a ship bound for Africa. It had torn Gabriel apart to leave Evan behind, but no one would know what had happened to them if he had not done so. The ship called the *Everson Solstice* was already a day at sea before Matt learned of it. There was nothing more he could do than to send a wire south to the main ports requesting immediate notification if the *Everson Solstice* came to port. With luck, the port authorities would notify him that the ship was there, and Matt could have the local authorities board the boat and send Evan home. Gabriel prayed that would happen, but the ship's captain had told him they would not see land until they were in Argentina. There was nothing more they could do other than pray for Evan's safety and return someday.

There was once a day when the love-filled Gray family started with a dream and excitement for Oregon's fertile Willamette Valley, but now, not one was left alive on American soil. Evan Gray was the only survivor, and that was questionable at best. Gabriel wondered if he'd ever see his adopted brother again. Life had not been fair to the Gray family, but no one would ever know that if they read Teddy Gray's grave marker. It was just a temporary name and date until the cedar rotted away.

Every experience in a man's life, whether good, bad, kind, or indifferent, was cataloged only in the man's memory. It didn't matter if a man was rich or poor. The fact was, someday, they too would be buried in the ground with a memorial marker with their name and a date etched in wood or stone. *The wife of, husband of, son of, and daughter of* were inscribed on some other markers, some in granite, some in wood.

Gabriel had been reading the grave markers, and it was strange how few mentioned a career or the amount in their bank account. The name and the year they were born and died were all that was recorded. Some granite markers had a cross engraved on them, and some of the cedar markers had a crossboard to make a cross. It was fitting, though. The only thing that truly matters at death is where one would spend eternity. No success or failure would be written in stone or mattered anymore. A man can be remembered for his triumphs and what he did or created while on this earth, but once buried, the only thing that mattered was their knowledge and relationship with Jesus, the savior of our souls.

The memorial marker waiting for every man and woman promises to have four words and two dates, but if a person's name is written in the Book of Life, they will never be forgotten and will live for eternity in Heaven. Gabriel gazed at the graves that surrounded him and wondered how many of the people were in Heaven and how many were in hell. On earth, it was peaceful and quiet, and one might assume the dead are gone, but the truth remains: human beings are eternal with a God-given soul that lives after death either in Heaven with the Lord or away from him.

The difference was a simple decision that every human being needs to make whether they believe in it or not. The decision is to accept the grace of Jesus and his gift of salvation or refuse to humble oneself to do so. The choice is not God's to make, it is the man's choice where they spend eternity. As the Bible says in John 3:16, *For God so loved the world that he gave his only begotten son for who-so-ever believes in him, will not perish but have everlasting life.*

The phrase *who-so-ever* makes it clear that everyone is invited to accept Jesus as their savior, as God does not want anyone, not one single person, no matter how badly they've sinned, to be lost. The Lord is full of grace and will refuse no one who comes to him. The truth is Heaven is only a decision away, but once the final date is engraved on a person's headstone, the decision is made and there is no going back. The Bible says in Hebrews 9:27, *For it is appointed for man once to die, and then the judgment.*

Such serious thoughts plagued Gabriel as he left the

cemetery and strolled downtown in the setting sun. He walked closer to the waterfront and past a few saloons filling up with men. Gabriel was wary of the saloons as the fear of being shanghaied again haunted him. He reasoned it was an unreasonable fear as he was on a boardwalk with many folks around him, but still, he couldn't shake the anxiety of his experience. He moved out onto the street to put some space between himself and the saloons and other businesses of questionable repute.

As Gabriel walked across a horizontal cross street, his attention was caught by a young lady wearing a pretty pink dress with a subtle white floral design walking toward him crossing the same street. The young lady was about his age, had blonde hair, and was quite attractive. She was carrying a bulky wooden box filled with heavy dishware in her hands. Gabriel silently cursed his bad luck of having a broken arm because he would have offered to carry the box for her. He couldn't take his eyes off her, and a chill fluttered in his chest when her lovely brown eyes lifted pleasantly when her gaze met his.

Gabriel couldn't help the shy smile that lifted his lips in response. He was going to say hello, but his left foot landed on the edge of a deep wagon rut on the cross street, causing him to stumble forward uncontrollably. Gabriel's shoulder hit the box of dishes, forcing it out of her hands while driving her down onto the hardened, rut-filled street. Her elbow took the brunt of her fall with a jarring ache followed by her back with the added weight of Gabriel landing on top of her. He quickly rolled off her and ended up face down on the street near a pile of dried horse manure. The crate of dishware landed abruptly on its side with a loud crash of breaking dishes and scattering silverware on the dusty street.

"Oh no!" she exclaimed quietly. She quickly got to her knees to check on the box of dishware. Seeing the broken plates and bowls, she leaned back on her heels, closed her eyes, deflated, and was about to cry. She rubbed her elbow and noticed a rip in the material, revealing an abrasion on her elbow that bled just slightly.

Gabriel was quickly on his knees and touched her shoulder with concern. "Are you alright? I am so sorry."

Laughter sounded from several men and a few women who had witnessed the fall.

She looked at the torn material and her voice quivered. "My new dress. Roy is going to kill me. I'm in so much trouble."

Gabriel repeated, "Are you okay, Miss? I am so...so sorry."

"Oh, no." She picked up part of a broken plate, and her body went weak as she dropped her hands in defeat and groaned. "He's going to kill me," she said with an increasingly higher-pitched voice. Her bottom lip began to tremble while her eyes grew thick with moisture.

"Hey, Ellie," a man hollered through his deep laugh at the step of the Wandering Goose Saloon. "Roy's right, you're clumsy as a blind, three-legged horse!" He laughed with a friend and went inside.

She sighed heavily, knowing she was trouble and looked at the young man who had knocked her down. She shook her head, unable to speak.

"My name is Gabriel. Let me help you pick this stuff up." He set the box upright and began picking up the broken pieces of the plates to do what he could to help her.

She grabbed the top of his hand. "You better go. If my husband sees you, he's going to be angry."

"Husband?" Gabriel questioned with surprise. She

wasn't wearing a wedding ring and appeared to be his age or younger.

She answered anxiously, "Go! I'm already in deep trouble for ripping my dress and breaking the plates. I'll be in more trouble if he sees you talking to me. Please, go!"

"But I'm the one that caused you to fall. It's my fault, so let me help you pick this up."

"No. Just go. Roy's going to tan my hide. Oh, Lord, I can't do this anymore," she whimpered with her hand on her forehead. "Roy's going to kill me. He just sold these."

"My father will pay for the damages and buy you a new dress if I ask him," Gabriel said to reassure her that he was taking responsibility to replace any damages. It was the least he could do. "I'm sorry, Miss. It was an accident. I tripped over a rut." He picked up broken pieces of dishware and set them in the box. He continued, "My name is Gabriel. What is your name?"

She began frantically collecting the silverware, her hands trembled. "I'll have to rewash these. I'm Ellie. Please hurry and leave before Roy comes out."

"If he does, I'll tell him it was my fault and my father will pay for the damages. I am so sorry, though. I didn't mean to hurt you." He touched her arm and leaned forward to look at her abraded elbow.

Roy's angry shout sent a chill down her spine. "Ellie! What the hell did you do?" His voice was deep and harsh. "You can't even carry a box across the street without dropping it! The easiest job in town and you're too incompetent to do it. You broke the plates?" He cursed bitterly as he approached with two friends walking beside him.

Ellie had jerked her arm away from Gabriel at the first sound of his voice. Her body began to tremble as she crumbled into frightened tears. "It wasn't my fault," she whimpered.

"The hell it wasn't!" Roy shouted. He was in his late thirties or early forties, about five foot ten inches tall, with a thin but muscular frame. He had straight, uncombed, medium-length black hair that covered most of his ears. By the length of the stubble on his lean face, it appeared he hadn't shaved for a week. His brown eyes were furious and grew colder as he approached his whimpering wife.

"It wasn't my fault," she squeaked as he neared her. She quickly protected her face in anticipation of being hit, but a pointed boot kicked her in the ribs. She collapsed to the ground, wailing in pain on the street. The laughter that rang out a few minutes before had ended as some folks watched quietly, but others turned around and went inside the buildings they were in front of, while some walked away, not wanting to witness or step between Roy Clegg and his young bride.

Roy didn't hesitate to kick her repeatedly as he shouted, "I should have left you shoveling pig crap on your brother's farm. It's the only thing you can do right without breaking something!" He kicked her again. "Are you too stupid to carry a box?" he hissed over her loud wailing.

"Hey, hey, hey!" Gabriel said, standing. He was stunned to see a man treat a lady in such a way. "It's my fault. I tripped and fell into her. It wasn't her fault. It was mine. My father will reimburse you. It's not her fault."

Roy turned to face Gabriel. "Oh yeah?" he questioned over Ellie's sobbing.

"Yes. I ran into her. I tripped over—"

Gabriel was unexpectedly grabbed from behind by a much larger man, who pinned Gabriel's arms behind his back.

"Let me go! It was an accident!" Gabriel shouted.

Roy grabbed Gabriel's hair with his left hand and held his right fist in front of Gabriel's face to show a big silver ring on his index finger. The large silver ring had the emblem of a white dice with four black dots in the corners. The four dots were raised metal studs intended to cut flesh. "See this ring? It wasn't made to scare fools like you, boy. It was made to scar you! And I will leave my mark on your rearranged face and strip those good looks from you! You're going to learn that you don't talk to my wife, and you sure as hell don't touch her! I saw you rubbing on her arm. For the rest of your life, when you look in the mirror, you'll see my mark, and remember you don't touch Roy Clegg's wife or anything that's mine!" He clenched his fist and plowed his fist into Gabriel's fore-head, leaving four dots of punctured skin that began to bleed.

Roy, filled with rage, pulled his arm back and swung with a mighty swing that connected to the side of Gabriel's nose, breaking it while tearing a gash across the bridge of the nose. Roy was filled with an exhilaration that surged through him at the sight of the boy's blood. He hit Gabriel's face repeatedly until the young man's face was dripping blood onto his shirt. Gabriel had no means of defending himself and was quickly too weak to stand.

Knowing Gabriel had gone limp, the big man that held him let him fall to the ground. Seeing the fresh white cast of Gabriel's broken arm, the big man stomped on Gabriel's plaster cast, breaking it. He tried to stomp on Gabriel's arm to break what was mended, but Gabriel, screaming in pain, tucked his arm to his side to protect it as the big man's heavy boot hit the hardened dirt of the street. Roy jumped to the ground and yanked Gabriel's hand outward, extending the broken arm so the big man could stomp on it.

"Stomp it into the ground, Grant!" Roy urged. Grant Gurley was a former lumberman, over six feet and well over two hundred pounds of brute strength. He had short and thinning light brown hair, a beard, and a mustache on his round face.

Roy's other friend, Doyle West, watched the street, threatening anyone who may try to stop the beating. No one on the street attempted to, as Roy and his friends had gained their ruthless reputation by earning it mercilessly. Doyle grinned, humored by the young man's loud cries as Grant stomped repeatedly on the crushed cast that offered no protection from the heavy stomps.

Ellie grabbed Roy's shirt, pleading with him to stop hurting Gabriel. After several attempts, he finally heard her say, "Leave him be, please, Roy. He offered to pay."

Roy released Gabriel's arm and stood. He quickly tossed a vicious backhand across the young lady's right cheek, stamping her face with his ring's mark and sending her to the ground. Roy's fury was not satisfied by seeing her on the ground holding her cheek. He stepped forward and drove a hard kick into her stomach, forcing the wind out of her. He bent over her, yanked her head up off the dirt by her hair, and jammed a blood-coated finger in her face. He screamed furiously, "I bet he did offer to pay you! He's your age and just happened to knock the box out of your hands? Right! It's more likely you dropped the box to proposition him like the whore you are!" He hit her in the face. "Am I right?"

"No," she whimpered, barely squeezing the word out. She knew Roy would beat her until she agreed, but when she agreed, the beating would become worse. There was no means of avoiding what was to come, and no one would help her without being beaten into submission, too.

"Yeah, right," Roy said, satisfied with her tears and crippling fear. He took a few steps over to Gabriel and told his friend Grant, "Stand him up. I don't think he's learned anything yet."

Grant pulled Gabriel to his feet, facing Roy. Gabriel's nose was bleeding severely, and there was a deep gash across his eyebrow from Roy's thick ring. His left eye was already swelling and turning black. Gabriel was whimpering in pain, and blood spewed out of his mouth as he gasped with the painful throbbing of his broken arm.

Roy grabbed Gabriel's chin and squeezed to get the young man's attention. "You owe me sixty dollars and I want it paid today. If I don't get the money today, I'll break your other arm. Do you hear me?"

When Roy let his jaw go, Gabriel said, "I'll tell my father."

"Good. You go tell your daddy to bring the money to the Half Moon Saloon and Trading Post tonight or bring something to trade of the same value for the damage you caused me, like a horse. I just sold that box of goods. You owe me a lot more than that, though. Tell your daddy to come see me, or my friends and I will find you and him. What's your name?"

"Gabriel Smith," he gasped through an exhaled breath. Blood trickled down his chin to drip onto the ground.

"You tell your papa Smith I'll do worse to him if he doesn't show up. I'm Roy Clegg, that's Grant Gurley, and that is my friend, Doyle West. He's the fastest gun in the West, so we're not people you want to mess with! Got it? We'll kill your papa and you, too, if he doesn't show up tonight." His voice was more threatening. "And you definitely don't ever want to mess with Ellie. She's my wife. My property! Got that?"

Gabriel nodded.

"Where's your pappy supposed to meet me?"

"The Half Moon Saloon and Trading Post," Gabriel said through his heavy breaths.

"Good. The price just went up. It's eighty dollars now or two horses. Are we clear?"

Gabriel nodded. "Yes."

"Think your pappy will show up or should I break your other arm now?"

Gabriel looked at Roy and closed his eyes with the unbearable pain that throbbed in his arm. "He'll be there."

"Are you sure?"

Gabriel's eyes lifted to meet Roy's. "He'll find you."

Roy nodded. "He better! Now get out off my street, and I better never see you around Ellie again."

Grant tossed Gabriel to the ground and kicked him in the ribs before stomping on his arm one final time. Gabriel laid where he was in severe pain, weeping.

Roy grabbed Ellie by the hair and dragged her backward across the street and into his saloon. She was screaming the whole way.

———

WHEN MATT RETURNED to the hotel from the Livengood Plantation, darkness had already set over the Columbia Gorge. Matt stepped inside the hotel and was informed that the town doctor had sent word that Gabriel had been hurt and taken to the doctor's office.

Matt hurried to the doctor's office and stared at his son's severely swollen black and blue face while the doctor explained the injuries. Gabriel's nose had been broken and although straightened, it may not heal as straight as before. Whoever had beaten the boy had intentionally stomped upon the plaster cast until it was shattered and offered no protection from a heavy man's powerful stomping that further damaged the broken arm, causing the doctor to set the bone and recast the arm once again.

Gabriel had nine sutures above his eye and three sutures on the bridge of his nose. Both eyes were swollen and blackened, and there was a cut on his cheek as well from the ring. On his forehead were four small red dots that Gabriel said came from a ring. The longer Matt gazed at his son, the more noticeable the red dots became, filling him with fury. He questioned his son carefully and listened to every detail Gabriel could remember.

Gabriel explained what had happened, and when he finished, Matt asked the doctor about Roy Clegg. The doctor had never met the man but had cared for a few men hurt by Roy and his small group of friends.

After taking Gabriel back to the hotel, Matt, William, and Morton walked downtown to find the Half Moon Saloon and Trading Post. It was located on a side street they had not been on before. It was close to the waterfront and in the heart of The Dalles City red-light district, an area Gabriel should have known better than to enter as the sun fell.

"There it is," William said, pointing at the business name painted on the windows glowing from the inside light. "Are we going in shooting or what's your plan, Matt? I don't want my back turned to the so-called fastest gun in the west when the shooting starts."

"I've never heard of Doyle West. Have either of you?" Morton asked.

"Nope," William answered. "But I look forward to meeting him."

Matt spoke evenly, "Just be nice until I'm not."

William laughed while nudging Morton's arm. "I love that calm-before-the-storm tone he gets. I love it."

Matt led the two others through the bat doors, let his eyes sweep through the building from left to right to place any apparent dangers, and approached the bar. The Half Moon Saloon and Trading Post was a large two-story building extending across an entire block length-wise. One side was the saloon with a bar, gaming tables, and a stairway leading upstairs, where Matt guessed the ladies of the evening's rooms were. The other half of the building was the trading post, which was open during the day and specialized in secondhand goods and some new merchandise.

Matt leaned against the bar and was quickly joined by William and Morton. He knew all eyes were on him. As a precaution, he looked in the mirror behind the bar to watch the room. It was a warm night, but the three men wore jackets to cover their badges. He figured some in the saloon may have known who he and his deputies were, but none had spoken too loudly about it.

"Can I help you, gentlemen?" an old man behind the bar asked.

William answered, "Three shots of your best."

"Yes. Sir."

Matt turned his head to watch the others in the saloon and see if he could identify the men who hurt his son. A moment later, William handed him a shot glass. "To get your blood boiling."

"It already is," Matt replied coldly. At one of the tables, four men were louder than the others, and the noisiest of them fit Gabriel's description of Roy Clegg, Grant Gurley, and Doyle West. The fourth man at the table was armed but unknown.

Matt waited, holding the drink and watching the table in the mirror frequently enough to know what they were doing. He focused on listening to their conversation as they were loud and annoying enough for him to do so.

"I'll bet you five dollars she does," Roy said to the fourth man with them. He turned toward the bar and shouted, "Arnie! Tell Ellie I want her to carry a tray with four beer mugs here. Arnie, I want those mugs full to the brim. No foam."

A few minutes later, Ellie came out of the back and, with trembling hands, took hold of the round tray and picked it up with four fully poured pint glasses. Matt watched her carefully as she cautiously carried the tray around the bar and between the first two tables to where Roy and his friends sat.

Roy turned around in his seat and glared at her harshly with an intimidating stare as she approached. He spoke kindly despite threatening her with his eyes. "Don't you dare spill a drop. I have five dollars on the line."

The threat in his cold eyes spoke louder than his voice. She knew he had made a bet of some kind and that causing him to lose the bet would be taken from her hide behind closed doors, but she didn't know what the bet was. Her hands trembled as she carried the heavy tray, but it was made worse when Roy extended a leg across the aisle, stopping her. "Let's see how long you can hold the tray without spilling a drop."

"Now, that's not part of the bet," the fourth man said on Ellie's behalf.

Roy waved a hand toward the man. "We didn't say it

wasn't. You'll pay one way or another if she drops it," Roy replied.

Ellie swallowed nervously. The heavy tray began to shake in her hands, causing the liquid to spill over the tops of the glasses. Overcorrecting the tray, she tilted it quickly, and one glass fell off the tray and crashed to the floor with a resounding hollow thud. The heavy glass broke. The tray was no longer balanced, and all three glasses quickly fell to the floor.

Grant, Doyle, and Roy laughed. The fourth man watched Ellie with empathy, knowing he was robbed of a five-dollar bet. Roy turned his head toward her as his laughter faded. Ellie began to shudder and fought against giving in to the sobs that pressed against her will.

Roy spoke coldly, "Are you going to stand there like a deaf and dumb mute or are you going to clean that up?"

She turned back toward the bar to get the broom and dustpan to clean the glass, squeezing her lips together tightly to hide her humiliation. She returned, swept the glass and excess beer into the dustpan, and carried it back behind the bar to throw away.

Roy yelled, "The floor's going to rot before you can get the beer licked up! Hurry up! I want you on your hands and knees, rooting like a pig licking the floor clean. In fact, I want to hear you snorting and squealing, too." He laughed with his friends.

Ellie had taken the broom into the back room and came back out behind the bar to grab a couple of towels. Her eyes were reddened and moist from crying in the back. Her cheeks were flushed while she kept her humiliated face downward. There were four small red dots on her cheek-bone that made Matt curious. They were the same marks on Gabriel's forehead.

Matt's heart went out to the young lady, and he reached across the bar to grab her wrist gently. He asked, "Miss, I don't mean to keep you from your work, but do you have mosquitoes with an engineering degree around here?"

"What?" she questioned, not understanding.

He pointed to her cheek. "You got four perfectly placed dots."

She forced an uncomfortable attempt at a smile. "I fell on something."

"Really?" Matt asked softly.

She held his gaze for a moment, somehow knowing the stranger's brown eyes had an empathetic kindness that could see through her best attempt at a lie. Her bottom lip began to quiver unexplainably as her eyes welled up with thick tears. She could not speak, in fear that she would start sobbing and not be able to stop until sixteen years' worth of hiding her sorrow burst through. There was something about the stranger's presence that touched her soul and comforted her yet scared her at the same time. She nodded affirmingly while her face struggled to retain its composure. Her eyes appeared a mile deep under the bulging tears that refused to fall as they remained locked on his.

Roy yelled bitterly, "Ellie, get your worthless ass over here and get this mess cleaned up!"

Her body twitched, startled by the sound of Roy's voice. She wiped the heavy tears away that suddenly fell as best she could before grabbing a towel to hurry to do as she was instructed. She was alarmed when Matt tightened his grip on her wrist firmly. "Let me go! I have to go."

Matt wrinkled his nose, unconcerned. "Tell him to lick it up himself."

"What?" she gasped. "No!" The terror on her face was clearly evident.

"Trust me," Matt said softly. "Step over there and tell him to do it himself." He added to his deputies quietly, "William, be ready, fast and accurate. You too, Mort." In the mirror, he could see William turn slightly to his left, using his elbow and forearm to move his jacket behind his holster, revealing his reversed Colt's ivory grip. His hand expertly removed the thong from the hammer in a slight turn of his body. Matt could see Ellie was terrified to do what he said.

"Ellie!" Roy's deep voice shouted irately. "Did you hear me? Crawl your ass over here now!"

"Tell him," Matt urged, with a soft smile, but his eyes had hardened, sending a chill down her spine.

Ellie's voice shook as she said loud enough for Roy to hear, "Do it yourself."

"Uh-oh!" Grant Gurley laughed. "Did I hear her right?"

Doyle West chuckled. "Sounds like she's stepping out of line to me."

"What?" Roy shouted, ignoring his friends. He stood and walked briskly toward the bar, spitting out, "Have you lost your feeble mind? You do not ever tell me no!"

She backed up hurriedly as Roy came behind the bar.

Matt reached his left arm across the bar to stop Roy. He sputtered, "She's too good for you and I'll free her from you, but before I do, how about I give you two bits for your worthless saloon?"

Roy turned toward Matt with an offended scowl. "Are you suicidal, you dumb son of a—"

Matt's right hand shot forward and grabbed a handful of Roy's hair, followed by his left, and using all his body weight, he slammed Roy's face down against the bar top.

He raised Roy's head with both hands and slammed his face down again with all the force he could. He did it once again with a cruel snarl on his lips.

Doyle West stood quickly from his chair, reaching for his revolver. He drew it from the holster and began to raise it toward Matt when William pulled the trigger, placing a .45 slug in the center of Doyle West's chest, blowing him over his chair and bouncing his body against the wall before falling to the saloon floor. Doyle gasped for his last few breaths. The frightened and startled men scrambling to get out of the way were the final sounds Doyle heard before he drifted into eternity.

William held his revolver toward the other men at the table while his eyes alertly roamed the room for another man willing to try their luck. Morton held his gun on the different customers while Matt beat Roy's face into the bar repeatedly until Roy had no strength to fight back.

The bar top was splattered with Roy's blood when Matt released the man's hair and took hold of Roy's right hand to look at the ring on his finger. It was a thick ring with the likeness of the number four on a gambler's die, the four dots were raised metal studs. Matt grabbed Roy's index finger and forced it back until it was disjointed from the palm while Roy screamed in pain.

Matt ordered Morton, "Hold his arm for me." Morton holstered his revolver and held Roy's right arm down across the bar top while Matt ripped the ring off Roy's disjointed finger. Matt forced Roy's ring onto his right-hand index finger, which is where the power of a punch is most significant. He held Roy's head down sideways against the bar and hit Roy's forehead five or six times, slicing his flesh with each hit. The hits were hard and brutal, without the slightest hint of mercy.

Matt picked Roy's head up by the hair and glared into his eyes. Matt's voice was fierce and cold. "Do you know who I am?"

Roy tried to shake his head. Blood flowed from his broken nose and gaping slice across his forehead. Two of his front teeth were knocked out as well.

Matt turned to the big man, Grant, who stood helplessly under William's gun. "Do you know who I am?" Matt shouted with a ferocious glare that scared Grant enough to begin to tremble despite his size.

"No," Grant said with a shaking voice. "And we won't speak to the law if you just go."

William chuckled. "Well, we'd appreciate that."

Morton smiled while holding Roy's arm, pinning him to the bar top. Roy tried to break free from Morton's grip, but Morton clenched his revolver, drew it, and slammed the edge of the butt down on Roy's extended index finger, breaking the bone. Roy cried out loudly. Morton slammed the butt down on the next finger, cracking it as well. "Stop fighting or I'll break them all!" Morton warned.

Roy screamed in agony and tried to pull free again. Morton slammed the revolver's butt onto another finger, breaking it. Roy began sobbing in pain but stopped struggling. "What do you want?" he cried out.

Matt lifted Roy's head by his hair and glared into his eyes to be heard. "I want your blood! I want you to suffer the pain that you and your friends put my son through today. You threatened to break my boy's other arm if I didn't come here, so here I am! And now I'm going to break yours." He grabbed Roy's left arm and dragged it across the bar top until his forearm was halfway over the edge, and then, using his body weight, Matt slammed his elbow down against the extended arm with a loud crack of the bone. Roy screamed in unbearable pain. Morton and Matt released him, and Roy slid back and fell to the floor behind the bar, sobbing in agony.

Matt went behind the bar and kneeled to rip Roy's gun belt off his waist.

"Please…stop. Please," Roy begged, weeping.

Matt stomped on the broken arm and watched Roy coil it close to his body with a pain-filled scream. Matt grabbed a man's half-empty beer from the bar and poured it out on the floor in front of Roy. "Grunt like a pig and lick it up!" Roy ignored him and continued to wail about the broken arm, teeth, and fingers.

William asked, "Hey, Matt, what about this big man? Mind if Mort and I have at him for what he did to Gabe?" He held his gun on the big man, waiting for an answer.

Matt shot a cold glance at Grant Gurley and answered coldly, "Make him hurt, William. I want his foot broken."

"With pleasure," William said. He spoke to Grant, "Draw your weapon or die where you stand."

"What?" Grant gasped.

"I said go for your gun, or I'll kill you."

"You'll kill me if I do," Grant said in a frightened voice.

"Yeah, but that's not my intention. You won't feel pain if I kill you, and I want you to feel the pain. You see? Now pull your weapon and take a chance, big boy."

"Why? I didn't do anything to you. I don't even know who you are or why you're here."

William smiled coldly. "You three hurt my nephew not two hours ago out on the street. I'm sure you remember that. I heard you took to stomping on his broken arm. He's actually my second cousin, but I think of him as my nephew. And that's too bad for you. Now you know why you're going to be crippled. I won't tell you again, draw your weapon. Go!" William shouted.

"But...but you're already aiming at me," Grant pointed out, beginning to sweat heavily.

"Darn if you aren't right. Sorry about that," William said, lowering his revolver as if he had forgotten about it. "On the count of three. One. Two. Three!" he shouted.

Grant was slow, but as soon as his hand touched the butt of his revolver, William pulled the trigger sending a .45 caliber bullet into Grant's right foot. Grant collapsed to the floor, screaming.

Behind the bar, Matt had stepped on Roy's broken fingers and kneeled, resting his weight on the fractured bones to encourage Roy to lick up some of the beer and snort like a pig. When Roy could no longer endure the excruciating pain, he grunted, squeeled like a pig and slurped up the beer. Only then did Matt remove his weight from Roy's broken fingers.

"I'll kill you, you son of a—" Roy began to shout. Matt slammed Roy's head against the beer-covered floor mercilessly and jerked his head up by his hair.

Matt shouted, "You think you're dangerous, huh? So am I!" He pulled back his coat to reveal his badge. "I'm Matt Bannister, and you were stupid enough to attack my son." He could hear Grant wailing in agony as Morton and William began taking turns stomping on his shot foot. Matt raised his brow with a slight shrug. "Your big friend won't be stomping on broken arms anymore. Your other friend is dead. And you're lucky I'm leaving you alive at all." He glanced at the end of the bar where Ellie was hiding in a corner with her hands near her mouth, shaking. "I'm taking your wife out of here. When the divorce papers arrive, you better sign them, or I'll come back and you will sign them then. I promise."

"You can't take Ellie. She is my—" he screamed as Matt grabbed his broken fingers and bent them backward, nearly disjointing them from his hand.

"I wasn't asking," Matt said. "Not another word or I'll knock more of your teeth out."

Matt left Roy to weep in the excruciating throbbing of his broken bones and approached Ellie slowly. She tightened herself closer to the corner like a terrified child, making herself smaller. He took a deep breath and exhaled. He showed his badge and explained, "I'm US Marshal Matt Bannister. I apologize for scaring you. It was my son, Gabriel, who accidentally ran into you today. He's beat up pretty bad, and I came here to give my eighty dollars' worth of damages to Roy." He paused while Grant bellowed out in agony.

Matt continued over the commotion in the saloon. "Do you have family around here that you can go home to?"

She shook her head nervously.

"Any family?"

She nodded. "My brother lives outside Salem."

"Can you live with him?"

She shrugged. "I don't know."

"Come with me and I'll get you a hotel room tonight. Tomorrow, we'll contact your brother and ask him." He pointed at Roy lying on the floor. "If you want to get away from that sorry excuse of a man, I'll make sure you have nothing to fear and he'll never bother you again. Are you okay with that?"

"I don't..." She paused, not knowing how to answer such a life-altering question. She was too afraid of Roy to say yes, although every fiber within her wanted to leave and go back home to her family.

"I hope you truly love him because both of his hands are broken, so you'll have to help him out in the outhouse every time he goes. Somehow, I doubt that you love him that much to want to stay here. If I'm wrong, say the word, and I'll leave without you."

"I'll go," she said quickly. "But what if my brother says no? I haven't talked to him for a long time."

"Then we'll find you somewhere else that is safe, but I won't leave you homeless. I'll make sure a wire gets sent to your brother in the morning. Go pack your things and tell this sack of crap goodbye because you won't be seeing him again."

CHAPTER TWENTY-TWO

"GOOD MORNING, MARSHAL BANNISTER," THE
manager of the hotel said as Matt came downstairs and
took a seat in the small dining room to order a breakfast
plate. "Did that Indian find you last night?"

"What Indian?"

"I guess not. I don't know his name. It was just some
Indian man who came asking for you. He said he'd search
for you at the doctor's office. I told him that's where you
went."

Matt shook his head. "I didn't see him. We brought
Gabriel here and then the fellas and I went to pay a debt."

"We don't let Indians stay here, but that's the owner's
rule, not mine. He seemed like a nice man. He came by not
long after you left."

"I didn't see him. Good morning, William," Matt said.

"Morning," William said as Matt sat across the table
and looked at the new ring on William's finger. It was
Roy's number four dice ring. "Thanks for the ring. I'm
lucky they had some lard to slide it off your big finger. I

thought it might be stuck for good, and Uncle Luther would be concerned that you took up gambling. He'd blame me for corrupting you."

Matt smiled as he took a bite of his breakfast. "I used it to hit with, that's all. I figured you'd like it more than I do."

"How is Gabriel doing this morning?"

Matt shook his head slightly. "Hurting. He didn't sleep well. He looks terrible. His mother is going to be so upset. She'll never let him out of her sight again, and of course, this happened when he was with me."

William smiled with a slight chuckle. "Well, you can always tell her we evened the score, maybe even added a little more to it."

"I don't think that would matter to her as much as it does to us." Matt's attention went to the door as Constable Perry Whitmore and Sheriff Cletus James entered. Perry pointed at the two men at the table.

"Do you want to tell us what happened last night?" Perry questioned irritably.

William twisted in his chair with a lowered brow. "Now, Constable, you haven't even introduced me to your wife, so nothing's happened yet."

"I don't like you, Fasana, so if I were you, I'd watch it."

William grinned. "I'll watch it. Yeah. So, what do you two scary boys want?"

Perry raised his voice irritably. "What do you think? You killed Doyle West last night and crippled two others. And where is Ellie?"

William glanced at Matt and then back at Perry. "I told you I haven't met your wife yet, but you can search my room if you want." His grin widened as he watched Perry's expression grow angrier.

"You son of a..." Perry paused short, noticing a family with two smaller children watching him two tables away. "Step outside with me."

Cletus spoke reasonably. "Perry, he's messing with you." He took a deep breath and asked Matt, "We need to know why Roy and Grant are broken up and why Doyle is dead. You men did a grand job at crippling them for a while."

"Thank you," Matt said. "That was our intention." He took a drink of his coffee.

Cletus was surprised by the answer. "Can I ask why?"

Matt's expression turned cold. "Go up to room seven and look what they did to my son for no reason. What they did to him was an invitation for what came to them. And Doyle West drew first. It was a fair fight."

William scoffed, "Fastest gun in the west, my ass."

"They beat up your boy?" Cletus asked to clarify.

Matt spoke heatedly. "Beat up? Gabriel had a broken arm and sore back from the train wreck. Those three men beat him to a pulp, and that fat piece of crap stomped on his broken arm repeatedly to rebreak what was just set days ago! Go look at Gabe. Go upstairs and look at what they did to him, and then I *dare* you to come back down here and tell me that you wouldn't do the same thing we did if that were your son."

Perry's eyes widened. "That's Roy's ring! You need to return that to me."

"Oh?" William questioned. "Well, it had my family's blood on it, so I figured I'd take it. Besides, Roy's fingers are probably so swollen right now that he won't miss it."

Matt spoke, "It was a fair fight all the way around. I won't apologize for it. That's what happened. I expected one of you to show up after the gunshots last night."

Perry answered, "I would have arrested the both of you right then and there."

Cletus spoke before either of the men could. "We had a murder of our own to try to solve."

"Did you find Isaac?" Matt asked.

"Yes. We found Isaac in the river. He wasn't murdered, though. His lungs were full of water. He drowned, no doubt about it. We found a dead Indian in the alley between Third and Fourth Streets. He had been stabbed several times and had his throat cut." He looked at the family. "My apologies for saying that in front of your children."

"Who was he?" Matt asked curiously.

"The dead Indian's name is Paul Strongwood. He was a teacher or something at the school on the reservation. He must have been up here visiting his parents out at the village. His father is a local chief, or so they call him. His name is Black Arrow. He's just an old man. I don't know what Paul was doing downtown after dark. He didn't drink or whore around that I'm aware of. But he's dead now. Cut to shreds, as a matter of fact."

Matt held his tongue from mentioning Paul may have come to find him for some reason. Whatever the reason, it got the man killed. He noticed the hotel manager behind the two men about to speak, but Matt put his hand to his chin and casually lifted a finger over his lips with a hardened expression in his eyes. The manager nodded with understanding and listened quietly. "Did you catch the killer?" Matt asked, scratching his mustache.

"No. As I said, Paul was found there. As far as Indians go, he was a good man. He was likable. My deputy is taking the body back to the village today. Perry and I had a busy night investigating those two deaths."

"Your deputy is taking the body back to the Livengood Plantation village?" Matt asked.

Cletus shook his head. "No. The fishing village out at Celilo."

Matt asked, "Just out of curiosity, what was the Indian wearing? I may have seen him in town earlier."

"Gosh, I don't...Paul's shirt was blood-soaked, but I think it was a gray shirt. Black pants and nothing too special."

"Mind if I take him back for you? I wouldn't mind getting out of town," Matt volunteered.

"Be my guest. Those heathens don't much like us coming into their little dump of a camp anyway."

Matt spoke sarcastically, "Well, William and I are both quarter-blood heathen, so we'll probably feel right at home."

Cletus sighed, realizing he had offended the marshal. "I didn't mean any offense."

"They're people, no different than you or me. They love their family as much as you love yours and grieve just like you would. And I'll remind you, Gilbert Redbird helped save your son and others. I'd say taking a loved one back to them deserves more empathy and understanding than you or your constable could offer, given your tendency to call them heathens. Get to know them and you might find they are some of the best-hearted human beings you'll ever meet."

Perry didn't want to hear it. "Yeah. Well, back to the point: where is Ellie? Is she here? Roy says you took her against her will."

Matt chuckled lightly. He ignored Perry. "Cletus, I'll bring Ellie to your office later, where you can ask her yourself if I forced her to leave. Your city constable is a jackass, and I'll have nothing to do with him."

Perry said a few choice words to Matt.

Cletus sputtered, "I'll need you to come down to make a statement about what happened last night anyway, so bring her. If she left on her own will, that's fine. She has that right. We'll let you men get back to your breakfast. We'll have Paul's coffin on the eleven o'clock portage train around the falls. They'll stop at the village to unload it. You can tell whoever is around that Paul was found dead and hop back on the train. My deputies do that because those folks out there can get a little hostile sometimes. We're not so welcomed out there as you can imagine."

Matt nodded. "I imagine you're not. How long will the portage train take to unload the folks and cargo from the sternwheeler and come back through the village?"

"An hour or two at most, usually. Depends on what is waiting upriver to load and come back this way."

"Can they stop and pick me up on the way back?"

Cletus shrugged. "For you, they will. Just let the engineer know. But I suggest you let the first Indian you see know Paul was found dead and get back aboard."

Matt wrinkled his nose with a slight shake of his head. "Like I said, William and I are quarter savage ourselves. I think we'll be okay."

"Matt, I didn't mean to offend you," Cletus said apologetically.

Matt tapped the table with his finger a few times before saying, "As the county sheriff, I would expect you to be more impartial and treat every man, woman, and child in this county with the respect they deserve, not refer to them as savages and heathens. They are human beings and deserve a full explanation of what is known about their loved one's murder. This man was murdered, and it's your job as the local lawman to find out who did it with the same intensity that you would if it was your son found dead in that alley. That's your job to bring justice to this man's family. And if you can't, my deputies and I will. And that's what I will tell this man's family."

"Tell them what you want, Matt, but a dead man in a dark alley doesn't leave much evidence to go on," Cletus said, suddenly annoyed.

"No. But talking to Paul Strongwood's family to see why he was in town might lead to something."

"You do that. Make sure I get to question Ellie privately when you get back. Let's go, Perry."

Once the two lawmen left the hotel, Matt asked the hotel manager, "Does the description of a gray shirt and black pants sound like the man who came here looking for me?"

"Yes, it does."

Matt looked at William. "What do you think?"

"I think we need to go to the village and find out why this fellow wanted to see you."

"Agreed. Tell Morton to get ready for a little train ride east."

"Are you going to send Gabriel home today?"

"No. My son is in too much pain to go anywhere."

CHAPTER TWENTY-THREE

THE OREGON STEAM NAVIGATION COMPANY monopolized the Columbia River with sternwheelers transporting people and goods from Astoria up the Columbia and beyond on the Snake River to Lewiston, Idaho. The Columbia River was divided into three main sections.

The Upper Columbia consisted of the hundred-and-twenty-mile section from Wallula, Washington, to a landing just above Celilo Falls near The Dalles City. A portage by rail delivered passengers and cargo twelve miles around the falls and a series of rapids down to The Dalles City.

The Middle Columbia was the forty-mile section of river from The Dalles City to just above the two-and-a-half-mile-long formidable rapids known as the Cascades, which became the namesake for the Cascade Mountain range. A portage railway once again delivered the passengers and cargo six miles around the raging river to the Lower Columbia.

The Lower Columbia River was the hundred thirty-two miles to Astoria and the Pacific Ocean. The Oregon Steam

Navigation Company had many sternwheelers along the Lower Columbia and Willamette Rivers, three stern-wheelers in the Middle Columbia, and several on the Upper Columbia.

The portage railway's steam engine pulled a tender of firewood, two passenger cars, and a flat and a box car. The cheaply made casket containing Paul's body was loaded for easy offloading on top of unlabeled wooden barrels that lined the length and width of the flat car. Random boxes and crates were stacked on the barrels and tied down. The box car was filled with the passengers' luggage and boxes.

Matt, Morton, and William entered a passenger car and found a seat. The train jerked to a rough start, but after a short eleven-mile trip upriver, it slowed to a stop beside the roaring Celilo Falls. The three men stepped off the train in the barrenness of Oregon's high desert. A few small trees and green foliage lined the river, but the high hills that made up the gorge were barren, with nothing more than brown bunch grass with some sagebrush. The thundering roar of the river's large waterfall and turbulent rapids was an impressive display of nature's power. A mist rose above the falls, giving it a rainbow reflection in the noonday sun.

Matt adjusted his hand-me-down hat, which was found in a pile of clothes donated by the townspeople. He stared at the majestic waterfall and watched in wonder as the men dared to stand on the edge of the slippery rock or wooden platforms built over the most violent water Matt had ever seen with long dip nets expertly catching salmon.

William nudged Matt's shoulder. "Do you want to try that while we're here?" he spoke in a raised voice above the river.

"I'm sure I'd fall in. I'm better off staying far from the bank. You?"

"I'm not a fisherman. Uncle Luther would, though. He and my pa would be right down there catching fish."

"True."

"Hey!" Morton shouted angrily. He began walking toward the flat car. The two cargo men who worked for the railroad had tossed the casket off the flat car without any care. "Where's your respect for the dead? Huh!" he shouted.

"What do we care? It's an Indian," one of the men responded as they retied the ropes that held the cargo down.

The train stopping there had drawn the village's attention, and they watched as Matt and William picked up the casket at both ends and began to carry it over the rough ground littered with exposed rock between the sagebrush. It only took long enough for the train to start chugging forward for several men to come up from the river, curious to know who the strangers were and who was in the simple pine casket.

An Indian man in his forties approached quickly, leading the others behind him. He was a stocky man with a bulky, muscular build with broad and thick shoulders. His round-shaped face had multiple pockmarks from some childhood disease. His dark brown eyes held a particular ferocity and determination, revealing he wasn't a man to tangle with. His black hair was dampened from the river's mist and rested loosely on his shoulders. The anxiety of learning who was in the casket could be seen in his expression and the faces of those who gathered around him. "Who?" he asked with a nod toward the casket.

Matt and William set the casket on the ground. "Sheriff James said his name is Paul Strongwood," Matt replied.

William was glad to set the casket down and stretched his sore back with a grimace.

The man gasped and lowered his head as an older man in the crowd stepped backward at the news and stumbled over a rock. Another man grabbed him to help him stay on his feet. "Open it," the old man said.

"I don't have a hammer," Matt answered.

The man spoke in his native Chinookan language, and several men moved forward to grab the casket. Lifting it together, they rested it on their shoulders and carried it toward the village. In the village, a few women watched the men carrying the casket and shouted to let everyone know the men were carrying a coffin.

The man with a pockmarked face looked at Matt's badge. "Who are you?"

"I am a US marshal. My name is Matt Bannister. These are my deputies, William Fasana and Morton Sperry. What's your name?"

"You people call me Walter. But my name is..." He spoke in Chinookan, which Matt did not understand. He translated, "It means Water-Turns-To-Stone. What happened to my friend?"

"He was murdered. The sheriff said he was found in an alley. From what I understand, you may not want to open the casket in front of any woman or children. They cut his throat and stabbed him multiple times." Matt understood that Water-Turns-To-Stone was the name given to him at birth by his parents or an elder. English-speaking Americans could not pronounce, let alone keep track of the many men, women, and children who were forced onto reservations with a variety of names. It was necessary to translate the Indian's native languages into English words to learn a man's name, but even then, it wasn't customary in English to use a phrase as a name. To add to the confusion, Indians didn't use surnames such as Jackson or Smith. Water-Turns-To-Stone was his name, period.

Matt didn't know if Water-Turns-To-Stone chose the name Walter or whether it was assigned to him by a government official. What Matt did know was using a phrase or description as a name made it hard to recognize who was related to whom and was confusing to the English-speaking government of the United States. English names were encouraged, and a surname was added to each family. The Indians could choose a name, but those who refused were assigned names.

It was clear by Water-Turns-To-Stone's bitterness that he probably refused to select a name, so Walter was most likely given to him. Matt guessed whoever assigned him the name would have to add a surname to the family, and since Stone was part of his name, his new surname and those of his wife and children would also become Stone, renaming Water-Turns-To-Stone to simply Walter Stone. Unknown to Matt and the Indians around the country, five years later, it would become a federal law to rename all Native Americans in such a way.

"Who killed him?" Water-Turns-To-Stone questioned with a twitch on his hardened expression.

Matt shook his head. "I don't know." He hesitated and asked, "Which name do you want me to call you?"

The man's tone hardened bitterly. "Walter."

Matt responded, "My cousin William and I are part Nez Percé, Walter."

Walter was unimpressed and raised his hand to reveal about an inch between his thumb and index finger. "You have Indian blood in your veins, but you have betrayed your people by becoming one of them that kill men like Paul. You wear a badge like them that forced us on a reservation and permitted us to catch the salmon in our own home. This is our home, not the reservation! No, you cannot call me by my given name. To you and the other whites, I'm Walter." He finished with a hardened glare. "You are not welcome here, but you must explain his death to his father. Follow me." He cupped his hands to his mouth and hollered in his native tongue to the men carrying the casket who had walked ahead not to open the casket when they set it down in the village.

––––––––

THE MEN HAD SET the casket in the center of the village and announced to Paul's father that the body the casket contained was his son. There were wailing women, some held others who were weakened by the shock of the news. A few individuals walked away to mourn alone. Paul's father, an old man with long gray hair that hung over his shoulders, stood quietly with tears clouding his eyes that refused to fall. He was surrounded by family members who wept. The old man spoke in his native tongue, and two men walked away and returned shortly with hammers. They immediately began pulling the nails that secured the lid down.

"I don't recommend that," Matt said as he entered the village with his deputies.

"He knows," Water-Turns-To-Stone replied harshly.

Matt waited while they removed the lid. The men stepped back and let the father and others gaze upon the blood-soaked and grotesque sight of Paul's body.

The father took a deep breath and looked at Matt with anger burning in his eyes. He spoke coarsely in Chinookan with a sharp glare at Matt, then turned his back and walked away.

Water-Turns-to-Stone translated, "He says, 'Paul, as you know him, went to find you and is now dead because White men always bring pain and death. He says his father and grandfather should have killed every White man that ever came on the river. He wants nothing to do with you. You can go.'"

Matt explained, "I have nothing to do with this man's death. I want to help find the men responsible for it. I came here because I understood Paul was looking for me. Does anyone know why he was looking for me?"

Water-Turns-to-Stone answered, "It doesn't matter. We must protect our people, and we will do so. His father warned him not to go, but he believed you would help, but there is no help from you White men, only sorrow. Now go away and don't come back."

Matt nodded with disappointment. Whatever the reason Paul came to see him was not going to be revealed to him. There was nothing more he could do. "My condolences to his family and friends." He backed away slowly, alertly watching the men around the village to ensure none were grabbing a weapon or becoming a threat. It had become clear that the death of Paul was a heavy loss felt by the whole village. The resentment toward their treatment by the White population and lawmen was thick in the air, and the threat of being ambushed in the heat of the moment was a concern that Matt wasn't taking lightly.

"Wait!" a man in his late thirties shouted as he exited a wood-framed hut.

Water-Turns-To-Stone shouted at the man, "You don't need them! We can protect you and your family."

George Tessay shook his head. "No, you'll only get everyone killed if you tried. Marshal, wait." He approached Matt. "My name is George Tessay, and I am the reason Paul went to find you. I watched them drown a man, and they want me dead. They came here to find me. Paul and the people here protected me. Paul spoke with them and they left with bad blood for him. They would have killed Paul if they saw him in town, and I think they must have."

"Who are they?" Matt questioned.

"Men from the plantation where other Indians work. I watched them drown their fat friend with a dip net. They saw me and chased me. I escaped into the river. They came here looking for me. One held a knife to Little John's throat. But my family did not tell them where I was hiding."

"Men from the Livengood Plantation?"

"Yes. I watched what they did."

"How do you know they were from the Livengood Plantation?" Matt asked, watching the man's facial expressions and body language carefully.

"Paul said they were. He recognized one man who had come to the reservation to talk our people into working for them."

"Do you know their names?"

"No."

"How many of them?"

"Three drowned the fat man. Five came here."

"Can you describe them or their horses to me?"

George nodded. "Yes. I can describe them all. I watched them from up there." He pointed at the roof of the longhouse.

CHAPTER TWENTY-FOUR

Upon returning to The Dalles City, Matt stopped by the telegraph office before going to the hotel. The hotel manager stopped them as they entered. "Marshal Bannister, while you were gone, Constable Whitmore came here with his deputies and dragged that young lady named Ellie out of here. He said her husband needed her. I would have liked to have protested, but I can't afford to lose my job. You know he's related to Cletus and Molly James, the hotel owners."

Matt glanced at the telegraph he had received from Ellie's brother. "Did she go willingly?"

"No. The young lady was quite upset, scared, and crying. She caused quite a commotion. That's why I say I would have liked to have helped her."

"Alright, thank you for telling me." He spoke to his deputies. "Let's go bring her back."

Morton asked, "Don't we have more urgent things to do? Those men might flee."

Matt shook his head. "They have no idea what we

know. They can wait. Let's go talk to Constable Whitmore first."

———

THE DALLES CITY CONSTABLE'S Office was several blocks away. It was like many other buildings on the downtown street: a wood-built two-story building with a false front rising above the roof line with bold lettering stating it was the constable's office. The ground floor contained the office area, while the jail cells were secured behind a heavy wood door upstairs.

When Matt and his deputies entered, Perry Whitmore was leaning against a counter, talking with two of his deputies. Perry ignored them with a sideways glance and continued telling a story to his two deputies despite the two constable deputies suddenly appearing uneasy.

Matt asked sharply, "Where is she?"

Perry smirked. He had expected Matt to come to the office when he heard the portage train's whistle returning to town. "She is back with her husband where she belongs. I understand that you were recently married and should probably be heading back home to your wife. This is our town, and you've overstayed your welcome."

"Have I?" Matt questioned.

"Yes, sir, you have. We don't need you here. Quite bluntly, we don't *want* you here. So, we'd all appreciate it if you'd move on. I'm sure your wife misses you."

William chided, "I don't think she does. No one misses him when he's away. Do they Mort?"

Morton shook his head. He had also been recently married and was anxious to get back home.

"I'm pretty sure she does," Matt replied to William.

"But, Constable Whitmore, I can't leave yet. We have a train robbery to settle and bring those who caused the massacre to justice."

"Massacre?" Perry questioned.

"Fifty-nine dead from an intentional act. What would you call it?"

"A tragedy."

"A tragedy is an accidental derailment or a trestle collapsing from shotty workmanship. With intent, it becomes a massacre, in my opinion. It doesn't matter what we call it, my deputies and I are very close to making arrests."

"Oh really?" Perry asked, stepping forward. "And who do you suspect now? Roy Clegg and his pals, which you three disposed of? That would be quite handy, wouldn't it?"

"It would be convenient if it were them, but unfortunately, not. Rest assured, I have a pretty good idea who did it, and you'll know before too long. I would think you would be more concerned about that crime or last night's murder of Paul Strongwood than a young lady leaving her husband."

"Roy is a friend of mine. So are Grant and Doyle, may he rest in peace. You three men had no right to do what you did. Ellie married Roy, and she belongs to him, body, soul, and mind. He especially needs her now that you broke his fingers on his right hand and broke his left arm. Roy can't even dress or feed himself. He needs his wife to take care of him as a wife should. She married him for better or worse. The deal was done when she said I do. You have no business interfering in their private affairs. No one does. They're married. It is as simple as that. I don't think you and your deputies deserve to be called lawmen for what you did. You're animals. We don't want you here."

William chuckled. "I like that. Thank you."

Perry raised his voice. "Yeah, you would appreciate that, wouldn't you?"

William nodded as Morton grinned.

Matt said, "I'll ask Ellie if she wants to stay with your friend, but the decision is up to her. It's not up to you to decide. If she wants to leave, I'll take her out of there and suggest you leave her be."

"It's her wifely duty to care for her husband," Perry spoke forcefully. "She'll stay with Roy and take care of him."

"I have doubts about that, but the choice is hers. If you're concerned about your friend, take him to your house. I couldn't care less about him."

"Leave her be," Perry warned, stepping forward.

Matt raised his brow. "Or what?" He watched the constable evenly.

Perry's courage faded as he watched Matt gaze at him without concern. "Just leave her be." His tone had quieted.

Matt said. "If she chooses to leave this time, you had better be the one that leaves her alone, or I will bust your head open. You've already seen what we can do. That's all I'll say. You're warned."

———

ROY CLEGG SAT in a padded high-back armchair with an angry snarl on his twisted lips. His nose had been straightened as much as it could be by the town doctor that morning. Nonetheless, the severity of his broken nose had left both of his eyes blood red, swollen nearly closed, and black and blue. His forehead was sliced open in several places from being hit with his ring, including four dots that penetrated deep enough to touch his skull. Roy's front two top teeth were knocked out. His left arm had been broken and was in a plaster cast, hung from a sling around his neck. The four fingers on his right hand had been broken and were wrapped in gauze, and a plaster cast over his palm extending to the middle knuckles.

Roy refused to be seen outside his apartment looking the way he did and wore a long nightshirt that came to his knees with nothing underneath to make relieving himself easier. A bucket under a wooden chair with the seat cut out was nearby for that purpose.

Sometimes, in a man's life, he hits a wall of grief and becomes despondent. His best friend, Doyle West, was in the funeral parlor. Grant had been shot in the foot, and the doctor was able to save the foot so far, but Grant would always be a cripple, limited to the use of a cane. Roy's reputation as a tough man had been humbled, and it hurt his pride to the point that he felt emasculated in front of his customers and friends.

Everyone who was in the saloon had watched him be thoroughly beaten, stripped of his custom-made ring and beaten with his own marker stamp. They heard him wail like a spanked child and grunt like a pig while licking beer off the floor. And when it seemed nothing could be worse, his wife left him on the floor weeping as he watched her leave with another man. It took his friend Perry Whitmore to bring Ellie home, and Roy was furious about her abandoning him.

He could not beat her. He could not hit her the way she deserved, pull a trigger, or hold a knife, which was lucky for her. Instead, all he could do was glare and yell.

He promised her that she would suffer the consequences for her betrayal in a few weeks unless she made up for it between now and then by following his orders as an obedient wife should. She could earn his mercy by feeding him, bathing him, dressing him, and doing whatever else was needed until his hands were usable. He also required her to oversee the finances and inventory of his businesses with him to ensure none of his employees were pocketing money or stealing merchandise. For the first time in their troubled marriage, he truly needed Ellie.

Ellie's hope of leaving Roy had been abruptly ended when the constable and his deputies entered her hotel room and forcefully took her against her will. She knew Matt had wired her brother over in Salem, but she did not know if he had replied about her moving in with him and his family. What she did know was she was back in her private hell, experiencing Roy's fury for her leaving him, which was unforgivable. He had a way of scaring her that no other man could. Even though he couldn't use his hands, he still terrified her.

Ellie had hoped Matt would save her from her prison of marriage to Roy Clegg, but hours went by and there was no knock on the door. She made Roy's dinner, hand-fed him, wiped his angry spit off her face, and continued to feed him. Ellie emptied his bucket of waste and cleaned up after him. She rubbed his feet and scratched his arm where the cast itched. She had become a personal slave to his every whim, and his needs were ever-growing to degrade and humiliate her as much as he could.

Her hope rose when there was a knock on the door. She had hoped Matt was returning to save her, but it was Roy's friend Eddy coming to talk about managing the saloon and store in Roy's absence. An hour later, there was another knock on the door.

"Come in, Eddy," Roy hollered. He did have a loosened tooth, but he hoped it would tighten up in his jaw in a day or two.

The door opened, and Matt Bannister stepped into the apartment with his two deputies behind him.

"What...what...what are you doing here?" Roy stumbled to get out of his mouth. He was alarmed to see the three men in his home. Constable Whitmore had reassured him that Matt would not interfere again.

The sound of William snickering at Roy's appearance came before Matt could say anything.

Matt ignored Roy and looked at Ellie. "I received a reply from your brother. He'd be excited to have you come back home. I'm assuming you don't want to stay here?"

"No," she said lightly. "My brother said I could go?" she questioned with watering eyes.

"You're not going anywhere!" Roy shouted with a mighty, resounding roar. It made her shudder in fear.

"Shut up!" Matt ordered coarsely. "You have no say in it. Ellie, pack what you want to take, and if I were you, I'd take half his money as well."

Roy stood defiantly. "Ellie, don't you dare leave with him! I told you what I'd do if—"

Matt pushed Roy back into his chair with a hard shove. "I said shut up! There is nothing you can say or do that will change anything! Ellie, get your things packed up."

William pointed at Roy's forehead. "It looks like you got a close-up look at my new ring." He showed him Roy's old ring with the four studs on a white-faced dice.

"That's my ring," Roy said, trying to contain his wrath. If he could, he'd shoot every one of them.

"Well, it used to be yours," William said. "If you want it back, I invite you to try to take it from me. But in the meantime, you had better sit here like a good little boy in your pajamas until your mama comes over to take care of you."

Roy's upper lip twitched with fury. "I'll kill you."

"Like the fastest gun in the west, did? That was very disappointing. I only had to fire one shot." William shrugged. "If I see you in Branson, I'll send you back home in a box."

"I'm ready," Ellie said. She had taken a good amount of money from Roy.

Roy gasped as if he ran out of oxygen. Fear of being left alone filled him, and he pleaded, "Ellie, I'm begging you. Please stay. I haven't got anyone else to care for me. Please, stay with me."

Ellie picked up the bucket partly filled with fresh urine and tossed it in his face. "Call one of your whores!" She walked out of the apartment without another word.

"You dirty little bitch!" he screamed as the lukewarm urine dripped down his face and chest. "Ellie! Ellie, come back. I'm sorry. Please come back," Roy yelled after her. A fear-filled desperation showed in his eyes as he yelled at Matt, "You have no right to take her!"

Matt smiled. "We'll close the door on our way out. Gentlemen."

William lingered just long enough to rub his goatee, revealing the ring with a chuckle. "I'm starting to like her. I might have to steal her from you, too. Hey, thanks for the good time and the ring. You have some yellow stuff dripping off your chin there." He laughed as he closed the door, leaving Roy alone.

CHAPTER TWENTY-FIVE

THE COUNTY SHERIFF, CLETUS JAMES, LISTENED to what Matt had to say before stating, "I don't know an Indian named George Tessay. I can't take his word for anything. Indians lie like a rug. I know Randy and all those men pretty well, and they didn't drown Isaac or rob the train. Like I said before, I think you're barking up the wrong tree."

"Do you have any suspects, Sheriff?" Matt asked.

He shook his head. "There's just no evidence to accuse anyone. I wish there were, but there is not. And an Indian's word is as worthless as a pound of donkey crap."

Matt scratched an itch on his head. "In my experience, White men lie far more often than Indians. I can't think of a lie that an Indian has ever told me. They are sincere people. Maybe you could explain why Randy and his pals went to the village searching for George if he didn't witness them drowning Isaac? Or why Rickson would get so uptight when I asked where they were last night."

"I don't know that they did go out there. Look, one of

the Indian's own kind was wrongfully hung and, unfortunately, decapitated. They're all mad about that and on the warpath, but they know they can't start a war, so false accusations are one way of getting even, right?"

"No," Matt said bluntly. "If that were the case, they'd be accusing Constable Whitmore since he was the idiot that hung Enzio Corrales, not Randy and the others that went out there with him. Why don't you ride with us to the Livengood Plantation and let me do the talking? Are you okay with that?"

Cletus smiled slightly. "Alright. I'll ride with you, but I think you're wasting our time."

"Just because you know these men does not make them incapable of committing a crime. You need to pull your head out of your boots a little bit and consider that maybe they could be involved. If you can do that much, then maybe you can give George Tessay the benefit of the doubt and consider that maybe they drowned Isaac because he was getting ready to crack under the pressure. I saw Isaac up close and personal, Cletus. Something wasn't right, and he was cracking when he saw all those bodies. I know that bunch of men blew that trestle and murdered those four young men to take the money. I'd appreciate it if you could do me a favor and put your friendship aside long enough to give it an honest look rather than immediately shunning the idea."

Cletus narrowed his eyes thoughtfully before replying. "Okay. I'll consider it. I'll keep my mouth shut while you question them."

"That's all I ask."

———

THE FOUR OF them rode out to the Livengood Plantation and passed by the large Emrick home to the bunkhouse where the plantation manager's office and rooms were for the field bosses. It was a long single-story building with Randy's office at the front end and five doors to the apartments where the field supervisors lived. The cookhouse and cook's apartment were in a separate building twenty yards away. Behind the bunkhouse, there was a pasture and barn for the men's horses. Knowing the office would be closed, Matt knocked on the first four doors without a response.

Finally, knocking on the fifth door, a coarse voice, sounding tired and irritable, yelled something from inside. A moment later, a short, obese woman wearing a cotton robe answered the door with a wrinkled brow and glaring eyes, upset about being woken up. She was in the midst of shouting, "It better be important to wake me up..." She paused when she saw the sheriff, Cletus James. "What's wrong?" she asked with a worried expression taking over her face. "Is Mark okay, Clete?"

William spoke before anyone else could answer. "Mark's never been okay, Peaches, you know that. Hey, you look as fresh and pretty as the day I first saw you."

She rolled her eyes with a good-natured smile to see William. He may have been a wandering spirit that would never settle down and could be irritating at times, but he was as refreshing to her gloomy spirit as a morning swim. Her countenance warmed with a welcoming smile. "What do you want, William? I told you to call me Clair. I'm a married woman now."

"Ahh," William groaned, "don't tell me that when I came all the way out here with money in my pocket. I was going to ask you to make me an honest man."

She snorted. "I don't think there's a woman in this world that is up to that challenge. So, really, what are you all here for? Nothing bad happened to Mark, has it?"

Cletus shook his head to reassure her. "No, Clair. I'm sure Mark is fine. These men just wanted to talk to him."

William asked, "Where is that rascal husband of yours? Have you got his leash tied to your bedpost like a castrated dog?" William asked.

"Leash?" she questioned with a raised brow. "If anyone has a leash on, it's me. I'm the one stuck at home. When's the last time you recall me going to bed so early, huh? Willy-boy?"

"I won't answer that question in front of my innocent cousin and his delicate ears. I'll just say not to sleep anyway."

"Well, nowadays, that's all I do, and I'm tired. So, why are you all here?"

Matt answered, "I wanted to ask Randy Paulson and the other fellas some questions. Are they around that you're aware of?"

"Questions about what? And you must be William's cousin, Matt Bannister?"

"I am. Miss, I wanted to ask about the hanging the other night. What they saw and such."

"I'm Clair Duffy, Mark's wife. I knew William years ago. He hasn't changed much, has he?"

"I'm afraid not. Is your husband available to talk with me about the hanging?"

"Ask Willy-boy there. He's the one who ruined that hanging for everyone. Mark was very upset with you, William."

"It's not the first time, and it won't be the last,"

William said. "He'll get over it or he won't. One of the two."

"Hmm." She grunted. "Mr. Bannister, Mark is with Randy and the others in town at the saloon, playing cards and having a few drinks. They always are at this time of night. It's almost a Livengood Plantation ritual. Clete, you should have known that."

Cletus nodded. "Oh, I did. The marshal was just anxious to get out here, is all."

"Well, I'm going back to bed. Goodnight, gentlemen," she said with a yawn and closed the door.

Matt looked irritably at Cletus. "You knew they wouldn't be here?"

With a vindictive smile, Cletus said, "I told you coming out here was a waste of our time. They will be in Gable's Steel Cable or The Witching House Saloon at this time of evening."

Annoyed, Matt said, "Maybe you should have mentioned that while we were in town."

"You were the one set on riding out here, not me. I told you I was going to keep quiet." Cletus smirked.

"Well, that's fine." Matt had hoped Cletus would at least consider that his friends may have been guilty of a crime, but it was suddenly clear that the sheriff had no interest in helping investigate the possibility of his friends being involved. "Since we're here, let's go talk to Rickson."

Cletus offered, "Rickson is most likely with the fellas in town."

"Then let's go talk with Cliff. He seems like an honest and upright man to me."

Morton spoke, "Last time that didn't go so well, Matt."

"This time may not either, but—"

Cletus sputtered, "I wouldn't bother the Emricks, Matt.

If you mention your suspicions, you'll mess with Randy and other men's jobs, which is not right. They worked a long time to earn their positions, and this isn't just their job, it's their home. I wouldn't go making unproven allegations against good men to their boss."

"You don't have to come with us, Cletus," Matt replied sharply.

Cletus sharpened his tone. "As I said, you're barking up the wrong tree. Even the railroad's detective doesn't suspect these men."

Matt was aggravated. "I hoped you'd give the idea a chance, but you clearly think I'm wrong and refuse to be of any valuable assistance. I'd appreciate it if you'd go back home. You are as worthless as your brother-in-law."

Cletus didn't say another word. He climbed into his saddle, shook his head with disgust, and rode away.

CLIFF EMRICK WAS SUMMONED by the maid, Anna, letting him know that Matt Bannister was waiting for him on the front porch. Curious, Cliff laid the book he was reading on his side table.

Marie Emrick's countenance immediately hardened. She said, "Send that man away, Anna! He has no business speaking to the likes of my husband."

"No, no. I'll go speak with him," Cliff said as he stood. "It might be important."

"If he makes one derogatory statement, send him away immediately. In fact, I better come along." She stood to follow. "This is my home too."

"Marie, please. You and him do not communicate well. So please, stay here."

Cliff stepped outside onto the front porch and closed the door behind him. "Marshal Bannister, it is good to see you again. Morton, William. What can I do for you, gentlemen?" he asked while shaking their hands.

Matt noticed the front door open just a crack as Marie listened in. "Mr. Emrick, I was wondering if I could speak with Rickson. Is he home?"

"No. Rickson is out with his friends. May I ask what this is about?"

Matt hesitated, wondering how much information he should share, if any. He usually would not share a thing, but his gut, his inner being, his conscience nudged him to be honest and forthright. "Okay. I won't share too much, but a man came forward claiming to have witnessed the drowning of Isaac and says it happened differently than your son stated."

"How so?" Cliff questioned.

"Let's just say it sounds more intentional."

"What?" Cliff gasped with a troubled expression.

The door opened, and Marie stepped heatedly out of the house, shoving a pointed finger at Matt's face. "Get off our property! You have no right to come here and make accusations against my son! What do you want to get from this? Money? Are you trying to blackmail us? How much Marshal Bannister? How much are you trying to swindle from us? Name your price and then leave us alone! Pay whatever he wants, Cliff."

"Mrs. Emrick, what a pleasure," Matt said sarcastically. "I don't want your money. I have reason to believe that Rickson may know more than he is saying."

"What reasons?" Cliff asked.

"Correct me if I'm wrong," Matt said to change the subject quickly. "I assume Isaac was a softer-hearted man than the others in your employment. Am I right about that?" Matt asked, ignoring Cliff's question.

Cliff turned his palms upward with a slight shrug of his shoulders. "Isaac answered to Randy and Rickson. I barely knew him. He seemed nice enough. Why?"

"The day the bodies were being identified at the railroad's warehouse, I stood back and watched everyone that entered and left. Isaac was distraught and hurried away after seeing me. He kept looking back at me to see if I was following him. I did follow and spoke with him and your employee, Mark. It appeared to me that Isaac couldn't bear the guilt anymore and would break down and start talking soon. I intended to catch him out here alone and talk with him, but conveniently, he drowned that very afternoon. Now, a witness has come forward to tell a different story than what Rickson told me."

"Who is the witness?" Marie questioned. Her scowl was stern and scornful.

"I'm not at liberty to say. His life was already threatened and I won't share his name until the men I'm looking for are arrested."

"I don't understand," Cliff said. His brow was furrowed with concern. "What are you thinking Isaac would have to talk about? And what are you saying? Are you accusing Rickson of being involved in something?"

Matt hesitated. "I believe Isaac and a few of your employees may have been involved in the railroad trestle being destroyed and the train wreck. I don't know to what extent Rickson is involved, but to some degree, I believe he is. I'd like to speak to him about it."

Marie stepped forward enraged, her lips snarled with hatred. Her two fists were raised and she pounded them against Matt's chest. "How dare you accuse my son! Get off my property. Don't ever come back! You atrocious human being!"

Cliff grabbed his wife, trapping her arms at her side. "Calm down! Marie, calm down. Go back inside. I'll take care of it."

"You can't let him take our son away!" Marie began to wail. "He's going to take Rickson away," she sobbed.

Cliff held her from behind as he guided her toward the door. "I'll take care of it. Go back inside. You're not making anything better. Go." He watched as she slinked back inside the house. He closed the door and turned around. "Rickson is in town with his friends. Marshal, I'd appreciate it if you'd let me talk to him first as his father to see if there is any truth to what you're telling me. You haven't told me much, but if he knows more about Isaac's accident than he's sharing, I'll know if he's lying. Please tell me, do you suspect he knows something about the train too? Is that what I understand you are suggesting?"

Matt nodded quietly. "It is."

Cliff gasped with an exasperated expression. "That wouldn't make any sense. What could he gain from that? We have money. I don't understand."

Matt shrugged. "That I don't know. Listen, I have my suspicions, but that's why I want to talk to him."

The concern was evident in Cliff's expression. "I don't understand what you suspect my son did, but if Rickson is involved in something illegal, I'll spend everything I have to get him the best attorney in the land. You need to know that. He can be a lot like my father, but Rickson is still my son. I love him."

"And your father was?" Matt questioned.

"Mean," Cliff answered. "He treated people like dirt.

Rickson tends to do that, too. I know when he's lying to me, Marshal Bannister. Please, let me talk to him first."

Matt nodded. "Alright. I'll come back in the morning. But if he runs. I won't have any mercy on him. You better tell him that."

"He won't run. I guarantee it. And thank you," Cliff said.

———

RICKSON EMRICK STOOD and raised his glass in the air to give a toast. "Gentlemen, raise your glasses to a year's harvest being done. To a good payday! And let's not forget our dearly departed friend Isaac Chandler. May his memory be long remembered and a cautionary tale for everyone to learn to swim!" He laughed.

"Cheers!"

"Here! Here! Jolly ole fellow he was!"

"To our friend," Mark shouted over the crowd of men in Gable's Steel Cable Saloon. "With the highest respect. Bon voyage, Isaac."

"I didn't know him, but thanks for the drink."

"He owed me a dollar."

"Is his horse for sale?"

"You could damn near make a blanket with one of his shirts," a man said to his friend.

Rickson shouted, "Norm, another round for everyone!" It was followed by loud applause. He watched the county sheriff, Cletus James, walk into the saloon. "Hey, Clete! Come join us. Norm, give Clete two or three shots of your strongest so he can catch up with us. We hate being more drunk than our friends, it puts us on different planes. Down those quick, Clete!"

Cletus held up a hand, denying the drinks. He stood beside the table where the group of friends, Rickson, Randy, Mark, Leon, Stan and Dave were seated. "Gentlemen, can I talk to you all outside?"

"For what?" Randy asked.

"Because I have to talk to you."

Rickson shrugged his shoulders. "Talk here. We're among friends," he said, indicating the room full of patrons drinking. "Hey, aren't you all my friends?" he shouted. There was a roar of agreement. "See?"

"You may not want them hearing this."

Randy asked, "What is it?"

Cletus kept his voice low enough so Randy, Stan, and the others could hear, but not the whole saloon. "I just talked with Matt Bannister. He is convinced you all are the ones who robbed the train. He's going to speak with Cliff about it."

"Why would he say that?" Stan questioned.

"Does he have some kind of evidence?" Mark asked.

His words had gotten all of their attention. All of their eyes were on him, waiting for an answer, except for Rickson, who was whispering in one of the ladies of the evening's ear. He patted her rump and watched her walk away with a grin as Cletus spoke, "He claims some Indian witnessed you drown Isaac."

Dave's head lifted with alarm. He sputtered, "Isaac fell in and couldn't swim. It's no more complicated than that. How does that tie in with the railroad?"

"How'd that Indian find him?" Randy asked without thinking about it.

Dave shot a hardened glance at his friend. He said, "Randy means what Indian? Did the marshal make this up or what?"

"Yeah, that's what I meant. What Indian?" Randy corrected, knowing he had spoken foolishly.

Leon rubbed his beard nervously.

"Listen," Cletus said. "He thinks Isaac was killed because he was going to break down emotionally or something. I know you guys didn't do it. I just wanted you to know Matt Bannister thinks so. Don't be surprised if he starts asking questions."

"Questions about what?" Rickson asked loudly. He had been busy talking with the lady and other people who thanked him for the drinks.

Stan tapped Rickson's hand to get his attention. "We'll talk about it later."

"Sounds good." He went to another table to talk to the men there.

"Thanks for telling us," Randy said to Cletus. "We'll have to let Cliff know it wasn't us."

"That's all I needed, fellas. I'm going home to see the wife," Cletus said.

"You tell her hello for us. And I'm glad she and your son survived that train wreck. It's hard to believe anyone survived it. It was horrible," Randy said, shaking his head.

Cletus nodded. "Thank you." He stepped across the room and turned to the table to look at the five friends. He remembered Matt saying he suspected there were five or more riders from the horse tracks available to see, even though the riders stayed on the gravel and rocky areas along Gypsum Creek. For the first time, Cletus wondered if it could have been his friends.

CHAPTER TWENTY-SIX

CLIFF EMRICK HAD STAYED UP LATE WAITING FOR his son to come home, but knowing Rickson may or may not return, he had gone to bed shortly before midnight. He woke up at his usual time just after sunrise, dressed for the day, and checked Rickson's room to find him sleeping soundly on top of his blankets, still wearing the clothes from the night before. The room smelled of stale liquor, proving his son had overdone his share of drinking at the saloon.

Cliff went downstairs and sat at the breakfast table with Marie and their daughter, Isabel. "I see Rickson made it home. He didn't even remove his boots before passing out on his bed."

Marie lowered her glass of fresh milk. "He got home around two, I'm guessing. I'm surprised you didn't hear him come upstairs."

"Did he wake you?" Cliff asked.

"I was already awake. I didn't sleep well."

Isabel looked at her mother. "Is something wrong? You look worried, Mother."

"No. I just couldn't sleep."

Cliff took a deep breath. "If I understand correctly, it seems the marshal, Matt Bannister, suspects your brother and the men in the bunkhouse of having something to do with Isaac and the train disaster. It truly makes no sense, but he's coming this morning to talk to your brother."

"Why?" she asked with a dumbfounded expression.

"The marshal is a lying thief!" Marie exclaimed. "I believe it's an attempt to extort money from us. Offer him five thousand dollars and send him away, Cliff. He might have some White man's blood in him, but he's no better than those thieving heathens."

"Mother, stop it!" Isabel snapped with a glance at their Indian maid, Anna. "The Indians are no better and no worse than we are. And I am tired of hearing you and Rickson talk like they are below you somehow. They are not. We're all human beings."

Marie tossed her napkin onto the table with disgust. "How you turned out to be like your father, I have no idea. Since you two love the heathens so much, maybe you both should marry one."

"Mother, I just might. I am liking Peter Tall Oak more every time I talk to him. A single father needs a good wife, and I'm not afraid to say I find him quite handsome."

Marie's eyes bulged with fury. "I'll have him run out of this state before I allow my daughter to marry a savage! Get that thought out of your head right now! I never want to hear those words come out of your mouth again, young lady. I'll close that school and send you back east, where you'll never see an Indian again!" She glared at Cliff and pointed at Isabel. "This is your fault! You treat them like civil human beings and they are servants! Maybe your father was right about your mother being unfaithful. You sure don't act like his son."

Cliff peered at his wife with annoyance. He sometimes regretted marrying her so much that it sickened his stomach. "I'm rather proud of that, Marie. And no, we won't close the school."

"Do you want her marrying a savage?" Marie questioned with disgust.

Cliff answered reasonably, "They'd run into some obstacles with the general public here and there, but if she fell in love with an Indian man and he loved her, I'd support them."

"You make me sick! And you..." she snapped at Isabel, "you disgust me." She walked away, saying, "I can't stomach either of you right now."

"Ditto," Cliff said under his breath. He turned his attention to his daughter. "Who is Peter Tall Oak?"

Isabel shook her head. "It's just a name I made up. He doesn't exist, but Mother wouldn't know that. So, the marshal doesn't think what happened to Isaac was an accident?"

Cliff finished his cup of coffee. "A witness came forward who claims it may have been intentional. That's all the marshal said. I have a hard time believing that's true, but the marshal's coming sometime this morning, and he has reason to believe it is. Grab a glass of water and let's go wake up your brother. I want to know what he has to say."

———

CLIFF AND ISABEL carried a glass of water upstairs and entered Rickson's spacious bedroom. Rickson hadn't moved from laying on his blankets and breathed deeply in his slumber. Isabel waved her hand in front of her nose. "It smells like a stinking saloon in here."

Cliff shook Rickson's shoulder. "Rickson, it's time to wake up. Hey, you need to get up. We have to talk."

Rickson groaned and swung his arm wildly to end the shaking of Cliff's hand. "Leave me alone!" he grumbled.

"Rickson, wake up! I'm giving you the count of five to sit up before I throw a glass of water on you."

"Go away!" Rickson shouted and turned his back to continue to sleep.

Cliff didn't have the patience to count. "Five." He poured the glass of water on Rickson's face.

Rickson yelled with a curse as he sat up, quickly wiping his face with a harsh glare at his father. "I'm trying to sleep! What do you want, you bastard!" he added a few curse words directed at his father.

Cliff struck his son's face with a rigid, open-palm slap. "Shut your mouth! I'm your father, and you won't speak to me like that. Not ever!"

"The hell I won't! You have no business throwing water on me. What the hell is wrong with you? What is she doing here? Both of you get out of my room!"

"Rickson, we just talked about your disrespect in my home. Remember, you can pack your things and get out right now if you don't like it here."

"And lose the plantation?" Rickson questioned angrily. "Is that what this is about, trying to make me mad enough to hit you? Are you trying to cut me out of your will?"

"Oh, my word," Isabel groaned.

"No, Rickson, it's about the marshal coming here to see you! What happened with Isaac?"

Rickson grimaced. "What the hell, Dad? Get out of my room and leave me alone!"

"What is going on here?" Marie demanded to know as she came into the bedroom. "Why is Rickson's hair wet?"

"He threw water on me, Mother."

"Cliff, why in the world would you do that? You know he was up late."

"You know why, Marie. Matt is coming here this morning to talk to him. I want to know if we need to get him an attorney." He turned to Rickson. "The marshal claims to have a witness that may be saying he saw you fellas drown Isaac."

Marie stepped forward to stand in front of her son protectively. "Of course, he did not do that! Tell him you did not do it, Rickson!" She pointed a finger in Cliff's face and spoke with a hardened scowl, "I will not lose my son or this plantation because of some damn half-breed's ruse! Offer him the money and send him back home."

Rickson sat on the edge of the bed, staring at the floor tiredly. He spoke calmly, "I didn't do it, Father. Are you happy now? Can I go back to sleep?"

"No, Rickson. Matt Bannister is coming here to speak with you. Do you think he'll walk away because you're tired? No. Get up and take a bath because you stink. Get dressed."

Isabel watched her brother carefully. "He's lying. Rickson, did you have something to do with Isaac drowning? Was it an accident?"

Rickson stood quickly and stepped toward Isabel angrily. He shoved a finger in her face. "I didn't! And don't say I did! He drowned, just like we said, Isabel. What? Are you trying to get me arrested so you can inherit the plantation? Your precious daddy will give it to you anyway because you are his favorite. Isn't she, *Daddy?*" Rickson sneered with a burning in his bloodshot eyes.

Marie added sharply, "Your brother didn't do anything to Isaac. The fool went fishing without knowing how to swim. Everyone knows those rocks are slippery. It was an accident! And I never want to hear you say something like that again, Isabel. Period! Rickson, get dressed. Isabel and Cliff, let's leave him alone."

"I'll be down in a minute," Cliff said softly.

Marie glared at her husband harshly. "Do not upset our son."

"I won't. Just leave us alone for a minute."

Once Isabel and Marie left the room, Cliff said, "Son, I need to know the truth. Did you have anything to do with Isaac's death?"

Rickson rolled his eyes and spoke strenuously, "No! I had nothing to do with it. He drowned, okay? I don't know what that Indian saw, but he didn't see us drown Isaac. There is no proof of that, no matter what that heathen says. Relax, Dad."

"Rickson, are you lying to me?" Cliff asked.

"Are you ever going trust me?" Rickson asked.

"Answer me honestly: were you or the men involved in the train accident? Please tell me, none of you were. Tell me the truth."

Rickson sat on the edge of his bed and rubbed his face with his hands. "For crying out loud, they were all working in the fields that day. Check the timecards. They were all here. You're worrying about nothing. I'll talk to the marshal and get this all cleared up."

ANNA, the middle-aged Indian maid, escorted Matt into the elegant parlor where the family relaxed in the evening. Despite the warmth and beauty of the room, Matt could feel Marie Emrick's hatred heavily penetrating the room's atmosphere. Marie stood next to a piano with her arms crossed over her breast. Her cold eyes burned into Matt like he was a diseased rat that needed to be disposed of.

Cliff stepped forward to greet Matt with a handshake. "Marshal Bannister, William and Morton, welcome. Thank you, Anna. Would you let Rickson know Matt is here, please?" he asked their maid with a kind smile.

"Yes, Mr. Emrick," she answered and left the room.

"Rickson will be down in a moment. Can we get you gentlemen some coffee, milk, or apple cider this morning?" he asked.

"No, thank you," Matt replied. "Did you speak with your son?"

"I did. I'm confident Rickson didn't have anything to do with whatever you suspect him of." His expression didn't appear to have the confidence that his words indicated.

"But you have some room for doubt?" Matt questioned with a slight hint of a knowing smile as he watched Cliff closely.

Marie dropped her hands to her side and quickly stepped to her husband's side. Her voice did not hide her contempt for Matt. "No, there's no doubt! Who do you think you are to come into our home and make these asinine accusations about our son? I despise you, Marshal Bannister!"

Matt wrinkled his nose and nodded understandably. "Cliff, if you don't mind, I'd like to speak to Rickson in private?"

"Absolutely not!" Marie exclaimed. "I will not allow you

the opportunity to put words in my son's mouth and arrest him for something he didn't do! You don't have to continue to play this game. You can follow us to the bank right now, and I'll give you snakes five thousand dollars each to leave us be."

"That sounds good to Mort and me," William said with a shrug.

Matt snickered lightly. "Mrs. Emrick, I could arrest your son right now if I wanted to. You have a choice: go sit down and shut up, or I'll arrest you for attempted bribery of a federal marshal on three accounts and take you to Portland in shackles to be held for trial. I do not care if you like me or despise me, but I am getting tired of hearing you. Sit down and shut up, or go into a different room."

ANNA KNOCKED on Rickson's bedroom door and knocked again when there was no answer. Slowly, she opened the door and peeked inside. "Rickson? Are you in there?" She opened the door and saw him lying on his bed, sleeping. He had bathed, dressed in a light tan suit, but had gone back to sleep. Anna entered the room and shook his shoulder gently. "Rickson, you need to wake up. The marshal is here. Rickson, you need to wake up," she said in a louder voice.

Rickson's eyes opened, and he rolled over to look at Anna. "What?" he snapped bitterly.

"The marshal is here to see you. They are waiting in the parlor."

Rickson sat up on the edge of his bed and rubbed his eyes. "Are you from that village on the river?" he asked her.

"What, sir?" she asked. Having delivered the message she was sent to give, she was leaving his room.

He waved for her to come back into his room. "Close the door for a moment. Are you from that village by the falls?" he asked.

Anna stood by the open door. "No, sir."

Rickson stood and stretched. "Will you grab my jacket over there, please?" The matching suit jacket was draped over the closet door eight feet from him.

An uneasy sensation stirred in Anna's stomach, but she stepped across the room to grab the jacket and turned around to see Rickson's bulging, enraged eyes inches from her face. His hands wrapped around her throat and squeezed, cutting off her air supply. He hissed fiercely, "I know all you savages have a communication line better than the underground railroads. Who saw us? What is his name? Tell me, or I'll snap your worthless neck!"

He eased his grip and she sucked in a breath of air. "I... don't know. Sir, I don't know." Terror filled her as tears slipped down her cheeks. "I swear I don't know. I've never been there before."

"Anna, I want that man's name. I don't care if you have to go to that village and prostitute yourself or any of the other girls from our village to find him. I want that man's name! If you don't have his name by tonight, I'll have the boys take your husband for a walk and you will never see him again. Am I clear?"

"Yes, sir," she wept.

"Once I go downstairs, I'll let my father know you're sick, and then you can go find Randy and tell them what I said. He'll know what to do. We have to find that savage and kill him, and you're going to help us. Right?" He squeezed her throat until she grimaced and her face turned red.

He eased his grip. "Right?" he repeated.

"Yes," she said through tears.

"Good." He forced a kiss and tossed her to the floor. "Get going." He picked his jacket up off the floor and put it on. "I'll tell my father you went home sick. Anna, remember if you don't have him here or his name when Randy brings you back, your husband will pay the price for your failure."

———

RICKSON ENTERED the parlor with a forced smile. "Marshal Bannister, it's good to see you again." He stepped toward Matt with an extended hand.

"I didn't think our last conversation was so stimulating that you'd be glad to see me again," Matt responded while shaking his hand.

Rickson's fake smile faded. "I didn't say I was glad to see you. It's just *good* to see you because I hear tales that I am being falsely accused of drowning my friend. Truly, is that even reasonable to consider? Isaac tried pulling one of those heavy fish out of the river with a net by himself and lost his balance. That's not uncommon. Once in a while, that even happens to one of the Indians who do that stuff every day by themselves. Maybe you should try it," he said with a wry smile.

"I've seen them doing it," Matt replied.

"Have you been to where we were? It's all volcanic rock that's pretty jagged, uneven, and rough ground, but it's constantly wet and slippery. It was at least a six-foot drop into the torrent of raging whitewater. Isaac lost his balance and fell in. He couldn't swim," he finished with raised shoulders in conclusion. "Of course, we tried to reach him with a dip net. So, if there was an Indian watching us, that may be what he saw and mistook that for us for trying to drown him. But unless you'd drown one of your friends," he said with a chuckle and a wave toward Morton and William, "then don't suppose we would ours."

"Well, that sums everything up pretty well. And it makes perfect sense," Matt said.

"Thank you. So, are we done?" Rickson asked.

Marie gently linked her arm with her son's with pride. "I would think so. Cliff, would you escort the marshal and his friends out."

Matt said, "I'm curious why your employees were twelve miles north of town in Celilo Village looking for the man who claims he witnessed you all drowning Isaac. Why were your friends causing trouble if they had nothing to hide? By the way, I never said it was Indian that claimed he witnessed it."

Rickson shrugged his shoulders. "Who else could it have been? There were not any White folks where we were. I have no idea why they went to the village. I can't control what they do in their free time. I brought the fish home for dinner. That's all I know."

Marie added, "Marshal, men blow off steam when they're upset. There is nothing new about that. I mean, Cliff and I were both raised on large plantations in Louisiana with many slaves."

"Marie, there is no reason to bring that up," Cliff complained. "I'm sorry, Matt, she's still bitter about the war and losing her family's fortune."

"Fortune?" Marie stammered. "Damn you, Cliff! I lost my brothers and father in that war. Of course, I'm bitter about it! My family owned the Westover Plantation, and then the Yanks came, and my family lost everything! I have every reason to be bitter, Cliff!"

"Well, I won't sit here and argue about the past. Your father should have been smart enough to sell out and come west with us."

Marie shouted, "My father believed in the Confederacy and was willing to fight to keep it. Not sell out and run away at the first sign of trouble. That is what a coward does!"

"Grandfather was no coward!" Rickson snapped at his mother. "He was brilliant."

Cliff shook his head, already tired of his wife's nonsense. "Well, at least we still have a plantation and wealth. The once prominent Westover family that proudly wanted to stay and fight to save that way of life are gone. My father may have been a lot of things that I despise, but he was smart enough to build *this*, and we're still alive and thriving. And you, my dear, can't say you don't enjoy it."

Matt spoke loudly, "Can you two argue about your past on your own time? Please?" He paused.

"Yes, I apologize," Cliff said, taking a deep breath.

Matt continued, "A teacher from the reservation was visiting his family in Celilo Village. Paul Strongwood was the man who spoke with your employees and recognized one of your men from a recruiting trip to the reservation. Your employees caused enough trouble out there that tempers got heated, and they were surrounded by several natives with rifles and told to leave. Your men threatened Paul's life the night Isaac drowned, and just so happens, Paul came into town that night to find me and was found murdered in an alley. His throat was cut and he was stabbed too many times for it not to have been personal."

Rickson shrugged. "It wasn't me. I was right here all that night."

"Yes, he was," Marie confirmed.

"That's true," Cliff stated.

"If you all don't mind, I'd like to speak with your employees and ask them some questions."

"Does that mean you're done with me?" Rickson asked.

"For now," Matt replied.

"We don't mind at all," Cliff answered. "Mind if I come with you?"

"They might be more willing to talk to me if you do."

Rickson felt a chill creep up his spine. He had ordered Anna to find Randy and ride to Celilo Village to locate the witness. He had been tired, hungover, and foolish. "I'll go bring them here," he volunteered. "I know where they are all working."

"No," Matt said, "we'll find them."

CHAPTER TWENTY-SEVEN

ANNA WALKED ON THE DUSTY ROAD TOWARD THE bunkhouse with the distress of a panic attack reeling within her chest. Her heart beat faster, occasionally fluttering rapidly as it stole her breath away momentarily. Her hands shook and her chest tightened. Fear stormed in her soul as she weighed the daunting task of finding a man she knew nothing about in a village of strangers who would not betray one of their own. Anna already knew it was a pointless venture, but failing to identify the man Rickson expected her to find was a threat to her husband being killed. The consequences of a doomed task scared her more with each step closer to the bunkhouse and reaching Randy Paulson's office.

Anna had worked inside the Emrick home for over twelve years and watched the Emrick children grow up. She never said too much during her long workdays, but her ears were open every single day. She knew far more about the Emrick family than she led on or would ever reveal to stay in the Emrick family's good graces. Anna had secrets she would never share with anyone, such as the bodies buried deep in the marsh of the Bottom Ten.

The Bottom Ten was a natural, low, bowl-shaped area of about ten acres at the base of four hills along Squib Creek. The area was a natural marsh, but Basil Emrick had built a dam across Squib Creek and created a lake for irrigation. In the spring and summer, it was a good swimming hole, but it was also a good place to bury things the Emricks and their employees never wanted to be found. Anna knew that disappearing from the plantation often meant being buried within the heavy mud of the marsh, such as the former missionary who was supposedly run off the plantation. Anna knew the man had insulted Basil Emrick one too many times, and he disappeared after being invited to dinner. The church was burned down soon after.

Rickson's threat toward Anna's husband had to be taken seriously. Rickson could come across as a nice young man, but he was a monster very similar to his grandfather. The only restraint that kept Rickson from becoming his grandfather was Cliff and, to a lesser degree, his sister, Isabel. His mother, Marie Emrick, was a heartless woman who could be as cold as ice and mean as Basil if Cliff wasn't there to keep her contained. Their marriage wasn't a happy one, and everyone knew it. Among the Indians who worked on the plantation, there was speculation that Rickson wasn't Cliff's son but Basil's. Such rumors were only founded by Basil's favoritism for Rickson over Isabel. The rumor was not true, but because Rickson acted more like his grandfather, it continued to convince some of the Indians that it *was* true.

The sound of horses caused Anna to turn on the road to see her employer, Cliff Emrick, riding beside Matt and his two deputies.

Cliff's brow lowered curiously as he pulled back the reins. "Anna, what are you doing? Are you going home?"

"Yes," she choked out. Her skittish eyes glossed over with the fear of losing her husband as she glanced at Matt.

"Are you not feeling well?" Cliff asked.

She nodded once while her bottom lip began to quiver.

"What's wrong?" Cliff asked. "Anna, what's the matter?" He knew her well enough to know something wasn't right. He had never seen her frightened, scared, or fighting her tears. "Anna, what is the matter? Please, tell me."

She pointed toward the bunkhouse as tears slipped slowly down her cheek. "Mr. Emrick, Rickson did it, sir. He wants me to find the Indian man so Randy and the others can kill him."

"Rickson told you that?" Cliff questioned as a cold chill went down his spine.

She nodded. "Yes, sir. In his room." She pulled her dress's collar away from her neck and lifted her head to show the red marks from being strangled. "He choked me and threatened to kill my husband if I didn't do as he said."

Cliff stared at the red marks on her throat with genuine disbelief. He knew his son had a mean streak, but he refused to believe that he was a danger to anyone. His voice cracked. "Go on home, Anna, and stay there. I'll take care of it." Without another word, he turned his horse around and gave it a hard kick to race home. He wanted to confront his son before Matt could.

Matt turned his horse and held the reins to speak to Anna. "He told you that this morning?"

She nodded. "Yes, sir."

Matt's lips lifted. "Thank you. I have been praying for a way to catch these men, and you just became the key that will open the floodgates. If you see Randy and his friends, say nothing about this or me for your own safety. Say absolutely nothing! Just go home." He kicked his horse to catch up to Cliff. His deputies immediately followed him.

———————

CLIFF JUMPED off his horse and ran into the house. "Where's Rickson?" he shouted at his wife.

Marie answered sharply, "He went back to bed for a couple of hours. Don't bother him, Cliff. He needs his sleep," she called as he ran upstairs. Curious, she followed.

Cliff burst into his son's room. "Get up!" He grabbed Rickson by the arm and pulled him out of bed onto the floor. "Tell me you didn't have anything to do with the train wreck! Tell me that at least," he said heatedly, with tears brimming his eyes.

Rickson was furious to be pulled out of bed. "What is wrong with you? You already know I didn't. For crying out loud, let me sleep, old man!" He stood from the floor. "I'm tired! Okay?" he shouted.

Cliff's chest rose and fell with his deep breaths. "I just talked to Anna, and Matt did, too. He's coming for you. He knows you want that Indian dead because he witnessed what you men did."

"We didn't do anything," Rickson said with a dismissive wave of his hand.

"Quit lying to me, Rickson!" Cliff screamed. "Please, son, tell me the truth so I can help you."

Rickson's eyes widened with alarm to see Matt Bannister step in the bedroom doorway. "I didn't do anything. I...I...don't know what Anna is talking about." He was beginning to panic.

Fed up with the lies and infuriated by fear, Cliff grabbed Rickson's shirt with both hands, yanked him close, and shouted, "Tell me the truth, damn it!" He threw Rickson across the room like a rag doll. Rickson stumbled forward out of control and ran into his dresser, driving his head into the dresser's mirror. The mirror broke upon impact, cutting Rickson's scalp while his hand knocked a bowl of wash water over, spilling it.

Rickson, leaning over the dresser, felt his scalp as he watched drops of blood splatter onto the white cotton doily that stretched across the dresser with lace trim. He looked up into the broken mirror and watched a solid line of blood running down his face as his scalp bled heavily. A snarl formed on his lips while his hand clenched the straight razor he shaved with next to where the bowl had been.

Cliff's anger had gotten the better of him, but seeing his only son's blood dripping from his scalp brought a sudden stab to his already breaking heart. He gasped. "Son, I'm sorry. Are you alright?"

Knowing his father was stepping toward him, Rickson turned quickly, slashing the razor in a wide arching motion that slashed his father open from his left shoulder down across his chest with a long and deep gash. "Leave me alone!" Rickson screamed. Cliff stumbled back and fell on the bed, horrified to see how quickly his shirt was saturated with blood.

Marie screamed and went to her husband's aid. To see the thick layer of bright yellow fatty tissue under his skin and the amount of blood flowing from his body shocked her. Marie's hands pressed the sides of her face as she repeated frantically, "Oh, no...oh no...oh no..."

Matt drew his revolver and aimed it at Rickson as he

stepped in front of Cliff. He shouted, "Drop it, or I kill you right now!"

Rickson's hate-filled expression changed in a flash to a dropped jaw while he stared at his father with a horrified expression. "Father, I didn't mean to. I'm sorry. I didn't mean to hurt you, Dad." He began to weep while still clenching the straight razor.

Matt had watched Rickson's expression change from an intent to kill to quickly becoming the sorrowful son. He wasn't buying the crying act, as Rickson shed no tears. Matt shouted to his deputies, "William, Morton, have their butler get Cliff to the doctor." He kept his revolver with the hammer pulled back level to Rickson's chest. "Drop the razor!"

Rickson tossed the razor down. "I didn't mean to cut you, Father," he said as Morton and William led Cliff out of the room. Marie, panic-stricken, followed.

Cliff looked back at his son as he reached the door. Love was the only emotion revealed in his torn expression. "Tell him the truth, son. Please. I'll do all I can to help you."

Matt's eyes weren't so kind as he glared at Rickson dangerously. "Why did you drown Isaac?"

"We didn't," Rickson answered without his usual arrogance. His attention was on his father being led out of the room.

The loud percussion of Matt's revolver echoed through the house as he pulled the trigger and fired into the dresser near Rickson to get his attention.

Rickson screamed, jumped into the air, and quickly moved into the corner, where he turned sideways to make himself smaller and used his hands to cover his face and body protectively. He shouted with a frightened, high-pitched voice, "Put the gun down! Put it down!"

Now that Matt had his attention, he hardened his voice. "Don't lie to me again! The next bullet will be a lot closer. Tell me the truth now!"

"What do you want to know? I didn't do anything, okay?"

Matt pulled the trigger and fired a shot into the floor near Rickson's feet. Rickson jumped in the air and screamed in terror. Matt shouted, "Last chance! Anna told me what you said. I saw the marks on her neck. I have all day to make you scream, Rickson, so you better be brutally honest. It is going to start getting painful now." He raised the revolver to Rickson's knee as he pulled the hammer back. The click of the hammer locking into its firing position sounded louder than it had before.

Rickson's heart raced. His face had gone ashen while his eyes darted around the room, helplessly searching for anyone to help him. His arms tightened around his body as he tried to force himself further into the corner to make himself smaller. His breathing became quick, panicked breaths until his emotions took over. His chin began to quiver, and his eyes filled with terror. "Okay!" he shouted and broke down into sobs as he held out a hand to stop Matt from pulling the trigger. He choked on his words as he spoke in a high-pitched, uneven voice, "We had to! He was going to talk about the train!"

"What about the train? Tell me!" Matt ordered.

"I wasn't there. But I know it was an accident. The train was supposed to stop before the trestle, but Isaac lit the fuse too late. It ended badly." He dropped into a sitting position in the corner and covered his face with his hands. "It wasn't supposed to happen like that. All those deaths, Isaac couldn't handle the guilt. That's why they killed him.

Stan said we had to kill him, or we'd all hang. We had no choice, but I didn't do it." He wept.

"Who all robbed the train?"

Rickson closed his eyes tightly as he wept. "Randy, Dave, Mark, Leon, Isaac, and Stan. They did it, not me. I didn't do anything."

"But you knew about it?"

"Yes."

"Who's idea was it?"

"Stan's."

"Who murdered the four boys?"

Rickson cupped his hands over his face and sobbed. "Randy and Stan."

"And Paul Strongwood?"

"Randy did that."

"Whose idea was it to blow up the trestle to rob the train?"

"Stan and Randys."

"What was your part in it?"

Rickson looked Matt in the eyes and answered truthfully, "I covered for them. I covered for our employees here and scheduled a meeting with the Stafford Milling Company to renegotiate our contracts. I requested to do it with Stan and Leon. They were supposed to be here all day, but they weren't. It was all a lie. That was my cut. It was supposed to be easy money, but it became a nightmare we couldn't discuss. No one wanted to hurt those people. You have to believe me. It was an accident."

"Accident or not, a lot of people died. You know I'm going to arrest you for it, right?"

Rickson covered his face and began a series of loud guttural sobs. "I didn't do anything. It was them, not me.

You have to believe me. I had nothing to do with any of it."
He wept.

"Yes, you did."

CHAPTER TWENTY-EIGHT

RANDY PAULSON WAS SITTING BEHIND HIS DESK in the plantation field manager's office when he heard the faint gunshots coming from what sounded like the big house. His head lifted curiously. He knew tensions were rising between Rickson and his father and wondered if Rickson had shot him. He knew a plan was coming to do away with Cliff, but it wasn't supposed to happen until after the railroad investigation was over. Randy stood from his desk and stepped out the office door to listen, but the silence suddenly felt eerie.

After a few moments, he watched the housemaid, Anna, nearing the office as she walked home. Puzzled, he checked his pocket watch. It was still early in the day. He hollered, "Anna, did it sound like those shots came from the big house to you?"

"I didn't hear anything," she answered nervously. Her shoulders tensed as the speed of her feet quickened to get past him. The last thing she wanted to do was speak to Randy. Anna could bury her emotions under a stoic mask and put up with being treated like dirt without revealing a twitch of her lips or a flicker of resentment in her eyes. There was only one emotion that Anna had a difficult time hiding: fear.

Randy's brow wrinkled. There was a sense of power in knowing the Indian employees were skittish of him, but he had said hello to Anna several times over the years, and she'd always been a stand-offish person, but not like today. "Anna, hold up. Why aren't you at work?"

"I...I...I have to go. I'm sick," she quickly replied, not slowing her pace.

Randy wasn't her boss, but he still held authority over the Indians who worked there. "I said stop!" he shouted and stepped toward her quickly. "You didn't hear two gunshots? I was in the office and I heard them. Are you telling me you didn't?"

She shook her head quickly. She kept her head downward, refusing to look at the man. Her arms crossed over her breasts.

Randy grabbed her chin with his left hand and lifted her face. "You look at me when I'm talking to you! I don't believe you didn't hear anything. Did those shots come from the house?"

Her quivering voice betrayed the muffled words she spoke through her pinched cheeks: "I don't know."

Randy intentionally applied more pressure on her cheeks to grind them into her teeth with a tight grip. Her hands grabbed his wrist to pull his hand away, but his strength was too powerful for her to do so. She whimpered as the taste of blood seeped onto her tongue. "Why are you hurrying home? What happened? Did Rickson shoot Cliff?"

He released his grip so she could talk. Anna spat out a

bit of blood. "I'm sick," she repeated. "I must get home." She quickly turned to leave, but Randy grabbed the back of her collar, scratching the back of her neck with his finger-nails, and jerked her backward, popping off the two top buttons of her dress. "Who fired those shots? Was it Rickson?"

"I don't know!" she shouted and then swallowed heavily.

Randy was losing patience. "If I find out you know and you aren't telling me for whatever reason, I will be very upset."

Anna's gaze quickly darted at Randy as a cold chill ran down her spine.

Randy's lips rose slightly now that he knew he had her attention. "Is Cliff dead, Anna? Did Rickson kill him?"

Anna's lips quivered. She had no idea what may have happened in the big house after hearing the shots. What she did know was she was told to keep quiet and go home. And there was nothing more she wanted to do than just that. "I don't know," she stammered. "The gunshots happened after I left."

"Why aren't you at work?"

"I'm...I'm sick," she stuttered uneasily.

"No, you're not." He slapped her across the face and then shook her violently. "What are you afraid of?"

"Rickson sent me to find you!" she blurted out when the shaking hurt her neck.

"Why?" he questioned with a fierce scowl.

"To find the Indian that saw you."

"I don't understand. Why did he send you to tell me that?"

Anna hoped to see some sign of fear flicker in his eyes

when she said, "The marshal is here. I don't know what happened at the house. He told me to go home."

Her hope was granted as a wave of alarm crept down Randy's spine. "The marshal is here?"

"Yes."

Randy bit his bottom lip as he looked down the road. He could see three riders in the distance as they crest the top of the highest hill between the big house and the bunkhouse. "Go home." He turned away from her and hurried back into the office to grab his gun belt and strap it around his waist.

———

RANDY WENT into his office and sat down behind his desk. He knew the end was near. He could feel it in his soul that his options were few and time was running out. He had no idea what happened at the house, but he knew Matt Bannister and his deputies were coming for him. He pulled a single bullet out of a cartridge loop on his gun belt, opened the revolver's cylinder, and placed a sixth bullet into it. To reduce the risk of an accidental shooting, Randy regularly kept the first chamber of the cylinder empty, but on this particular occasion, he wanted a full cylinder. The riders were coming fast, and he knew he did not have time to go to the stable, saddle his horse, and ride out across the many acres to gather his men and fight together. He was on his own.

He sat behind his desk and squeezed his thighs together to hold the revolver on his lap underneath the desk. He pulled the hammer of the double-action Remmington .38 back until it clicked and positioned the barrel straight ahead. There was no faceboard on the desk to interfere with the bullet. He hoped to raise the barrel just enough to miss the desktop but hit a man's groin, and in the chaos, shoot the next man and drop himself to the floor to not become an easy target and continue firing.

Randy knew the odds were against him, but it was his only chance to live. If he surrendered, he would be hanged. The others might be lucky enough to get a long sentence in prison. But for Randy, death was coming unless he could surprise the marshal and his deputies and catch them off guard just enough to kill or severely injure all three with six shots.

Surrendering was not an option because Randy could not stand the idea of the community he loved knowing that he was to blame for the train disaster and the heartless murder of four young men that he personally knew. All of those deaths were to steal the money that many people in the community were relying on. His actions were as treasonous and heinous as if he had intended to blow the trestle just to watch the people die. Now, he had no choice but to fight for his life, and if he failed, his sacrifice would at least give his friends the chance to live if he killed Matt or one of his deputies.

He heard the horses come to a stop outside his office. He squeezed his legs together and adjusted the revolver on his thighs for a final time before quickly grabbing a pencil to appear to be doing some paperwork.

It seemed an eternity as he waited, but he knew it had only been a minute before Matt Bannister stepped through his office door, followed by William Fasana and Morton Sperry.

Matt tossed a pair of shackles onto the desktop that landed with a jarring bang. "Put those on and tell us where Dave Ruddick and Mark Duffy are. You're under arrest for the murder of fifty-nine people onboard the train and four young men whose names escape me. But you can add the murders of Isaac Chandler and Paul Strongwood to your list as well. The other crimes you could be charged with won't matter."

Randy could feel the pressure of having Matt Bannister's hardened gaze fixed on him and felt the cold chill of terror run down his spine, which was only comparable to watching the train plummet over the Gypsum Creek Gorge. Matt's reputation was well known, and from a distance, a man could think about what he was planning to do and think it would be easy until they faced the man. The severity in Matt's eyes when his hand was within an inch of his famous sidearm had a way of scaring the fight out of a man.

Randy had a plan, but he wasn't expecting shackles to be thrown on the desk or deputy Morton Sperry, a shootist in his own right, to be holding his gun at waist level pointed at him. To see William Fasana's fingers tapping the ivory grip of his revolver like a countdown to draw. Everyone in town knew Doyle West was quick with his gun hand, but William Fasana outdrew him. Seeing the three men in front of him shook Randy's courage. His breathing grew shallow and hurried as he changed his gaze to the shackles on the desktop.

"Put those on and stand up," Matt ordered.

From his general appearance, Randy remained stoic and controlled, but inside, he could feel the panic rattling his best efforts to stay calm. "Where's Rickson?" he questioned. "It was his idea. I did what I was told to do. That's all."

William was the first to answer. "Oh, don't worry about him. He's tied to a wagon wheel in the carriage house. I must tell you, Rickson was so excited to start talking about you and the others planning all this stuff that we had to gag him just to shut him up. It was great!"

The cruelty and magnitude of their crime would leave no escaping the death penalty if he were to put on the shackles lying in front of him. His breathing quickened even more, and his throat tightened, knowing his life was about to end. He could surrender and plead innocent in a court of law, but being the leader of the other men, he would be the first to be crucified with the nails being driven through his flesh to secure his death by the very attorney the Emrick family was sure to hire for Rickson. He was alone and had only one option against three men who were tough as nails and used to killing.

William asked, "Where can I find Mark? As his friend, I should be the one to arrest him."

Matt was losing patience and asked sharply, "Are you going to put those on or do I have to do it for you?"

Randy took a deep breath and reluctantly picked the shackles up with his left hand and then quickly tossed them at Matt's chest while simultaneously reaching for the revolver set on his thighs. He did not have time to aim the weapon at anyone. He pulled the trigger, firing the bullet from under the desk. His bullet hit the wall between Matt and William.

The shackles hit Matt's chest and bounced off while he pulled his revolver. Morton fired first from his hip, hitting Randy's far left shoulder. Randy pulled the trigger again, and this time, Matt grunted loudly and turned sideways with a hop on his right foot as he fired his first shot, which hit the wall. The outside of his left leg burned like someone held a match to his skin. He could feel the warm blood running down his leg.

William fired his revolver, hitting Randy square in the chest, combined with Morton and Matt's repeated shots as both men fanned their hammers while holding the trigger down. Randy's body was exploding with torn clothing and blood spatter. His chair fell back against the wall, bracing him in a leaned-back position, already dead with thirteen bullet holes riddling his body. The sound of his gun falling from his hands to the floor was the last sound Randy Paulson had ever made.

Matt kept his left foot held up off the ground while a pool of blood was forming under his boot.

"Matt, are you hit?" William asked anxiously, looking at his cousin.

Matt hesitated to say the words he had never spoken before. "I've been shot." He holstered his weapon, loosened his gun belt, and tossed it on the desk. He undid his pants and let them drop to see the wound. He feared the bullet had entered deep and torn through his muscle into the bone with the amount of blood he could feel running down his leg, but his fears were relieved when he saw the bullet had grazed the outside of his mid-thigh, leaving an open gash that was bleeding heavily. The bullet had ripped a hole in the front and back of his pants.

"It doesn't look like you'll lose your leg, but you're going to need some sutures, maybe. You need to get to the doctor, Matt," Morton said.

"No time. The others will be coming." He pulled his pants back up and buttoned them. He grabbed his gun belt and strapped it on. "We have no idea where the others are coming from, but we know they'll be coming here after hearing all that shooting. Morton stable the horses so they won't be seen. William, push Randy onto the floor and lock the door. We'll hide in the bunkhouse rooms and wait. Dave Ruddick and Mark Duffy will come back here."

"Mark's wife runs the village store. I think I'll run over and see her. Are you sure you're going to be okay, Matt?" William questioned after Morton left the office.

Matt answered with a painful grimace, "I'll be fine. My leg hurts like a son of a gun, but I'll be fine."

"Are you sure you won't bleed out and die on me?"

"I bled worse just the other day. I think I will be twenty pounds lighter when I get home just from blood loss, but I'll be fine."

CHAPTER TWENTY-NINE

DAVE RUDDICK HEARD THE DISTANT SHOOTING and furrowed his brow questionably. He could not count the number of shots being fired as it happened so suddenly, but he knew it was odd to hear. There was a plan in the works to kill Cliff, but the last he heard, it was on hold until after the investigation was finished. He wondered if the Emricks were doing some target practicing or if Mark and Randy were. Either way, he was checking the fields and young crops on the farm. He didn't have time to waste shooting at tin cans.

An hour later, it was time for lunch, and he rode back to the cookhouse to get some food but found it empty. The cook was not in the kitchen, and no food was being prepared. Cursing the cook, an old man named Harold, Dave stormed out of the cookhouse to Harold's room and banged on the door. "Harold, you old drunk, wake up and get some food on the fire!" He opened the door and entered to find Harold's room empty. "Where are you?"

He left Harold's room, walked to Randy's office, and

tried to enter, but the door was locked. He looked through the window and could see the empty desk. Dave entered his bunkhouse room, shouting, "Randy, where is Harold? I'm starv…" He stopped when he realized Randy wasn't in their shared bunkhouse room. "Where the hell—" He stopped when he heard the door close behind him. He turned around to see Matt Bannister standing behind the door, holding Dave's single-shot shotgun. Startled, he stuttered to speak, "Wha…what do you…doing here?"

"Slowly unbuckle your gun belt and kick it over here," Matt said. He had been waiting for over an hour. They had sent the cook, Harold, away with a firm threat not to speak a word of their presence. As an innocent man who didn't want any trouble, Harold took the day off and went to town to visit his daughter and grandchildren.

"Are you going to shoot me with my own shotgun?" Dave asked as he slowly unbuckled his gun belt. He let it drop to the floor and kicked it across the small room, stopping short of reaching Matt.

"If I must. Turn around and get on your knees. Place your hands behind your back."

"Am I under arrest for something?" Dave asked, unable to keep his nerves from showing.

"I don't think you need to ask. Do you?" Matt replied.

Dave exhaled heavily. "No. Am I going to be hung, Marshal?"

"That's up to the court."

Dave lowered his head and slowly turned around and noticed Morton Sperry suddenly standing in the darkened doorway of his bedroom, pointing his revolver at him. Dave knew he was beaten and got to his knees and slipped his hands behind his back. Morton stepped closer and kicked Dave forward, forcing him face down on the dirty floor. To

Matt's surprise, Dave didn't try to fight or mumble a word as Morton shackled his wrists together. Once Morton helped Dave back to his feet, Matt commented, "I was expecting more of a fight from you."

Dave shook his head slowly. "There wasn't much I could do except be killed, now is there? It wasn't supposed to happen the way it did. No one was supposed to be hurt. No one. I'll pay my dues." His eyes rolled as they filled with moisture. "Money…it was all for money. I've never been a good man, Marshal, but even I found myself going too far for that damn money. No one was supposed to die. Honest."

"But they did, and many burned to death while you cowards rode away. I have no mercy for you!"

Dave gasped as he looked upward toward the ceiling. "Do you think God will have mercy on me, or have I condemned myself beyond saving?"

Matt limped forward. He had tied a cloth around his leg to slow the bleeding. "You're never so far gone that God won't forgive you. All you have to do is ask him to."

Dave asked, "Would you believe I was raised going to church every Sunday? My father was an upstanding elder in the church, but at home, he was anything but that. My father was a drunk, a wife-beater, and a hard-hitting disciplinarian that was so damn abusive to all of us children. I swear I was beaten black and blue before I could talk. My siblings certainly were. He killed my baby brother. Babies cry, Marshal Bannister, and he beat that baby to death because he was crying. Everyone thought little Henry died in his sleep, but that was a lie. I swore at an early age that I would never become like my father. I wanted to be a better man, and I thought I was, until the train wrecked. I killed far more people than he ever did, including children. I know I deserve hell. But at least I didn't pretend to be a Christian like my father did."

Matt exhaled heavily. "If it's any consolation, God knows his sheep from the goats. People can fool others, but God will not be fooled. Not by any means. I will tell you, if you knew the Lord all those years ago and walked away, he's still waiting for you to come back like the prodigal son. That story wouldn't be in the Bible if it weren't true. God will be there waiting for you with open arms, and the kingdom of heaven will be ready to celebrate. That is how much Jesus loves you and wants you to return to him. Right now is *always* a perfect time to pray and get right with the Lord, but until your last breath is taken, he is willing to forgive you."

Dave's voice cracked for the first time as he said, "Will you pray with me, Marshal? I'm afraid the Lord won't hear me."

Matt grimaced in pain as he leaned against a chair to ease the weight off his leg. "I could pray with you, but the truth is Jesus wants to hear you pray. In fact, he draws near just to listen because he longs to forgive you. Jesus lived and died so that he could save you from your sins and the guilt you carry. He will gladly cast those sins as far as the east is from the west and remember them no more because that's how much he loves you. All you have to do is ask. Jesus will hear your prayers no matter where you are or how badly you messed up. The Bible says his mercy is new every single day. He will hear you pray. I'll pray with you, but you need to ask Jesus for his forgiveness. I can't do it for you. Let's pray."

———

"WILLIAM, WHAT WAS ALL THAT SHOOTING?" Clair Duffy asked him as he entered the store. William was looking for Mark and hoped to find him there.

"Oh, Randy challenged us to see who could hit the target the fastest. I believe we humbled him. I was strolling by and thought I'd stop in and say hello."

"Well, hello." She smiled. "You don't give up, do you?"

"Give up?" he questioned.

"On stealing me away. I already told you I'm in love with my husband."

William grinned with a slight chuckle. "Oh, Peaches, if you came with me, you'd just work yourself to the bone to support me."

"I bet so. Still gambling, William?"

He held out the ring he had taken from Roy Clegg. "In more ways than you know. Win some, lose some, but I always come out ahead, even when it's not money we're talking about. Take you for example, you would be the queen of the Monarch Hotel if you had come with me. Fancy dresses and elegant rooms, fine food, and the best living conditions a woman could ever ask for. But no, you stuck with slow wit, Duffy. Listen, Peaches, you broke me up. I was devastated when I left here."

"You were not." She laughed with a wave of her hand.

"Hmm. Well, maybe not, but I thought of you every time I saw a peach. How's that?"

She laughed. "Get out of here, William. It sure is good to see you, though."

He smiled. "You too."

"MARK, your wife is right over there in the store. So why are you here pestering me again?" Isabel Emrick asked. She knew very well why he was there, and like many times before, she had been trying to send him away. She liked Mark as a friend, but she drew the line there. It was lunchtime, and the children had half an hour to run home, eat lunch, or go outside and play. Isabel sat at her desk eating a fruit.

"Because I like talking to you, and this is the only chance I get to. I can't just show up at the big house without Rickson thinking I'm there for him, and you never come to the bunkhouse."

"You're married. So why would I do that?"

"I don't know. For something to do."

Isabel grinned with a scoff. "I have plenty to do."

"All right. I'll let you enjoy what's left of your lunch. But tomorrow, you better be more talkative."

"I have my doubts."

Mark laughed lightly. He enjoyed Isabel's no-nonsense humor, and pestering her was fun entertainment. He left the school and stepped toward the store to escort Clair to the cookhouse for lunch. He stopped when he saw William exit the store and come down the three steps onto the road. "William, what are you doing talking to my wife?"

William wasn't expecting to see Mark walking toward the store. He was about thirty-five feet away. "You caught me red-handed, Mark. My memory has me hungering for a free peach," he said with a troubled yet friendly grin.

Mark stopped walking to twist his body with frustration. "Darn it, William. I told you I don't appreciate that. We're married now, and I'm getting sick of hearing you say that kind of thing about my wife."

William stopped walking forward, leaving twenty feet

between them. It was safer for him to be at a distance to make an arrest than to be close, where a physical altercation could take place. He groaned. "Then you're not going to appreciate this. You're under arrest, Mark, for the train and all the folks you fellas killed. Drop your gun belt, old friend, and your knife. I have to take you in. Matt's waiting on me."

"William, are you joking?" Mark gasped, suddenly beginning to tremble. He knew he was no match for William with his sidearm, but he also knew there was no man alive who was going to separate him from his beloved bride.

William gave a sad shrug of his shoulders. "I'm sorry old friend, but I'm afraid not. I'm dead serious, Mark. Drop your gun belt."

Mark's breathing grew erratic while he shook his head, refusing. "I can't go to jail. I...I have Clair to take care of and this farm to run. Trust me, I didn't do anything! I didn't kill anyone. I'm innocent, William. You have to know that!"

William spoke sincerely. "That's not my job to say. My job is to take you in, and I'd like to take you in alive. Please, Mark, loosen the gun belt and come with me without a fight. I'll speak on your behalf, but it's the court that decides. Lay the gun down and come with me, old friend."

Mark's hand crept closer to his sidearm. "I'm innocent. William. Let me go. I'm begging you. Please?" He choked on the words.

William pointed with his left hand warningly. "You can't beat me in a draw, Mark. Don't try it. Don't make me kill you. It's not worth it." He stepped his right leg forward, turning his body parallel to become a smaller target.

Mark's hands shook noticeably. "I didn't do anything to deserve this." His eyes went to the store longing to see Clair. "William, can I have a moment with my wife?"

William relaxed and nodded. "Sure."

The distraction he needed was at hand, with William moving his hand away from his reversed revolver. As fast as he could, Mark unsnapped the cover over his holster, grabbed his revolver, and jerked it out of the holster. He barely cleared the barrel from the holster when he heard the sound of William's .45 and felt the strike of a bullet shatter his sternum and rip through his chest as he fell back onto the dust of the Livengood Village street. His gun bounced once as it left his hand. A strange hum filled Mark's ears as he heard the faint scream of his beloved Clair.

"Mark! Mark!" Clair screamed as she ran past William to her dying husband. "Mark!" she bawled, cradling his head. "Don't you leave me! Mark, don't leave me!" she sobbed.

William lowered his head and stared at the ground, feeling the heavy burden of having killed his old friend. He listened to the wails of Clair and gently kicked the dirt with his toe when an unexpected bullet buzzed past him by several feet. Startled, he stepped back and looked up to see Clair twenty feet away, kneeling beside her dead husband, holding Mark's gun pointed at him. Smoke was rising from the barrel as she pulled the hammer back.

"Why?" Clair screamed. She pulled the trigger again, missing William by a few feet again.

William held out his left hand to reason with her while his right hand rested on his holstered ivory handle. "Put it down! Listen," he shouted urgently. "Mark gave me no choice, Peaches. I had to." He had no desire to draw his weapon on her.

"I'll kill you!" she screamed and fired the revolver for the third time.

William shouted, "Clair, stop! Please, put it down!"

She fired again, this time coming much closer to him as he heard the bullet fly past him. She refused to listen to him and pulled the hammer back to fire another shot.

Her aim was narrowing in, and William had no choice. He drew his revolver, allowing his hand to follow his gaze, and pulled the trigger, placing a fatal bullet into her heart, killing Clair instantly before she could pull the trigger again. "I didn't want to do that, Peaches!" he exclaimed angrily. "Damn it, I didn't want to shoot either of you!" he shouted. The school teacher, Isabel Emrick, stood on the school steps, covering her mouth in shock.

Morton galloped his horse into the Indian Village and pulled the reins to a quick stop. Seeing the two bodies, he asked, "Are you alright?"

William looked up at Morton and took a deep breath as he holstered his gun. He motioned with his thumb toward the two bodies. "I didn't want to do that."

Morton nodded understandably. "Let's take their bodies back to town and arrest the others, William. Matt said tomorrow, we're going home, and we can put all this behind us."

William spat on the ground and shook his head, disheartened. He took another deep breath and exhaled. He said, "I'm afraid that might be easier said than done this time, my friend. Let's finish this and go home."

CHAPTER THIRTY

ALEXANDER WENTWORTH WROTE QUICKLY IN HIS notebook as Matt told him what had happened at Gypsum Creek. "And," Matt continued, "that is how it ended. The trip home was uneventful except for Elizabeth, Gabriel's mother, who was absolutely horrified to see Gabriel all beat up and with a broken arm." Matt smiled. "She swore she would never allow him to go anywhere with me again. I got quite a verbal beating from her. William thought it was funny, and so did Morton. They harassed me about missing part of my rear end after that butt-chewing all the way from Willow Falls to Branson." He chuckled lightly, reflectively.

"What about Stan Meldrum and Leon Goodrich? Did you forget about them?" Andrew asked as Matt stood and stepped across the room to a display case, sliding the glass door open to grab something out of it.

"No," Matt said. "We took Rickson and Dave to the county jail, along with the bodies of Randy, Mark, and Clair. It took Dave's testimony to convince Sheriff Cletus

James that I was right. We had Cletus and his deputies join us, and we went to the mill where Stan Meldrum and Leon Goodrich worked and had them surrounded and arrested without any trouble. Oh, Stan jumped into the river and tried to swim for it, but he came ashore after a bit. We arrested or killed them all that day to the great aggravation of the town constable Perry Whitmore and Marty Rook, who was in charge of the railroad's investigation."

Matt took a breath. "Stan Meldrum and Dave Ruddick were both found guilty and hung. I did not attend the hanging. If I recall, Leon Goodrich was sentenced to thirty years in prison and served several years before dying of natural causes while in prison." Matt handed Alex a railroad spike that was bent and warped by the combination of heat and pressure. "That spike is from the trestle. It shows how hot the fire was. The day that spike bent is the day all those folks died, and I got this scar." He bent his head down to show a narrow scar on his head.

Alex held the spike in his hands and could see the evidence of Matt's split-open scalp. Matt returned to his seat beside his beloved bride.

After looking at the railroad spike, Alex asked, "What happened to Rickson Emrick?"

"I do know a little bit about all that. I stayed in contact with Cletus James for several years until he passed away. Rickson Emrick had the best attorney money could buy and was sentenced to a year in prison for his part, but being a rich kid, he got out after a few months. I read that a few years later, Rickson was assassinated along the road to the Livengood Plantation. Someone shot him, but no one was ever arrested for it. My guess is that it was one of his Indian employees tired of being mistreated.

"Rickson's mother, Marie, took Rickson's death very

hard and died not too long after from alcohol poisoning. It was the beginning of the end for the Livengood Plantation. It doesn't exist anymore. It was sold off piece by piece when Isabel Emrick inherited it after her father passed away. She wanted nothing to do with farming, so she separated it into parcels and sold it to several of the Indian families, including the Redbirds, who I understand are thriving there to this day. Isabel had married and was raising her family in Portland at the time. I don't know who she married or anything else about her."

"Do you know whatever happened to Ellie and Roy Clegg?"

"I have no idea. Ellie went to live with her brother, and I have never heard from her again."

Alexander looked at Matt awkwardly. "Did Perry Whitmore ever lose his position for hanging an innocent man?"

Matt grunted. "That's another story I'll have to tell you sometime. But not today."

"Marshal Bannister, you mentioned you four had gone back to Portland to testify at Felix Rathkey's trial. I'm curious, did the young man shanghaied with Gabriel, Evan, I think his name was, did anyone ever hear from him again?"

Matt smiled as he took hold of Christine's hand. "Evan Gray, yes. About three years later, Evan came back to Willow Falls. He came by my office to say hello. Evan goes by Captain Gray now. Evan took a liking to the sea and remained a sailor on an ocean-going steamer up and down the West Coast for several years. He is a pilot of one of the sternwheelers on the Lower Columbia and Willamette Rivers. He has a family and lives outside of Portland. He and Gabriel are still best friends."

Alex closed his notebook and put it in his leather bag. He leaned over his knees and spoke pointedly, "Marshal

Bannister, as you know, when the Branson Gazette newspaper building burned down in 1895, so much of our local history was lost. With your permission, I would like to write an ongoing series of forgotten stories that have been lost in the fire. Your legacy to this town and the whole community is important enough to resurrect those lost stories while we can. May I come back next week to hear another story and tell the world about it?"

Matt looked over at Christine. "My lady, what do you think?"

Christine looked at the display case of items he had collected over the years, such as the warped spike from the collapsed trestle next to Alex's hand. "Matt, this whole room is nothing except a collection of a lifetime of memories and stories that you and I know but the world has forgotten about. When our lives are gone, that bent railroad spike will be a bent spike and probably thrown away without any significance. To make all these items relevant and to mean something to our grandchildren or anyone else, you must tell the stories behind them, even the stories that are hard to tell. I say we do it while you and I still can."

Matt gazed at his beloved bride while holding her hand. He took a deep breath and exhaled, and after a long moment, he turned his attention back to Alex. "Because you're Jed Clark's Grandson, I'll invite you to come back next Sunday after church. Christine and I will feed you lunch and tell you another story. But I'll warn you, one lie, false allegation, or try to make me sound like a bigger hero than I really was, and you won't be welcomed back. I read enough dime novels about me in my time that it makes me want to puke. Don't be like one of them lying writers. Just tell the truth. That's all I ask."

Alex stood to shake Matt's hand again. "I will do so. Thank you for trusting me."

Christine clapped her hands. "Well, now that you have a story. How about a piece of Rory's famous strawberry shortcake?"

"I'd love some. Yes."

"Good," Matt said, standing. "How about I show you my office so you can see where your picture will be added if you do me wrong with this article? I always keep an empty picture frame handy for my next victim."

Christine laughed and slapped his hand. "Stop teasing him, Matthew. Give me a push into the dining room so we can eat."

Matt stepped behind her wheelchair and unlocked the brakes. "Follow us, Alex. Let's get some dessert."

Alex followed and then stopped in the hallway where an enlarged photograph of Christine and Matt dancing together on a large dance floor was hanging. They were both young. Alex was amazed by how beautiful Christine was and the love clearly expressed between them as they gazed into each other's eyes. "Excuse me, when was this taken?"

"Long time ago," Matt answered. He returned to stand beside Alex. "Christine was a dancer at a place called Bella's Dance Hall. That's where I met her. She was the most beautiful and best dancer of them all."

Alex lowered his voice. "May I be so forward to ask why she is in a wheelchair? Can she walk?"

Matt took a deep breath and patted his shoulder with a heavy frown that twitched his lower lip. "Come eat. That is another story for another day."

A LOOK AT: CAUSTIC OCTOBER

(The Jessup County Chronicles Book 2)

From bestselling author Ken Pratt comes a thrilling new chapter in the Jessup County Chronicles, set in a world where past and present collide.

It's 1932, and journalist Alex Wentworth is eager to unearth the forgotten stories of Matt Bannister's legendary past. While seeking to revisit the Hollister Sheep Shooter's War, Alex instead discovers a chilling account that picks up where the war's tragedy left off—a tale hidden since the Branson Gazette went up in flames.

Months after surviving a brutal assault, fifteen-year-old Laura Whitehead is trapped in a nightmare. Forbidden from seeing her beloved Jake Thomas, and reeling from the revelation that she's pregnant by one of her attackers, Laura faces her father's desperate attempts to end the pregnancy at any cost. But the shadows deepen when Jesse Helms, one of the men responsible, learns of the child and plots to claim it for his own.

With the help of his embittered aunt, Mattie Sperry, Jesse devises a sinister plan: kidnap Laura and force her into captivity, raising the child as his own. For Mattie, it's a chance to rebuild her shattered life. For Laura, it's a descent into horror.

As Laura vanishes, U.S. Marshal Matt Bannister and his deputies, Morton Sperry and Truet Davis, are thrust into a desperate search. With no leads, no motive, and a ruthless gang covering its tracks, Matt faces his toughest challenge yet. Can he unravel the twisted conspiracy before Laura's fate is sealed?

AVAILABLE NOW

ACKNOWLEDGMENTS

For all the years that I have been writing, my family has always been the most supportive of me. So, with that, I want to thank my wife, Cathy. Without her support and encouragement, I wouldn't be able to do as much writing as I do. Our children are also very supportive, and I want to thank them for being encouraging as well. Mike, Jessica, Chevelle, Katie, and Keith...thank you. My son Keith deserves more credit, though. He reads everything I write and is not shy about telling me what he thinks and offering suggestions that quite often I follow. His interest in the books and the hours he puts into reading them, marking them up, and sharing his opinions while doing his college work to keep his grades up are admirable. Thank you, Keith.

I also want to thank Micheal Gear and Kathleen O'Neal Gear for their help and suggestions with this book. Their keen wisdom and knowledge of how to tell a story were a feedback that I certainly appreciate.

Finally, I want to thank CKN Christian Publishing, Patience Bramlett, Sharmaine Gobind, Ellie Folden, Mike Bray, Jake Bray, and the rest of the team who make CKN and Wolfpack Publishing the fantastic company that it is.

ABOUT THE AUTHOR

Ken Pratt and his wife, Cathy, have been married for twenty-two years and are blessed with five children and six grandchildren. They live on the Oregon Coast where they are currently raising the youngest of their children.

Ken grew up in the small farming community of Dayton, Oregon, where he worked to make a living. But his true passion always lay with writing.

Having a busy family, the only "free" time Ken has to write is late at night—getting no more than five hours of sleep every day. He has penned several novels that are being published, along with several children's stories.